Annie Eliot Trumbull

White birches

A novel

Annie Eliot Trumbull

White birches
A novel

ISBN/EAN: 9783337046590

Printed in Europe, USA, Canada, Australia, Japan

Cover: Foto ©Andreas Hilbeck / pixelio.de

More available books at **www.hansebooks.com**

A Novel

BY

ANNIE ELIOT

NEW YORK
HARPER & BROTHERS PUBLISHERS
1893

TO

S. R. T.

WHITE BIRCHES

CHAPTER I

"Speak, I am bound to hear."

"We stand in the heart of things.
   The woods are round us, heaped and dim ;
  From slab to slab how it slips and springs
   The thread of water."

THE clump of aspens across the field quivered in the breeze, their dancing leaves, turning now this way and now that, reminding him more than ever of the advertisements of Ivory Soap in the shop-windows. Dreamily he watched them, half expecting to read "It floats" as they twinkled hither and thither. Where was it there was one of those signs? At the corner store in the village. It was an extraordinarily metropolitan acquisition for the corner store, and the "Ivory Soap" winked itself into "It floats" just as you reached the church-gate, and imparted a slightly supernatural charm to the dress-braid and lemon candy in the window under it. It was a curious thing—that effect of changing the angle of observation—he wondered if he changed his angle of observation of those aspen-trees—and with a slight groan of pain he sank back again on the deep moss. He must have been getting a bit sleepy, his

1

mind wandered off so easily into all sorts of absurd directions.   It was partly the plashing of the waterfall that
soothed him ; that unlucky waterfall that he had come up
to see.   It was worth seeing, to be sure, and, crossing his
arms under his head, he turned away from the aspens and
looked back at it where it pitched forward over the cliff and
fell uncertainly downward forty or fifty feet, catching here
and there on projecting rocks, laughing meanwhile at its
own temerity.   Worth seeing, to be sure, but hardly at
the cost of twisting his confounded leg.   He wondered
what the deuce he had done to his leg anyhow.   He had
passed the period of thinking he could make his way back
unaided, which had been his first impulse after his fall,
and the following one—of cursing his own stupidity and his
luck—had also gone over his head in the hour or two since
it happened.   Now he was reduced to a state of calm
wonder as to how and why he had done it, and how he was
going to get out of it.   That a climber of his pretensions
should have slipped on a rolling stone, saved himself by
springing to another coated with wet, green moss, and gone
down between two uneven rocks, was bad enough in itself,
but that this not altogether unheard-of performance should
have ended in giving his leg an ugly wrench that made it
impossible for him to do more than crawl a few steps to the
soft moss—this was without precedent.   Why couldn't he
have had a little of that flimsy waterfall's imperviousness?
It was a fragile, evasive, foolish sort of thing, but it fell its
fifty feet and ran on without stopping, while he, in the full
possession of athletic manhood, slipped a few paltry steps
and found himself helpless!   How long would he have to
remain there—that was an interesting question too.   Not
all night, of course, but, as it was yet early afternoon, this
was not in itself immediate consolation.   By nightfall the
people at the Clocks' would begin to wonder where he was,

for he left word that he would be home to supper; but it would be some time before they concluded that any accident had happened to the best climber in the valley, and felt authorized to go after him. He reflected with grim amusement on the spectacle of his own towering rage if nothing had happened, and he, simply taking his own time to return, had been met upon the road by a posse provided with lanterns and anxiety. It would be just like that atrocious little Mrs. Needham to suggest it. There was nothing she liked better than going about after presentable men, with or without a lantern, and she had already shown a well-defined inclination to watch over him, just now the only thoroughly presentable man at hand. She was no fool either, that same little Mrs. Needham, which made it the more difficult to avoid her and at the same time increased his anxiety to do so—for this man had all his sex's toleration for a pretty woman, who is also a fool. Well, she was safe to see that he didn't stay out all night, as he'd made some idiotic promise to sit on the stile with her, at the end of the garden, and see the moon rise. She had drawn from him the object of his walk that day too, so she might follow if she could find anybody to drive her to the bars—he remembered hoping they would all be busy haying. So she might make her appearance before lantern-time. Austin Medcott uttered a groan of deeper impatience than physical suffering had drawn from him, as he realized that he was unconsciously placing his most vital hopes upon Florence Needham.

But meanwhile—it was early afternoon, and even Florence Needham wouldn't come for two or three hours, and, in all human probability, no one else would come at all. The hush of noon still lay over the valley. Through the length and breadth of it not a sound was stirring. Away over there, too far for any shout to attract attention, lay the ugly

little buildings that constituted the village; ugly, but not
destitute of a certain picturesque dignity, since in them people lived and worked and died, and these great facts must
leave an impress that is never all commonplace. On all
sides rose the mountains, strong, still, and protecting, but
unassailable. From the forests that covered their sides
came the sound of distant brooks, audible in the sunny
quiet, and now and then broke in the flute-like sweetness
of the wood-thrush, while nearer at hand, but illusive and
uncompanionable, was the restless tinkle of a cowbell; but
no sound of human presence came from mountain or forest.
Austin made up his mind to the inevitable, and looking up
into the blue sky just visible over his head through the tall
trees, he waited quietly. Nearer and nearer drew the sound
of the cowbell—mysteriously near, for no animal came in
sight, and there was no accompanying rustle of four-footed
existence and motion. It was as if a lonely bell were making its solitary way in curiously persistent fashion through
the woody glades. How could anybody speak of a peaceful cowbell! It was irritating in the extreme, and yet when,
irrelevantly and purposelessly it died away and he heard
only the faintest tinkle now and then, he felt an unreasonable increase of the sense of desolation. For half an hour
the waterfall plashed, the brook purled, the shadows grew
and the aspens fluttered, and then a sound which was
neither plash nor purl nor flutter came to Medcott's ears.
Faint at first, somewhat broken by distance, and by the
singer's evidently uneven steps the notes of a song drifted
from the direction of the rocks above the waterfall. Medcott raised his head and listened intently, resolved, if the
voice showed signs of straying off to either side, to shout
for assistance. But instead, without any of the evasive
quality of the cowbell, it came straight on, and he now distinguished the words of the Eton boat song—

       "'Twenty years hence, such weather,'"

sang a girl's voice quite near at hand and then ceased, as its owner evidently needed all her available breath to climb some sharp ascent. Then she began again,

       "'We may be long on the feather,'"

and to Medcott's eyes, steadily fixed on the opening in the trees through which she must come, appeared a beautiful girl, whose flushed cheeks told of a hard pull through the ill-cleared path, and whose brown hands, and clothes of ordinary material and country make, hinted that she was not unused to such effort. She paused, looking about for the easiest way down the slippery and jagged rocks, covered here and there by the quick sweep of the stream itself and everywhere moist with spray.

The afternoon sun, penetrating the foliage here and there, threw flickering bits of light over her face and figure. By her side clustered three or four slender white birches, like her in their suggestions of freedom and girlishness, and she laid her hand on the graceful branch of one of them, bending it towards her, as she waited. Medcott feared to startle her, and yet it seemed better to speak now than to wait until she came quite near, when the surprise of seeing a man lying on the ground might be more of a shock, especially if it should happen as she was crossing the ungovernable brook on that slippery tree-trunk. He raised himself on his elbow and then hesitated. What should he say? And he ran over in his mind the different salutations proffered to strange young maidens according to the best authors. "Fair Lady" and "Beautiful Being" both seemed a little strained. "Look here, my girl" a trifle Early English in its tone. If he were a seafaring man he could say, "Heave ho, my hearty," or something like that. "My hearty," now —that wasn't a bad idea—rather a pretty, old-fashioned sort of name for that sweet, strong, beautiful girl. The branch of the white birch swung back from the detaining hand, she made a step down.

"I beg your pardon," said Medcott.

The girl stopped and looked about her.

"Here I am," said Medcott again, leaning forward and pushing aside some obscuring shrubs.

Then she looked down and across, and their eyes met, while the swift color leaped into her face.

"I am afraid I have startled you," he went on, "but I had to speak before you really walked over me," and he smiled. "You must be coming across to the path—I only wish I could get out of your way."

All this time she had not uttered a sound, neither did she seem frightened, she simply stood still and looked at him. Medcott began to wish she would evince emotion of some sort, if it was only curiosity. Except for that first flush, theirs might have been a most conventional meeting.

"What is the matter?" she asked. He knew already that her voice was sweet, and though she spoke shyly, she was evidently not inclined to run away like the chronically startled fawn.

"That is just what I can't tell you," he replied. "But I've turned my ankle or sprained my knee or some other idiotic thing, and can't walk home, and I shall have to ask you to send me up a man and a cart from the village, if you are going that way."

She came rapidly down, her feet, clumsily clad, stepping lightly from rock to rock, her short skirt escaping the little wet pools, her coarse straw hat pushed back from her wonderful eyes and low, broad forehead. Without a moment's pause of uncertainty, she crossed on the green, mossy tree-trunk, and made her way up the few steps from the brook that Medcott had first traversed with such pain and difficulty.

"I will send my brother up," said she, standing and looking down at him. "But—" and she hesitated.

"You can't think how I am abusing my own stupidity, in having to give you all this trouble."

"It isn't your fault," she said slowly, "and it won't be any trouble anyhow; but I was thinking—it will be some time before Jib can get up here. Don't you think"—and then she paused again ; there was something disconcerting in the very respectful gaze of the deep gray eyes and the half-amused, half-exasperated smile of the very firm mouth under a drooping moustache. Her shyness was increasing, but she put it aside.

"Don't you think that you could walk, leaning on my shoulder, as far as the road? Then, perhaps, some of the other folks will be going by."

"I'd like to think anything you thought I'd better," said Medcott with deceptive meekness, "but I really do not think I could do that. I tried it by myself, and it was too many for me, and as for your helping me, I cannot consent to incapacitate you for further action also."

"I'm very strong," answered the girl.

"I am sure of that"—he had already noted her look of superb health and strength—"and I am very grateful for the suggestion, but I really think it would be impossible. I shall be as patient as a rubber doll now that I know help is coming—and this isn't at all a bad place to wait in."

"No," she assented, "it's a pretty place." Still, she hesitated. Her shyness had given place to a feeling of pronounced friendliness. She did not like to leave him alone and helpless. All the pent-up irritation of the afternoon overflowed Medcott's masculine soul. It was too exasperating that he should lie prone before this splendid creature, this beautiful woman, helpless as a log, dependent upon her for physical assistance! He was unused to the pose of weakling.

"What a fool you must think me!" he broke out. "Lying here like a babe in the wood! And no prospect of getting home unless you send for me! It's outrageous! I won't come out again without a keeper."

This outbreak, instead of dismaying his companion, rendered her more completely mistress of the situation. She had seen the spectacle of helpless and impatient manhood before. Whether the victim reclines in a not ungraceful attitude on shaded moss, in velveteen jacket and knickerbockers with an impatient frown disfiguring his handsome forehead, and eyes whose appealing quality has an undeniably sulky light in it, or sits about the farm-kitchen in overalls and a flannel shirt, swearing at his pipe because he doesn't enjoy it, and kicking over a three-legged stool because it looks so cheerful and comfortable—they are each individuals of the same class, and not an unfamiliar one.

Around the girl's waist was a cord with a tin cup attached. She went swiftly down to the brook, and filling it with the cold, clear water, brought it back to him.

"You must be thirsty," she said.

"Thank you," he said gratefully, "I am very thirsty."

While he drank she added quietly,

"Now I'll go as fast as I can, and that's not very slow," and before he could take the cup from his lips to speak, she was speeding away from him over the rough ground.

"Please don't run," he shouted after her imploringly.

She looked around and nodded, and was about to run on again in defiance of his entreaty, when a sudden thought seemed to strike her, and she slackened her pace to a swift walk, and soon passed out of sight.

"Jove! but she's fair to see," thought Medcott, "and wasn't it nice of her to put on the brake because she knew it would make me uncomfortable to have her run. What eyes and what a figure ! And what a delicious combination of shyness and unconsciousness !"

He felt again the cool touch of her fingers when he took the cup from her hands, and was glad that not a look had betrayed his inclination to take them in his. Silence fell again, save for the sound of the waterfall, the undertone of brooks, the far-off song of the wood-thrush, and the spasmodic tinkle of a cowbell. But it was not an oppressive stillness, and the cowbell no longer irritated him. It was a silence full of suggestions of beauty and movement, and of past memories and future possibilities.

CHAPTER II

"For every passion something, and for no passion truly anything."

"It would be argument for a week."

"SHA'N'T I read to you?" asked Mrs. Needham, laying down her cut work and leaning over towards Austin with her bright, hard little smile and her pretty blue eyes raised to his.

Medcott turned away with a slightly bored expression from the window, whose splendid outlook embraced a wide semicircle of hills rising one beyond the other, in varying shades of green and misty blue, and holding in their midst the beautiful sweep of meadow-land with the clear, narrow river flowing through it. If only she would let him alone for a while, so that he need do nothing but listen to the sound of the river and watch the shadows drift over Monument, and wonder where and when he should meet Rhodope Trent again. But she had let him alone for five minutes or so, and he was disgustingly ungrateful to wish to ignore her pitying companionship! His injured leg was supported in front of him as he lay at ease in the long lounging-chair whose lazy comfort should have checked the restless sighs that now and then rose from its depths.

" I'm afraid that means that I've been brutally cross, and you don't know what else to do with me," he answered.

" It certainly doesn't mean that I think you are blissfully happy."

"I ought to be," he said, looking with such emotion as he was capable of into the challenging eyes so near his.

Florence Needham was a remarkably pretty woman. Her most intimate enemy could say no worse of her personal appearance than that she was getting too stout. Her face was round and babyishly pretty, her curly hair was wound in many little golden braids at the back of her small, well-shaped head, and charming rings of it escaped here and there after the manner of hair of this description. She was always exquisitely dressed, and her small hands glittered with gems, hard, bright, and sparkling as her own personality. After Medcott's last speech, she looked at him a moment in silence, and then she laughed—a high, bell-like little laugh.

"Why?" she asked; "because you've sprained your knee and the doctors say you are not to stir for a fortnight? And because you are precisely the kind of man to thoroughly enjoy watching beautiful Nature from a steamer-chair when it is just the weather for climbing and fishing?"

"No," said Medcott lazily, "I hadn't thought of those advantages. Because I am at present the recipient of Mrs. Needham's exclusive attention."

"That is why I think you need a change. Since you have been suffering my exclusive attention you have sighed three times, stifled two yawns, looked longingly out of the window four fifths of the time, and generally misconducted yourself. Never mind explaining—what shall I read to you?"

"Anything you'll be good enough to read to me," he answered penitently. "'The volume of thy choice'—except perhaps some 'humbler poet'—I don't feel like a humbler poet this afternoon."

"Mr. Steven says 'To-morrow' is very good," and Mrs. Needham took up a volume from the table that stood near her.

"It can't be worse than yesterday," said Medcott with lazy petulance.

"Or to-day for that matter? Never mind, my poor boy, the first week one is shut up is always the worst." Mrs. Needham turned the leaves of "To-morrow," but she did not seriously open it.

"You are always quoting Mr. Steven," said Medcott with the fault-finding spirit of invalidism. "I'm sure I don't see why."

She looked up with a sharp, questioning glance in her round, blue eyes.

"Why," she said, "he is so literary—isn't he? I supposed he'd know."

"I can't see that he knows any better than other people," answered Austin, playing impatiently with the curtain cord. "You recommended that 'Story of a Window Seat,' on the strength of his opinion, I believe."

"Yes."

"Well, it ought to be an infringement of the law of nations to reprint such stupidity! I couldn't read it."

"Neither could I," said Mrs. Needham, seriously and thoughtfully, "but I thought it was good. He said so. I supposed he knew," she added again, and looked absently at the first page of "To-morrow." "Perhaps this isn't good either," she said after a moment.

Medcott watched her with a slight smile that she did not see and would not have understood if she had. What an artificial creature she was anyway! And then he turned wearily to the open window again.

"You are not a bit interested in me," said Mrs. Needham, shutting up "To-morrow" and putting it back on the table.

"Oh, but I am," asserted Austin, "but I am not interesting—that is the matter with me."

"I wish you weren't," pouted Mrs. Needham. "Then I shouldn't care."

"I only need the assurance that you care, to be anything you like," said Medcott, resigning for the second time the outside for the inside view, and making an effort to speak less perfunctorily.

He had had a good deal of this sort of thing for the last three days. Mrs. Needham had frankly expressed her satisfaction with the fate that had thrown the most interesting man about, upon the tender mercies of indoor companions. "It is more than I had a right to expect," she told him, "that you should be laid at my very door. I hate walking and I hate driving and I hate everything that one generally has to do in the country as means to an end. And here is the end right at my hand without bothering with the means at all. There's nothing left for us to do except to be mutually entertaining." Entertainment and flirtation were practically synonymous terms in Mrs. Needham's vocabulary, and Medcott had tamely acquiesced, in a measure, but to Florence Needham's practised eye it was acquiescence, not interest, and she speculated somewhat concerning the reason.

There were no depths in her eyes as they met his, but they were of a very pretty color and were capable of a touch almost of softness now and then. As Medcott looked into them, by very force of contrast another pair came into his mental vision—eyes, penetrating, deep and grave, which, though meeting his fearlessly, were quickly veiled in a pretty sort of shyness if he looked too long. His expression, although painstaking, grew indifferent notwithstanding, and Mrs. Needham's hard little laugh broke out again.

"Oh, Austin Medcott!" she exclaimed, "how badly you do it. You are almost as unsuccessful as—as Charlie Needham himself."

Conscious of his failure, and yet willing to repay her for her real kindness during his helplessness in the only coin which was acceptable, Medcott breathed a sigh, half real, half simulated,

"There it is—a woman's way! Make victims of us and then laugh at us! Poor Charlie—and most unhappy I!"

Even as he spoke a swift change passed over his face. The bored look left it, and his sunbrowned check flushed a little deeper. Florence Needham saw the change, and as she was about to speak checked herself, and, leaning forward, looked out of the window in the direction of his gaze.

"Oh," she said under her breath. A little path wound from the nearer hills through the meadow to the road. It strayed now this way, now that, crossing a tiny brook by an uneven, tilting board, and avoiding the overflow of a hidden spring by a sudden curve. On either side the flat greenness stretched away till it met the duskier green of beech and pine. Along this path came Rhodope Trent. Twenty times had he thought of her as he saw her first in the wood; and now as she moved, tall and straight, through the meadow, a big bunch of sweet-peas in her hand, her beauty was no less remarkable than it had been then. She was a figure fit to give the human element to this scene of lofty peace and sunny freedom. Suddenly his three days of mingled sentiment and cynicism with Florence Needham seemed singularly pale and empty. Such intercourse bore the stamp of the city's lightness and unnaturalness. It lacked the truth of cool woods and high hills and murmuring waters.

But Medcott was accustomed to feminine scrutiny, and it was with the most discreet interest and his usual expression of nonchalance that he said to his companion,

"There is the young woman who found me in the woods the other day, and sent her brother to bring me home. I should like to thank her if she comes near enough to let me."

Florence's lips curved into a smile.

"I fancy she will," she observed. "In fact, it would not surprise me if those sweet-peas had been gathered in view of some such contingency."

Medcott was annoyed, and almost unwise enough to make this plain.

"I do not believe it would occur to her to think of strewing the recumbent hero with flowers," he said with a frown. "Such attentions are reserved rather for the criminals in the large cities."

"Really a village belle!" murmured Mrs. Needham, leaning farther forward, so that her blonde head was very near Medcott's dark one. "Beauty, badly fitting clothes, and a bunch of posies."

Nearer, in her rough straw hat, her clumsily made gown, and her fine unconsciousness, came Rhodope.

"She is not at all my idea of a village belle," answered Medcott quietly. "She is too statuesque." He knew it was most ill-considered on his part to use the one word that could never be applied to Florence Needham's beauty, but he had been goaded into it.

He longed to go out and, meeting the girl, take her around another way out of reach of these comments, or, at least, give her the protection of his presence.

"Oh, it is to your artistic soul that she appeals, of course," went on Mrs. Needham, with a furtive touch of sharpness in her incisive little voice. "You artists always rave over those large women. You didn't tell me you were rescued by a rustic beauty."

"No, I didn't mention it," said Austin dryly. "I knew if you ever saw her you would not need to be told."

Certainly he was acquitting himself most unwisely.

Just then at one of the many turns of the wayward path the girl under discussion raised her eyes, and looking straight before her saw the picture framed in the window of the large farm-house whose wide-open doors and piazza full of easy-chairs suggested such summer ease and hospitality. She made an instant's pause, and the deep flush, that Austin recognized with a thrill of pleasure, dyed her face and even her throat. Then, averting her glance, she came straight on her way towards them, the intentness of Medcott's attitude and gaze, and the pretty, curious face so near him, photographed distinctly on her memory. When she looked at them again she was just before the house, and Austin was leaning over the sill, and on the doorstep stood Mrs. Needham in her exquisitely fitting gray gown and her bright little smile.

"Won't you please come in," she said, "and let us thank you? Mr. Medcott tells me if it were not for you he would be up at the Cascade yet."

The "us" in the sentence produced all the effect she hoped from it. It filled Medcott's soul with impotent wrath, and touched the spirit of the girl whom she addressed with vague and unrecognized discomfort.

"Do be so good as to grant me this other favor," said Medcott's musical voice. The girl looked at him with her shy smile, hesitated a moment, and then slowly crossed the road and came in at the gate. Mrs. Needham watched her coming with a curious, cold look about the corners of her mouth.

"I want you to thank your brother for me," added Medcott.

"Will you tell us who you are?" asked Florence with an air of good-natured freedom.

"Miss Trent need not do that," interposed Austin quietly, "her brother gave me his name—perhaps he told you that mine is Austin Medcott."

"Yes," she said.

"Oh," said Mrs. Needham, airily, after one of her quick, surprised glances at Medcott. "Mr. Medcott did not call you by name in the description he favored me with; Miss Trent—is that it?"

"Yes," said the girl again, with her grave, direct look which made Mrs. Needham seem unreasonably frivolous and ephemeral, "Rhodope Trent."

"And I am Mrs. Needham," went on Florence. "Do come in and stay, won't you? Mr. Medcott and I are bored to death, and we long for something diverting—something interesting, he would say," and she glanced at him laughingly around the doorpost. "I am usually considered interesting—very—by men of taste, but I've sung my best songs and danced my best dances and told my funniest tales this afternoon, and Mr. Medcott is still bored, and naturally I am by such an unappreciative audience. So as the rest of the boarders have all gone on a picnic and "—she sank her voice to a transient whisper—"and the Clocks are all slow—excuse me, but we make that joke regularly once a day—there is nothing left unless you come in and amuse us."

She delivered her analysis of the situation with her usual accompaniment of bright, unmeaning laughter, watching all the while the beautiful face of the girl before her, whose expression of mingled questioning and dismay made Austin long to shake the speaker.

"I cannot come in to-day," Rhodope answered at last, with the dignity of sincerity in which Florence Needham was so notably deficient.

"Come another time, then," she said in honeyed tones. "We shall always be glad to see you. What beautiful sweet-peas!" she added, before Medcott, who felt angrily helpless, as a man always must between two women, one of whom is bent on putting the other at a disadvantage, could speak. "I am sure you must be taking them to some one

—those colors would cheer the most disconsolate invalid."

"I am not taking them anywhere," said Rhodope frankly, holding them out, " I picked them because they were so
pretty.   Won't you have them?"

"Mrs. Needham, herself, could not have put in a neater
thrust," thought Medcott, with satisfaction, as he noticed
the swift change of expression that showed that this development was unexpected.

"Oh, thank you!" said Florence effusively.   "I will
gladly take some if you do not want them, but I really
think you ought to give half to Mr. Medcott—he is the one
that needs all the petting and spoiling just now, you know.
I persist in considering him your patient too—I am sure he
is inclined to so consider himself."   She had taken a part
of the bouquet from Rhodope's hands as she spoke, and now
watched her as she stood irresolute, with the same curious
interest.

"She is resolved to make us both uncomfortable if she
can," thought Medcott angrily, as he, too, looked at Rhodope, whose eyes were on her flowers while she hesitated.
"If you will give me a few," he said aloud, "you will add
to the list of your benefactions to an unworthy, but not an
ungrateful object.   Do give them to me, Miss Rhodope,"
he added pleadingly.   He felt impelled to use her odd,
inappropriate name.

Still looking down, she drew nearer the window, and as
she reached it, lifted her eyes together with the flowers
towards him.

"You are very welcome," she said.   There was that in
the sweet, glowing beauty of the blossoms like that of her
face.   Suggestions of the sunlight of the wide, green meadow and of the depths of the cool mountain shadows were
concentrated for him in her eyes and smile.   In the fra-

grance of the sweet-peas, he forgot to be on his guard, forgot Florence Needham in the doorway, and looked into her face with a feeling he did not hide.

"Thank you," he said absently.

"We will see whose last the longest," laughed Mrs. Needham from the doorway, and the spell was broken.

"Please tell your brother," said Medcott, earnestly but conventionally, "not to think that I did not appreciate his care and strength the other afternoon. I want to see him again to tell him myself."

"Jib didn't think he did anything," she said, going back to the path. "I guess you didn't make any trouble. I'm glad it's no worse," she added. "Good-by," and with a farewell smile to Mrs. Needham she passed out of the gate and down the unshaded road with the free, easy motion that spoke of the absence of fatigue and indolence. Mrs. Needham turned slowly into the house and came back to Austin's chair.

"What a pretty little idyl!" she said in her light, mocking tones. "It is so evident, poor child, that she has never seen quite such an interesting invalid before. She fancies you as gentle and helpless as you seem—just the person to be reached by the fragrance and innocence of—sweet-peas!" and she laughed again.

Medcott said nothing; he felt that he might hit upon something rude by way of reply.

"It is only hardened souls like mine that learn," she went on with a sigh, "that you attractive men are just as exacting and as heartless when you are drawing upon all our womanly sympathies."

He looked up and recognized the sentimental gleam from under her drooped eyelids.

"And yet you give them to us all the same," he said with an effort, his fingers playing caressingly with the flowers on the window-ledge.

"Yes," she answered slowly, her glance wandering to them for a moment. "Oh, yes, we give them to you."

Medcott said nothing for a moment. He blamed himself for his irresponsiveness. Why not amuse this pretty woman as she wished to be amused? But he was out of conceit with her and her prettiness, and he did not speak. She did not give him long to make up his mind. The sentimental gleam gave place to a harder one.

"Now," she asked, "will you put them in your autograph album and press them and date them 'Given me August tenth by the fair hands of Rhodope'? or will you let them lie and spend their brief existence by your side, while you forget them?"—she was pinning her own to her dress as she spoke—"or—"

"I will put them in water and keep them as long as I can to remind me of her," he answered defiantly. "That is," he said, with the smile which she had sought to bring to his lips before, "if you will add to all your many acts of grace and give me that dainty vase in blue, cracked glass, decorated with red and blue pictures, from the shelf."

"So I must minister to what I foresee is going to be good for neither of you," she said as she turned away. "At least it is well Rhodope won't see them. She would be so flattered because they were put in what she is sure to consider an artistic object. She is probably educated up to scrap pictures," with which Parthian suggestion she went into the next room for water.

Medcott's irritation most ungratefully grew with her absence. That meeting in the woods and the subsequent fancies were no longer between him and her alone; this sharp, hard little woman had made her way into the charmed circle of their acquaintance. He had thought of how, as soon as he could walk, he would find her out and thank her and see again her beauty and her fleeting shyness and her simple, direct glance. He had dreamed a dozen things about this meeting, and now—and he bit his lip with vexation as he recalled how she must have seen him through the window, alone with Florence Needham, her fluffy, blonde head so near, and her ringed fingers resting on the arm of his chair. And how should her innocence know that it was but the perfectly aimless coquetry of an unmitigated flirt who cared no more for Austin Medcott's attention than for that of any man who should turn up in this quiet place! An enterprising bee had already discovered the sweet-peas. His buzz in the quiet room was unusually intrusive. Why could not bees and Mrs. Needham leave his flowers alone!

Florence returned with the vase of water. It increased his irritation to see the blossoms at her round little waist. In a moment she would begin her odious chaff about "Rhodope." He wished she had not discovered her name. But instead she was quite silent as she took the sweet-peas from his hands and arranged them with quick, skilful fingers in the cheap little vase. Only once she uttered an exclamation when the bee which Medcott thought had gone flew out from the purple petals. He was seized with remorse.

"It did not sting me," she said composedly enough, "but it was a narrow escape."

It was with a remark on an utterly different subject that she placed them near him and took up her work again.

CHAPTER III

"ORLANDO.   Your accent is something finer than you could purchase in so removed a dwelling.

"ROSALIND.   I have been told so of many ; but indeed an old religious uncle of mine taught me to speak.."

"RHODE !" called old Denver Trent from where he sat in the living-room of his small but comfortably furnished house.   It was raining, and the fire on the wide hearth conquered the slight chill of the dampness that came in through the open door.   The sturdy old man did not seek its warmth, however.   Rheumatism had marked him for her own and imparted a decided limp to his left leg, but dampness was none the less a thing to be ignored, and a fire in August a pitiful concession to weak womanhood.   The personification of weak womanhood to whom this concession had been ungrudgingly, if somewhat scornfully, made, was at present outside in the cool dampness, her buoyant health untroubled by hints of deleterious influences, while she rejoiced in the thought that Uncle Denver was at least in the room with a fire.   Such are the mutual forbearances from heights of conscious superiority.

"Rhode !" called Denver Trent a second time.   Jib looked up from the book which he was devouring in an attitude suggestive of indigestion rather than assimilation, his head being some inches lower than his heels, which were waving with temporary irresolution to and fro as he lay, face downward, on a cushioned bench upon which he was too long to find ample accommodation.

" She's round on the side piazza," he remarked cursorily, and returned to " The Haunts of the Prairie Dog," a work teeming with illustration and adventure.

" Of all the uses to put a side stoop to," commented Mr. Trent, "about the foolishest is usin' it to set on. It's a good enough place to stand barrels, or shell pease, or hang dish-towels to dry, but as for settin' on it—that's a trick she's learned of the summer boarders—blessed if they don't come up here more'n a hundred miles from home to see how it feels to set on a stoop! Wonder they don't buy themselves one where they come from."

Rhodope had entered in time to hear the conclusion of her uncle's speech, and she now stood before him, looking down and smiling.

" And I suppose you were not wont to sit on the side stoop and watch the hills long before any summer boarders found out there was such a place as this," she said. In this sentence there was a touch of a certain quality that distinguished Rhodope's speech from that of the ordinary countrywoman. Many people noticed it, but few recognized the reason of it. Brought up as she had been, and always having lived in this quiet, ignorant valley, she had none the less absorbed a somewhat unusual education. She, like her brother, was fond of reading, but, unlike her brother, her taste was for the best procurable class of literature.

Denver Trent, a remarkable man in more ways than one, had been for these parts a most extensive buyer of books, and odd volumes had a way of drifting to his table and book-shelves. Sometimes they were sent or left by summer travellers who knew his tastes; sometimes bought from the train newsboy, who had relatives — apparently a most incongruous thing for a train newsboy—near by, and who occasionally stopped overnight, varying for a few hours his dizzying round of dropping novels and railway guides into people's laps for future recovery, and his presumably exclusive fare of apples, bananas, and fresh caramels. It was a motley collection, this library of Denver Trent's, of cheap editions, sensational novels, memoirs and classics, but they meant literature, and some of it the best literature, and out of it certain phrases found their way into Rhodope's speech. Hence with the utmost simplicity of manner and language were blended suggestions of bookish expression which had an odd, half-stilted, half-amusing effect on the ear of the listener. She dimly felt a shade of difference between her own mode of expression and those of the villagers, but of what it consisted she was absolutely unconscious. Her books were as real to her as living companions, and she did not dwell upon their dissimilarity. Upon Jib this love of reading had, as has been hinted, a totally opposite influence. Whether or not it was because he habitually read with his head down and his heels up, he seemed to assimilate nothing. His favorite literature was that of fire and flood, sword and pillage, but his manners and disposition were of an extreme mildness. He held, with the partially domesticated newsboy, long discussions anent the comparative value of the fiction of certain depicters of life in the Far West, and the tamer but more cosmopolitan merits of the works of Mr. Archibald Clavering Gunter. To Jib this newsboy represented that rung of the literary ladder achieved, to those of wider horizon, by the critics of the large metropolitan journals. He picked up all sorts of news of contemporary literature in the tasks he daily perpetrated, and which seem so like that of the daughters of Danaus — always emptying a rack of books and a box of assorted candies, only to fill them up again immediately with the same ones. When a treasure, pronounced by this authority to be most blood-curdling, fell into Jib's hands, he would rise from its perusal to the performance of any domestic duty with calm and unheated imagination, and chop wood at his sister's request with as sweet an expression and as lazy a smile as were presumably those of his favorite heroes as they wielded the marline-spike or the battle-axe. Uncle Denver was vastly amused by the literary proclivities of his nephew, and listened not unsympathetically to certain thrilling experiences detailed at second-hand. When well-meaning people, as occasionally happened, remonstrated with him about some of the undoubted trash that found its way into his family, he would smile and observe that the valley was pretty quiet—wasn't much doin' there in the way of scalpin' and ridin' tournaments, and cuttin' off people's heads with swords, and he guessed he'd just as lief Jib 'd take it out in reading about their happenin' in foreign parts as be lookin' up jobs about home. He might happen to fall on to somethin' worse—he knew them as had.

To which there was little for even well-meaning persons, who have a proverbial fund of disagreeable anecdote and illustration, to reply, for the state of morality in this small, out-of-the-way place was not very encouraging, as is so often the case in these spots favored by Nature above others, but not a word was ever breathed against the good-natured, stalwart character of Jib Trent. When Uncle Denver added that, for his part, he'd as lief have second-hand murders around the house as first-hand whiskey, the subject was usually dropped, only to be supplemented, if the well-meaningness of the person had not destroyed his judgment, by the arrival of "Treasure Island," or some equally exciting and unobjectionable book of adventure. ·

Rhodope stood smiling at her uncle, and he looked up with a half-shamefaced twinkle in his eye.

"Well," said he, "I don't say anythin' against looking at the hills. I reckon that's what they're put there for mostly —but that ain't what the summer boarders set on the piazza for. They seem most as scared of gettin' too well acquainted with them as if they was likely to turn up and worry 'em in the city after they get home. Where's the glue-pot, Rhode?"

A long love of Nature, and an extended, though intermittent, acquaintance with the summer visitor, had taught Denver Trent a number of things about both.

Rhodope went after the glue-pot and brought it to the old man, and then, resting her hand on his broad shoulder, stood watching him a moment as his big fingers manipulated the broken chair he was at work on. But her gaze wandered; she glanced out of the window, went over and put a stick of wood on the fire, and then spoke.

"What you reading, Jib?" she asked.

"'Haunts of the Prairie Dog,'" he answered.

"Good?"

"Fair to middling."

"Ain't all dead yet, I guess," put in Uncle Denver. "Jib thinks it ain't, so to say, a first-rate book while any on 'em's left alive."

Rhodope smiled and walked to the doorway, through which one looked across the branches of a whispering poplar straight into the green hillside opposite, which might extend up, up, up interminably, for all one could see. There she stood a moment, glanced back into the room to see if her uncle wanted anything else, then stepped out and went around again to her big chair on the side piazza. But she did not sit down in it immediately. She paced up and down once or twice, leaned against the rough, unpainted support of the roof, looking off to the distant peaks, and then came back and threw herself into the weather-beaten chair. This restlessness and this idleness were alike unusual with her. She had less household tasks than most of the village girls, for her uncle was well-to-do, and they had helpers in kitchen and field, but she always found something to be done, especially on rainy days. This morning, however, she could settle upon nothing in the way of employment. She did not even want to take up a book. She was never as easily absorbed in a book as Jib was, and to-day she did not feel in the least inclined to one. She wanted to be out-of-doors; she sighed for freedom and action; but it was too wet to walk far, and she had nothing to go for, no errand to do until mail-time anyway, then she would go after the paper. Gray mists floated down the blue sides of Mystery. Now its summit was veiled entirely by the thick, low-lying clouds, and then it pierced through them, and the scraps of mist, torn from the enveloping folds, slipped down into the valley, caught here and there and rent with further fragments which melted quickly into invisible showers. Nearer at hand the straight, fine rain fell softly and persistently on the grass. The house was not on the village street, and there were no unsightly puddles and no deep, muddy ruts to illustrate the annoyances of a rainy day, and no brick walls and sloppy pavements and wet umbrellas to make it seem aggressive. All about the mountains looked on calmly and not unsmilingly at the pretty downpour. Rhodope watched it without further occupation, and wondered if the summer boarders Uncle Denver had spoken of were doing the like. She did not believe they were so indifferent to her dear and beautiful hills as he had implied. She thought they spent a great deal of time investigating their beauties. What had he gone up into the woods for, if it were not to see the cascade—for no possible purpose except that it was beautiful? Rhodope was ignorant of the significance of the sudden change of personal pronoun. He was an artist, Jib told her when he came home, and Jib had also volunteered the observation that he guessed he had good grit, because between him and the doctor they hurt him like thunder and he didn't let on. Among qualities native and ineradicable of the female character, tutored and untutored alike, is the admiration for the faculty of showing good grit when one is hurt like thunder, and the observation, though not a surprising one, had had its full effect upon Rhodope. It must be wearisome for him to stay indoors so long. It was a week now since it happened. To be sure he had many people to prevent his being lonesome. She saw again the picture framed by the farm-house window—certainly, he had not been lonely that day. As Medcott had realized, to Rhodope's simplicity that glimpse had meant more than experience would have seen in it. Mentally she reviewed every line, every detail of Florence Needham's dainty prettiness. It was not yet time for her to contrast it with her own deficiencies of manner and costume; she did not put herself in juxtaposition with this charming woman at all. Yet, without comprehension, without preparation, it flashed across her that it was at her, not at Mrs. Needham, that he had looked, when she first caught that intent gaze in the meadow; that it was she who had seen that long, eager glance that had said something — what, she did not know—when he had taken the flowers from her hands. This was not a thought, it was a realization—and she turned from it with a frightened shyness, but it had come, not without results. She remembered vaguely that his companion was Mrs. Needham; she was married then; but she did not formulate her sense of a certain incongruity between the fact and her view of their relations. She was too unheeding to do this, and innocently and naturally what she had retained of the little scene she had witnessed was that commonly accepted impression suggested by the sight of a handsome man with a pretty woman by his side. She was as far from being troubled by the social aspects of the question as from deliberately analyzing the scene at all. Her reverie this morning was a succession of fleeting reminiscences, as vague, intangible, and shifting as the mist wreaths on the sides of Mystery Mountain. Yet with the same sense of relief that he had experienced, her thoughts flew back to the quiet wood where she had first seen Austin Medcott.

"Miss Rhodope," said Belinda Thompson, coming around from the back door, "will you please come and see about the butter?" Belinda's given name was Jane, but she shared the literary proclivities of the family whom she helped now and then with the butter sufficiently to confide to Rhodope that she had become dissatisfied with the bald simplicity of Jane, and that even Jenny failed to satisfy her completely, and consequently she begged her to give her a choice of book-names. With this request Rhodope had complied, and it had resulted in the semi-adoption of Belinda, by which name Miss Thompson was known to a limited but increasing circle.

The butter had been seen to, and had come out in delicious, creamy balls. It still rained, and Rhodope started down the lane for the daily paper. Jib had offered to go, and Uncle Denver had made a feint of sending him; but Rhodope would not listen to either of them, and the fact of her going out in the rain did not call for a second thought. It has been frequently observed that the old-fashioned waterproof, worn before these days of mackintoshes that cheat you into believing that they are meant for pleasant weather, lacked artistic charm. It was one of these that hung upon Rhodope's superb figure. It was too short, and somewhat too narrow across the shoulders; moreover, the little slits for her arms to come through had very much the air of being in the wrong place. She wore a cap of Jib's, which was masculine without being jaunty, and, altogether, it was quite fortunate that it was a beautiful woman and not a plain one who had involved herself in these disadvantages. She went to the post-office, which lacked its fair-weather environment of lads in tennis clothes and lasses in imitative flannels, and presented only its normal features of waiting teamsters, patient market-wagons, intermittent loafers, and unhurried conversation, all engulfed in an atmosphere of mud, dampness, and general want of enterprise. On her way home, with the paper hidden in the angular recesses of the old-fashioned waterproof, she looked up and before her with the thought, " It will clear, the clouds are breaking away from Monument "—and it had stopped raining when she came to the little lane. Towards her was coming a wagon with a single occupant, who waved his hand to her and spoke as she was about to turn off the road, and she waited until he drew up his horse beside her. As he did so his expression grew to one of wonder and surprise. Jib's cap was pushed back, her brown hair clung to her low forehead, and she had let the waterproof slip away a little from her fine throat. Tom Davenant nearly stammered as he said,

" Pardon me for stopping you—but I thought you might be able to tell me if I am on the correct way to the abode of one Israel Clock." He spoke slowly, with a detaining drawl, and his face was perfectly serious, unlighted by the glimmer of the smile which would have been the homage paid by most men to Rhodope Trent. As she answered him she felt none of the swift embarrassment, the thrilling consciousness which had surprised her in her first meeting with Austin Medcott. She saw and liked his solemn countenance, which bore unmistakable signs of ill-health, and which, in spite of the cynical twist of the mouth and the little frown between the eyebrows, was an attractive one.

"You follow this road," she answered, "until you come to one that crosses it by a house with a windmill; then your way lies westward and turns into a field, and leads you where you see the house—it's the only one anywhere near."

"Thank you," he said, "I will proceed to search for windmills with all the ardor of—" he felt that he was making a foolish allusion for the circumstances, and paused.

"Of Don Quixote," said Rhodope simply. "Well, you won't find but one round here."

Tom Davenant was a man so rarely surprised that the two shocks he had experienced in the last five minutes threatened to overwhelm him, but, with much presence of mind he repeated,

"Of Don Quixote—exactly, thank you again," and, raising his hat for the second time, he drove on, and Rhodope turned into the little lane.

"Bless me!" ejaculated Davenant, as he left the scene of the interview behind him. "Is that the common wayside species about here? If it is, I don't wonder Medcott fell down and hurt himself. A man has to prostrate himself before such divinities. I'm blessed if she didn't know who Don Quixote was, as well as looking so disgracefully pretty in that old waterproof! I say it's an outrage." And as his horse, somewhat spent by a twenty-mile drive, jogged slowly on, he pulled a note-book out of his pocket and made an entry or two. "Valley—setting sun breaking through—mountain mists—regular thing. Wet road—golden rod—tall, beautiful girl—irregular thing—Naiad in a waterproof—incongruous." He perused this fragmentary description with some satisfaction. "Not a bad idea—that last," he concluded, with some complacency, and picked up the reins.

"So my way lies to the westward, does it?" he meditated later on, as he reached the house with the windmill. "Now what, in the name of the Yankee dialect, made her say that! I believe she's a masquerader."

The second week of Medcott's helplessness found him outwardly resigned, as the object of so much unremitting attention from all the occupants of the Clock house could not fail to be, but inwardly somewhat inclined to fret against the overrulings of Providence. He was out on the piazza to-day, and was turning to the account of one of his fellow-lodgers some of his monotonous moments by criticising the sketches of a young woman who was bent upon reproducing some of the scenes which so deeply impressed her susceptible soul. The fact that if she drew a hawk it was as likely as not to look like a handsaw would have discouraged some critics with half Medcott's ability; but he was very good-tempered and tolerant of harmless pleasure, artistic or otherwise. As he raised his eyes and his arm to point out some peculiarity by way of instructive illustration, he disconcerted his pupil by a sudden exclamation,

"By Jove! That looks—it certainly is—old Tom Davenant!" All the occupants of the piazza-chairs looked up the misty road.

"Who?" exclaimed Mrs. Needham incredulously, from the other end of the piazza.

"Tom Davenant," repeated Medcott, noticing nothing unusual in her voice, his eyes being fixed upon the approaching wagon from which Davenant was waving his hat. Mrs. Needham rose and went to the edge of the piazza. She flushed deeply and then the color faded, leaving her a little paler than usual. She was in the shadow of the vines, and from there she watched the arrival and Medcott's enthusiastic greeting.

The ambitious pupil had disappeared, and only two

women, one of whom was reading aloud to her companion, remained on the piazza. She stepped quietly forward and held out her hand.

"How do you do, Mr. Davenant," she said, her blue eyes meeting his with that trick of softness in their shallow brightness. If she had expected any unusual development, she was disappointed.

"Florence, upon my word! How do you do, Mrs. Needham," drawled Davenant, shaking her hand cordially.

"Any more old friends concealed about the vines?" he asked, looking anxiously behind her. "Well, I'm glad to find you so's to sit up and take a cracker, Medcott. Thought as I didn't have anything particular to do—never do it now-a-days if I have, you know," and he smiled his brief, melancholy smile—"I'd look you up and cheer your hours of suffering. Didn't know you had Mrs. Needham to do it for you," and his eyes rested on her with that tolerant solemnity which was characteristic.

"I can't cheer him," laughed Florence, a little nervously; "I can only pacify him, and read him things he doesn't want to hear. I need cheering myself."

"Don't believe it," asserted Davenant calmly. "You were always cheerful. One of the most conscientiously cheerful people I ever saw in my life," he added slowly, as she disappeared in the doorway. When she looked back from the foot of the stairs with some idea of answering him, he had seated himself by Medcott's side, and was giving some directions about his horse to the man who had come to take it.

She went up the stairs biting her lips, and did not come down until supper-time. Then she came, looking charming in a blue gown, which to every end of its watered ribbon was a daintiness and a provocation.

"I found my way here," said Davenant at the table,

"thanks to a most exhilaratingly pretty young person whom I met in the road. She had beautiful eyes joined to a lamentable ignorance of that fact, which was a snare in itself. I have reason to think that she lived up a lane, and her clothes were most inappropriate."

"Oh, Rhodope Trent, of course!" exclaimed Mrs. Needham, with her sparkling laugh. "Don't say any more! So you fell in with her too! She seems to go about succoring distressed gentlemen — something between an ambulance and a sign-post. We are all in love with her."

"I should know you were," drawled Davenant. "I don't wonder, I'm sure."

"I'm not such an authority as Mr. Medcott," said Florence, her voice harder and brighter than ever. "He knows all about her."

"Oh, no, not by any means," said Medcott from his sofa, "I only know she is one of the most beautiful women I ever saw in my life."

"Ah," said Davenant sadly, "my dear fellow, you confirm my gravest apprehensions. I'd begun to fear the same thing about my own experience. Thank you, Mrs. Needham, I will have some berries, please."

It is to be feared that the pronounced hostility Mrs. Needham had begun quite early to feel towards Rhodope was in danger of being increased, rather than lessened, by circumstances.

CHAPTER IV

"By indirections find directions out."

"If she grow suddenly gracious—reflect. Is it all for thee?"

FLORENCE NEEDHAM was a victim of social ambition, and, like the lunatic of Scripture, she was sore vexed by this disorder and ofttimes it cast her into the fire. The most disastrous example of a catastrophe of this kind, one to which she looked back with a regret, the special bitterness of which is one of the penalties of this form of disease, was her throwing over Tom Davenant when they were both very young. Her subsequent marriage with Charlie Needham, though not to be classed as a social failure, lacked that distinctive success that she had hoped from it, and, when contrasted with what might have been the results of that other, acquired the properties of a mistake. But when Florence Evans was eighteen and Tom Davenant was twenty-four, and her beauty was turning the heads of most of the men of her acquaintance, he, though belonging to an unexceptionable family, and sustaining excellent, though somewhat limited social relations, was only a rather lazy, easy-going young fellow, whom his friends called clever, and who was culpably indifferent to what is ordinarily considered success either in life or society. He fell in love with Florence Evans the first evening he saw her, and, somewhat perplexed by the strength of his own emotions, he tried hard to win her. It was the first time he had tried hard to do anything, and he developed a good deal of persistent power ; and as Florence had told herself since, with irritated frankness, she had liked him quite well enough to marry him. But he was not rich, and his undoubted talent, the belief in whose existence she took, as she took every other conclusion she had ever come to in her life, from the authority of some one whom she recognized as competent to pronounce, seemed of the untransmutable kind, and she saw no prospect of achieving any particular position as his wife. He was so incomprehensibly indifferent, too, to the advantages within his grasp, so given over to liking the people who pleased him and associating with those whom he found congenial, without reference to more solid, social grounds, that she felt him to be beyond reformation. Meanwhile Charlie Needham, the only son of a very rich man, who died just as Charlie reached his majority, a young fellow also of thoroughly respectable social conditions, popular, and though somewhat light, not by any means stupid, and unreasonably in love with her, put his name and fortune at her disposal. It was not surprising that without even a temporary mislaying of the calculating faculties of her pretty head, she made her choice between these two suitors, and married Charlie Needham, while Tom Davenant went to Europe. For a time her husband's beautiful presents and the honors of her new position completely satisfied her, and she saw her dreams realized; but those same calculating faculties were by no means sunk in the sloth of a grand passion, and she very soon perceived that her career was not to be from glory to glory, but rather, she must learn to be contented in the unexceptionable, though somewhat commonplace, environment in which she found herself. She had fancied that she could rouse Needham's ambition, of which he had seemed to have enough, and, with his fortune to help her, could make her house a resort for the richest and greatest of the circle of which she formed a part, and herself become a social leader of wide acknowledgment. She had known that her husband was entirely under her sway, that he admired her beauty and her taste, and was the willing slave of her charm, and she thought that she could do with him as she chose—a mistake made often enough, and upon slighter grounds than there were in this case. But she had reckoned without one fatal defect in Needham's character, knowledge of which had been slowly coming to her, that of his dissatisfaction with whatever he happened to have within his grasp. To be sure, he was still the admirer of her beauty and taste, still her lover, but her influence was no longer paramount. He knew her character more thoroughly, of course, and though he did not recognize her shallowness, he had begun to question and to doubt. He wondered if he had been quite wise in marrying her, even as he looked at her with passionate admiration. It is only fair to Florence to admit that had she been a creature quite too bright and good, Charlie Needham would have questioned and doubted with equal dissatisfaction. Now, had he been like some other men, this very quality might have proved a stepping-stone of ambition. It might have roused him to make some sort of advance in life outside of his home, and she might have attained her ends the more quickly. But it was not so with Needham; he simply lost much of the interest she had awakened in earlier days; and admitting the misgiving that it was not all he had fancied to have a beautiful wife and a pretty house, he found amusement in speculation and his club, making up, in small, daily excitements, for the lack of one powerful motive of existence. Florence herself had a certain vogue, but, after all, her position was only that of countless other pretty, rich, young married women, and she longed for something more elevated and more distinctive. There were exacting circles into which even Charlie Needham's money and her beauty and aplomb did not take her, where she aspired to shine. Having reached what had once been the acme of her ambition in the way of dinner-service and gowns, she naturally looked higher. In this situation she found herself when Tom Davenant returned from Europe and the irony of fate was manifested. While abroad he had met with divers experiences. He had undergone a bad attack of Roman fever, which had left him a good deal of an invalid, and he had written certain letters for various periodicals which had directed towards him the applause of a class whose approval is best worth having. He came to New York and went into journalism with the way made plain before him by popular appreciation. Since then he had written a successful book, and though his ill-health forced him to make his application somewhat desultory, his acknowledged talent obtained for him plenty of well-paid opportunities for such work as he chose to do. He would probably never be rich, and apparently cared not at all to be, while he had money enough to prevent his being cut off from any rational pleasure: but he went where he chose, and was much in demand at all sorts of exclusive entertainments. Florence Needham read his name as one among the people invited to meet the latest celebrities, and laid down the paper to remember, with pitiable clearness, that this Tom Davenant, the cleverness of whose verses was proverbial, had once been writing sonnets to her eyebrow, or something very much like it. It was three years ago that he had come home and found the entrance into that charmed circle open to him, and she had never seen him until he stepped down from the wagon in front of Israel Clock's. It had not been her fault that this was so. She had sought in more ways than one to bring about a meeting; she had even invited him to her house ; but he travelled a great deal, he affected no wide social popularity, his work and his health both forbade it—and chance, aided by his disinclination, had made her unsuccessful. As she stood in the shade of the vines and saw his meeting with Medcott, she was startled at the change in him. He had not been so thin and so melancholy-looking in the old days, and she felt with a thrill of unmistakable satisfaction that the exile, from which he had returned a different man, had been her doing. If he had avoided her these three years, it must be because he still feared her power, and it was with this thought that she stepped forward and called him by name. His matter-of-course way of receiving her greeting had been a surprise, but, with the obtuseness of a pretty woman, she could not believe that Tom Davenant, with the same odd, bright manner of speech, the same drawling intonation, the same easy naturalness, unspoiled by flattery and success, was not the same Tom Davenant still. This morning she watched him from her window, as in a suit of unimpeachable flannels he stood beneath her by the piazza steps talking to Medcott.

"Do you know of any place around here," he was saying as he lit a cigarette—he was one of those men who always seem to be lighting a cigarette—"where there isn't any waterfall, or any brook, or any view of the mountains—any exacting view that is to say—or anybody playing tennis within hearing, and where it is shady and cool and nobody else goes, and that isn't more than an easy quarter of a mile off?"

Medcott pondered a moment, lazily smiling, his arms under his head.

"Well, as it happens, I do," he answered, "but I don't know that you deserve to be told, coming over here into our quiet valley and making your requisitions. What do you want to cut yourself off from human companionship for?"

"I have a book that must be reviewed before to-morrow.

It's neither very good nor very bad, so I'll have to put my mind on it to make a readable notice. After it's done, I am at your service."

"Go through the field to the left," directed Medcott, while Mrs. Needham leaned a little forward and listened intently. "Climb the fence where there is a broken bar, and you'll find a cow-path; follow it and you'll come to a scrap of pine woods that ought to serve your felonious purpose."

With a nod Davenant picked up his book and walked off through the field, Florence following him with her eyes. He was not the same Tom Davenant. That one would have never walked carelessly from the house which held her; but he had not married, at least, and people talked about an unhappy attachment, of course—they always did under such circumstances, but no one knew quite as much about that as she did. She looked in her mirror and smiled; she had grown stout, to be sure, but she hadn't gone off much since Tom Davenant loved her. Half an hour later, avoiding the piazza by a wide circuit, she stood at the fence where one of the rails was broken.

Davenant had written a few lines of his book-notice where he sat at the foot of a pine-tree, enjoying the stillness of the woods and their fresh fragrance. Suddenly this silence was broken by the swish of a woman's dress, and the sound of quick steps in the direction from which he had come.

He raised himself from his half-reclining position and looked curiously around. As he saw Mrs. Needham's face and figure and caught her smile of greeting, with the silent ejaculation "Given away, as I'm a sinner!" he rose with all the alacrity of a civil welcome.

"So you *are* here!" exclaimed Florence. "To tell the truth, I wondered if I shouldn't come across you. I wanted a walk, and so I half fancied did you. This little path keeps straight on and comes out on the road. Did you start to find it and become discouraged?"

She stopped as she spoke and, a little out of breath, leaned against the nearest tree, swinging her parasol idly.

"I came out to find a book-notice and became discouraged," he replied gravely.

"Does that mean that I am discouraging you?" she asked saucily, but showing no sign of departure.

"Oh, no, you came along just as I was sighing for an inspiration," he drawled; "nothing could be more opportune."

"Then why don't you ask me to stay, now I'm here?" she said laughing.

"I was waiting to find out whether you mean to do that, or to have me go on with you to the road," he replied immovably.

She gave him a quick glance of interrogation.

"You speak as if you were ready to do what I wanted you to," she said, as she sank down on the carpet of pine-needles.

"That is a manner of speaking," said Davenant coolly, as he seated himself beside her and put his pen in his pocket. "It saves me a great deal of trouble and gives pleasure to the hearer."

"And doesn't mean anything, I suppose."

"Few of us ever mean anything," he asserted. "We all find that out early in life—so much the better for some of us—Mrs. Needham included, without doubt."

The conversation bade fair to take the sentimental tone she longed to give it, but there was an absence of regret in his tone which was not altogether encouraging. On the whole she concluded that to sigh and look a trifle pensive would not be detrimental, which conclusion she carried

into immediate effect.   Davenant watched her, his serious
mouth taking on its cynical droop as he studied every item
of the beauty he had once found so powerful.   With his
cigarette between his teeth, and without a shade of the
emotion that had once thrilled him, he marked the curve of
the cheek, a little fuller than it had been, but still almost
faultless, the babyish mouth, the upward tilt of the eyelashes from the lowered lids; it was so long since he had
seen them that it was an idle pleasure to revive his memory of each detail.   Conscious of his scrutiny, Florence
kept her eyes down and her head averted, until the silence
grew too long, then lifting her liquid blue eyes to his with
all the air of one who, in a few suffering moments, has said
good-by to a too sweet past, said softly,

"You didn't call me Mrs. Needham once—I don't like
the sound of it."

Davenant removed his cigarette, while a look of dim
amusement came into his eyes and vanished again.

"No, I didn't," he answered easily, "you know it might
have created remark at the time.   I never saw you after
you were married, so I was obliged to call you Miss Evans
to the last."

She smiled, and then drew her red lips together with an
air of affront.

"You used to call me Florence," she said quickly.

"In moments of expansion—yes," he assented thoughtfully.   "So I did.   It wouldn't surprise me if, in moments of
expansion, I should call you Florence now.   If I do, I trust
to your memory to pardon the indiscretion."

"Why have you avoided me all this time?" she demanded boldly.

"Avoided you!" he exclaimed with lazy injury, "when
I've come all the way from Stonewall Pond to put up at the
house where you are!"

His deliberate evasions irritated her.

"Did you know I was here?" she asked heedlessly.

"That is neither here nor there," he replied with exasperating coolness. "But if I had, I assure you I shouldn't have stayed away. You are most unjust," he added with melancholy gravity.

"I heard early in the summer that the Swains were coming here this year," she said. The amused look dawned again in Davenant's eyes. He knew so well the key of this not very complex character. He had wondered what had brought Florence Needham and her likings and her extravagances to this quiet place when there was so little chance to display either.

"Yes," he replied.

"I wonder where they went," she resumed.

"They are at Stonewall Pond." She glanced at him sharply.

"Did you see them?" she asked.

"Been staying with them," he replied, leaning forward to light another cigarette. She was silent a moment. Here was another adverse turn of the wheel her own hands had set in motion. As Tom Davenant's wife she might have stayed with the rich and artistic Swains.

"Well," she said at last, "they're nice people."

He nodded in assent and idly pitched small lumps of loose earth at a caterpillar whose furry existence was thereby endangered.

"Have you known Austin Medcott long?" she asked.

"Very long."

"He's an attractive man," she remarked impersonally.

"Too attractive by half. He has gone about being attractive long enough. He ought to marry and settle down."

"Do people cease being attractive when they marry and settle down?" asked Florence with alarmed coquetry.

"Not if their settling down is of the butterfly order," he replied with a slow smile. "Then it is merely an added opportunity to show off one's advantages."

Florence was only partially appeased by the flattering implication.

"But Mr. Medcott is no foolish butterfly, I suppose?"

"No," he rejoined; "but you must allow me to point out, by way of avoiding future recrimination, that you, not I, applied the adjective. I should never dare call so brilliant a thing as a butterfly, foolish. It sometimes seems to me," he added thoughtfully, "that they have quite as much worldly wisdom as, for example, the chastely adorned bumble-bee."

It had always been an objection to Tom Davenant, in Florence Needham's eyes, that he had a way of saying things whose meaning one could not be quite sure of. She was by no means a dull woman, and she naturally resented this. The introduction of worldly wisdom would not have troubled her particularly if she had been quite sure it contained a personal allusion, but she did not wish to make a mistake. Consequently she left the observation unanswered.

"I've often heard the Mevans speak of him," she said— "the Rodman Mevans, you know. Perhaps," and she laughed, "he may find his inspiration in Rhodope Trent."

"Ah," said Davenant to himself, "so at last we have gotten round to Rhodope Trent! He may," he assented aloud. "Now that you suggest it, it seems to me not unlikely."

"Oh, I don't suggest it!" disclaimed Florence. "It is already suggested. I am sure that would be settling down —very much indeed."

"I suppose it would be pretty decisive," said Davenant absently. "She strikes me as a woman who would absorb a man's best efforts."

"I declare," said Florence, rising and shaking the pine-needles from her gown with quick, impatient motions, "I believe I'll ask this"—and she hesitated.

"Juno—Hebe—I beg pardon! Sign-post—Ambulance," murmured Davenant.

"This paragon to go with us next week to the Pond—we are planning a picnic—and give you and Mr. Medcott a chance to see how she appears in polite society."

"How nice of you!" he said admiringly, as he picked up her handkerchief. "I hope it won't rain, because if it does she'll wear that waterproof. Now she's nice in that waterproof—no one knows that better than I—but my diseased fancy longs for something more brilliant, of gayer plumage—something less like a chrysalis."

"Oh, she'll be gay enough, I've no doubt," laughed Mrs. Needham. "She'll probably wear a green and blue plaid skirt and a red jersey—beaded—with white cotton lace in the sleeves. We dress a good deal for picnics up this way!"

The pine-trees shot up far above into the hot morning sky. Their spicy fragrance mingled with that of Davenant's cigarette. The rough path wormed itself into a hollow and disappeared. She stood beside him, her cheek flushed with annoyance, but her white teeth gleaming in her ready smile, while he, lying on the warm ground, looked up at her from under the turned-down brim of his felt hat. With that swift association of place, persons, and perfume that we have all experienced, there flashed into his memory a similar scene, years ago—he had hardly thought of it since. They two had been in a wood together then, and he had lain at her feet and looked up at her, a vision of utter loveliness, and she had smiled down into his eyes, reading easily what was written there. And now—she was Charlie Needham's wife and a good deal heavier, with a bitter little way of her own; while he—pshaw! he was no emotional boy to be the slave of a pretty face—but a more or less successful man of his world. He flung away the end of his cigarette and stood up.

"Are we going home?" he asked.

"You may go to the bars with me," she answered. "Then you may come back and do your writing."

They made their way slowly along the narrow path, she laughing as he held the branches back for her, as if they had not touched—as in truth they barely had—on anything as dangerous as reminiscences. He took down the bars for her; and, when she had passed through, they stood a moment on either side, he leaning argumentatively on the top rail, and she playfully forbidding his coming farther. They looked across the field to the house. There, on the piazza, they saw a new figure—a man, tall, slight, restless, who now tipped his chair back, now rose and leaned against the house as he spoke.

Mrs. Needham paused in the middle of her sentence.

"Who is that?" she said.

"I don't know, I'm sure," he answered. "That settles it. I shall come with you and find out."

"No," she said, turning to him and laying her hand a moment near his on the upper rail. "Don't come with me —please. I know who it is. It's Charlie Needham;" and picking up her dress she walked swiftly towards the house. Davenant stood looking after her.

"So!" he said to himself. "She wanted me to think that Needham might resent seeing us together of a summer morning in the seclusion of a forest path?—in view of past events. Well, perhaps he hasn't changed as much as I have. If he had, he'd envy me my position of disinterested spectator."

Then he made his way back to his retired spot, and took

out his pen again. Before he began his review, however, he opened his note-book and wrote as follows: "Summer morning—woods—woman once madly loved—breath of the pines—white clouds—suggestions of the past—man busy— wishes she'd go."

CHAPTER V

"He may not, as unvalued persons do, carve for himself."

"She had
A heart—how shall I say?—too soon made glad."

"WOULDN'T you have said you'd go, Uncle Denver?"
said Rhodope in surprised tones, her star-like eyes wide
open, her brown cheek flushed as she looked at him, half
in question, half in remonstrance. Down the lane from the
house a little carefully, on account of round stones and
high heels, was disappearing the pleasing figure of Florence
Needham. Denver Trent watched her to the high-road before he answered.

"Well, yes," he said slowly, "I guess as likely as not I'd
'a' said I'd go."

"Well, then," demanded Rhodope.

"Well," he said, still thoughtfully.

"Do you think I ought to have said I wouldn't?" she
went on quickly.

"No," he rejoined quietly—"no, I don't think you ought
to have said you wouldn't." Rhodope went over and stood
by his side where he leaned against the door-post looking
out.

"Uncle Denver," she said, "it is borne in upon me that
you don't think I'd better go. I'll run after Mrs. Needham
and tell her—only"—and with a girlish petulance unusual
with her, added, "only I do want to go!" Denver Trent
looked down at his beautiful niece and his keen old eyes

softened with the fondness that was never far off from
them.

"Easy," he said, "easy now! There ain't any call for
you goin' after that smoothly runnin' little machine. And
there ain't any call for you stayin' at home either. Of
course you can go on this picnic. Anybody that likes better to eat their vittles off an open lot stead of a wooden table never'll be held back by me. Of course you'll go," he
reiterated, and, to dismiss the subject, turned into the house
to light his pipe. But Rhodope was not yet entirely satisfied. Her whole heart was glad with the thought of the
morrow's pleasure. What might it not be to go with all
those gay people to spend a whole, long day! She knew
the place well enough—its beauty had no surprises for her—
but to see it with them, in an atmosphere so different from
that of her strolls, alone or with Jib—that would be something altogether unexperienced. Her thought of the day
was permeated with a warm glow of some undefined pleasure, some satisfying companionship that was waiting for
her. It was like looking to the top of one of her unclimbed
hills. On those heights of shining distance, what unex-
plored delights might lie! Yet her very anticipations made
her afraid. This vivid rose color was not like the cool
grays of her daily life, and there was something in Uncle
Denver's manner that made her hesitate. As she stood
where he had left her, with his assurance in her ears, and
his doubt in her heart, Jib came up the lane with his fish-
ing-basket on his arm. She was glad to see him, perhaps
his encouragement would be without reservation. He had
been off since morning, and as she helped him take out the
fish and watched him put up his rod, she asked him some
questions about his luck, all the time with this other question near her lips, but withheld. He hadn't had his usual
luck, he admitted in a rather shamefaced way, with a side

glance at his uncle. Hadn't gone far, anyway. Found it pretty hot. Thought he'd get enough for supper and come home. There was a suspicion of hurry in his arrangements, and signs of an absence of mind in his way of dropping his possessions about the room. As he was making his way out of the door, his uncle removed his pipe from his mouth, while his eyes twinkled quietly as he asked,

"Been reading any to-day, Jib?"

Jib turned back and laughed a little.

"Well," he said slowly, "I ran across Tim down at the Corners. He was waitin' for the up-train, and he said he had just the book for me to go fishin' with. He said I could bet my life it was pretty lively readin'. So I got it of him, and I've been sort of lookin' it through," and he drew a somewhat rumpled paper copy of " She " out of his pocket and handed it to his uncle. The smallness of Jib's basketful was explained as he turned the leaves, and together they discussed the unqualified praise which the newsboy had lavished upon it.

"Jib," said Rhodope, as she came into the room again, which she had left with the plate of trout, " I'm invited to go on a picnic with the folks from Clock's. Would you go?" and she looked wistfully down at her big, good-looking brother, who was considering just then that nightmare situation of the hero who is pulled up from the bottomless abyss, as portrayed in a dizzying frontispiece.

"Picnic," he repeated vaguely. No wonder it seemed somewhat tame.

" Yes, a picnic," repeated Rhodope patiently. " We're to go up to Shadow Pond and stay there all day. Wouldn't you go?" she repeated.

" Why, yes, I'd go," said Jib readily.

Rhodope felt disproportionately glad of his encouragement.

" I don't suppose," went on Jib with some of his sister's wistfulness in his eyes, "that those city folks do anything particular on picnics. They won't have any fighting, or anything. If it was the centre of Africa now !" and with a sigh Jib returned to a consideration of the grewsome pleasantries of untamed savage enterprise as set forth in the pages of " She." Rhodope took up a piece of work and seated herself by the window in the afternoon sunlight. In a few minutes she laid it down, and leaned her head against the pane, looking out. They did not either of them understand. Uncle Denver thought it was foolish to make a time about doing a thing she had done often enough before—go for a row on Shadow Pond. And Jib—Jib thought it was more interesting to read about African merry-makings than to join in those of the valley. How should it mean to either of them what it meant to her ?—a day in another world, with all the possibilities and alluring impossibilities of another world. Perhaps Uncle Denver, who was leaning back in his chair smoking his pipe, while Jib had sauntered out under the trees, had a clearer conception of what it meant than she thought. He had seen Rhodope, without appearing to see her, when Medcott had come up with Davenant, to make a call of acknowledgment, as soon as he was able to get about. He noticed how quietly she sat and how sweet was her rare smile when Medcott spoke to her, and how long she stood out on the piazza after they had driven out of sight. He saw this, and Tom Davenant had seen it too. He liked the man, though Davenant, with his droll speech and supernatural gravity, had pleased him more, and he felt there could be no reasonable objection to their acquaintance with his niece. Denver Trent's position was too secure for him to trouble his sensible head about social distinctions. Before now, brilliant birds of passage had passed in and out of his doorway, and their migratory propensities had left life there quite undisturbed. But there was something in the air this time that directed his watchful eyes to Rhodope's face more than once, and which had almost led him to deny her the proposed drive. But, after all, it was only the vague uneasiness of deep affection and a keen perception of the problems and conditions of life that lent anxiety to the glance which rested on the girl as she sat with her head against the window-pane in the warm rays of the declining sun.

"There isn't any use crossin' bridges before you get to 'em," he said to himself at last, "and Rhode may as well find out one time as another that to-day's plenty don't mean to-morrow's dinner, and that it takes more'n good looks and a character to take the fancy of a little woman like that one that just went out of here. If I was to tell her so every day it wouldn't be worth as much as one of their picnics—likely as not that's what they're for."

It was after tea at the Clocks' that Mrs. Needham chose to announce the result of her afternoon's expedition. They were all sitting about on the piazza as usual. Old Israel Clock had been milking, and was carrying the brimming pails into the side-door. The quiet household sounds that somehow betoken that work is nearly over for the day were heard about them. The chill that follows the disappearance of the sun was just beginning to make itself felt. Mr. and Mrs. Needham, Medcott Davenant, and Miss Screed sat in a little group by themselves.

"Rhodope Trent is going with us to Shadow Pond to-morrow," said Florence.

"Rhodope Trent!" exclaimed Medcott. "What do you mean?"

Davenant raised his eyebrows, but said nothing. He had looked upon Mrs. Needham's proposal to ask her as a bit of petulance, and supposed she had forgotten it immediately.

"And who may Rhodope Trent be?" asked Charlie Needham, as he flicked the leaves of some purple asters with his cane.

" Oh, how nice !" murmured Miss Screed, who hadn't the remotest idea whether it was nice or not.

" I mean," answered Florence, looking at Medcott, and ignoring her husband and Miss Screed alike, " that I went up there to-day and asked her to go, and she was only too glad—really, if I may not be considered as reflecting upon her statuesque "—she paused to accent the word—" immobility, I should say she jumped at the chance."

" Fancy !" drawled Davenant; " with what a nice fly Mrs. Needham must have baited the hook which is afterwards to make things so unpleasant for the victim !"

" I don't know, I'm sure, what you mean by making things unpleasant !" Florence said crossly. That was a nasty way Tom Davenant had of going to the root of the matter ! He looked blandly forth, and answered, " Oh, I don't mean to make it unpleasant for her, you know. I was only following out your simile—jumped at it—bait—hook—unpleasantness !" and his voice fell into hesitating silence.

" And who may Rhodope Trent be ?" repeated Needham.

" You'll know to-morrow, my dear boy, probably to your sorrow," answered his wife. " She is the village beauty whom Mr. Medcott, assisted by Mr. Davenant, longs to draw from her obscuring retirement, and I am offering my humble aid and getting snubbed for it."

" I'm very glad she is going," said Miss Screed, honestly. Mrs. Needham had not paid any attention to Edwina Screed since they met. She was a quiet girl, with ineffectual features, well bred, not in the least assertive, and childishly artistic. Florence had decided she would not repay cultivation, so did not feel called upon to make any reply, but listened for what Medcott would say.

"I think it was an unfair thing to do," he broke out. "She'll be thoroughly uncomfortable. What does she know about a picnic? She probably thinks we all go from a genuine love of nature!" Mrs. Needham's ringing laughter followed his speech.

"How he resents his goddess being brought down to the haunts of men!" she cried. "She is no associate for the likes of Miss Screed and me!"

This, together with a covert kick from Davenant, cooled Medcott's unwise remonstrances.

"Will she wear the beaded jersey?" asked Davenant, with kindly interest. "I'm afraid you forgot to speak about that. I long to have Needham see her with all the adventitious aids of effective costume."

"I'm not finding fault with you, Mrs. Needham, you understand," said Medcott in his usual tone. "It was nice of you to ask her."

"Yes," put in Davenant, with a heartiness that made Florence long to push him over the railing on which he was balancing himself, "it was indeed."

"But it is hard on my deliverer to put her in competition with the rest of you accomplished women. My natural gratitude leads me to deplore the circumstance."

Mrs. Needham was entirely satisfied. She had paved the way for Medcott to be ashamed of his enthusiasm for a country girl, and at the same time had led him into an ill-timed effort at protection. If it had not been for Davenant's comments she would have felt that she had been as skilful as she had been successful. As it was, she looked forward to the happy consummation of her plans on the morrow.

"Well," said Davenant, as he sat smoking with Medcott later in the evening, "I've heard of men walking into traps before, but I've seldom witnessed the spectacle of a man charging for one like a bull of Bashan, as you did this evening.

Mrs. Needham got just what she wanted in the way of seeing your sensitive anxiety."

" I know it," said Medcott with some penitence. " I behaved like an idiot."

" I should say you did," with which frank reflection Davenant smoked in silence for a few moments. " What the mischief is it to you, anyway," he began again with slow inquiry, " whether that girl has a good or bad time on that picnic to-morrow—as she's foolhardy enough to go?"

"I suppose it's not an altogether unheard-of piece of chivalry for a man to dislike seeing a beautiful woman made uncomfortable, particularly when she pulled him out of an awkward hole three weeks ago," replied Medcott gloomily.

" No," and Davenant tipped back his chair in greater insecurity and deeper comfort, " but there's no use in goading Florence Needham into sticking pins into her, with your chivalrous emotions. She has a large number of pins about her person, warranted every point of 'em."

" I don't care," broke in Medcott with sudden ardor. "I'm ashamed of myself for being troubled about her! "I'm ashamed of myself for trying to shield her! But I'm more than all ashamed of myself for temporizing as I did a while ago, and trying to laugh at my own enthusiasm! Good heavens!" and Medcott's chair came down sharply on four legs, "isn't that girl above any defence of mine and above any of the pin-pricks of an envious woman? and oughtn't I to be proud of knowing that she is and saying so? I've no right to insult her with my protection, but at least I needn't conceal my admiration!"

" That's all very well," commented Davenant quietly, " very proper indeed. But there was a man once gifted with somewhat remarkable powers of practical observation, who advises his readers to answer a fool according to his folly. You think this over and look at it on all sides as you're apt to do, and you may come round to Solomon and me."

Ignorant of all the comment that the prospect of her presence had provoked, Rhodope stood, the next morning, waiting for the buckboard. Her attire, though neither waterproof nor beaded jersey, was a different affair from the trim and picturesque walking-dresses of the party she was to join, but was not destitute of the attractiveness which always belongs to what is entirely appropriate. She knew what walking in the woods meant, and she had never in her life aspired to the city styles, an aspiration which leads some women into the unmitigated errors which Mrs. Needham had hoped to see exemplified in her person; therefore there was a fitness in her appearance which pleased the eyes of at least two occupants of the long buckboard as it drew up at the roadside where she waited.

As she saw them approach a rush of shyness overpowered her. For the first time she realized what she was doing—going away from her own associations into a circle where she would be a stranger as thoroughly as if she spoke another tongue! But as the high, clear treble of Mrs. Needham greeted her, and the sound of laughter reached her with the suggestions of lightheartedness that seem wafted from such a party, no matter what individual annoyances make it up, she looked into the eyes, not of Mrs. Needham, but of Austin Medcott, who was driving, and with a swift thrill which said that the sunny day and the vague delicious anticipations were not in vain, she lost her sense of strangeness with all fear of what it might mean. In an instant Davenant was on the ground to help her in, and Medcott was moving baskets and wraps to make room for her.

" On the middle seat, please," said Mrs. Needham from her position by Medcott's side, and Rhodope climbed in and took her place by Miss Screed, surrounded with this atmosphere of attention, welcomed by smiles, feeling as if she were *en route* for pleasures beside which the imagination of Jib's favorite authors might indeed falter.

The arrangement of the buckboard was a triumph of Florence's diplomacy. This day was to be at once a bitter lesson to the girl whose head she assumed to be turned by the visible effect of her beauty, and to the two men who had dared so openly to express their admiration. With this end in view she had placed herself in front with Medcott, where he would find it impossible to talk connectedly with any one else, and where he might nevertheless be the helpless observer of all the awkwardness and ignorance of this country beauty. Behind them, with Rhodope, was Miss Screed, a nonentity whose very want of character would make her a helpless follower of her lead, while Rhodope should be witness of her own intimacy with the man who was undoubtedly deified in her rustic imagination. In the back seat were Davenant and a Mrs. Rois, who, without Mrs. Needham's beauty, or her sparkle which passed for wit, was quite capable of monopolizing the attention of any man whom chance threw in her way, and who, to do her justice, had seldom time or inclination for the furtherance of schemes outside this attractive monopoly. It was an arrangement evincing considerable strategic skill, and ought to have been successful, and for a time it was. In Medcott's breast wrath might burn and sear, but the capacity of looking at a question from all sides, to which Davenant had appealed, assured him that the wisest thing he could do was to fall in with the arrangements. Davenant, from the back seat, might twist his solemn mouth into its most cynical expression, as in three distinct lines of thought he listened to Mrs. Rois, admired Rhodope's profile, and condemned Mrs. Needham's sagacity, but he, too, acquiesced. They had a good pair of horses, and the buckboard kept the lead gayly, for there were two or three carriage-loads behind them, and for a short while, with the swift motion, the exhilarating air, the laughing company, Rhodope felt no diminution of her pleasure.

"I'm so glad we are keeping ahead," laughed Florence. "Don't spare the horses, Mr. Medcott; Charlie is in the last cart but one. Please pretend that you are running away with me."

"With these unsympathizing companions behind us?" asked Medcott, hearing with Rhodope's ears as well as his own.

"Oh, we won't think about anything but the enraged husband," rejoined Florence. "Look behind, Laura, please, and tell me if his suspicions are aroused," and she glanced back, taking in Rhodope with the downward sweep of her eyelids. If she was trying to shock her, she failed to elicit striking testimony to her success. Rhodope was looking at her with a perplexed smile, and, still smiling, her look passed on to Medcott, as if to ask him for the key to this conversation. But his eyes and attention were naturally on his horses.

"The enraged husband," said Mrs. Rois, "is at present lighting a cigarette in the inside of his hat, and his features, doubtless contracted in a spasm of jealousy, are therefore hidden. I have told you four times, Mr. Davenant, that it is not customary to put your umbrella into the basket that holds the butter, and you have prodded it harder each time."

The conversation flew back and forth over Rhodope's head, varied by allusions to people and things of whom she knew nothing, a thread so elusive that she could not grasp it—

"Just as she seemed about to learn,
Off again—the old trick."

All the time, right before her eyes, Florence Needham's piquant, fair face upturned to the handsome man beside her, who was obliged to bend low now and then to catch the words which she interpolated in low tones, when the conversation was supposed to be general. Once or twice Medcott turned squarely about and addressed Rhodope directly. Then, unconscious of Florence Needham's hard scrutiny, the color came to her face and that shy confidence to her eyes which half intoxicated him with its sweetness. But Florence saw it too, and, with an added bitterness, she barbed the arrows of subtle irritation. Now and then she addressed words enough to Rhodope to save her from the charge of the most undisguised ill-breeding; but for the first hour, save for an occasional question from Mrs. Rois, who was really not ill-natured, but only occupied, a straightforward remark from Davenant, who carefully refrained from fanning the flame of Mrs. Needham's resentment, and rather timid little conversational offerings from Edwina Screed, Rhodope sat almost in silence. Certainly Florence Needham had reason to congratulate herself. The sunlight was as joyous, the deep green of the hills as satisfying, but strange, perplexing discomforts had taken hold of Rhodope's heartstrings and crept into her eyes. Something had gone ; the warmth, the kindliness that had seemed to envelope her like a protecting garment, had vanished somehow, and left her only an unnoticed observer of the happiness of others.

Not in the least morbid or inclined to fancy herself neglected, Rhodope, if she had led a somewhat colorless life, had found it the freer from disappointment, and there was something she could not understand in this sudden dying out of the intensity which had seemed to glow through all her thoughts of this happy day. With sudden homesickness she thought of Uncle Denver and Jib up in the dear, quiet, old house, while she was here with these strange, gay people, and her lip trembled. It was then that a strange thing happened. It was a thing that Mrs. Needham never could have anticipated. It was a thing that Mrs. Rois observed with good-natured approval, and that was noticed with large, present encomiums and much future acknowledgment by the two men. It was a thing strange in itself, but not unprecedented in the history of certain kindly but uninteresting people. It was this. Miss Screed rose to the occasion. No one could tell precisely how it occurred. Miss Screed herself said that she only asked Miss Trent the name of a wayside flower. Mrs. Needham was heard to declare the next day that it was only a part of Miss Screed's everlasting artistic pose. Medcott thought that it was her innate kindness of heart and good manners. Davenant secretly expressed his conviction that it was but another instance of the weak things of the earth being chosen to confound the mighty. Be this as it may, in a few minutes Rhodope and Miss Screed were talking like two girls of the same associations and the same interests. Rhodope's eyes were bright, and her low voice was ready with replies. Underneath Miss Screed's ignorance of perspective lay a genuine love of Nature, and she was unaffectedly delighted with Rhodope's knowledge of woodcraft and general acquaintance with hills and streams. Rhodope, doubly sensitive to friendliness that was not within the strange shadow that had fallen across that of these other people, responded heartily, and found positive pleasure in the acquaintance. Still, underlying this new pleasure was a new, dim sense of distrust and pain. Was there a disappointment in store for her here, too?

Nevertheless, when they left their carriages for the climb

up to the lake, and again there was a going hither and thither, and a bright commotion, though Rhodope might have experienced defeat, thanks to Miss Screed it had not been an utter rout.

Here Medcott asserted himself as he had not been able to do before.

"Miss Trent," said he, coming to her side, "will you show me the way up?"

She assented gladly, and felt, as they climbed together the steep path, that the day had but begun, and much might yet be in store—what, she never asked herself. But a doubt had shadowed its brightness; she had felt the chill of the winds that blow on the clearest hill-tops, and it would never be quite the same day again.

CHAPTER VI

"She gave her a nasty one now and then, I must admit," said Davenant thoughtfully, as he pushed himself back more comfortably into the fragrant haycock and dug his heels into the ground more thoroughly to secure his position. Medcott lay on the ground face downward, leaning on his elbows and looking now off into the distance, now at Davenant, and chewing conscientiously the end of a long wisp of hay.

"And the peculiarly trying point of the situation," went on Davenant, "was that the poor girl never knew what hit her."

"It was a confounded shame!" said Medcott hotly; "having asked her to go on the thing, she might at least have let her alone."

"That wasn't what she asked her to go on the thing for," returned Davenant sapiently.

"She came out of it well."

"Yes, she did. If Florence Needham had been in her place she would have cried and gone home. But Miss Trent was grandly unconscious to the end. That is where that sort of woman scores. She is too ignorant to cut herself through laying about her with her adversary's weapons."

"And every time I tried to make her more comfortable I let her in for more of it," declared Medcott with angry penitence.

"To carry my simile over into fire-arms," stated Tom, as one pleased with his own argument, "when a man takes a hand in women's warfare, the recoil of his weapon generally knocks him over and insures his missing fire."

"I'm tired of your theories."

"I've noticed that more than once lately," admitted Davenant, with entire evenness. "It's a bad sign. It shows that you are given over to personalities."

After which he smoked in silence a moment, and Medcott contemplated the horizon and began on another piece of hay, which he selected with care.

"Now there's Miss Screed—"

"Is she coming?"

"No, she isn't yet. I spoke figuratively. There's Miss Screed, I would say. You don't feel called upon to grind your teeth over the fact that she is not entirely happy on a picnic."

"No."

"Well, then, I say—"

"Oh, bother your comparisons!" exclaimed Medcott impatiently, which, considering that he had given him no time to make any, was both rude and illogical. Davenant looked at him quietly through his half-shut eyes, as he leaned back in the hay and inhaled the smoke of his cigarette. "You can generally be trusted to make your own comparisons, I know," he said at last.

"I'd like to paint her," said Medcott, with apparent irrelevance, a moment later.

"Who?" drawled Davenant, "Miss Screed?"

"Rhodope Trent," returned Medcott defiantly.

"To be sure, Rhodope Trent. I wouldn't, if I were you."

"I'm not a figure-painter, or I would," asserted Medcott with unnecessary perverseness.

"That's what I meant," agreed Davenant with perfect amiability. "You're not a figure-painter."

"I could put her into a landscape, though. Leaning on a stile, or coming down one of these forest paths—or standing with her hand on a white birch-tree."

"Or why not try her in another setting?" suggested Davenant in his hesitating way. "In a city room, with a tea-table and — and a ginger-jar — or under a chandelier at a ball, or looking into a shop-window—those are the things that please the populace."

"Hang the populace!" was the impolitic rejoinder, in the spirit, if not the letter, of a great man.

"By all means," assented Davenant. "Here comes Miss Screed."

Medcott sprang to his feet and hastened to meet her. She came uncertainly across the field, along the path Rhodope had trodden with such free, swinging grace. She carried her sketching-stool, umbrella, and portfolio, and as she snatched a fearful joy from the prospect of the morning's occupation, and was consequently somewhat agitated, she held them in an irresolute fashion, which caused her to surrender them to Medcott's care with real gratitude. It was in the current of grateful feeling produced by her cordiality to Rhodope that Medcott had offered to take her sketching, in order, as he modestly put it, that he could offer a few suggestions that she might find useful. The idea of enjoying the advantages of a morning's work with an artist of Medcott's standing made her apprehensive that she might not profit by them to the expected degree. He longed to assure her that his anticipations of results were most moderate.

For half an hour longer Davenant lay in the fragrant field

enjoying the warm scents and sounds of the late summer, and reviewing his conversation with Austin. It had been no idle suggestion of his, this fancied transporting of Rhodope Trent to another atmosphere than that in which she had been until now. He saw that Medcott's imagination, possibly something deeper, was strongly affected by this beautiful girl. But he knew also that, together with the susceptibility of his temperament, Austin possessed to an unusual degree that faculty, to which he had already appealed, of looking at a thing upon all its sides. His hint was intended to call this faculty into action before his emotions had led him any further. Austin Medcott sometimes passed for vacillating, and to a certain point perhaps he was, but, after all, this was not a fair criticism. As is more often the case than is generally admitted, his artistic temperament, emotional, intense, susceptible, was united to that judgment which sees, feels, and recognizes from many standpoints besides its own. When once he had made up his mind, he was fearless and direct of purpose, but so many factors went to his conclusions, so wide an appreciation of disadvantages as well as advantages, that he seemed to swing from one side to the other without due balance. It had been so with his choice of a profession. He had always loved painting, and cultivated his talent for it, but when it came to the time that he must make a choice that should be for life, he felt so clearly the many things in the way of such a career—the discouragements, the shortcomings, the inevitable disappointments—that he hesitated. He must be sure that he had the power that alone makes the path of art unmistakable, before he would enter it, and this question was not to be decided in a hurry. It was a calm, temperate conviction that overcame this hesitation, rather than the legacy of an uncle to which public opinion assigned the cause of his taking up definitely this congenial work. The decision once

5

made, however, there had been no further delay. He had studied in this country and in Paris; everything else had been subordinated to his profession; though with the breadth which ought to belong to a true artist, he had led no narrow, one-ideaed life, but had seen, heard, and enjoyed beyond the limits of his special aptitude. It was this man whom Davenant knew well when he brought forward the picture of Rhodope in another world and under other conditions, in order to check possibilities which might be disastrous in their consequences.

At the end of half an hour Davenant began to find the sun uncomfortably warm, and, picking himself up, he lazily brushed off the clinging wisps of hay from his coat. Then he stood undecidedly a moment, his hands in his pockets, looking about him. Coming to a decision, he pushed his soft felt hat back from his forehead, and walked slowly across the field in the direction opposite that of the Clock domicile.

On the Clock piazza sat Mrs. Needham, Mrs. Rois, and two or three of the other boarders.

"I use the heavier gold thread," had said a few moments before a small, sharp-featured woman, who abounded in embroidery designs.

"Does it really wash?" asked Mrs. Rois.

"Oh, some of it does," she replied with the unreliability of an advertisement.

"I had rather do cut-work than anything else," said Florence, looking off and seeing that Davenant was still lying where she had seen Medcott leave him.

"It takes forever," objected Mrs. Rois.

"Leila White does the most exquisite cut-work," said the first speaker.

"Doesn't she?" exclaimed Florence effusively. "You mean the Leila White who was such a belle last winter?"

"Yes, I know her very well?"

"So do I," Florence hastened to add. "I met her first at luncheon at the Adells'—a small luncheon."

For a moment she forgot her interest in the distant hay-mow. The small, dark needle-woman said, "Oh, did you?" and was silent for a moment. The shot had told, she had never been to luncheon at the Adells'.

When Florence looked again, Davenant had risen and was looking undecided. In her anxiety to have him come back to the house she laid down her work. A large, placid woman in the corner, with the surprising quickness of large women, noticed the movement and followed her glance.

"How our young gentlemen do scatter in the morning," she observed, as Tom walked off across the field. With a flush of vexation Florence took up her scissors.

"The village has attractions that we cannot hope to rival," she said with a hard laugh.

Florence was not altogether contented this morning. Even her undoubted success of the day before was not quite satisfying. She bitterly resented the part that Miss Screed had taken, but circumstances forbade her to declare it. Her irritation against Davenant was increasing, though she did not believe in his indifference; she was sure that some of the old emotion would yet awaken. This irritation circumstances also prevented her from evincing. Each hour brought new evidences of the social advantages that lay in Davenant's hands. She plied him with questions which bored him greatly, but which he could not refuse to answer, and she felt that no larger piece of luck could have befallen her than this accidental renewing of an intimacy which years had threatened to annihilate. Whatever happened she should not quarrel with Tom Davenant, but peace had begun to be difficult. Together with these sources of annoyance was the feeling that she had for Medcott. Florence Needham was as incapable of startling

imprudence for the sake of love as for any other indec-
orous cause; but whether it was Medcott's fortnight of de-
pendence, or his preceding most transitory and conventional tenderness, or his good looks, or his general air of
prestige, it is certain that he had for her a deeper interest
than any of the observers—certainly than Austin himself—
would have believed possible. It was something that had
gone beyond wounded vanity, that made her jealous of
Rhodope. It was with something deeper than the insati-
able desire of conquest that she longed to command Medcott's devotion. And all these emotions that she could
not reveal, the expression of which was forbidden her by
feeling and prudence alike, concentrated her hostility to
Rhodope Trent. She needed an object for her irritation
to expend itself upon, and she found it in this girl whose
beauty had called forth the homage of these two men which
she wished in vain for herself. It made her clever in de-
vising ways of annoyance; but as the penalty of ill-temper
it rendered her not blind to, but heedless of, the unfortu-
nate effect it produced upon both Medcott and Davenant.
She did not mean, however, to abandon her attentions to
Rhodope.

Davenant left the fields behind him, struck the road, and
sauntered down towards the post-office. On the steps
leading to that fount of perennial interest sat several na-
tives of the valley whose occupations were of that desultory nature that admits of certain intervals to devote to the
amenities of social intercourse. Two of them edged an ap-
preciable distance in opposite directions in a manner heedless of contact with the rough and dirty boards, and Davenant passed between them to drop his letters in the box.
Inside he delayed a few moments to purchase some stamps,
and conversation which had been somewhat at a standstill
for want of material was resumed with a new impetus.

" Lazy sort of chap," commented some one.

" Bet you spruce gum he ain't as lazy as he looks," remarked an older man with the courage of his convictions.

" Well, I guess he can stand bein' spryed up a little by this here air," hazarded the first speaker.

" Wal, I d'know but what he can," admitted the second.

The silence of assent ensued, and Davenant came out of the post-office.

" There comes Denver Trent," said a tall, slack youth who stood about with that aimlessness of demeanor observable in villages wanting in business activity. Just then the United States mail, in charge of a small boy and drawn by a horse whose daily trips of two miles to and fro from the station were an exhausting drain upon its resources, arrived at the door. Davenant waited to see if there was anything for him, and so met Denver Trent as he walked up, his stiff leg imparting almost a seafaring roll to his progression.

" Well, sir," said the new-comer with a smile as he recognized Davenant. Denver Trent's smile was something out of the common. It was so sweet and childlike that it made his rugged face a most attractive object; men, women, and children felt its charm, and it was a trait which had manifested itself in another generation. Jib and Rhodope both had it, but with them it was less a surprise than a part of their youth and beauty.

" Well, Mr. Trent," replied Davenant, "you are just in time for the mail, sir."

" Mornin', Denver," remarked one and another of the bystanders.

" Mornin'," he replied. " Seems to be a good deal doin' to-day." Davenant was inclined to suspect a satirical implication, but as he saw that the circle about the door was rapidly enlarging, and met Denver Trent's honest gaze, he felt that it was only the result of intelligent observation. The periphery of the circle was composed of the transient population of the village, to whom calling for the mail was rather a social episode than a daily incident, and their light, quick speech and laughter seemed like the demonstrativeness of foreigners, by the side of the slow, rare words of the nucleus of the group. As soon as the window was opened this periphery closed in and called for its mail with varying expressions of pleasure and disappointment, while the nucleus waited until such time as it could claim the postmaster's undivided attention.

"You see, they've only got all the time the' is," said Denver Trent with a shrewd twinkle in his eye, as two laughing girls hurried by with the exclamation "I knew he'd send it to-day!" "and then it's with them the responsibility of the mail mostly lies. There isn't much of any mail when they ain't here. We know that, and so we sort of stand by and give them first chance."

"I see," said Davenant smiling. "They can have my chance. I'd be obliged to them if they'd take my letters, too."

In a few moments the two men were walking together up the road. They had contracted a mutual liking, based largely upon taciturnity, and were quite at ease in each other's presence.

"Might walk up along with me," Denver had suggested, "Jib's fishin' again to-day. Might come up and see if he's had any luck."

"I'd like to," said Davenant heartily. They both recognized this as a mere pretext for further intercourse.

"Well, now, I'm sort o' surprised that you've got time," said the older man after they had walked a few rods. "Most of you young fellers who come up here hardly have time to turn round, what with walkin' and drivin' and climbin'—seems as if they thought the whole valley'd get away, 'less they sort of run it over."

" My dear sir," said Davenant, "I assure you on my word of honor I have time to make a perfect teetotum of myself if I feel inclined. I wouldn't detain the valley a minute beyond its appointed time either. It's likely to stay here as long as I do, and meanwhile I intend to enjoy myself."

Denver Trent laughed softly. He liked Davenant's drawling laziness.

"I guess," said he a few moments later, "that you're a pretty sensible sort of feller."

"I guess I am," said Davenant with entire gravity. "I guess that's exactly what I am."

When they reached the wide, open door of the little, old house, they found no one within.

"They ain't back yet," said Denver; "I guess Rhode's gone too."

"Is your niece a fisherwoman?" asked Davenant. He was disappointed not to see Rhodope.

"Considerable of one," replied her uncle. "I'll tell you, they're only just down at the foot of that next lot. You see where them rocks are? You just foller them around and you come out right over the brook, and I guess they ain't far up it. Perhaps you'd like to go see, while I set here and read the paper. Then you can come along with 'em and have some of the fish for dinner."

" Thank you very much," said Davenant; "I don't believe "—then, as he looked at the old man, he saw that he really wanted him to accept his careless invitation, and he altered the close of his sentence—"I don't believe it'll make any difference to the Clocks, and I shall be very glad to, indeed."

Denver Trent watched him as he strolled along in the direction pointed out to him.

"He's the kind of man I'd like to have for company," he meditated. "I'm surer of that than I would be of the one that's got the good looks of the concern."

It was a rough and overgrown path that Davenant was following, and it led him through an amount of underbrush that made him reflect in mournful Phrygian strain upon the future state of his white flannel trousers. At last he came to a break in the foliage, and, walking to the edge of the ascending bank, he looked over. There, some distance below him, was a pretty sylvan scene, and he studied it with appreciation. The brook, clear and narrow, babbled of green fields, as it ran on under overhanging branches and over smooth stones. The noon sun made warmth but not glare in the deep shade. Jib's line was in the water, and Rhodope, her lips a little apart, leaning forward, sat by his side, watching with absorbed interest the floating thread. Beyond them both, almost hidden in the thick grass and shrubs, lay a third person, his eyes also fixed in suspense upon Jib. This third person lacked the beauty of the other two, and introduced an element of worldliness into the rusticity of the group. One felt instinctively that, though he might mingle freely in the sport of the hour, it was with a certain condescension, as of one to whom busier scenes and more exciting contests were familiar. He was a small, slight youth, with an expression of not unhappily blended astuteness and good-nature, and was a stranger to Davenant. It was Tim, the train newsboy, taking a day off. As Davenant looked down at them it was like a well-set tableau—the immobility of the figures, the intent expressions, the quietness of the little glade.

"There!" exclaimed Rhodope, and the spell was broken. The curtain was down, and Davenant was behind the scenes. With a quick motion Jib landed a fair-sized trout, and Tim crawled along to inspect it.

"Well," said Jib, laying aside his fishing-tackle, "I said I'd only wait to catch one more. We may as well talk awhile."

"Gorry!" exclaimed Tim, "I'm tireder holding my tongue than you are hauling in those fish!"

"Yes," said Rhodope, glancing up at the sky, "we needn't go home quite yet—we may as well talk."

"But," said a slow, drawling voice from the distance above their heads, "I'm afraid I can't hear all you say." They started and looked up, and Rhodope's surprised gaze brightened as she saw Davenant, though even with her smile of recognition went an eager glance behind him, as if there might be some one else. Davenant saw it and knew what it meant. Jib and Tim looked at each other and laughed in some embarrassment without replying, after the manner of boys confronted with social problems, but Rhodope said,

"The path is farther on. I guess you'll see it."

"He's one of the dudes from Clock's, ain't he?" asked Tim in a stage-whisper as Davenant went on to find his way down. Tim was often noticeably inelegant in speech.

"He isn't a dude at all," said Rhodope with decision. "If he talks with us you will like to hear him," which, for one whose ideas were somewhat hazy on the peculiarities of the species referred to, was not demonstrating her point badly. The boys were both accustomed to accept Rhodope's judgment as infallible upon all subjects not immediately connected with either sport or literature, so Davenant found a far from hostile circle open to admit him.

For an hour the four sat on the border of the babbling brook and talked, Davenant keenly enjoying the unconventional natures and their differences. The boys at first had been constrained, but Tom possessed in a high degree that enviable faculty of meeting people on their own ground without patronage, difficulty, or affectation, and there soon existed that hearing and speaking eagerness which is the touchstone of profitable conversation. Most of all he watched Rhodope, and found her a different person from the Rhodope of the drive. The consciousness that she felt in Medcott's presence was gone, as was also the perplexed shyness produced by unwonted ways and surroundings.

Here, in her own woods, with all the dear sights and sounds of the forest and the hills about her, her two devoted admirers by her side, and Davenant, with whom from the first she had felt at ease, seeming for the moment her own familiar friend, the full charm of her freedom, her quaintness, and her simplicity, as well as that of her great beauty, was manifest. She had a positive delight in the growing, moving things about them. The birds and the insects acquired the attributes of persons beneath her comment. An oriole flashed by them and perched upon a not distant branch.

"See," said Rhodope, "he has a June-bug which does not want to be eaten. Watch him deal with it."

"Not an unnatural frame of mind, I suppose," commented Davenant; "few of us would care to be intercepted for that purpose."

"And that June-bug never thought that it would be eaten," asserted Rhodope gravely. "It was so safe inside its hard little shell! But it is just those things that go boom, splash, right into danger—remember that, Tim!" She smiled at the boy, as one who knows admonitions are wasted, and therefore harmless.

The oriole put its head on one side and knocked the recalcitrant bug hard on the branch of the tree.

"I'll bet on the fire-hanger!" remarked Tim.

"Poor little stupid June-bug!" exclaimed Rhodope; "it is having its brains knocked out."

"It has no brains," consoled Davenant; "hard-shelled things never have—wisdom is sensitive."

"No, it's only that ignorance doesn't know what hurts it."

Davenant glanced at her with quick interrogation. Was she thinking of what had made the substance of his and Medcott's talk that morning? Evidently not. She was smiling still, as she watched the bird with a pretty intentness. The oriole flicked the branch with the now quiescent bug more decidedly, and then nodded its head with a funny little air of triumph, combined with a final setting aside of all opposition on the part of his victim—a nod of negation and of exultation.

"It is all over," sighed Rhodope. "Why is it we are not more sorry?" she demanded, turning to Davenant.

"Well, something will happen to the bird," he answered, trying to rise to the philosophic level of the occasion, "and we'd have to be sorry for that—and we can't go on being sorry forever."

"Do you suppose there are people like that?" she said softly—"people that are sorry forever?"

"I am afraid so," he answered seriously.

Tim was bored by these reflections.

"Aunt Matilda ain't," he observed. "I don't believe Aunt Matilda was ever, so to say, sorry in her life."

The seriousness vanished from Rhodope's eyes.

"Not when you made the sawdust pie and sent it in her name to the sewing society?" she asked.

"No," declared Tim, "she wasn't anything but just sizzling mad then."

"Aunt Matilda?" repeated Davenant.

"Matilda Spore," said Tim promptly; "that's my name, too—Timothy Spore. Don't you know Miss Matilda Spore, in the village?" he asked curiously.

"Miss Matilda Spore," repeated Davenant slowly—"I can't say I have that pleasure. I haven't been here long, you know."

"It don't take more'n a minute to know her real well!" exclaimed Tim, with the appreciation of peculiar traits one finds within the immediate family circle. "She's my aunt—maiden aunt—and I tell you, she's a hummer, ain't she, Jib?"

"Well, yes, I guess she is—considerable of one," assented Jib, with an evident disposition to be just.

"She can find more fault inside of five minutes than the best floor-walker ever was made. She's the only relation I've got, and I'm the only one she's got; so all the fault she'd find with a large family, if she had one, she has to find with me. I tell you, she don't lose a minute."

Davenant might have found this free analysis of character embarrassing, if the calm assent of Jib and Rhodope had not made it clear that it was merely the statement of accepted facts, rather than the indulgence of private feeling.

"A most entertaining old lady, I've no doubt," he observed.

"Bet your life!" affirmed Tim; "she'd entertain a graven image—and find fault with it for not answering back."

The alleged performance of this somewhat remarkable feat passed without question, in itself no mean tribute to Matilda Spore.

"She is fond of you, Tim," said Rhodope.

"I guess she is!" Tim's conversation was distinctly ejaculatory. "What 'd she do without me, I'd like to know. I tell you I'm all the family she's got to find fault with! She just treasures me like the apple of her eye, and she'd better."

There was an entire absence of resentment in Tim's enlargements upon this theme which was attractive.

"Perhaps she would have been fonder still," went on Rhodope, gently, "if it hadn't been for the jumping-jack."

"The jumping-jack wasn't anything! 'Twas the toad."

"I should not pick out a jumping-jack and a toad as natural cementers of affection without further evidence," remarked Davenant.

"A jumping-jack at the Church Sewing Society! Oh, Tim, it was bad of you!" Rhodope's eyes were glistening with a child's enjoyment of mischief, while she reproved him.

"I tell you, 'twasn't the jumping-jack—'twas the toad. When they cut the sawdust pie, they touched the spring and it hopped." The cynical malevolence of Tim's smile was irresistible. "They fell over chairs, they were so scart —and they thought 'twas Aunt Matilda put up the job on 'em. I traded two good books and one without a cover for that wooden toad," he observed with the not unsatisfactory reminiscence of a railroad magnate referring to an advantageous deal.

"'Twas awful good crust," observed Jib; "Miss Matilda needn't have minded that part."

"Yes, 'twas good crust," assented Tim.

"The crust of lots of things is good," remarked Davenant oracularly, "the insides of which are 'hollow—hollow— hollow!' I am sure Aunt Matilda, from what I hear of her, is too clever a woman to have been surprised by that."

"Rhodope made it," remarked Tim.

"What!" exclaimed Davenant, turning upon her in exaggerated but actual amazement.

"Oh, Tim, I did not!" she exclaimed indignantly, but looking like the discovered culprit she felt herself to be. Tim winked at Jib—further than this there was no comment.

"But," began Rhodope again, after a moment's timid silence, "I knew Belinda was making it"—desperately—"and I knew what it was for!"

Davenant laughed one of his rare laughs, and Rhodope joined him.

"In spite of her seriousness," thought Tom, "Miss Rhodope has not outgrown her girlhood yet."

"Got any new books, Tim," inquired Jib, as he lay on his back, looking up into the sky.

"Well, no, I haven't, Jib," replied Tim, candidly, "not any that you and me'd care about. There's a few of just the reg'lar thing—girls and fellers—you know, sittin' round and talkin' and mixin' things up that any fool could straighten out, and gettin' thin over it—you know the sort —I don't read 'em myself."

Jib made an indistinct sound of assent and indifference. Davenant was immensely pleased with this open-air criticism, and Tim's position of intelligent reviewer.

"Now, I tell you, that last one I brought you was a fine one, wasn't it?" demanded Tim.

"Fine," answered Jib with cordiality.

"'She' was a dandy, wasn't she?"

"Yes, she was."

"I bet that 'She' 'd have gotten the upside of Aunt Matilda," and Tim breathed a sigh over the short-comings of the actual female character as compared with the idealities of "She."

"I like the 'Vicar of Wakefield'," said Rhodope.

"Oh, I say, Rhode;" Tim spoke with patronizing impatience, "you've got the queerest ideas about books. Pickin' out that humdrum old story. Why, I ain't sold a copy of that on the cars, I don't know when—I don't know as I ever did."

"Well, now, Tim," said Davenant, in moderate defence, "the 'Vicar of Wakefield' isn't so bad."

Tim looked at him a moment doubtfully.

Davenant's previous conversation inclined him to consider favorably what he might say.

"No, it ain't so bad, perhaps," he admitted. "But there ain't much to it. I wouldn't have read it if Rhode hadn't made me."

"What are you doing, Jib?" asked Rhodope suddenly.

Whatever his employment, Jib had been completely absorbed by it for some minutes, as he lay on the grass in his favorite attitude.

"Do you see that beetle?" he asked, pointing to a little spotted lady-bird. "He's trying to get to the top of that blade of grass; he's fallen back half a dozen times besides the times I poked him down."

Rhodope's eyes flashed indignation.

"You shall not poke him!" she exclaimed, going swiftly to his side, where she knelt on the ground. Davenant applied himself to looking at the beetle too.

"This has been for me," he remarked, "a morning of most unusual attention to the habits of the animal kingdom."

Laboriously the tiny thing made its way up the blade of grass, which swayed and bent under its weight. More and more slowly it crawled as it neared the top. Down it slipped twice, though Rhodope held Jib's hand so that he could not touch it. They watched it breathlessly.

"Wouldn't it be fair to poke it *up*?" asked Davenant in a whisper as it fell the second time, and they all laughed.

"What will the blamed thing do when it gets there?" speculated Tim with that contempt for inadequacy which was born in him.

"Wait and see," said Rhodope.

The third time, by hard endeavor and delicate balancing, it crawled on and on till its little body clung fast to the very tip of the green, slender, trembling stalk. There it paused in the perplexity of achievement, and then — it opened its wings and flew away.

"Smart, wasn't it?" jeered Tim.

Rhodope looked up at Davenant. "And it had wings all the time," she said, half sadly.

"Yes," he said, "things might be easier if we knew!"

She was grateful to him for his quick comprehension. She was yet to learn how distinguishing was this comprehension of his.

"It will seem so easy when we get to the top," she sighed. "Come, it is noon," she added, "we must go."

Jib picked up his tackle, Tim took his hat off a neighboring bush, and Davenant stood aside to let her pass.

CHAPTER VII

"A truant disposition, good my lord."

"What man would read and read the selfsame faces,
And, like the marbles which the windmill grinds,
Rub smooth forever with the same smooth minds,
This year retracing last year's, every year's dull traces,
When there are woods and un-man-stifled places?"

A TALL, dark woman of between forty and fifty stood at
the door of a tent, looking off towards the west, where beyond the smoky haze of a manufacturing town loomed
faint shapes, suspected, rather than visible, in the light of
a late moon, shapes which meant the neighborhood of mountains. A flaring torch stuck in the ground near her side
threw its fitful light over her striking features, which to-
night bore a shade of wistfulness somewhat at variance
with the general aspect of her good-natured mouth, bright
eyes, and brilliant costume. The tent stood on a slight
eminence, and just in front of her was a wide, open space
filled with an indiscriminate litter, in the midst of which
rapidly moving figures were taking down, with shouted words
of direction, a mammoth tent, that made the one by which
she stood look a very pocket-affair. Here and there were
other flaring torches throwing their fantastic light on the
ground with its scattered peanut-shells, dirty sawdust, torn
papers, trodden and dusty spots, and on the faces of the
men, tired, laughing, spiritless, and scowling. On the borders of the field, unreached by a hurrying, pushing crowd
that had but lately left it to this semi-desolation, stood the

6

starry asters and plumy golden-rod, waving in the night
breeze, bathing in the pale light of the moon, as heedless
and natural as if this atmosphere, permeated by kerosene
oil and roasted peanuts, had not made its way to their very
roots; and beyond them, away from this noise, this commotion, and this splutter, was silence, reaching, it seemed, to
the very hills themselves.   Perhaps the contrast struck the
woman as she stood idly in the tent-opening, for she scarcely noticed the disappearance of the huge spread of canvas,
and the progress of the packing and stowing that went on
about her, though usually she was ready enough to order
and advise.   Not that she was specially susceptible to the
incongruities of the scene; it was much of it too accustomed
a one for that.   Even the sudden appearance of a painted
harlequin figure in white and red, close at her elbow, as it
crossed a lighted space under one of the lamps and disappeared in the shadows beyond, did not startle her with its
suggestions of sad-hearted mockery.   To her it was no possible frequenter of a Walpurgis Night of revelry; it was only
Bob Stein who hadn't yet had time to change his clothes.
But, nevertheless, more clearly with her mental than her
physical vision, she saw that line of high hills on the near
horizon, still, calm, and watchful, and above the shouts of
the men and the falling of poles and the rattling of metal,
she seemed to hear a distant sound as of the purling of in-
numerable streams, and, shutting her eyes, the kerosene-
weighted atmosphere grew heavy and stifling, for she almost
caught the woodland fragrance of sweet-fern, pine, and elder.
Suddenly she started from her half-dream and smiled.   Into
the midst of this grim, smoky artificiality there broke a harsh,
discordant sound, which seemed for a moment to banish all
the puny, human discordance with its pitiless ferocity, a
sound which no amount of gaudy show and commonplace
trappings can make anything but a natural sound—the howl

of a wild beast. The woman smiled—it was as if for a moment she felt the freedom that it recalled.

A man's figure approached her, stopped, and turned back, while he shouted a word or two, and then came on. The work was almost done. The torches were flickering themselves into oblivion, the moon was regaining her legitimate pre-eminence, silvering, with generous largess, even the dirty sawdust, and the voices had grown quiet.

"Well, Nick," said the woman in a pleasant voice, as the man paused in front of her. He was a strong, not ill-looking fellow, with a certain shrewdness tempering the otherwise somewhat expressionless good-humor of his blunt features.

"Pretty good receipts for a small town like that yonder," and she indicated the direction of the smoky cloud.

"Pretty good," he assented.

She felt a note of dissatisfaction in his voice, for she asked, "Nothing gone wrong, is there?"

"Nothing much," he answered, his hands still in his pockets, and a look of somewhat apprehensive perplexity on his face, which his wife saw and could not account for. But she waited, feeling sure that she should know its cause before long.

"It's this, Marcella," he went on in a moment—"Georgiana says she won't ride in the procession to-morrow."

"Well, Georgiana had better not be giving herself airs!" exclaimed Marcella, who was a stickler for discipline.

"You see, she did turn her ankle a bit, and she says it tires her to stand up in one of those dratted go-carts—those being the words she used—and she isn't going to do it if she's expected to go on in the evening. Now, you know we've got to drive Georgiana with kind of a loose rein," and Nicholas looked up into his wife's face, sure of being understood.

"Yes, I suppose so," she answered slowly; "she's the only rider we've got that the public cares anything about. Why not drop her out of the procession entirely?"

"That's just what we can't afford to do," replied Nicholas decidedly. "We haven't got any great shakes of a procession anyway. It isn't as if it was the whole regular show," he went on as apologetically as if his wife had been the public to whom he appealed. "But, you see, we wanted to do it cheap up here in the country, and I've dropped a feature here and a feature there, till there ain't much left."

It was evident that Marcella did not take this lamentable picture of her husband's condition literally, for she did not look at him to mark the hinted-at devastation.

"Yes, I know," she assented thoughtfully.

"We haven't but a few wild beasts, and a regular job-lot of camels," went on Nicholas pessimistically, "and it's the floats and the Roman chariots that fetches 'em generally, anyhow, and we're mighty short of them. We can't drop a blamed chariot," he declared again.

"Well, then, let somebody else drive it," suggested Marcella.

"There it is! There isn't anybody to do it! There isn't a man or woman about the place that hasn't more than they can do. I've had to take Rip out of the panther's cage and put him in as the Goddess of Liberty, as it is, because we can't get along without her and Diany the Huntress, and when you've said Diany and the Goddess you've said it all," asserted Nicholas gloomily.

"Then I don't see what we'll do—unless you want me to drive the Roman chariot," and Marcella laughed an infectious, gurgling laugh. "I ain't *much* more afraid of those ponies than I am of the lion and the panther put both of 'em together."

Nicholas laughed absent-mindedly, while the apprehension deepened on his face.

"No," he said, hesitatingly, "I don't want you to drive it, but I don't see why Elizabeth "—then he paused.

"Elizabeth!" exclaimed his wife. She had slipped out of the tent-door and walked a few steps with him, so that they should not be overheard ; and as she spoke she glanced back over her shoulder as if in fear that their voices should reach to the dim interior. "Elizabeth!" she repeated. "Why, Nicholas French! And you promised me, promised me over and over, that our girl should never have the first thing to do with the show! Are you forgetting everything?" and she faced him angrily. It seemed as if she would say more if only her surprise had not clogged her tongue.

"There, there," said the man soothingly, "I promised, and I'll stand by my word, and I don't want Elizabeth a circus girl any more than you do. And she sha'n't go a step unless you say she may."

"I should think not," interjected Marcella.

"But one swallow doesn't make a summer, after all. And it's only for this once," he went on coaxingly. "And think how pretty she'd look in Georgiana's train and handling those ribbons. *She* ain't afraid of anything that walks."

"No, she ain't," admitted her mother, her swift indignation beginning already to evaporate. "But—"

"Bless the woman's heart!" went on Nicholas. "Does she think I want my little Liz to do anything that's going to hurt her any way at all? If it was a city we were going to, now, I should say right off, 'No, *sir*, she won't ride through all those streets with people staring at her!' But up here in this little town, why, it'll be an amusement for her."

He paused to let this argument have all its weight, but

Marcella still shook her head. "It's a different thing, that's what it is. And who's going to know who she is, and if she helps her old father out, who's going to say as she oughtn't?"

"I don't want her mixed up with the circus," repeated Marcella decidedly.

"No more do I," said Nicholas, honestly. "But once ain't mixin' up. And I tell you what it is," he went on in a lower tone, "if Georgiana once sees Elizabeth dressed up and looking forty times prettier than she ever could, there won't be any more shirkin' processions."

Marcella smiled and nodded. She knew the force of this, and it appealed to her mother's vanity besides.

"And such a little quiet country town as we're going to next—it isn't anything but a parcel of boys and girls and a few farmers and their wives that'll see her anyway."

"You're sure you can't drop it out altogether," said Marcella doubtfully.

"Certain sure."

Marcella knew that her husband was as unwilling as herself to have their daughter become a part of the circus performances, though he was less sensitive to details, and she began to yield. How pretty the girl would look in the gaudy, golden equipage, and how she would enjoy the excitement! and, after all, it was only just for the drive.

"Where is it we're going next?" she asked.

"To North Lanes."

North Lanes! It was the very town she had been thinking of. She had not realized they were quite so near. The folks from all about would be coming to town to the circus. How well she remembered one such day.

"Nick," she said suddenly, "North Lanes—that's where I saw you first. Do you remember?"

The man started in his turn.

" So it is, Marcella," he exclaimed. " Dashed if with all
the going and coming we've done since, I hadn't clean forgotten the name of the town ! We've been there since then,
haven't we ?"

" Yes," she answered ; " once, when Elizabeth was a
little thing. That was when we brought the elephant," she
added with professional pride.

" Yes, and a nice time we had with it, too! Well, if I'd
forgot the place I haven't forgot the luck that came to me
there, Marcella," he said with rough tenderness. Marcella
looked up at him smiling. The torches had gone out altogether, and they stood in the light of the waning moon.
" No, I guess you haven't, Nick," she replied. " And over
there in the valley," she went on after a moment, " is where
I used to live. I've been sort of thinking about it to-night.
I wonder if I'd know anybody there now. I suppose they'll
all be over to see the show."

" Of course they will," replied Nicholas, who knew, without exaggerating, his commanding. if isolated position. To
Marcella's dramatic instincts there was a strong appeal in
the thought of her pretty daughter riding, in all the imperial
triumph of a Roman chariot, into the little town from which
she had run away twenty years ago with the handsome
young ringmaster. She had been a pretty girl herself
then, and she had made a genuine love-match in spite of all
the arguments advanced against it. The ringmaster had
been detained in North Lanes by one of the various acci-
dents that may befall the members of a travelling circus, and
had employed his spare time making love to pretty Marcella
Brown.

The day before he left she slipped away to the next town,
where she met him and married him, leaving all the gossips
to lift up their hands over the headstrong whims of that
Marcella, and her probable future misery. How she had

revelled in the excitement! How her romantic soul had admired the elegance of the magnificent ringmaster!

"Marcella," said her husband as they turned back to the tent, "when you was thinking about the valley then—you wasn't thinking you was sorry you left it, was you?" There was a diffidence in the tones of the powerful circus manager that was flattery in itself.

"No, Nick," said the handsome, dark woman, pausing as another low growl from the cages fell on their ears, and then going on, speaking softly, lest her rich voice should disturb the sleeper near at hand. "No, I haven't never been sorry." She lifted the flap of the tent and went in. On a couch of boughs, beyond the light of the small candle that was burning slowly, down in the farther corner, lay a young girl asleep.

"I sha'n't take much of a nap myself," said Nicholas from the doorway. "You'd better try and get one, but we'll start before light. I'll sort of look round," and he turned towards his own quarters.

"I guess I'll let Elizabeth go," whispered Marcella.

"I guess you will," he answered with a smile.

Early in the gray morning the strange train wound along the country road. Mademoiselle Georgiana, the celebrated equestrienne, was accommodated with the manager's family in a comfortable enough conveyance in the rear of the line.

Half asleep, the jockeys and beast-tamers rode, in a hit-or-miss fashion, whatever seemed handy.

Looking across the dewy fields through the misty air, one might have seen two or three camels patiently poking their way along, probably wondering why they had been brought to a country where the remarkable domestic arrangements of their insides were really of no particular advantage, since water was to be had on every side. An observer would have rubbed his eyes to make sure that it was not a stretch of sandy desert with a pyramid in the distance that made the landscape which bore their moving figures, instead of the pale bloom and dampness of the New England country.

Huge, misshapen forms draped in disguising folds spoke of uncertain magnificence later to be revealed.

Everything was vague, mysterious, awful. So, quietly, suggestively, secretly, the circus train stole into the outskirts of North Lanes, to make ready for the grand parade at nine o'clock.

CHAPTER VIII

" It is common for the younger sort to lack discretion."

" She should never have looked at me
If she meant I should not love her!"

" There are fireflames noondays kindle
Whereby piled-up honors perish, whereby swollen ambitions dwindle."

IT is a person of small imagination that finds himself entirely indifferent to circus performances. Beyond the satisfaction of natural curiosity with foreign elements, beyond that of the ear in the stirring strains of a brass band mingled with those of the mysterious calliope, beyond that of the eye in the brilliance of gold and spangles and strange exotic magnificence of chariots and houdahs—beyond these is an appeal to the deeper if vaguer instincts of humanity. Perhaps it is the chord of wildness in all of us that vibrates at the sight of those strange, fierce creatures with their associations of pathless jungle and burning desert; perhaps it is the shudder that the sight of anything lawless and uncontrolled brings to our careful civilization. These emotions have each a force of their own; but, besides these, there is in the spectacle an undeniable pathos. There in the cage with the wild beasts sit men whose life and limb are at the mercy of a savage impulse, a careless motion; the cruel little whip in their hands the only bar between them and a tearing asunder, their coolness the result of a long training in jeopardy every hour. There are the gayly dressed women in golden equipages, whose life, to the open-mouthed looker-on, seems a beautiful Olympic dream of high carnival on the top of elevations precarious as those of political eminence, and who are doubtless weary of the stupid, laughing, cruel crowd with a weariness that makes their mouths bitter and their eyes hard. Slowly they all pass by for the amusement of a marvelling people, that cares not a whit for them or their fate, but loves the sight because it is human nature to love it—it is almost a Roman holiday. So it looks to the impressible outsider; and though the carping and the worldly-wise laugh and tell him that the wild beasts are gorged with meat and cannot be roused from their stupor, and that the weary women are only men dressed up and probably swearing at the heat—nevertheless, to him the underlying pathos remains.

It was no jaded sight-seer that stood on the little porch of Matilda Spore, in company with her accomplished nephew, waiting for the grand parade. Jib Trent had left the valley early in the morning, that he might be in time. Uncle Denver would drive Rhodope in later to see the circus proper, and wagons would be coming in all day from the country round, including a large party from Israel Clock's, but Jib could not afford to wait; he could not lose one of the many excitements of the day. He had never seen a circus, and he knew not what of strangeness and wonder was in store for him. He awaited it here with Tim— Aunt Matilda's porch being a favorable situation—underneath his calm exterior a prey to impatient excitement. Even Tim, with all his memories of past circuses and his indisputable vantage-ground of outlived emotions, was not free from a thrill as the first stirring sound of the somewhat curtailed drums and trumpets of the procession reached his ears. The crowd on the narrow little sidewalk had increased, Aunt Matilda came to the door, there was a hurrying and pushing of expectation, and the train began to go by. Tawdry, trite, and disillusionizing enough, the circus keeps its hold because, after all, it is made up of real-ities—it is not the clever illusion of a stage, however suc-cessfully deceptive, and Jib's imagination, fed by long pas-turing in the fields of romance, was ready to invest it all with a halo of Oriental brilliancy.

"Of all days," said Miss Matilda Spore, "for a circus, seems to me Thursday's the worst."

She was of the tall angularity of the typical New England spinster, and her glasses seemed endued with a peculiar sharpness for detecting motes in her surroundings. Tim's attention was not so absorbed by the approaching proces-sion that he could not transfer a portion thereof to Aunt Matilda.

"What's the matter with Thursday?" he inquired.

"Well, you're home for one thing," said Aunt Matilda with perfect readiness. "Seems as though that ought to be rampagin' enough for one day."

"It's fine weather for it, anyway," said Jib absently.

Miss Spore looked about her, up into the clear sky, across to the sunny hills.

"It ain't anythin' but a weather-breeder," she said.

There never is anything to say to those people who can't rejoice in a fine day without adding that it is a weather-breeder. It is too vague a term to admit of circumstantial disproof—and Jib wisely refrained from further comment. Tim indulged in a wink apparently for his own sole enjoy-ment, and then gave his undivided attention to the circus.

"Seems to me," said Aunt Matilda, after a pause, during which even her carping spirit was quelled by the novelty of the scene, "them camels is dretful moth-eaten."

"Yes, and they've got humps!" said Tim scoffingly; "and they ain't very pretty anyway. I suppose you'd like 'em to be kind of smooth and regular like the parlor andirons, wouldn't you? Gorry! Aunt Matilda, you'd like a giraffe to have his head set right plum down between his shoulders!"

"There ain't any sech a thing as a giraffe in the hull lot," replied Miss Spore with that dexterity in turning an adversary's argument to her advantage for which she was remarkable. "'Tain't much of a circus without a giraffe."

Jib did not make any comments at all. Leaning forward, his arms resting on the low gatepost, his straw hat pushed back from his handsome forehead, the deep, rich brown of his tanned cheeks making his hair lighter and his blue eyes bluer, the strength of his tall figure perceptible in the loose, careless cut of his rough clothes, he was devouring the scene with all the intentness of a child. It was as if there were unrolling before him some of the pageants which until now had but wended their glittering way through the leaves of his books. The camels with their uncouth riders were bearing untold riches in an Arabian caravan ; the horses with their booted and spurred riders might break any moment into a gallop, which should distance the officers of the law, and the wild beasts were crouching for the death-spring in the hot, stifling forests of Africa.

"Them is the *tamest* wild beasts I ever laid eyes on," said Aunt Matilda. "Guess you could yoke up a couple of 'em and drive 'em to pastur'."

"Now you'd better let them wild beasts alone," said Tim, whether with liberal or metaphorical significance it was difficult to say.

"They come awful short in spots when they got to that leopard," went on Aunt Matilda with annoying impartiality. "There ain't a dozen of 'em altogether—small ones."

"I suppose you thought he'd be laid out like a crazyquilt, didn't you ?" inquired Tim. "One of them fine ones with fancy stitches between."

What Aunt Matilda might have replied, strong as she was in the fact of the leopard's spots being, as it were, vouched for by Holy Writ, is uncertain, for just now the trick ponies began to go by, and in the midst of them, on a large horse, with the bearing of a Roman general, cut off from all work-a-day associations by the adoption of a suit of purple corduroy, chastely ornamented with gold lace, rode the owner of the circus himself.

"I declare to glory!" exclaimed Miss Spore, "if there ain't Nicholas French that Marcella Brown ran away with twenty years ago!"

"Which of 'em?" demanded Tim sceptically. "Do you mean the Arabian Chieftain or the full-blooded Indian Bravo what's ridin' barebacked? You're always recognizing somebody that's about as much alike as a trout and a tree-toad."

Miss Spore was too much excited to heed her nephew's impertinence; she only settled her glasses more firmly on her nose.

"That's him," she said, "the one in the middle with the purple clo'es and the long whip." She nodded frantically, for even Matilda Spore was not above the natural human pleasure in recognizing and being recognized by those of even temporary high degree. Nicholas, however, perceived in this only a tribute to him in his official capacity, and never having known Miss Matilda save by hearsay, he saluted with his whip, without disturbing for a moment the majestic calm of his demeanor.

Tim and his aunt were both obliged to shout their observations at each other, for the noise of the band and the commotion on the little street were quite overpowering. Jib heard them without heeding. He only moved his shoulders a little impatiently to throw off the influence that would seek to introduce anything so belittling as the private position of any individual of this glittering whole.

"I wonder if she's along," speculated Aunt Matilda; "but probably he's married half a dozen since then," she added in an undertone of hope and charity—"I ain't got any faith in circus men."

"Here she is!" said Tim, waving his hat with frantic enthusiasm, the ice of reserve that a cold world had engendered having rapidly melted in the heat of experience. "Here's Columbia, the Gem of the Ocean!"

"Laws!" said Aunt Matilda contemptuously, "she ain't anything but a stuffed doll." There was a moment's pause; there was some delay in the line ahead, and the trumpeters had come to the end of their tune.

"Well, she's a mighty smart stuffed doll," Tim piped up in the comparative silence. "She winks regular, and she just says to the driver, 'Go easy, for my helmet's blamed topply,' and the driver says he, 'I will, Rip.'"

The bystanders in the immediate vicinity laughed, and Aunt Matilda hastened to reply in a tone which freed her from all suspicion of being disconcerted,

"Well, I should say his helmet *was* topply."

The procession began to move on again. Really, it was a very creditable one. There was a louder clash from the instruments. What was coming now? Jib turned his head and then stood still waiting, his head raised, breathless, his blue eyes deep with some new excitement, as he looked at this feature of the grand parade. In a gilded cart, upon the adornment of which, it seemed to his thrilled fancy, the riches of no clime had been spared, behind four fiery little ponies, the reins of which her small hands held with an easy strength, her small head encircled with a shining crown, her straight, slight figure draped in the long folds of some wonderful statuesque garment, stood a girl, and, as she held in the prancing ponies behind the drums and the cymbals, she raised her eyes and they looked straight down into Jib's as he waited by the roadside, and he forgot the visionary splendors of the equipage, and only saw the piquant, dark beauty of her oval face, the curls of black hair under the heavy golden crown, and the subdued laughter of her dark eyes. As she met the sudden, startled—what, she did not know—in the glance of this handsome young countryman so near her, but beyond the staring crowd of boys and girls in the roadway, she looked down, her lips quivered as if she would have laughed if she had dared, and she gave her attention to her long whip, while the impatient ponies danced along the dusty road. Jib never turned his eyes away from her until the last sparkle of her golden circlet was lost in the distance. Gone were the barbaric glories of Bedouin, lion, and bear-tamer. It was as if some rare and radiant maiden had come from the distant, and by no means geographically certain, Aiden of his wildest romances. It was as if all the deeds of derring-do performed by his favorite heroes on what, it must be confessed, had seemed to Jib the insufficient grounds of love for some perverse, if affectionate, heroine, had suddenly become natural and unexaggerated. It was as if a princess who lived in the Court of the Lions, and walked upon gold and silver, and laughed at the threatenings of an adversary's triumph, had deigned to wend her way up the village street. These are a few of the things that it seemed to Jib had taken place when Elizabeth French drove the circus ponies through the town of North Lanes, arrayed in the gorgeous raiment of Mademoiselle Georgiana, the celebrated equestrienne.

"Those ponies ain't very well matched," said Miss Matilda Spore. "I could 'a' told 'em where they could get better ones."

"And you could have drove 'em better, too, couldn't you?" asked her irreverent relative.

"I'd 'a' put my mind on it more than the one that is doin' it," retorted Aunt Matilda. "She see a good deal besides them ponies. She's the very moral of what Marcella Brown was twenty years ago," she went on thoughtfully. "I wouldn't wonder if it was her daughter. Pretty kind of business for Marcella Brown's daughter to be at—drivin' them godless ponies!"

Jib roused himself from the fit of abstraction into which he had fallen since the tail of the procession had disappeared down the street. He had not heard a word of the conversation.

"I'll meet you here, Tim," he said lazily, "in time for the show," and, going out of the gate, he joined the pushing and laughing crowd moving down the street.

Matilda looked after him for a moment; then she said, in a tone of reminiscence,

"Denver Trent used to know Marcella consid'ble well. She mittened him the year before Nick French come here."

"Hum!" commented her astute nephew contemptuously; "mighty sight of a fool a man is to get mittened by a woman."

"And a mighty sight fooler a man is if he don't ever give a woman the chance!" returned Miss Spore with a promptness which seldom failed her, and to which Tim yielded an ungrudging admiration. She darted into the house and shut the door with her last words, leaving Tim with, for a wonder, no reply upon his lips, seated in state upon the gate-post. He smiled and shook his head at the closing door, and then observed to himself,

"Gorry! I d'know but the old lady's right," a reflection which showed him to be open to the convictions of a liberal philosophy.

7

The circus performance was nearing its close, but was still in full swing. Bob Stein was being uproariously funny, as the frequent bursts of applause from within the tent fully testified. Mademoiselle Georgiana was making up for any prestige she might have lost earlier in the day, by marvellous feats and by unmeasured prodigality in the matter of spangles. The cages of the wild beasts were nearly deserted, not being at present features of the in-door entertainment. There were not many of them; a wild-cat or two, the disillusionizing leopard, several of those creatures whose labels present absolutely no suggestion to the untutored mind, but whose personal oddities are an attraction, and a lion. Nothing can ever belittle a lion, and an exhibition, however small, always acquires a certain dignity from its presence. In front of its cage stood Jib and Rhodope. She had felt the close, hot air of the tent unpleasantly, and had asked Jib to take her out. He was only too glad to come, for the brilliancy of the spectacle to which he had looked forward for weeks was a dim neutrality, for nowhere about the stage or in the audience was to be had a glimpse of the dark eyes and close-cut curls of the occupant of the Roman chariot. How eagerly he had waited for the appearance of Mademoiselle Georgiana, and what a sigh of disappointment had mingled with the easily excited applause. He was restless, though enchained by the novelty of the scene, and gladly seized Rhodope's suggestion that they should wait outside for a while. To-morrow, he felt sure, the broadsides of humor delivered by the clown and the ringmaster would overwhelm his whole being in the recollection, but to-night—and he took a long breath of the cool night air without, as he and Rhodope passed through the opening of the tent.

Outside there were glaring torches and people passing here and there, and subdued sounds of confusion and creature complaint, but the contrast with what they had left was strong enough to make it seem quiet and refreshing.

Rhodope looked into the other cages with a transient interest, but before the lion's cage she paused fascinated. She had never seen a lion before, and as she watched the steady up and down, up and down pacing of the superb creature, her deep eyes glowed and she held her breath with excitement. Jib moved about restlessly. He had been from cage to cage several times already, and although it had been a momentous experience, he was not under the spell like his sister — possibly a stronger spell had taken hold of his imagination. The small tent before which Marcella and Nicholas had talked the night before was pitched, as usual, just outside of the circle belonging to the circus proper. It looked dark and deserted. As Jib moved on, from one object to another, leaving his sister to her preoccupation, he drew near this quieter part of the grounds. Finally he stepped outside of the circle of light, and stood leaning against a tree, nearly facing the tent and its surroundings. He could see Rhodope ; she was not far off, and he was going back to her in a moment, but just now a bit of freedom was what he wanted. He scarcely saw the little tent a stone's throw to his right as he stood half turned away from it. The late moon, upon which the valley revellers depended to light their way home, dimly outlined his figure and the tall tree against which he rested his broad shoulders. The flap of the tent was moved cautiously aside. A small, dark, curly head was put out and quickly withdrawn, and the flap fell. Apparently encouraged by the quietness, and possibly by maternal inattention within, a second time the folds parted and Elizabeth stood in the opening. She was another person from the barbaric chieftainess of the morning. In a plain, dark dress, the crimson flush of excitement replaced

by a soft glow of color in her brown cheeks, she was quite
as pretty if less magnificent ; her short, dark curls still fell
about her forehead and the curves of her throat, as they had
fallen under the golden crown. The morning's experience
had been for her, too, an unsettling one. Besides the natural
exhilaration of her young soul in reducing those cavorting
ponies to the decorum of a procession, there had been the
atmosphere of admiration that no woman, however young
and inexperienced, can breathe with entire unconsciousness.   As she thought of her triumphal progress, Jib's face
came back to her, the startled look of his handsome eyes
as they met hers. At first she had not been much struck
by it ; she had looked along the way through which she
passed for other similar impressions, but she had met none.
Looks of admiration she had had in plenty, but nothing
like that quick, intense glance, and nobody half as good-
looking had she seen at all. To be sure, Mademoiselle
Euphemia, who had driven the other chariot, had had any
number of such experiences on the way, and had seen
scores of attractive people in her time ; but Elizabeth had
not, and consequently Jib recurred to her memory with a
decidedly particular interest. To-night, when she saw him
coming out of the tent with a beautiful girl who must be his
sister from the resemblance between them, she could not
resist the temptation to give some sign of her presence ; but
with feminine consistency she waited until he could not see
her without a special effort. Half with a child's love of
mischief, half with a woman's impulse towards sentiment,
she drew aside the curtains, stood a moment, and stepped
out. Jib stood motionless in the shadow, looking towards
his sister. Elizabeth moved a few steps forward into the
light of the torches and gazed in an absorbed way at the
zebra.

   "Elizabeth !" called Marcella from the tent. "Elizabeth!" Jib started and turned in the direction of the sound. There she stood, the vision he had sighed for! He recognized her instantly, though her panoply of gorgeousness was absent, and with the simple directness of his nature he went towards her. But she had started too, and with a sudden shyness and fear of consequences, now that the attention of this stranger had really fallen upon her, and a little dread of reproof, she sped back to the tent, and the curtains fell together behind her. Quickly Jib's stride brought him to the tent, and there he paused, not near enough to hear what the low voices said that were speaking in the interior, but near enough to make himself heard should he be so minded. A man of more sophisticated impulses might have hesitated in Jib's position, and possibly have abandoned the idea of speaking to the girl at all. But he thought of but one thing to do. He glanced about him. Rhodope was still in front of the lion's cage; there was no one very near, few people were outside at all. He turned again to the tent.

"Elizabeth!" he called out. "Elizabeth!"

The voices inside ceased; there was a moment's pause before the folds were drawn aside and Marcella appeared in the doorway. She looked angry. "Young man," she said peremptorily, "I want none of your impudence. You can stop calling my daughter by her name and you can go away. This isn't part of the show!"

If Jib was unsophisticated, he had the courage of his calm temperament, and fortunately he hit on what happened to be the best thing to say.

"I didn't know what else to call her," he said simply. "My name is Jib Trent. I want very much to see her."

"Jib Trent?" said Marcella, her voice, in spite of its righteous indignation, softening a little. She, too, had been watching the crowd this evening; she had seen Denver

Trent go in with Rhodope. She expected to hunt up some
of the valley folks before they left.

"Are you anything to Denver Trent?" she asked.

"He's my uncle; I live with him."

"You ought to be a good young man, then," she said
impulsively.

"Well, I guess you needn't be afraid of me," drawled
Jib, "you, nor Elizabeth."

Marcella's good-natured laugh rose to her lips.

"Well," she said, "if you want to come round after the
show and bring your Uncle Denver along, I guess you can
see us both."

Jib looked back again to the lighted tent. The performance was over; he heard the crowd moving towards the
ways of exit.

"All right," he said, and went back to Rhodope. He
had been away only a few moments, but it seemed a long
time. Some of the first people to come out passed near
them. Their voices were different in quality from most of
those about.

"It is difficult for me to decide between the claims of
Mesdemoiselles Georgiana and Euphemia," hesitated Davenant. "Georgiana is the greater *artiste*, but Euphemia has
the *esprit*. In speaking of professionals of any sort, one
falls involuntarily into the French language," he added with
some regret. Rhodope did not heed the crowd nor their
voices. Human beings were so small and trifling beside
the tremendous animal she was watching. How weary he
was of this circumscribed pacing—this creature who had
had miles of wilderness to traverse! How awful that co-
lossal head with its tawny mane! Rhodope shuddered as
the restless, impatient eyes of the animal looked, unseeing,
unheeding, into hers—eyes of a ferocity chained, but all untamed.

"Behold!" said the high, thin voice of Florence Need-ham in half-suppressed tones, "the lion is now exhibited with Una in attendance. The faithful beast is, however, submitting to temporary confinement, lest he attack Una's other admirers."

"And the gentle knight now comes, pricking out of the circus tent," suggested Davenant, as Medcott's tall figure appeared in the midst of the crowd. Austin was compelled to make a détour to rejoin his companions, and in so doing passed close to Rhodope.

"Have you enjoyed it?" he asked. "I saw you in the tent."

Rhodope started and looked up into his face. She forgot even the lion, which still paced restlessly so near her.

"Yes," she said, "it is all so new. I think it is wonder-ful."

Florence Needham's lips drew tightly together as she watched them. She could not catch their words, but she could see their faces.

"But," went on Rhodope, "it is cruel to keep him shut up," and she turned back to the caged beast. "He ought to be free."

Medcott looked into the cage. "He is no worse off than the rest of us," he answered. "We all ought to be free, and we are all bound and caged." He spoke with sudden vio-lence. Rhodope did not comprehend him. She perceived that the others were waiting for him.

"Come, Jib," she said, "we must go."

Medcott lifted his hat and made his way to his party. "I'll wager a penny," said Davenant, as he joined them, "that you've just been getting off something epigrammatic —or, say, an aphorism. You have just that look." Med-cott did not reply.

"Perhaps it was only a successfully appropriate quotation like Mrs. Needham's and mine," Davenant continued to speculate, as he elbowed the crowd away from Edwina Screed, "there's no mistaking the air of that sort of thing."

" I suppose it does give a man a distinctive look to have spoken the truth," said Medcott grimly.

" There !" said Davenant calmly in Miss Screed's embarrassed ear, " he has begun to be epigrammatic and he can't stop !"

CHAPTER IX

> "A crowd is not company; and faces are but a gallery of pictures;
> and talk is but a *tinkling* cymbal, where there is no love."

> " The forests had done it: there they stood:
> We caught for a moment the powers at play."

MEDCOTT paused in his rapid walk up the hard, gravelly
road. It was a pleasure to feel like himself again, to be
able to go forth with his long, swinging stride, to discover
some of the secrets of the hill country, to leave behind him
the pettinesses and the worryings, as well as the light jollity of the farm-house with its circle of high civilization. It
seemed to him that the air was freer than ever, and that
he could walk on and on for uncounted miles. He had
wanted Davenant to go with him, but Davenant had declined.

"I'm not a climber," he said; "to me the summit of a
hill is very much like the foot, only harder to get to. I
know you can see more at the top, but I am pretty well
used to seeing things that are out of my reach—it's hardly
worth using myself up for. I think I'll stay in and about
the Hive"—this being Davenant's term for the Clock household.

"You mind the stinging as little as anybody," laughed
Medcott.

"Yes," he replied, "it makes very good material sometimes. That's where we literary fellows have the pull over

you artists. We don't have to wait for the picturesque.
We can make a page out of nothings."

The spot where Medcott paused was just before his way
turned from the road into the trail that led up the mountain, and the cool shade, by the river that appeared suddenly under the trees, flowed under a wooden bridge, and
disappeared suddenly under the trees on the other side
of the road, tempted him to linger a moment and look
back on the valley, and then down at the water. Finally
he seated himself on the edge of the bridge, his back turned
to the road, one foot hanging over, and gave himself up,
half to an artist's pleasure in the scene, half to the recollection and anticipation that were becoming so large a part
of his life.

Every time he saw Rhodope Trent she impressed herself
more and more on his imagination; but he felt as if at every
interview there had been misunderstanding, misinterpreta-
tion—as if matters would never be set right, so that there
could be full comprehension, each of the other.

Yet he knew that there were nearer, deeper, truer bonds
between himself and Rhodope than existed in his careless
intimacy with all the other companions of the valley. He
knew this instinctively, certainly, and yet ever between
them was a shadow, a stumbling-block, an intervention.
Was this the result of circumstances only, such as Mrs.
Needham's jealousy and Davenant's hints? or was it his
own knowledge of what was best for them both?

The river, which, when it burst out from under the close-
growing alders and overhanging trees, rejoiced with a little
laughing utterance to find itself free, and chattered encouragement to the ripples which were yet behind, tossed up
wavelets in pure wantonness of pleasure, and when the
branches of brushwood dipped into the stream, broke and
climbed over them in teasing spurts of playfulness, as if

to mock their superior solidity with its affectation of defiance.

He sprang to his feet and looked up and down the road. With a quick surprise, a sudden acceleration of his heartbeats, he stood an instant motionless, then with long, even stride he went on, past the point where the well-known trail led up the mountain, past the unfrequented road which turned off a stone's throw beyond, up to a straight figure which moved along lightly, with well-poised head and ill-fitting drapery.

"Good-morning," he said behind her, lifting his cap. Rhodope turned instantly and smiled up into his face with swift illumination.

"I did not hear you," she said, "and neither did I see any one on the road as I came into it."

It was as if she were unconsciously apologizing for not being aware of his presence.

"So you came down that lonely road," he answered, looking with eager satisfaction at her beautiful face, feeling as if it made not much difference what he said or what she said, now they were alone together on this sweet country highway. It was as if the shadow between them had suddenly melted away in the morning sunlight. "I knew you could not have passed me; I was on the bridge below there."

"Are you perhaps going in the same direction with me?" she asked with an innocent curiosity that almost made him smile, it was so devoid of coquetry. "I am going to Shadow Pond," she added, that there might be no mistake.

"What luck!" exclaimed Medcott with unblushing readiness; "then you will show me the way. I was half afraid I might lose it. That is, if you will let me go with you." He spoke rather anxiously: perhaps her shyness or some unwritten rule of the valley etiquette might interfere.

"I shall be glad of your company," she said with perfect simplicity. "Jib was coming with me, but he had a new book, and though I might have prevailed on him to leave it, it would have been just his good-nature," and she looked at him, smiling. "Jib is very good-natured—it seemed most too bad to ask him."

Medcott inwardly called down Heaven's blessing upon the author of the book which had kept Jib at home.

"That brother of yours is a very fine fellow," he said aloud, by way of compensation. Rhodope's eyes grew shining.

"I think he is," she said; "I think"—and then she paused a moment—"I think he might have sat at the Round Table."

Medcott looked at her with the same sensation of surprise that had attacked Davenant when she understood his allusion to Don Quixote. Moreover, it took a moment to adapt himself to her point of view. At first, he was rather staggered at the thought of exchanging Jib's flannel shirt and brown corduroys for a coat of mail, but as he thought of his handsome face and figure, and the straightforward, serene nobility of his expression, he recognized that it would be hard to find a man who would appear more knightly in the accoutrements of that period. Moreover, he knew something of the young man's character.

"So he might," he answered thoughtfully, "and who should he have been?"

"I hardly know," she said.

"You would not have put me there at all, I suppose," he said, with a jealousy that amused him. She looked up at him as he walked beside her, in the strong sunlight and the sweet air, and it seemed for a moment as if this were a world of romance again. Then she reddened swiftly, and her eyes fell, for she thought of no one but the typical lover, handsome, strong, and valiant—but he, as he looked down at her, thought neither of Elaine nor of Guinevere. Then she broke into her rare laugh as she answered, still flushing,

"It is late for seats at the Round Table. Uncle Denver says what between Jib's African queens and Rhode's stories, the valley's gettin' to be a mighty unsettled place." Medcott was glad to see that she was not always grave. He joined in her laugh, and King Arthur and his knights, who had led them both back into the unreal past, were lost in the fresh reality of the present.

"Speaking of unsettlements," said Medcott, "isn't this the landslide?"

They stood at a point high above the valley, where before them, in the distance, the hills opened, one beyond the other, the long, white streamer of a waterfall waving on the rocky side of one of them. Close by their side the mountain went down in craggy forest to the lower levels, while on the other it went steeply up to its summit, jagged with lofty pines. Between these precipitate slopes wound the road, covered just here with a deep layer of sand perhaps fifty feet broad, which extended downwards, and showed by the upturned roots of trees, the rough stones and other débris there half buried, as well as by the hillside above, that it was the result of the breaking-away of masses of earth thereabouts.

"Yes, this is the landslide," said Rhodope.

Slowly they moved through the heavy sand. There was a sort of excitement in it. The valley lay so still and peaceful before them, the hills stood so grandly quiet above them, and yet a quaking of the treacherous sand, a crumbling of the unsteady rock, and instead of the quietness would be a sudden turmoil, a rushing and a destruction. When they reached the other side, and stood again on the firm road, it was as if they had been through a bit of peril together, though in all probability the path had been absolutely safe as far as they were concerned.

It was not a long walk to the pond. When they came in sight of its guarded beauty as it lay silently between the silent hills, Medcott uttered a sigh of satisfaction and Rhodope smiled as if she had met a friend.

"How delightful to be here without all those people who were with us the other day!" he exclaimed. She looked at him in surprise.

"Why," she said, "are you not always glad to be with your friends?"

"Friends!" he said contemptuously. Her surprise grew puzzled and a little pained.

"I thought—" she began, and paused to think further.

"Yes, one friend of mine was with us," he amended, "Davenant."

"Yes," Rhodope said, "but the others? Mrs. Needham," she went on with a simple directness—"you must know her very well?"

Medcott kicked a stone out of the way. He could not express the impatience he felt.

"I have known her a month," he answered, "nearly."

Rhodope was silent again. She had thought them such old friends; it was a sudden pleasure to know that it was but the acquaintance of a summer. Still—was this all it meant with these people—this whispering intimacy, this warm friendliness of word and manner?—just the careless, irresponsible acquaintance of a month? With sudden misgiving she realized how short a time it had been that she had known him; barely four weeks, and she had only seen him half a dozen times. Was this a careless intimacy? She did not believe it possible; it was a sensation rather than a thought, and flashed across her consciousness and was gone.

"Will you let me row you across the lake?" asked Medcott, as they passed into the shadow of the woods which grew close to the water's edge.

"Yes," she answered, "willingly."

It was new to her, this formal courtesy. Had she been with her usual companions they would have climbed into the boat, and either of them, as the case might be, have taken the oars and pulled out without further words. She accepted it, however, with a pretty, natural dignity, and a silent perception of something new in the familiar scene.

"You think my friendship not much worth having?" asked Medcott suddenly. They were coming down a steep little path leading to the tiny landing-place where a boat was moored. He was before and below her, and turned as he spoke, to help her over a jagged rock. She gave him her hand mechanically, and paused as he paused, looking down at him.

His warm, strong grasp of her fingers, the undertone of earnestness in his words, made it difficult for her to answer him.

"Your friendship?" she repeated, while the color rose in her cheeks, though she did not take her eyes from his.

"Yes," he answered, "you think it a poor thing, do you not?"

His friendship—she tried hard to think what it might mean. Perhaps this was all: a courteous manner, an interested glance, low tones, a clasp of the hand—and nothing more. She looked away from him, her hand still in his, to the quiet lake, to the stern hills whose bluff precipices no adventurous climber had ever scaled, to the thick woods which kept their secrets safe, and the deep, unbroken peace. It was so different a thing from the scene of which they had spoken, where there had been the trampling of horses, echoing laughter, and loud, careless voices, that the sentiment she had associated with that scene seemed necessarily ephemeral, exaggerated. For a moment she caught an unrecognized glimpse of the contrasts that were constantly present to Medcott.

"Perhaps I do not know what friendship is," she said slowly, "I know little of its mere appearance."

He felt a reproach in her words, though she had intended none.

"No," he said, "no one would ever insult you with the offer of the appearance of anything."

Rhodope moved forward; he let her hand fall as she passed before him, and followed her down to the miniature landing. In a few moments they were on the water, floating about through its sunninesses and its stillnesses. The first were rarer than the second. The little lake lay so low in the hollow of the hills that they overshadowed it, and rose like cathedral walls on all sides, letting only the light from high above shine down into its deep, religious peace. There were no cross rays and reflections of earth—all the light that penetrated to the surface was that coming straight from heaven, and beyond that radiance it was tranquil, cool, and colorless. Only their voices broke the silence that Nature keeps within her precincts. Rhodope sat in the stern, her deep eyes softly radiant, a smile, whose presence she would have found it difficult to account for, touching her grave lips. Now and then Medcott pulled a few strokes which sent them closer in the shade of the deep woods, or out into the warmer sunlight, and then, lifting his oars, they drifted back again. while he looked at the hills and at Rhodope.

"I feel a little as if I were in church," he said. It was not only the effect of the landscape. He felt dimly a sense of having made confession when he had stood and held Rhodope's hand.

"It always seems like that to me," she answered softly. "It is as if you had come in and shut the door."

Medcott's thoughts reverted again to their past visit with a sense of exquisite pleasure in the present.

The foolish, laughing crowd, with their crudities of lunch-baskets, were gone, and there was nothing to encroach upon Nature's solemnity, a solemnity sweetly thrilled and permeated with a something distinctly warm, human, and personal —no one but their two selves—and truth and serenity and uprightness.

"How those people did disturb the service the other day," he remarked lazily. Rhodope hastily glanced towards the shore as if she half expected to see it inhabited.

"That day was very different," she said; "but I guess," she added thoughtfully, "they liked it better that way. I've noticed that about the people that come here—they don't like our places just as they find them, but want to make them over into more like what they are used to." She felt the difference less consciously but not less acutely than he. It was to her only as if all the pleasure and brightness that that day had promised and had somehow missed had gone over from the merriment and confusion and concentrated itself in this beautiful quiet. As for Medcott, he knew well enough that it was because he had his wish to-day which had proved vain then—the exclusive companionship of this exceptional woman.

"Did you ever read 'Pilgrim's Progress?'" asked Rhodope.

"Why—er—yes, of course—certainly," he answered. To be sure he must have read the "Pilgrim's Progress," but for the moment the inquiry puzzled him, because he could not say just when it had been.

"Don't you like it?" she asked, with a soft light of pleasure in her eyes.

8

"Oh, very much," he hastened to reply, convinced that of course one liked it, and with uncertain recollection that Macaulay had said it was very fine, and a determination not to disappoint that look of pleasure, anyway; "but you see—well, it's some time since I read it."

He instantly recalled a large copy with colored pictures he had had as a child, and resolved to look it up when he went home.

"Don't you remember when they saw the mountains—Christiana and Mercy and the rest?"

"I don't know that I do, exactly," he submitted, adding, with the diplomacy of a school-boy, "you go on and then I'll see."

"Oh, it is nothing of importance," answered Rhodope; "only these mountains about here always make me think of those, and I have named them after them, Mount Marvel you know, Mount Innocence, and Mount Charity."

"Which is which?" he asked, lamentably conscious that he could not say anything that would touch the heart of the matter in the way of appropriateness, and meekly contenting himself with encouragement.

"That is Mount Marvel," said Rhodope, pointing to the majestic mass of the hill that rose most precipitately from the water. "No one has ever climbed it, you know—not even Uncle Denver. And see how dark the woods are—and often there are clouds on the top. There is room for many marvels up there," and her eyes searched for a moment the gray cliffs and the dusky green of the steep mountain. Medcott was moved by a vague impulse to make a landing and go up.

"And there is Mount Innocence," she went on; "that has more sunlight than the others. and you can trace the course of several streams—do you see? And the woods are not so thick, but they are cool and fresh—I have climbed that myself—and they are full of birds; and that long, broad mountain is Mount Charity. Do you see how it sweeps about the others like a mantle, and how it holds the head of the lake, and seems to protect it?"

"Yes," answered Medcott, as he followed her glance from one hill to the other, "I see."

The fancy touched him—it seemed so fitting a one for the place and for her, this simple, strong, imaginative woman, brought up in the shadow of Marvel, Innocence, and Charity—these three.

"Speaking of names," he said a little later, "may I ask how you came to be called Rhodope? That isn't out of— er—'Pilgrim's Progress,' is it?"

If she had told him that Rhodope and Apollyon fought with Master Faithful and Master By-ends in the Valley of Humiliation he would have accepted it with a simple faith which had never before seemed a part of his character.

"It was Uncle Denver's choice," she replied smiling.

"My father and mother—they died when I was very little —told him he could name me, for he was very fond of me even then, and he found Rhodope in a book, and liked the sound of it—it's the name of some mountain somewhere, isn't it?"

"I believe it is," replied Medcott vaguely, who began to feel that, between literature and geography, his attainments were little less than despicable.

"And he said that I was going to be brought up among mountains, and he'd like to have me get as much of them as possible," she concluded.

"Henceforth I shall not hamper myself with derivatives," said Medcott lightly; "it has but one association for me. It means—*you.*"

His voice took a dangerous intonation with his last words, an intonation he had not quite meant it to have.

If Rhodope had had a morsel of coquetry, she would not have let it escape her. As it was, she felt it as she felt every change, every impression of this man; she was learning, almost, to take her impressions through him—but it only startled her a little. Naturally, she expressed the idea that was farthest from her inclination and nearest to her conscientiousness—after the New England fashion.

"I think I must go back," she said, "I only came for the morning."

Medcott turned the boat towards the landing. He would have liked to prolong the morning indefinitely, but he did not rebel even silently against her decision. He was wise enough to be content with the satisfaction that had been his. He recalled his angry impatience when he had seen Rhodope at the circus. It had seemed then as if everything in the way of physical disability, social difficulties, petty enmities, and friendly prudence had conspired to keep them apart. To-day he found, as we all of us have often found, that while one has slept the enemy has not sown tares, but instead some good angel has been at work uprooting and smoothing out, so that the way seems suddenly fair and open. Florence Needham and society, Tom Davenant and criticism, were afar off, and he and Rhodope were alone, marking out for themselves the path which they should follow. Rhodope had brought some sandwiches, which in a pretty little way she offered to share with Medcott as they went through the woods. It made her feel as if she knew him well to laugh with him over her bread and butter, and have him praise it as Tim might have done —it was as if she had known him always. And to him, too, it brought her nearer, it gave a touch of the sweet familiarities of ordinary life to the fineness of her nature.

A heavy wagon with four horses was ahead of them as they drew near the landslide on the road to the village.

"Isn't it a dangerous crossing for such a heavy load?" asked Medcott.

"I should think so," said Rhodope, looking forward closely at the horses and their driver, "but the man knows all about it—I know who he is; he has preferred to take the risk rather than delay by taking the lower road. Yes—I thought he would get down himself."

The heavy cart was now close to the place in the road covered with the sand and gravel. As the feet of the slowly moving leaders struck it the driver climbed down and walked a little ahead. Evidently the familiarity of the danger made him careless of it, and in fact the ground looked firm and solid enough as the horses made their way over it. Medcott and Rhodope stopped at some little distance and watched their progress.

"Come on!" shouted the man to his animals, and his voice rang out in the peaceful air as if it were the only human element in it. The gravel creaked under the stout wheels, and the horses kicked the pebble and sand before them.

"He has taken a good deal of a risk," said Medcott, "if what the people about here say is true."

"Uncle Denver says John Dibson had always rather risk his life than tire his limb by a little extra work," said Rhodope. "There is danger—it is true enough."

The wagon had reached the farther limit of the slide; the driver already stood on firm ground and was cracking his whip at the straining animals. They watched breathlessly as the horses—the front wheels—the hind wheels—passed slowly and safely beyond the line—when Rhodope drew a little, quick breath of relief, and they both laughed at their own anxiety. A pebble or two rolled down; the driver climbed back to his seat, and put on his break for the descent that followed, and the other two went on their way. As they in turn came to the place of danger, he said, smiling,

"I fancy our weight will not convulse Nature if she will bear an unruffled brow in the presence of a coach and four."

"No," answered Rhodope, moving lightly on, "I guess we are safe enough."

But whether it were that the mass of the débris had been loosened, or whether it were that Nature's time had come to push this little handful of rocks and earth over this hillside of hers—for one reason or another, just as they reached the farther limit where the deep ruts of the cart-wheels grew less marked on the harder road, there was a slight rattle, an ominous roar, a crashing and breaking, and Medcott, feeling the ground move beneath his feet, instinctively caught Rhodope in one arm, and, throwing the other about a tree that stood at the edge of the road, swung them both out of the path of the downfall of stones and earth. If he had not been at the very edge of the peril he could not so have escaped it; but as it was, they were in safety, and stood in silence watching the mass tumble into the valley below. It was not an avalanche, but enough power had suddenly been cast loose to have hurled them both down that rough and craggy hillside, and covered them with stifling stones and dust. Medcott still had his arm around Rhodope as she, unconscious, save of their narrow escape, gazed with startled eyes at the devastation. He looked at the soft lines of her cheek and throat, the turn of the eyelashes up from the lowered lids, the masses of hair, that almost touched his lips, as they clustered about her half-averted head, and he thought of how cut and bruised that beauty might have been, and shuddered.

"Thank God, you are safe!" he exclaimed.

"Thank God, we are both safe!" she said. Then the

swift waves of color breaking over her face, she drew herself away from him, adding softly,

"And thank you for doing the only thing that could have saved me."

He did not answer immediately. His gaze had not left her face, raised now to his. It had all taken place so quickly. The dust of the slide was settling again; the reverberation of its crash had entirely ceased, the valley lay below them as serene as it had ever been, but in that one brief moment these two had been together in danger, and had come out of it—still together.

They could not either of them quite forget. But Medcott did not care to exaggerate any such element of intensity.

"I do not think I did the only thing," he said lightly, "probably there were a dozen other things we could have done. We might have gone part of the way, you know, and clung pale and bruised, but still alive, to a frail tree, and I would have rescued you with pomp and circumstance."

She looked at him, but did not speak. She could not answer him in the same tone. She was deficient in the art which turns one's deepest feelings into light appropriateness, and her feelings, as well as deep, were complex. So they went on together, both conscious that somehow a rush of emotion had come into their lives which had not died away with the rattling of the last pebble and the final echo among the hills.

" He's gentle, never schooled and yet learned, full of noble device."

> " The West is tender, hardly bright,
> How gray at once is the evening grown,
> One star its chrysolite !
> We two stood there with never a third,
> But each by each, as each knew well :
> The sights we saw and the sounds we heard
> The lights and the shades made up a spell."

IT was late afternoon, the shadows were long in the village street, the legend of Ivory Soap which Medcott never saw nowadays without a mental transition to a cool wood and a sensation of pain, twinkled in the window with all its accustomed hilarity. Outside stood General Jim Downing, a man of thirty odd, and the proprietor of the store, Abijah Stetson. They called Downing the General, not from the love of military title, considered by transatlantic writers to be an integral part of the American character, but from what is a much dearer national characteristic, the love of incongruity. Jim Downing never went anywhere or did anything, and yet he always spoke as a born leader of men ; so they called him General, with an irony which he appreciated, but consistently ignored. Abijah Stetson was older and much stouter. His flannel shirt presented such wide acres of unoccupied space that the suspenders which made their precarious way over it seemed discouraged from the outset.

"No, we 'ain't got any butter," Abijah was saying to a

woman with a shawl over her head. "No, I dunno' as we shall have any, not to sell. Perhaps you can get a pound over to Gapp's; they churned yesterday." The woman passed on, and Stetson settled his large shoulders more firmly against the doorpost with the fine indifference to the possibilities of trade evinced by merchants whom no danger of competition disturbs, and whose social position does not at all depend upon their business success.

"Yes, that's Marcella French's gal," he went on, taking up the conversation where it had been interrupted, "she that was Marcella Brown. She turned up over here to North Lane the day of the circus, and Marcella she kinder talked with some of the folks and seemed to hanker after staying in the valley a bit, so she and the gal are putting up over to Dust's."

Jim Downing shifted his quid of tobacco and nodded.

"I didn't get over to that circus," he observed thoughtfully.

"I thought you was makin' up a load?"

"Wal, so I was; but what with one thing and another we didn't get off," replied Jim with his usual air of mild surprise at the failure of his plans.

"Wal, General," said Abijah, "I guess you'll get off one time when you've kinder calculated on goin', and that'll be when they come after you with the hearse."

"Mebbe," replied Jim, not caring to resent any satirical implication that might be in the grim suggestion.

"There she comes now," said Abijah, looking up the straggling street.

Both men watched Elizabeth French's slight figure as she came buoyantly along the road. There was this suggestion of buoyancy in all her movements. She was not tall, but she held herself straight as an arrow, and her coronet of short black curls, her laughing dark eyes, and her brilliant color made her a very striking young person.

"Good-afternoon, Mr. Stetson," she said, pausing in front of the store and looking up at the two men with an upward slant of her chin and a downward slant of the eyelashes she lowered to shield her eyes from the level rays of the westward sun. Then she hesitated a moment. She was not quite used to the place yet, and it was not her idea of shopping to question the proprietor of the bazaar while he took his ease on a three-legged stool outside. Her sauciness had had its immediate effect on the General. His inefficiency fell an easy prey to the striking in female beauty. He involuntarily straightened himself, immediately abandoning the support of the dusty wall, and adopted something that might be considered as an attitude of respectful attention. But Stetson was less impressible. In his line of business he was exposed to so many visits from pretty girls, indigenous and exotic; and they so seldom knew what they wanted, and when they did, so often showed a disposition to subordinate it to the pleasure of conversation with other customers, that he never allowed his interest to become active.

"A'ternoon," he replied, as one who would say nothing he might be sorry for.

"Can I get some dark-green dress-braid here?" inquired Elizabeth.

"I guess you can get it here if you can anywheres in the village," answered Stetson immovably.

"I thought so," said Elizabeth with much tact. There was a pause. In the face of her pretty manner and her charming hesitation, the General felt his companion provokingly unresponsive, and cleared his throat and hit a packing-box with his foot, to imply that he might feel a desire to say something himself if this went on much longer.

"Wal," said Stetson, "I dunno' as I've got any dress-braid at all."

"Oh," said Elizabeth, "never mind, then," and she turned to go, half suspicious that he was chaffing her.

"I dunno' but I got some dark red," said Stetson. "Dark red won't do you, will it?"

"No," she answered, "I don't quite think it will."

"Wal," said the enterprising Stetson, "I'll go in and see."

This was a relief to the feelings of the General, who couldn't bear to see even the whims of such a beauty in a way to be disregarded. As Elizabeth followed Stetson inside, he strolled in after them, and took up his station on the edge of an empty barrel with careless but none the less actual interest in the transaction. Inside there was the usual variety of wares: dried peaches, brown calico, and several antique chocolate mice being among the most prominent. It smelled chiefly of what might be string. Stetson took down a box labelled "Peppermint Lozenges," but that only held several rolls of tape; then he took down a box labelled "5 lbs. Candles," but that only held darning-cotton; at last he found a box labelled "Gumdrops," and that held the dress-braid. He set it down before Elizabeth with an air that suggested she might take it or leave it, and went to the other side of the store and measured out two quarts of split peas for some mysterious but unforgotten patron. Having twisted them up in a paper bag, being watched silently by the General with fascinated eyes which would much prefer to have watched Elizabeth, but were withheld through embarrassment, he returned and stood opposite to her.

"Got some new mackerel," he said to the General, over her head.

"Hev?" said the General, with fictitious interest. There was a moment's silence.

"I will take these," said Elizabeth. A shadow shut off part of the sunlight from the door just behind her.

"H'are you, Jib?" said the General.

"H'are you, Jib?" said Mr. Stetson, nodding in dignified greeting.

Elizabeth did not turn, but she dropped one piece of dress-braid and picked up another just like it and looked at it earnestly while Jib returned the salutations. Jib never wasted time in circumlocution. He walked straight up to the counter where she stood.

"Well, Miss Elizabeth," he said. Elizabeth turned her little curly head sidewise, and glanced up at him with a suppressed smile.

"Oh, is that you?" she said. "How do you do?"

Jib leaned on the small show-case, beneath the glass of which the chocolate mice gazed thoughtfully, almost hope-fully, at the two sticks of licorice and a bunch of white elastic, and, with an entire indifference to shopping, looked down smiling at Elizabeth. She looked away from him to the dress-braid, and again to Mr. Stetson.

"I'll take four pieces of this, please."

Mr. Stetson hesitated, and poked about in the peppermint lozenge-box doubtfully.

"I guess that's all there is, ain't it?"

"Yes," answered Elizabeth, "that's all."

"Couldn't get along with two, could you?"

"I don't believe I could," she replied, in some embarrass-ment.

"Wal," he said, unwillingly, "I suppose I'll have to let you have it. First thing I know somebody else 'll be in after some. It keeps one handlin' it all the time when I hev to get a new lot of such things. I'd ruther you'd 'a' left a piece."

Elizabeth was unused to these economics of trade, and so smiled with some perplexity. Stetson, seeing that she did not change her mind, wrapped it up and made change

for her with an appearance of high-minded protest, while
Elizabeth still ignored Jib's glance and gazed interestedly at
a highly colored portrait of a child of a truly abnormal health-
fulness, produced by the exclusive use of a certain cereal.
When he had almost forgotten to expect her to look at him,
and was studying her quite at his ease, she flashed her eyes
back at him.

"Did you come to shop, too?" she asked.

"No," said Jib, not in the least disconcerted, "I came in
because you were here."

"Ah," said Elizabeth, with a suspicion of a smile at the
corners of her mouth, "it's almost a pity you gave yourself
the trouble—I'm not going to stay very long. Thank you,"
she said to Mr. Stetson as she picked up her change.

"You'll be staying just about as long as I calculate to,"
said Jib easily as they went out together. The General
watched them absorbedly. He even nearly upset the barrel, leaning forward to watch them across the street.
Abijah, however, had seen too much of this sort of thing to
waste much thought on it. He slowly replaced the peppermint, candle, and gumdrop boxes, set the bag of split peas
in a prominent position on the counter, and sauntered outside again, whither the General immediately followed him
with that somewhat slavish adherence which was part of his
character.

Jib Trent, according to Uncle Denver, had signed considerable of a contract when he fell in love with Elizabeth
French. The magnitude of the undertaking, however, impressed him not at all, for the simple reason that he gave
not a thought to its possibilities. Men who are building
towers and going into battle sit down and count the cost of
it as far as their limitations admit, if they are wise, to be
sure; but, after all, it is only for the sake of making a good
start and being unhandicapped by avoidable drawbacks.

Nobody really thinks that he has counted it all; and those who build the best towers and fight the best battles are those who grapple best with the unforeseen. Jib Trent was conscious of nothing except a never-failing impulse to seek the society of Elizabeth French. His favorite books were neglected. Tim recommended "That Frenchman" in vain. For the first time in his life Jim found fact more absorbing than fiction. Upon Elizabeth this devotion had a not uncommon effect. It was something to amuse one—even to interest one—something of a fashion quite new; but owing to the fact that it was so readily come at, something not to be superlatively valued. She was one of those women who need no artificial incitements, no cynical experiences, no envious emulations to develop a latent sense of coquetry. She had been sent to a good school, and was by no means ignorant. She did not often travel under the canvas wing of the circus; it was only on short, out-of-season tours like this last that French was accompanied by his wife and daughter. Nicholas French was an unusual man in some respects. He had associated all his life with horses without being brutalized thereby; he had a genuine love for animals which extended even to the vicious and the outcast. He was still in love with the woman who had run away from her home to marry him, twenty years ago, and proud of the daughter who was such a credit to them both. He had made money enough to live in a less precarious style, but as it is hard for a Cromwell to lay aside his sword, so is it hard for a man or woman, much of whose life has been lived within the circus ring, to return to a respectable but monotonous side street. Nicholas French would have been unhappy without a horse, would have felt bereft of luxury without a trick pony, and would have experienced a genuine deprivation in the loss of the society of a wild-cat. Marcella, though at first her interest had been purely vicarious,

had also become fond of the distinctive features of their
life. The same impulsive love of the romantic which had
led her to throw aside her comfortable country home for
the vicissitudes of one with a ringmaster, led her to enjoy
the novelties, the excitements, the very makeshifts of the
business. So Nicholas, without being any longer the slave
of his fortunes, was generally doing something or other in
the circus line, and Elizabeth, though carefully shielded,
with what might seem unusual discretion, from that which
could easily have proved harmful in the life, picked up, together with her school duties, a good deal of information
and experience which made her more interesting than most
girls of eighteen, whose conventional advantages had been
greater. In fact, she was exceptional enough in her character and training to prevent the veil of romance and magnificence with which Jib had enveloped her from the first
from being drawn aside by the hand of more familiar acquaintance, and revealing only the dulness of the commonplace.

"Where are you going?" asked Elizabeth, demurely, as
they turned up the village street.

"Let's go up on the mound," replied Jib; "there is time
enough before supper."

His assumption that wherever he went, she was going
too, amused Elizabeth, but did not displease her.

"I don't know about that," she demurred; "I expected
to take this dress-braid home to mother."

"I guess your mother isn't in any hurry," said Jib with
masculine incredulity concerning the imperative importance
of dress-braid; "please come, Elizabeth."

Elizabeth had only been waiting for that look of anxiety
in those handsome blue eyes, and she went on with him
readily enough. The mound was a mild sort of bluff about
half a mile long, in the middle of the valley, not high

enough to be called a hill about here, but reached by a steep little ascent, and forming a pretty place of lookout.

It was crossed by a fence or two, crossed in their turn by several stiles, and was a favorite walk for those who found the village street too densely populated and who yet did not care to seek greater and more distant seclusion.

"Mother is ever so much pleased to see your Uncle Denver again," said Elizabeth, as they passed beyond the scattered houses into the solitude of the country road.

"I don't know when I've seen Uncle Denver so lightened up as since your mother and you came here," replied Jib; "he talks more about it than he does about most things. Not but what he's always pretty noticing—but this seems more like real pleasure to him."

"Most people like mother," said Elizabeth with satisfaction.

"I guess Uncle Denver used to love your mother," went on Jib simply. "He hasn't ever said so, but I've mistrusted he did. He don't seem noways ashamed of it. I wouldn't ever be ashamed of loving a woman like — like her," he added, with a shy glance at his companion, who colored a little and smiled, which encouraged him to proceed.

"All the men that I've ever read of that were worth anything were in love with somebody."

"I guess it don't always depend on their being worth anything, though."

"No," answered Jib, momentarily chilled, "I don't suppose it does. But then you don't want to read about the other kind, you know"—a remark, by the way, showing small literary discrimination—"and all those who fight and ride and get into the hands of the enemy—they always love somebody."

"Well, if I loved anybody"—she spoke with a charming disregard of any personal application—"I should want him to do something for me besides fight and ride and get into the hands of the enemy."

"I guess he wouldn't do that any more than he could help," said Jib lazily; "he'd rather stay with you."

"Oh, don't be ridiculous," said Elizabeth, with a shake of her curly head, immediately followed by a smiling salutation to a good-looking young fellow in mountain costume who passed them on the road.

"Who's that?" asked Jib.

"Oh, he stays over to Dust's," answered Elizabeth with an air of marked indifference. "He's from New York—I've talked with him some."

Jib was not rendered in the least uneasy by this incident, but it changed the current of their conversation.

"You've seen a good many people, first and last, haven't you?" he observed as they reached the first stile. Elizabeth perched herself on the top before she replied, while he stood leaning against the post beside her.

"Well, yes," she said, "I suppose I have seen a good many people—seen them, you know. I haven't known very many. And a good many animals too," she added, without cynical intention.

"And you've seen cities, too?"

"Oh, yes, I've seen cities too. Haven't you ever?"

"Never," answered Jib unblushingly. It was impossible for her not to feel a little superior, but she answered truthfully enough,

"The country is a deal prettier—though I don't know as I'd rather always live in it. But my! it's a great deal prettier. Mother always said it was, too."

"I don't know as I'd always rather live in the country either," said Jib, gazing up into her pretty face.

He was leaning forward, his arms on the fence, precisely as he had been when she first met his eyes the day of the

9

circus procession. He did not think of it at all, but she did.

"I don't know as I will. I mean some time to go where things are done such as we were speaking of along back."

There was a pause. Elizabeth had taken off her hat, and she gave her head a little turn and smiled, but said nothing.

"Did you ever see a herald?" asked Jib.

"A newspaper, do you mean?"

"No, a herald—a man."

Elizabeth's sense of urban superiority vanished suddenly.

"No," she said. A moment of unconscious cerebration connected heralds with sandwich-men, but she repeated, "No, I never did. Why?"

"Oh, nothing. I was only thinking," and he slipped into silence a moment. This silence was so full of her and he was so ignorant of women that it did not occur to him to tell her that he was thinking of her. She grew a little impatient of his abstraction. She had become accustomed to his devotion, and with true femininity felt aggrieved by the least lucid interval. She swung her hat by its string, looked around her, down to the village street, invisible but not entirely inaudible, and finally half rose to go.

"What would you want your lover to do?" inquired Jib suddenly, "to show that he loved you?"

Elizabeth abandoned temporarily her intention of going home. The seriousness of the question was somewhat disconcerting, backed up as it was by the good looks and immediate proximity of the questioner. It was difficult for little Elizabeth to maintain the utterly impersonal. The utterly impersonal is a product of the higher civilization.

"What would I want my lover to do?" she repeated with red cheeks and a would-be defiance in her eyes.

"Yes," assented Jib, seriously. "You have said what you didn't want him to do."

"Oh, yes," she laughed, "fighting and getting into the hands of the enemy. Well, you know that wouldn't be real satisfying."

"I suppose not," said Jib with imperturbable directness. "What would you want him to do?"

A girl's first genuine lover is a disturbing element, even when Nature has provided a disposition quick to adapt itself to such disturbances. Elizabeth had all her sex's aversion for direct questions and direct answers.

"Oh, so many things," she said lightly, standing up and stepping down the first step of the stile. "It would take too long to tell and it's too late to begin."

He stood silently where he barred her way down, and she waited. He was not yet experienced lover enough to be tyrannical, or he might have taken advantage of this circumstance to make her explain herself. Perhaps Elizabeth half fancied that he would. Instead he moved one side as he pleaded, "Can't you tell me one thing?"

His prompt submission emboldened her coquetry — it could not throw away such opportunities.

"Yes," she said, with audacious seriousness, looking down at him, "I can tell you one thing. I would ask him to help me down off the stile and take me home."

The two figures disappeared through the tall meadow-grass, the soft, late twilight settled down into the valley and brightened towards the hill-tops. The wood-thrushes called back and forth to each other in the stillness. The distant murmur of the streams assumed an importance it had lacked when human voices were at hand. The world was afar off, the earth with her voices spoke to those who could hear.

From the other side of the fence came a soft, steady rustle in the dry, feathered grasses and clinging vines of the field. It was too measured a sound to be the stir of the wind which was breathing across the valley. It was Rhodope's step, who, after the early tea at the cottage, almost always strayed away from its open door, over the warm grass to this particular stile. To-night the air was full of expectancy, the quietness of the hour was thrilled with unquiet possibilities. These were days when things happened—much had happened yesterday—which things were not to be forgotten and which filled such hours as this with remembering as well as anticipation. She climbed up the stile and sat where Elizabeth had perched an hour before, clasping her hands about her knees and gazing over to the dark hillside whence rang the voices of the thrushes. In the opalescent green of the sky floated pink snatches of cloud, both of which blended into pearl farther away. Rhodope thought of Elizabeth and Jib; she had seen them walking together, from the cottage window, and Jib had come home to tea with a gleaming illumination in his steady gray eyes. She was much interested in what it might mean. She was deeply devoted to her brother, and she was fascinated by this new, brilliant Elizabeth, whom she could not in the least understand. She speculated about their relations with her eyes on the hills, and was glad and was sorry—and was conscious that, absorbing as it was, it was not this that gave its peculiar meaning to the August evening; that back of all this speculation was something more absorbing still. Up, over the edge of the hill that separated the mound from the plain, came Medcott. She turned her head and saw him, and immediately all the unrest went out of the night and all speculation ceased, and there was nothing to do but to wait quietly while he came straight towards her.

"I hoped to find you," he said, as he reached the stile.

"I am glad you came," she answered; "it is so beautiful here."

"Yes, it is beautiful," he assented, as his glance went

over the tinted valley and back again to the girl above him, whose figure and pure profile were outlined clearly against the sky behind her, as she looked away from him.

"I have been wondering what it is that the thrushes say," she said after a moment. "It is something glad, and yet—it is not all glad. It is triumphant, but it is not—exulting. I guess you can tell better than I," she concluded. Medcott leaned his head on his arms on the stile and listened. They were both silent, waiting, and it was after a longer interval than usual that a hidden bird uttered its few notes. Down in the country road a heavy wagon creaked slowly by, and it seemed as if the tide of travel was importunate. The world seemed to belong to them and not to feverish travellers. But alas! it did not. The song of the wood-thrush broke forth again.

"It is 'Why? why? why?'" said Medcott sighing.

"I think it is 'Yes, yes, yes'," said Rhodope.

The colors were fading out of the sky; the distant peaks were faintly blue and shadowy, those near at hand were dark and massive. The sweep of ripened grass about them grew ghostly instead of golden. Over the top of Mystery Mountain appeared a little bit of a moon. It looked so small and far off, and the top of the mountain was so black just under it that they seemed to have a little world of their own up there to illumine and to reflect—and all they could do, too—without bothering about the lowlands. Medcott banished the questioning and gave himself up to the actuality. He talked of what was nearest to him, he brought certain of his feelings and aims to the judgment bar of her intuitions. He let what was best in him speak, and he listened to what she said with a certain reverence mingled with his tenderness. He did not tell her that he loved her, though the words were very near his lips more than once, she was so beautiful and so sweet and so single-minded, and her simplicity was never folly. It was no doubt of his feeling that withheld him, it was rather an instinctive unwillingness to disturb her peace, and a delight in the present which would not be hurried or ignored; nor did she listen for him to say that he loved her, but she did not need to tell herself that she loved him. Why pause to analyze the varied forces of a current that is sweeping us along? She knew it for the first time, and doubted it as little as if she had long known it. He seemed to her faith what a man always seems to a faith like hers. He was a tall, well-made man with somewhat more than indispensable regularity of feature, talking, as he leaned against the fence or straightened himself and walked a few paces up and down, with earnestness and decided picturesqueness of description and allusion, or listening to her with an attention that made her words seem suddenly freighted with something precious; but she would have rejected this description from its baldness. He was a hero. He was—she did not stop to think what he was—she loved him. It was a strong, deep conviction which she faced and realized and thought upon with the strength and simplicity of the nature that was hers.

When the little moon with a fine audacity had made good her claim of a broader field for the assertion of her privileges, and had really become an important little factor in the universe, so dim was the sky and so heavy the shadow in the valley, Davenant started across the field in the direction of the village. Neither Rhodope nor Medcott saw him, but he saw their silhouettes by the stile, and recognized them. For an instant he paused and then went seriously on his way. Apparently he was thinking earnestly, and his earnestness was tinged with something that was not pleasant as he made a détour that led him to the Trent cottage without passing the stile. On the piazza sat Denver Trent and Needham, who was making one of his flying visits to the valley. They were talking with some animation as Davenant approached, and apparently changed the subject as they saw the light of his cigarette. He stopped and talked to them a little while, and then strolled down to the Clock's with Needham.

"All humbug," said Needham as they made their way with some difficulty along the dark country road. "Now, tell me what would you give to be walking along a decent side-walk with an electric light instead of that inefficient moon overhead?"

"I mightn't have to give anything," said Davenant pensively. "A pickpocket or a sandbagger might take it, you know."

"Oh, come," said Needham, "talk sense. We are neither of us afraid of pickpockets nor sandbaggers in the city, and we don't either of us like a—a confounded ditch"—and he stepped down with unforeseen suddenness—"better than a curbed pavement! George! This is worse than Philadelphia."

"Well, I never said it was New York; it is almost a pity we can't call a cab."

"And it's all humbug, Medcott's staying up here on account of art. He's staying up here to philander with that handsome woman, old Trent's niece—she's out with him somewhere this evening."

Davenant kicked a quiescent pebble out of his path. "Well, philandering is capable of being developed into Art," he drawled.

"Well, let 'em call it by its name, that's all I mean," said Needham, not wishing to be disagreeable. "It's the humbug I object to."

Charlie Needham was one of those persons who think that every emotion they have not themselves felt is necessarily a counterfeited emotion, that every enjoyment they have not felt is an unreal enjoyment; that every taste that is not theirs is an affected taste. Such men pride themselves on their ability to discern sham, and on their own genuineness, and they are not infrequently genuine in a limited sense. They have penetrated some of the insincerity of the world, and with insufficient logic they fancy that all they have not penetrated is insincerity too. In their anxiety to prove their superiority to certain affectations, they fail to perceive that they are making themselves a heaven-appointed standard for the race.

When the two men reached the Clocks', Needham went inside to find his wife, and Davenant went to the lamp in a small room off the hall, where he began to write in his note-book:

"Evening—pink and gray and green. Loneliness—girl at the stile," he wrote. "Suggestions of sentiment in the environment." He paused a moment here, and then went on: "Man (more worldly) leans on the fence—air of isolation—usual thing." Here, with what for Davenant was suddenness, he drew his pencil thrice across what he had written, put book and pencil back in his pocket, lighted an incomputable cigarette over the lamp, and went out on the piazza and stood gazing into the semi-darkness.

"Why? why? why?" sang a wood-thrush.

CHAPTER XI

" Envy is a gadding passion and walketh the streets, and doth not keep house."

MEDCOTT looked out upon the silence of the city roofs. In the cold, clear west the sky was reddening in the early sunset. Beyond, and beyond, and beyond stretched the plain of roofs, rising here, falling there, but all inequalities almost lost in the general level. Over, and straight, and obliquely, apparently at cross purposes, or utterly at random, from height to height, concentrating here at some lofty corner in a hopeless tangle, widening there into hundreds of hair-like lines, the telegraph wires cut the clearness of the sky. The flare of the tall chimneys turned slowly, fitfully, now this way, now that, moved mysteriously by draughts of air unfelt in the lower atmosphere. On commodious ledges the cockney sparrows fluttered and lunched and sported. The dull roar of the city was beneath, but above was the silence of an unoccupied world. Unoccupied! And under all these roofs, stretching away almost to the cool horizon, were human lives and human interests countless and conflicting, with death and sorrow and shame and suffering and disgrace. So many! So many! And each to the other but a shadow, but a nonentity, and all alike, in the eyes of an Omniscient and Omnipotent. Trite thought— but universal conviction—too overpowering for long reflection! Medcott's eyes fell upon the sparrows, secure, optimistic, unforeseeing. More value than they? Why should they be?

Upon the easel stood the picture he had been at work upon while the work lasted. The room was filled with the hangings, the bits of embroidery, the odd and curious things that seem to grow up about those who represent the artistic in life, seeming an indigenous growth or a painful exotic according as the representation is of genuine or artificial affiliation. There was a smouldering coal-fire in the low grate and an odor of tobacco in the air. On the writing-desk lay a number of recently opened letters, pamphlets, cards, and so on. One epistle on tinted paper, with an unexceptionable cipher, was conspicuous from its length.

It was almost the first time that Medcott had had time to think uninterruptedly since he left the valley. He had been summoned thence by a telegram from his mother's physician, saying that she was very ill. He had spent several anxious weeks with her and with his sister at their home on the river, had then made a visit or two, and had come back to the city a few days before, oppressed with the fact that winter had come in earnest, and that somehow the weeks of the fall had slipped away in the unaccountable way known to those who have been watching an invalid. Medcott was devoted to his mother, as, too, was his sister, but the son had always been the favorite, for the daughter, with the best intentions, was too apt to succeed in being antipathetic rather than sympathetic.

"I am glad to see you, Austin," said his mother when she was able to speak, "Bertha is a dear child, but there were times when I knew she thought I ought to prepare for a better world, and it irritated me. You see, with that pain it never occurred to me that another world was in the least likely to be worse."

Bertha Medcott was not perhaps any more keenly alive to the claims of another world than her mother, but she was always oppressed by the idea that she ought to be doing something she wasn't, and might live to repent it. In this sensitiveness to what might be future reproach she occasionally disregarded the possibilities of the present reproach of other people.

Since his hurried departure from the valley Medcott had thought many times of Rhodope, but not in a connected strain, and insensibly she had glided back, as interests which seem to us the most absorbing will, to a secondary place. He admired her none the less. Were she present he would be no more indifferent to her charm, but he had had no time to devote to their possible relations. During these hurried weeks she had become an influence to revert to, instead of one claiming part of his daily life. This afternoon, however, as he gazed out over the silence of the roofs, towards the clear, green, western sky, the spell of those other, so different, silences, was upon him—those of forest, lake, and mountain—and with these, as an indwelling presence, came the vision of Rhodope. He had been so sure that last night, when he stood with her by the stile, that he should tell her soon that he loved her, so sure that without her life would be a poor thing, limited, artificial, and that in spite of the difficulty she would find in adjusting herself to an existence less serene and simple, he could make her happy. He had been sure of all this. Now these weeks had brought him back within another horizon. He felt that his was in reality another world than hers and —was it not best as it was? He had said not a word of love to her. He was sure her peace was untroubled as yet. They had spoken of friendship—had they not been wise to speak of nothing else?

There was a knock at the door. "Come," Medcott

called out, and turned back to the dim room in which the shadows had fallen swiftly the last half-hour. "Hold on a moment, though, whoever you are," he added, as the door opened, "till I get a light, or you'll fall over something."

"So you've come back," observed Davenant from the doorway.

"Oh, Tom, so it's you? how are you? Glad to see you. Perhaps you can find your way. Not a confounded match in the box, of course."

With the natural impatience of one who, though he has been watching the sun set, finds the room has taken advantage of his inattention to grow dark behind him, Medcott was industriously feeling for a match in an ash-receiver at the wrong end of the mantelpiece.

"I can see well enough," said Davenant calmly, making his way towards the fireplace. "I didn't come in out of the glare. I had to feel my way along your hall, by the wall."

"Drunk again," observed Medcott briefly as he lit the gas.

"Oh, no," began Davenant mildly, "it wasn't for the support."

"The janitor, I mean. I don't want to be hard on a janitor, but I wish he'd wait till after candle-light."

"He'll give you all the light you want some time, and burn the building down. When did you get back?"

"A week ago," answered Medcott, "though I've been here off and on before."

"Heard of you now and then at the club. Going to dine anywhere?"

"I hope so; times are hard, but I mean to get a bite."

"Dine with me, then. I fell in with a clever newspaper man from the West last night. You'd like to hear him talk, and he and Wills are going to meet me for dinner."

"With pleasure. Who is he?"

Their talk drifted from one thing to another as they sat before the fire whose smouldering inaction had been enlivened by another lump of coal.

"Did you stay long at the Hive after I left?" asked Medcott at last

"No, not long. About a week. Spent most of it with Denver Trent." Medcott felt a spasm of sudden jealousy. "Charlie Needham was there the last few days, and we used to go up and smoke and talk with the old man."

"And Miss Trent—Rhodope?"

"Sometimes she listened, sometimes she didn't," he answered briefly.

"I found among the letters that didn't get forwarded to me," said Medcott, leaning forward and taking up the tinted note-paper from the table, "one from Mrs. Needham. It was written soon after I left, and it came to me like a breath from another world."

"Warm in tone, probably," commented the other.

"A warmer world than this, anyhow," laughed Medcott. "She was sitting on the piazza when she wrote—she says that you have just left"—he ran his eyes over the pages as he spoke—"that nearly everybody has gone, in fact, but that she and 'dear Edwina Screed'"— he paused and looked at Davenant, who smiled his enigmatic smile as he said,

"Yes, to be sure, that was after you left—'dear Edwina Screed' didn't come till almost too late. You know when you were there it was 'that little Screed woman!'"

Medcott nodded as Davenant knocked the ashes off his cigarette. "One day she was talking of Art, and I was trying to listen, and Mrs. Needham was trying to prevent me, when she said of some plate or jug or other that it was owned by her cousin, Mrs. Adell. There was a sudden cessation of interruption and sarcasm, but Miss Screed went on placidly—you know her placidity?"

"Yes," answered Medcott, "I know."

"'Your cousin?' said the other. 'My cousin, Mrs. Adell.' 'Which Adell?' 'Why, Mrs. Leavenworth Adell,'" answered Miss Screed, who was somewhat startled by this sudden interest. Then there was a silence. To me it was like the silence of the tomb—" and he paused to light another cigarette—"because I knew if it was filled with anything, it was with promises of future amendment; and then Mrs. Needham said, 'What were you saying, Edwina dear, about the ancient potters?' and it's been her 'dear Edwina' from that time to this."

Medcott laughed. "You're not at all cynical, are you, Tom?" he said.

"No, I try to be, and now and then I make a pretty good showing, but I've a beautiful faith in my fellow-men when you get down to me."

"I believe you have more than most men," assented Medcott.

"But we get after a while so that we read words of two syllables at sight," said Davenant slowly. "We can't help it; it's the natural result of practice, and we can't help the knowledge that comes to us with it. Great Scott! how I did admire that woman once."

"She was a great beauty."

"Yes, she had great beauty—she has now—and she had other qualities, too, which are going to last her even longer. I tell you," and he clasped his arms behind his head and gazed into the fire thoughtfully, "Cupid is painted blind because he hasn't any foresight, but he's got an awful lot of hindsight. Go on, did she give you any more news?"

"She says, 'I see the errant Rhodope now and then; so far, I think she has found no more knights to succor.'" Medcott turned the leaf impatiently.

"Small-minded women," announced Davenant sententiously, "never know when they have had enough of their own *bon-mots*."

"'I told her the other day that you—'"

"Go on."

"It's only some of her maliciousness," said Austin angrily, breaking off the sentence.

"I can fancy," said Davenant, "just the sort of thing she told her for her good."

"'The little circus girl—'"

"Isn't a circus girl, by the way."

"'The little circus girl is still the Boadicea, or the Fairy Princess, or the Rosalind, or whatever you like, of the literary Jib, and is weaving the fascinations of the ring about young Schumacher, who is still a member of the Dust household, and rendering Jib's life and that of young S.'s mother alike an apprehensive one.' That's all the valley news, I guess," and he tossed the letter back on the table.

"Leaving out the undoubtedly intentional error of the reference to the ring, there must be a good deal of truth in that last. It began before I left. That little Elizabeth is a young person of unlimited coquetry, and she hasn't lived long enough to know what Jib Trent is worth. Get your coat, Medcott, I guess we've exhausted the social situation of the valley."

The Western newspaper man not only managed a newspaper, he was a bit of an inventor as well. He had knocked about the West in its early days, and had gained a breadth of view which knocking about over such wide areas naturally imparts. He was constantly entertaining and occasionally brilliant, and the fact that he must leave on an early evening train, on business connected with what he had invented last, was the only drawback to the enjoyment of the occasion.   As they came out of the dining-room they passed a small room reserved for private dinners, where evidently a very gay party was being entertained.   The dinner was just over, and there was that indiscriminate sound of moving of chairs, voices, and laughter which follows.   A man turned quickly as the four went by the half-open door, and, coming out, followed them.   It was Charlie Needham; his cheeks were flushed with wine, and he was in high spirits, but there was a deep line between his eyebrows, which gayety had not smoothed away, and his eyes were more restless than usual.

"I say, Davenant," he called out, "beg pardon for detaining you.   Let me speak to you half a minute."

The other men went on, and Davenant and Needham stepped one side.

"I've been trying to make up my mind to speak to you for a week," he said rapidly.   "Then, when I saw you through the door, I thought I must do it.   Seemed providential, you know.   That is, if the finger of Providence ever points through a half-shut door after a champagne dinner," and he laughed rather loudly.

"May be all the more necessary," suggested Davenant quietly.

"Yes, that's so.   I need some one to look after me.   Fact is, I'm in a tight place, Davenant; that's what I want to see you about.   Give me half an hour to-morrow, when you are not busy.   Any time you like."

"Say about noon—I'll come to your office.   Shall be down that way."

Through the door of the brilliantly-lighted room came the sound of voices, not loud but gay.   Men were passing through the hall, nodding to one another, sending messages, lighting cigars. The line on Needham's forehead deepened as he indicated the room he had left with a half-nod.

"They're going to the theatre," he said; "I haven't time —too many other things to think of. See you to-morrow at noon."

The colloquy had only lasted two minutes, and Davenant passed on, buttoning his coat, while Needham stepped back to the door—then he stopped, turned, and came back and added, laughing,

"I don't know just why I come to you, Tom, but you've always been a good friend of mine." He paused an instant and then went on, still with the laugh about which there was more than a touch of recklessness. "You ought by rights to hate me, you know."

"Oh, no," answered Davenant with a slight smile, "I don't hate you, Needham, at all," and he rejoined his companions at the door of entrance, while Needham returned to the room which the theatre party were just leaving.

"That's an odd burst of sentiment," thought Davenant, as they walked up towards Forty-second Street. "I haven't ever been anything particular in the way of a friend towards Charlie Needham. Something must be up. He's in that mood when ordinarily decent treatment assumes the proportions of the relations of Orestes and Pylades—it's not an uncommon thing—usually means there's danger of losing even that. I wonder if he doesn't really know the favor he did me." Wills had left them, but Medcott kept on with the other two, and he was talking with the journalist about a recent publication they had both been reading, while Davenant considered the Needhams. "Can hardly be money, except that Needham has always fancied gambling—and when a man does that, it's pretty likely to be money—still, I thought he could afford to play with stocks; wonder why he comes to me—there's a lot of richer men in his intimate set."

10

The truth was that men were very apt to go to Davenant if they were in difficulties. He was wont to assure them that he never kept anything by him for those who fell by the wayside, except the oil of "worse things might have happened," and the wine of "any fool might have known it," but perhaps these remedies possessed simple curative properties unknown to priests and Levites. Certainly they were in more or less demand. A pretty wide, and by no means shallow, knowledge of human nature and entire absence of conviction regarding the duty of "improving the occasion" are apt to render people esteemed confidants.

Later, he dropped in at Daly's with Medcott. Ada Rehan's voice was vibrating through a delighted house, and Lewis, the very wrinkles in whose coat are mirth-provoking, was the victim of some delicious anxiety or other. The fragrance of the flowers worn by the pretty women in the audience was now and then wafted across by the waving of a fan, and the odor of a cigarette drifted in with the entrance of a dress-coat. In a stage-box sat the party of which Florence Needham was one. In a ravishing costume of green and silver, her charming profile outlined against the hangings, her piquant beauty sparkling like the brilliant lights and the diamonds in her bonnet-strings, she sat listening with a smile to the man behind her. When she spoke herself, he laughed, and indeed most of the others did. She was in excellent conversational form to-night. It was natural she should be. She was with quite the right sort of people, exquisitely dressed, in the front of the box, and a pretty woman. She saw the two men as they came in and took their seats not far off. Her color changed, for she had not seen Medcott since the summer, and he had not answered her letter. A short note just after he left the valley being the only word she had heard from him for months. Davenant she had seen now and then. Medcott was very handsome to-night, and through the play itself, and all the laughter and persiflage which apparently occupied her whole soul, she never altogether lost sight of his distinguished face and figure, as he sat before her, his eyes turned towards the stage, save when he exchanged a word or smile with Davenant. The evening ought to have been a great success; it was something of a triumph for Florence. The party was made up of the elect. It was given for a foreigner of note, and he had shown a marked interest in Mrs. Needham. With the nicety of a qualified judge she knew what it was worth—and it was worth a good deal. Yet when it was over and the door of her own house had closed behind her, and she had gone upstairs to her room in silence, being informed that Mr. Needham had not yet come in, it was with the impatience of chagrin that she pulled off her gloves and tossed down her ornaments. "I would rather have had those two men come and speak to me than — than all the rest of it!" she exclaimed angrily, "and they—they never looked at me! Austin Medcott might at least have the simple decency to come and call after the summer. I wonder how long he has been in the city." Her maid took her heavy evening wrap and put away the things she threw aside. When she had gone for the night, Florence dropped into a chair in front of the mirror, and looked at her own reflection frowning; then, remembering that frowning produced wrinkles, her brow cleared.

"He never looked at all," she said again. Her thoughts succeeded each other in angry confusion. The sight of Medcott's handsome head and broad shoulders had called up all the sentiment that had been overlain since her return by the requirements of daily life. His mingling of deference and indifference was the very charm to fix her volatile fancy. She wished passionately to break through that indifference and to inspire that deference with something deeper than courtesy. When her beauty had failed to do this, she had exerted all the fascination—and it was no trifling amount—of which she was capable, and when this, too, had failed, she had annoyed and irritated him in the bad temper of disappointment. At least she had produced effect by her flings at Rhodope Trent. Rhodope Trent! There it was, the secret of her failure. How she hated her! If she had but stayed away, Medcott would have found all the entertainment he wished beneath the Clock roof-tree. Florence knew she was too pretty a woman for a man to feel deeply the necessity of looking further; but that awkward, ignorant, good-looking girl must needs come across his path with her pose of ingenuousness and air of woodland poesy, and all the rest of it, and appeal to his susceptible artist's soul in a way that she could not, and which was, moreover—this at least was a comfort—pretty sure to produce a misunderstanding on the girl's part. Florence rose and moved restlessly the silver trifles of her dressing-table, then she walked to the hearth, where the fire was just dying out. Yes, misunderstanding, of course, and that would annoy him, and she, Florence, would always understand, and he might find that out in the reaction. What a pleasure to have the distinguished Austin Medcott her devoted attendant! What excitement in the devotion itself! What avenues might it not open to her! But to gain all this she must reach him—must have him at hand —and how to do this? Ah! the lamentable conventions of society! It is a proof of the unconsciousness of deep emotion that this heretical exclamation passed through her mind without producing a shudder. Her only hold on him was through Davenant—Davenant who once loved her— who might love her still. Her meditations were a curious mingling of genuine feeling, prudential foresight, and social mathematics. Almost the last image in her mind that night

was the annoying one of Medcott and Davenant at the theatre never once looking in her direction, but to this succeeded a glimpse of the distinguished *personnel* of the dinner, and she sank into a deep and refreshing sleep.

She was mistaken, they had looked at her several
times.

"The front of the box," had said Davenant pensively,
"that is the place for Florence Needham. You observe I
speak enigmatically—in a metaphorical sense," he added
in kindly explanation, "referring as it were to life as a theatre, and so on."

"It's a benefit to the rest of the house," replied Medcott; "she's a marvellously pretty woman."

"So she is," said Davenant; " I hope the time may never
come when a too exacting socialism will cut out the parts
of such ornamental lookers-on."

"I don't believe it is coming in my time, or in yours."
Medcott was a persistent optimist.

"Such sentiments were rife in the critical time of the
late esteemed Noah."

"Oh, I say! you don't believe we are dancing on the
verge of a crater, or skating on the thin ice over a cataract,
and all the rest of it, any more than I do."

" I don't believe anything about it," replied Davenant
calmly. "It is not the business of a humble newspaper
man to believe anything, but merely to hold himself in
readiness not to be surprised. The business would go to
the dogs if we allowed ourselves to become critical about
the truth of a statement, or to be surprised."

"Do you mean you would not be surprised at a French
Revolution breaking out under our feet?"

"Oh, very much. A progressive newspaper man cannot
fail to perceive that New York no longer slavishly gets her
fashions from Paris. She sets her own, but a good deal of

the stock-broking and the starving has got to be stopped some time, you know."

"Yes, I suppose it has," assented Medcott—"undoubtedly it has."

"And when a good many people think certain things have got to be done some time, some fools are likely to take it upon themselves to set the clock ahead."

"There's truth in what you say, Tom," said Medcott. "We all know that; but from the glittering generalities of your style I should say you were working off one of your half-columns on me."

"Just the introduction for a metropolitan letter to a provincial journal," replied Davenant with perfect fairness. "Glad to see it strikes you favorably."

They had been talking during an intermission, and as the curtain went up for the next act, the orchestra, which had been playing a medley of popular songs, struck into the air of the boat-song which had been so popular in the summer, and which Rhodope had been singing when she found Medcott in the woods. He had not heard it since. From that moment on, he never lost the thought of her. Socialism and politics were forgotten. He joined in the laughter, he noted the brilliancy of stage and audience, but it all seemed only to mark the contrast with another life. She —his beautiful, strong, free Rhodope—she could never live in this artificial atmosphere. He had done right, he had done the best thing for them both. Suppose he might have made her love him—even supposing the worst—suppose that he had made her love him, how much better for her a little regret among the mountains, and then peace, than a life-long uneasiness and pain. Yes, he had done the best thing. As usual, Medcott was in danger of losing a fair estimate of the arguments on one side from his disposition to give their full weight to those on the other. The two men came out of the theatre together and turned up-town. They spoke of indifferent matters as they passed through the glare of the brilliant lights, but as they turned into one of the quieter cross-streets, where Davenant lived, a short silence fell between them. The moon was shining, and here one might be allowed to perceive it, without manifesting undue rusticity and an unfashionable familiarity with the almanac. The houses seemed suddenly so tall and dark, it suggested the idea that they grew like Jack's bean-stalk in the night. The dash of a cab on the stones was infrequent, and became an event. An elevated train shot across the opening of the street on one of the more distant avenues.

"Davenant," said Medcott, pausing an instant and laying his hand on the other's shoulder, "do you think she could ever be happy here? Tell me as you hope for happiness yourself."

Davenant's lips drooped into his curious, pleasant, cynical smile.

"Can't you think of a better invocation, my dear fellow? Have I ever struck you as a person who pinned much faith to his own hopes of happiness?"

"Tell me," said Medcott impatiently, "do you think she would?"

"Of whom might you be speaking?"

"You know whom I mean—Rhodope Trent."

"Do I think she could be happy here?" repeated Davenant as they moved on again. A look, half tenderness, half regret, crossed his face. •"I think she could—so far as women ever are happy—under the right conditions. I don't think she would find her true happiness in always being in the front of the box, but with the man that loved her—"

"Well!"

"Then I think it would be just the same old risk not

materially increased," he concluded, glancing at his companion.

"I love her," said Medcott in a low tone.

"Yes?" observed Davenant quietly.

"Yes. I don't know whether I have known it before or not. I know it to-night; but rather than bring her here to be unhappy, or to be happy in losing that singular strength and sweetness that distinguishes her—" he paused a moment.

"Men are apt to think there is something singular in the women they love, I fancy—before they marry them," commented Davenant.

"And after, too. This is no case for satire, Davenant, and you know it."

"Well, then, why should she lose them? They are part of her."

"Why do we ever lose what is best in us? Because we are stifled! Rather than that—I would never see her again. I would only remember her always," he went on almost passionately. "To have her sensitiveness touched by insinuations and ridicule—her ignorance made a discomfort—her very truthfulness a disadvantage—to have repeated some of the scenes we saw last summer, Davenant—and I—I could not protect her; a man cannot always protect a woman! Heavens! It would be like bringing one of those delicate ferns from its forest freshness to blacken in the gas-light of a city parlor."

"A little worse, perhaps."

"If I only knew, if I could only tell—whether I was shutting away my own best happiness or only saving hers, that is the question."

"You talk curiously for a man in love. You ought to have no doubts—and then vainly repent afterwards."

"I know—I know, but it is love, just the same. I am pretty well acquainted with myself, Davenant. That is the reason. I know the perfect charm of her fitness in the place. I know the glamour that Nature casts over men of my temperament. How much did all that influence—not my conception of her—not that, Tom—but that of my own faith and devotion to the ideal? I distrust myself, I might now and then feel that I must slip back to a lower plane."

"I think it extremely probable," assented Davenant. "You wouldn't care for the mountains all the year round, but neither do I think it a foregone conclusion that she does. I wish you might see how she would adapt herself to other conditions."

"I wish I might," said Medcott briefly, "you understand me, Davenant; it is her happiness I am thinking of."

"Yes, I understand you, and, what is more, I believe what you say. With most men I should conclude that this hesitation was the reflection of their doubt of their own happiness, but I do you no such injustice." His voice had dropped its tone of half-mockery, which somehow people never found unsympathetic, and he said with earnestness as he stopped with Medcott at the foot of the stone steps,

"But tell me this before I go any further—have you ever said to her a word of what you have been saying to me?" Medcott shook his head. "Wait a minute, I know that you may have said a dozen things that you had better not have said. One doesn't float around on Shadow Pond or watch the sunset at the stile with an utterly inexperienced person without slipping most heedlessly into these things—but have you ever said to her that you love her in such terms that she can be saying it over to herself now?"

"It is well that no one but you ask me that question, Davenant," said Medcott, his voice low and tense; "but I will answer you. I never have," he added solemnly, "so help me God!"

CHAPTER XII

" Mais savez vous quelle est la différence entre l'erreur des hommes et
l'erreur des femmes ? Non, vous ne le savez pas ! Voila en quoi elle
consiste : un homme pourra dire, par exemple, que deux et deux ne
font pas quatre, mais cinq : une femme dira que deux et deux font une
bougie de cire."

> "And she—I'll tell you—calmly would decree
> That I should roast at a slow fire,
> If that would compass her desire
> And make her one whom they invite
> To the famous ball to-morrow night."

DAVENANT found Needham alone in his office the next
day at noon. The latter was not in the good spirits of the
evening before; certain lines about his mouth and eyes,
which had not been evident then, were easily to be seen
to-day, and, though his manner was quieter, there was in it
a marked restlessness and constraint, the more perceptible
that he tried to be unusually cordial and at ease. He
pulled up a curtain with a jerk, shoved a chair out of what
was not in the least his way, kicked the waste-basket aside,
and made other hospitable demonstrations. Meanwhile
Davenant took a chair and lighted a cigarette.

"Been so busy all the morning that I haven't had time
to cool off," said Needham, throwing himself down into his
revolving chair; "so busy I haven't had time to do my
wife's commissions, by the same token," he added, glancing
at a twist of paper on his desk. " She wanted me to leave
an order for some flowers—doesn't trust me with commissions often," and he laughed, "but she couldn't see her

way out of it this morning. I sha'n't earn her lasting ingratitude, however, if I forget 'em—she probably expected me to. Wants flowers for that Adell musicale." He seemed to be talking against time. "That's another confounded humbug," he asserted positively, causing Davenant unsmilingly to consider whether or not the implied former one was Florence. "Music! Who in possession of his faculties wants—really wants—to hear music?" He waited apparently for an indignant response, but Davenant only said,

"It depends a little upon what faculties one possesses, doesn't it?"

"All humbug! All sheer humbug and affectation!" said Needham violently. "It's the fashion—that's what it is! And people are persuading themselves that they'd rather hear it than eat! Most of 'em would give a dollar to get away from the best musical show going. I'm not musical myself."

"No?" interjected Davenant in mild surprise.

"No, I'm not. And consequently I'm not afraid to say what I think—and I think it's all a confounded humbug."

"I suppose there isn't anybody else in the world, Needham, but you and me, who isn't afraid to say what he thinks," observed Davenant lazily. He didn't believe Charlie had summoned him to shed new light on the question of music, but he was quite willing to let him take his own time.

"Precious few," assented Needham. "I'm not—and I believe you're not. But we can't either of us say that about many people we know."

"I don't believe I'm not," reflected Davenant. "I'm afraid now to say I enjoy music. I thought I did rather—just a little now and then, you know."

"Oh, *rather!*" and he pushed a paper-weight from one side of the table to another. "That's another thing. But these people that rave, you know, and that are so uplifted by it and find it the great gift of inarticulate expression. Great Scott! as if they hadn't rather articulately express themselves over a chicken-fight!"

Davenant suspected that Florence had been indulging in a burst of well-regulated enthusiasm which had proved irritating, as her bursts of enthusiasm sometimes were to people who saw the source of the inspiration.

"The Adells rave over it, you see, and the Adells are pretty honest sort of people as people go," he said, to keep up the conversation. "I never caught them at liking anything recklessly because it was the fashion."

"Oh, the Adells!" repeated Needham, who had not meant to be suddenly confronted by the Adells, who straightforwardly indulged their own tastes, having no social axes to grind. "They say they do."

"Oh, well," drawled Davenant, "if it comes to a question of personal veracity, we're all likely to have the other man's word taken, you know."

There was a tap at the door, and a young broker who occupied the next office came in.

"You're here, Needham," he said, nodding to Davenant whom he knew slightly; "I met Slyck outside and he asked me to give you this—he was on the way to the station. Good tobacco you're smoking, Mr. Davenant," and with another nod he left the room.

Needham read hastily the note the man had given him and then pitched it into the waste-basket with the monosyllable that ought to receive a most grateful public recognition, so overworked is it by the whole Anglo-Saxon race.

"Another bit of my cursed luck!" he said. "The truth is, as I told you last night, I am in a tight place, Davenant. I want a few thousand dollars in a hurry—and I don't want to borrow it around here," he added significantly. " I know you haven't anybody dependent on you, and after seeing you this summer and reviving old times more or less, it seemed to me easier to go to you for a friendly turn than to anybody else I know. Then, again, you haven't got any of that cursed Pharasaism that's going to make your friendship worse than an enmity to lay hold of !"

He had poured out his words in the same nervous, restless way in which he had arraigned music-lovers, and now he paused suddenly.

" Go ahead," said Davenant, taking his cigarette out of his mouth to speak. He would have been surprised, if anything in the way of reverses in fortune surprises an American, for he had believed Needham to be a rich man.

" I am going to tell you the whole business, and then you can do as you please. I've been gambling, of course, a little in stocks and a good deal at the poker-table—naturally the former has been the more expensive. I've had the devil's own luck against me in both, Davenant—and I've spent money that I ought to have shot myself before I touched—there ! that's the matter in a nutshell."

His bravado failed to cover his real shame and mortification. As the light smile he had maintained through much of his talk left his lips, he looked thoroughly worn and harassed. He was not of the stuff of which successful sharpers are made, and the perquisites of dishonesty had not been sufficiently large to make them look like the guerdon of honest toil. Davenant was sorry for him, and as he thought of Florence and her utter inability to be anything but an added burden under such complications, his former envy of this man seemed as unreal as a shadow.

" I like your telling me the whole business," he said slowly, "but I don't see how I'm going to help you, Needham. I haven't money enough in the world, probably, to pull you out of the hole you're in."

"I don't want much," said Needham eagerly; "that's the worst of my luck! If I can get over this place, I'm all right—I know I am. I can see my way clear. But just now I'm pinched, and I must pay a debt that not to pay means—" he paused, and laughed unmirthfully—"well, means the bow-wows and no mistake."

The brilliant sunshine poured in under the curtain Needham had pulled part of the way down. The roar of the street came up to them, and there was the sound of voices, gay or abrupt, hurried always, and the passing and repassing of busy feet just outside the door. The whole situation was trite as possible.

"Well, I guess we'll have to throw a stick at them anyway," said Davenant.

"I knew you would give a man a leg up!" said Needham, resting his folded arms on the table, and leaning over towards Davenant. For the first time since the interview began, he remained in one position for more than a moment. "It's chiefly on account of Florence I care, of course. It's no easy thing to tell a woman like that that you can't pay her bills."

Needham did not mean to be cynical, he only thought of this contingency as the most natural one to bring out the unwelcome truth. Davenant saw this, and fancied that he perceived also that Needham meant to call upon his past sentiment for Florence and his unwillingness that she should suffer, as an unmentioned ally whose presence he had felt in his first impulse towards him as a confidant. In Davenant's silence there seemed no lack of sympathy; he was thinking of his own affairs in the light of this appeal, and apparently so Charlie understood it, for he was the first to speak again. Evidently he found in confession the usual relief.

"Do you remember that old man up in the valley?" he asked suddenly.

"What old man? Denver Trent?"

"The same," with an accent of jollity which his voice immediately lost. "Well, I don't know what devil prompted me, but I talked speculation to him."

Needham paused, for Davenant had risen and looked at him with a certain quiet scorn.

"Go on."

"On my honor, it was in all honesty, Davenant—these things hadn't happened then."

"Well?"

"And he caught the fever a little—the longest-headed will get it, you know; and more on account of that niece of his than anything else, he gave me a few hundreds to turn into thousands, and—and," he concluded defiantly, looking away from the contempt of Davenant's eyes, "I've got to make some payments there, among others, and I haven't the money to make them. There you have it."

"So that is what you were doing those September evenings that we sat by his fire and smoked his pipes?" said Davenant slowly.

"Confound you, Davenant!" said Needham in a burst of humiliated remorse. "I won't let you or any man talk to me as if I lay in wait to beat an old man out of his hard-earned savings if I *am* down on my luck! I did it to make him more comfortable—that's God's truth."

"God's truth!" repeated Davenant. He spoke quietly, and the hesitation of his speech was increased rather than lessened, but its force was none the less unmistakable. "This is a crime that you have committed, Needham—a crime. I don't object to your playing for high stakes down here in any infernal business where everybody knows the dishonesty of the game—"

"Go on," said Needham sulkily, "kick a man when he's down—it's the safest time."

"But that fine old fellow up there! To take the money that he has won by hard work, of which you men down here know not the first stroke or indication—money that he has wrung out of a reluctant earth and kept by actual privation—and I'm not giving you a fancy sketch of a New England farmer, either, I'm talking of what I *know*—and that you have tossed into your game of taking out of somebody else's pocket"—Needham sprang to his feet and struck the table with his fist, but Davenant did not stop and he was not interrupted—"the funds to buy what nobody owns—when you run a risk of losing this, that he looks on as an assurance of future comfort—you commit a crime."

His indignation had carried him further than he had meant to go. It was true that it was in Denver Trent's person that he felt the wrong and the injustice of it, but the knowledge that it was not he alone that would suffer—the thought of Rhodope—had stirred him to a degree of emotion that he rarely permitted himself to reach. "The only excuse for you," he concluded, "is that it is not the crime of an individual, but that of a body of men—which ought to make it worse, but doesn't."

"Why don't you add a few more bits of information and then send for the police?" asked Needham, still sullenly. "Is that all?"

"No, it isn't all," answered Davenant in another tone, his oddly attractive smile coming back for an instant to his lips. "How much must you have?"

Needham looked up quickly from the chair he had dropped into after his explosion of temper.

"I believe you're one of the best fellows in the world," he said.

"If you go on believing things of that sort without looking into them you'll never keep out of trouble," observed Davenant coolly. "Now look here."

It needed but a few minutes more to bring the interview to a close, and Davenant, declining to lunch with Needham, whose sense of relief had restored a languishing appetite, left him with a mild amusement underlying his half-contemptuous interest. He was sorry for him—his volatility and want of steadfast purpose in any direction drove him from one excitement to another, almost of necessity, but he could not pardon him the unscrupulous thoughtlessness which had threatened to wreck the modest and dearly bought prosperity of a man like Denver Trent, with that of his adopted children. Jib, of course, could make his own way, but Rhodope—!

"I am several kinds of a fool," he remarked to himself, without bitterness, at this point, as he crossed one of the unfashionable avenues. "I could have knocked Needham down when I heard his blessed statements, and yet I was perfectly conscious that I was filled with unmitigated gratification that it was in my power to do something for Rhodope Trent. Something that she will never know about either. Of course," he continued to speculate, with his smallest smile, "I'd rather she would know. If she could find it out in some way utterly unknown to me, and reflecting much credit upon my careful method of concealment, and in a burst of gratitude should hail me Benefactor and Friend—I should like that better. But I don't know just whom I could depend upon to tell her without letting me suspect—Hullo!"

The interjection was addressed to a small girl carrying a large basket and draped in a shawl folded cornerwise, and which, being intended for a full-grown woman, dragged fore and aft, in spite of her efforts to hold it up. The complexity of the situation was momentarily relieved by her falling apparently flat on her face so suddenly that Davenant nearly fell over her. He picked her up and waited for her to cry; but though she had barked her wrist and banged her knee, with the patience of a frequently barked and banged childhood she did not weep, the luxury of indiscriminate grief being one of the many confined to the wealthy classes. She carried her wrist to her mouth, while she carefully examined the contents of the basket, after which she looked up at Davenant, whose assistance she had received with as thorough inattention as if it had fallen from the skies.

" Nothing injured, I hope," he said politely. As her large eyes and small face remained quite unintelligent, he repeated the substance of his inquiry, and she shook her head.

" Does your wrist hurt you ?"

She looked at her wrist and then at him with a wise little smile.

" Not as much as a lickin'," she replied.

" No," he assented, " not nearly as much."

As he spoke his thoughts flew back with a sudden sense of the drollness of the contrast to the other distress he had just been witness of, and the different manner in which it had been borne. Somehow this seemed the more real.

" Here," he said, " is a small piece of money which I am going to give you. It comes under the head of indiscriminate alms-giving, which has gone by, and, moreover, I rather hope you will spend it foolishly."

The child's eyes were fixed on the coin, and she did not understand a word he said, but she listened, fascinated by his smile.

" In order that I may not be too unenlightened," he went on, " I give it for an object, the promotion of stoicism among the poor. I am glad to contribute something towards its support. It comes high, but the poor must have it."

Without a word the child took the money and went rapidly on, the point of the old shawl dipping here and there in wanton irregularity, her swiftness suggesting the presence of a fear that the gentleman might think better of it.

It was late in the afternoon that a half-formed intention that had been floating about in Davenant's mind ever since the night before took a shape which led him to Needham's house up-town. He must call on Florence, to be barely civil, and as a result of his attention so lately directed to the Needham family, and a sort of curiosity to note the difference between the husband and the wife, due to his habits of observation, he was led to go there the same day.

Mrs. Needham was at home, and in a few minutes he found himself by her daintly appointed tea-table and her still more daintily appointed self. She wore a somewhat daring tea-gown of pale yellow with shaded effects of golden-brown velvet, and here and there, at odd times, a good deal of cream-colored lace. The result with her blonde hair and soft complexion within the light of the many lamps was distinctly fetching. Her thoughts were pleasant ones. A visitor of social prominence, who was a great bore, had just left the room, and although Florence was of too lofty a nature ever to be really bored to the annihilating degree suffered by less elevated spirits, even she could not prevent a lulling sense of physical relief from permeating her relieved frame. She was going to the Adell musicale this evening, and although, to be sure, it was a large one and a lot of people were asked, still it was a pleasant thing to go to the Adell's at all, and she would wear a gown which would go far to make such discriminating people regret not having asked her oftener. The door was opened by the servant, and she looked up and saw Tom Davenant. For the moment she felt that she was really in perigee.

"Why, Tom," she exclaimed, coming forward with a charming impulsiveness. "I mean, How do you do, Mr. Davenant?" she supplemented with her sparkling laugh.

"Well, Florence," said Davenant, and then with immediate imitation of her own manner, "I mean, Very well, I thank you, Mrs. Needham."

She was prettier even than she had been in the summer. The finish, the luxury of her surroundings, the soft-tinted illuminations, the perfume, the studied and undisturbed perfection of color and outline, suited her better than the freer, plainer, natural surroundings of country life.

He looked at his chair, then at hers, with a slight anxiety, after they were seated.

"I was afraid I had taken the most becoming chair," he murmured, "I knew you'd never forgive me if I had. It doesn't matter to me, you know—when you've once made up your mind to be good rather than pretty, you don't mind things like that."

"I thank the Providence that on my birth has smiled," she said gayly, "that I can be pretty in any kind of chair, and as for my being good—"

"That kind of chair hasn't been invented yet," finished Davenant lazily. "The stool of penitence comes first besides."

Florence laid down her sugar-tongs and looked at him. She felt a little reckless this afternoon—success is apt to make us so. She fancied that even a confession of wasted hopes from Tom Davenant might be impending.

"Do you really think that I have much to repent?" she demanded, looking into his eyes. She dwelt slightly on the first pronoun.

"Oh, my, yes!" answered Davenant easily, as he looked back. "And wouldn't you be sorry if you hadn't! Show me the woman that wouldn't. Who is it says one of a woman's sweetest pleasures is to cause regret? it's the same thing."

"One certainly need not weep over having caused that sort of regret. It doesn't last long enough for one to get at one's handkerchief."

"Most beautiful things are evanescent," he admitted.

Florence was a little provoked, and she shut the lid of her tea-pot with a snap.

"I believe you come to see me just to laugh at me," she asserted.

"It is you I come to see, just the same." There was a touch of seriousness in his tone which mollified her. That which he said was true at least. She glanced up in quick recognition, and then went on pouring tea. Her sparkling fingers, her sparkling eyes, and her sparkling silver produced a general effect of gleam and glitter.

"You ought to keep smoked glass for the benefit of your visitors," he said as he took his cup. "You are a strain on the eyes."

"That's the sort of thing you have always said to me," she pouted. "Always about the effect I produce, or wish to produce. Just as if that was all there is of me."

Davenant checked an impulse to say that he guessed it was.

"Well, you like a successful effect, don't you?" he suggested.

"I don't know that I do. I have a great deal in my life that people don't understand," she averred, with a transparent little sigh. "Perhaps it would be better if I did."

"Now you take my advice, Florence," said Davenant honestly, "and don't you go in for being a genuine, candid sort of person—it wouldn't do at all. I know it's the fashion, but one has to have certain natural qualifications."

It was singular how old habits asserted themselves after

all these years. He talked to her with the old ease and familiarity, and she listened with the shrewd half-comprehension with which she had always listened to him. Only in him was wanting that which had once made their talk—his lecturing and her speculations—but the foam on the current—the passionate longing which had thrilled every moment, to touch her hand, her cheek, her hair, and to hear her say she loved him. That deep undercurrent had swept itself away, but on the surface of the quieter pool the bubbles of laughter, admonition, and resentment tossed as lightly as ever. She was not in the least angry at his last remark. Instead, she turned it over in her mind.

"Do you really think so?" she mused, looking at him thoughtfully.

He nodded. Evidently what he had said influenced her, but she changed the subject.

"Are you going to the musicale to-night?" she asked.

"I believe I am. Who is the young woman they have there—from the South or something?"

She hesitated a moment.

"I don't know," she replied. She had not known there was to be any one of the sort, which was an occasion for a sudden, sharp regret. She was glad she had found out before she went.

"She's an original young person, I believe. Unconventional and clever. Never has been anywhere before. It's quite a card to have that sort of person at one's entertainments nowadays. Rouses the jaded interest."

Florence stirred her tea, and thought.

"So it is," she assented. Davenant had spoken idly, with no thought of the effect of his words, but now as he noticed Mrs. Needham's thoughtfulness, and recognized with amusement the fact that she was running hastily over in her mind all the unconventional people she knew, with the idea of finding somebody to present at her next entertainment, a sudden suggestion came to him. Was not this just the opportunity that Medcott had wished for? He did not stop to consider all the manifest disadvantages of the scheme. For one of the few times in his life, Davenant spoke from impulse.

"Why don't you get Rhodope Trent down here?" he asked lazily; "she'd combine well."

"Rhodope Trent!" repeated Florence, sitting up straight in her chair.

"Yes, rather unusual type of beauty—would look well in your parlor. Out of place, but that is interesting and would make you the more harmonious, you know."

Davenant spoke indifferently, but he watched with interest the effect of what he said.

"She'd have a pleasant winter. I fancy she'd attract some attention. I admire her uncommonly myself."

"So does Mr. Medcott."

"Yes, so does Medcott. He'll probably want to make a study of her."

It was an unscrupulous proceeding, this of Davenant's, but the idea having once recommended itself to him, he gave the same attention to carrying it out, by playing upon Florence Needham's well-known characteristics, as he would have given to the development of a piece of literary work. It amused him to see the effect of his suggestions. To Florence the idea came also as the solving of a problem. Its fulfilment would insure Tom Davenant's presence; more than that, it would bring that of Austin Medcott. What had seemed the night before so difficult of attainment would follow in the natural course of things. Her feeling for Medcott had drowned for the moment her jealousy of Rhodope. She must see him—of that only was she conscious. And then the social advantage of bringing forward a country girl, over whom a man of letters like Davenant and an artist like Medcott had lost their heads. Why had she not thought of it before?

"I think I shall ask her to come," she said.

Then their talk fell naturally on the valley and the past summer, and Mrs. Needham guessed why it was that Medcott had not answered her letter when Davenant told her how he had been shut away from the city and all news of it for weeks.   She would have liked Davenant to dwell on him and his affairs—she liked even to hear his name—but he did not.

CHAPTER XIII

" They do best, who if they cannot but admit Love, yet make it keep quarter."

IT was Sunday noon. Service in the little church was nearly over. Deacon Bunt, who sat in the front seat, and listened to the word of God with kindly tolerance every Sunday, glanced at the hymn-book to see that it was in readiness for the last hymn. Mrs. Roble, a large woman, whose breathing had been audible at intervals during the sermon, discomposed herself into a final effort of attention.

Tom Furwin shifted a morsel of tobacco, which had been administered surreptitiously within the last few minutes, from one cheek to the other, and, meeting Rhodope Trent's eyes at that critical moment, colored violently under what he felt was her disapproval, and moved his heavy boots noisily from a secluded spot under the bench. Denver Trent's fine, gray head was thrown back a little, as his upturned eyes followed the clergyman's gestures, the directness of his attention itself an inspiration in such an audience. With the choir, to which were dedicated those seats, at right angles to the others, immediately about the melodeon, sat Elizabeth French. She had become a little

sleepy, but just now she caught Jib Trent's unsmiling eyes,
and flushed into a perturbed wakefulness. Against the
whitewashed wall, her ears hearing the clergyman's words
and her thoughts wandering abroad, leaned Rhodope. She
had not even marked the delinquencies of Tom Furwin,
when her glance had revealed his shortcomings to his own
startled consciousness. She had let her gaze slip from the
speaker to Tom, and from him to the uncurtained window
against which a pine-tree shook now and then its snow-
weighted branches, and, scarcely conscious of this small
breach of attention, had returned to the legitimate occupation of the hour, and fixed her eyes on the preacher's
face. The little church was a cheerful, peaceful place in
summer, when to the picturesqueness of an utter simplicity, which is, after all, as symbolical as sumptuous decora-
tion, were added the sweet scents of the fragrant season of
the year, and the lazy hum of the holiday of the insect
world, coming in through the open door and the raised
window. Then the now snow-weighted pine gently waved
green plumes in the sunlight, promising shade and coolness ; then the squares of free air within the window-frames,
towards which the eyes of impatient youth so often turned,
throbbed with the promise and exultance of welcoming Nature, and the fancy wandered beyond the waving branches
and the blue sky, there visible, to unseen delicious freedom
and delights. Then the religious feeling that stirred the
exhortations of the preacher, and that breathes through the
Christian hymns, seemed a natural and simple emotion.
The world was a world of peace and pleasantness, Nature
was at one with the Christ who so loved it and so studied
its beautiful appropriateness ; the universe was God inspired, and thrilled and glowed with the love and the light
that is about us, and over us, and beneath us like a garment.

But to-day the glow and the freedom were absent. In winter the doors and windows were shut tight and the outside air, when it entered, was an unwelcome intruder. The heat from the iron stove reddened the cheeks, made the eyes heavy, and benumbed the senses of the hard-working men and women who sat rigidly upright in painful conscientiousness, or drooped in the relaxation of forced inaction. And up there in the pulpit some one was telling them to do certain things that were very hard, and utterly opposed to all naturalness and longings of man whatever.

"Be not weary in well-doing," exhorted the preacher.

It was his concluding sentence that he was beginning with this repetition of his text. Rhodope had followed his words, sometimes absently, sometimes attentively, and suddenly it seemed as if her whole being was permeated by a sense of the weariness of this very struggle that all the teachings and interests of her life were holding her to. If there were more to fight, it would not be so difficult—but who is able to stand up against weariness?

Four or five months ago it had not so come home to her —this realization of the effort of trying to do the best that in her lay. It had seemed that her life was opening and developing into what were its best possibilities, in joy and calm. Fulfilment after fulfilment seemed to lie before her ; the religion which had long been part of her existence had appeared to manifest itself in the assurance of happiness. But of late this inspiration had somehow disappeared. Life seemed weary and yet restless. The apostle knew of what he spoke. It is not the satiety of evil, it is not the fatigue of labor, it is the weight of exhausted enthusiasm that burdens the hands of those who would lift the world. The clergyman closed his sermon, offered a short prayer, and with much shuffling of feet and the usual air of factitious activity the audience rose for the last hymn. Elizabeth, as she shook out her draperies, cast a furtive look at Jib, but he was stolidly gazing at his hymn-book, and with a little toss of her head, thoroughly to convince herself that she did not in the least care whether he looked or not, she addressed herself to song. Every syllable uttered by her fresh young voice reached Jib's ears so acutely that it seemed to fill his brain. It was as if no one else was singing, so conscious was he of the clear, sweet soprano that lifted the somewhat depressing words of the hymn into an atmosphere of encouragement, almost of gayety. He knew just how she was holding her book, and just how often she glanced away from the page, and yet he never looked from his own book upon which the printed words met his unseeing eyes, while they came with such swift interpretation to his ears. The benediction was pronounced, and the little audience filtered out through the door, beyond which there began to be the sound of sleigh-bells and much stamping off of snow. Rhodope looked anxiously at Jib and then quickly towards Elizabeth, who was exchanging elaborate civilities with Tom Furwin's mother. She laid her hand on her brother's arm.

"Wait for Elizabeth, Jib," she said. Jib did not reply, but she knew he had heard her. He did not shake off her hand or in the least resent her suggestion, but he went quietly on his way down the aisle.

"Jib," she repeated, "now you wait for Elizabeth."

He looked at her and smiled in tolerant kindliness, and she dropped her hand and shook her head regretfully. She knew this mood of her brother's very well. It was rare and it was one against which beating was in vain. He would not answer her further, and he would not be influenced by her—he would take his own way. It was now and then after this fashion that Jib Trent evinced a sternness of purpose that seemed utterly foreign to his nature, and which,

while she lamented it, called forth from Rhodope a devotion which would not have been so complete had he
been always as yielding as he sometimes seemed. And
it was this trait that had caused Denver Trent to observe
with a chuckle that "Generally speakin' it was awful
easy to tow Jib home, but now and then when you picked
up the rope you found he'd got up steam to go t'other
way."

Outside, the white snow stretched itself over the hills,
flung the ends of its mantle across the hollows, and swept
with its fingers the leafless trees and the stalwart pines.
Heavy, awkward sleighs stood about the entrance; their
owners were climbing in and tucking dingy buffalo-robes
about their feet. There was a good deal of excitement
when Mrs. Roble was being assisted into a quite narrow
sleigh. It seemed once or twice as if it wasn't going to be
done. Several persons of wide sympathies desisted from
their own similar efforts to watch hers. When she was
fairly in and had turned about with the genial smile with
which people, stout and unashamed, reward such friendly
interest, there was a general sense of relief. The rude
sleigh-bells jangled, and slowly the group on the wooden
steps grew smaller.

"I never could abide that kind of a stove anyway," said
a familiar voice just behind Rhodope. "It's one of them
stoves that the more fuel you put into it, the more it just
kinder winks, and you'd never know it had had anything at
all. You can git it red-hot if you want to, and then you can
sit and freeze."

"I thought t'was pipin' this mornin'," said a mild voice.

"Well, 't warn't," was the uncompromising rejoinder.
"'T warn't a mite above sixty-five. I felt cold."

"Well, I felt hot," said the other with more firmness than
would have been anticipated from such a voice.

"*Felt!*" retorted the first speaker. "'Tain't any sign how ye *feel*. If there'd been a thermomety there, I tell ye it wouldn't have riz above sixty-five—I 'ain't been so cold this season."

"How d'ye do, Miss Matilda," said Rhodope, turning around, "I didn't know you were here."

"I didn't hardly know as I was either. I come over for a little change. Ashur Dust sleighed me over yesterday. He said 'twas dretful good sleighin'. I guess we'd 'a' come better on wheels. We slumped *and* slumped."

"How's Tim?" asked Rhodope; "I don't see him much in the winter."

"I guess there ain't anythin' the matter with him. I ain't very well."

"Why, I'm sorry—"

"Oh, there ain't any use bein' sorry. My food don't set well, that's all. I came over to see how Roxana Dust's would go. It's my belief she raises with yeast-cake. I can smell a yeast-cake as fur as I can see it. She's stopped to speak to the minister, and Ashur he's gone off after the sleigh. I can't hear more'n half that minister says. I ain't deaf either. I guess he ain't got much of a delivery. That's Marcella Brown's girl, ain't it?"

Out of the church-door came Elizabeth. She was talking with two of the village youths, but her glance scanned swiftly the group outside, and then followed Jib's figure up the road. His pace was leisurely but unloitering. Her voice fell a moment and then rose in its gayest tones as the two boys went forward with her to the old sleigh which Ashur Dust was just bringing up.

"Yes," said Rhodope, quietly, as she watched the pretty girl, "that's Elizabeth."

"I didn't see her this mornin'—she spent the night over to Clock's," continued Miss Spore. "Well, I never see such airs as she puts on. And what ails that hat? You don't suppose her head's *made* one-sided, do you?"

Elizabeth paused just as she was climbing into the sleigh. "Where's Miss Spore?" she asked.

"She's comin'," answered Ashur. "You get up here along of me."

Elizabeth looked back and saw Rhodope and Miss Matilda; they were almost the last people on the steps. She turned away from the somewhat inefficient youths and waited for them.

While Miss Spore climbed into the sleigh assisted by the even-tempered Roxana, and remarking that she'd rather climb into a cistern, Elizabeth said with an affectation of entire indifference,

"Seems to me your brother is in a dreadful hurry to get home, Rhodope."

"I don't believe he is," answered Rhodope, looking straight into Elizabeth's eyes, in which there was a suspicious mistiness. "I don't believe he's in any hurry at all."

"Oh, well, it isn't anything to me," and she threw back her head with a trifle more spirit than was called for by complete indifference.

"Isn't it?" said Rhodope slowly. "Then I'm very sorry."

Elizabeth looked at her a moment as if she would speak, but as the inefficient youths called out, "I guess we can h'ist you in now, Miss Elizabeth," she bit her lip, turned away, and climbed lightly up to the place by Ashur's side. From there she nodded a farewell, and they lumbered down the rough road with that apparent gayety that sleigh-bells lend to any sort of locomotion, however impeded. Rhodope looked after them a moment. The glare of the noon sun dazzled her eyes, but up the road she could see Jib's dark figure against the white fields, swinging strongly on. Before and behind him were other dark figures, little groups

of two and three, but he joined none of them, greeting one
and another, but passing by. She wanted to run after him
and walk home with him; it should not be that they should
both be lonely while they had each other. But she checked
the impulse, and with a farewell glance at the shining peaks
that stood about her, she entered the church-door again,
her Sunday duties not yet over.

Meanwhile the Dust sleigh reached and passed the groups
which were making their way along the road and narrow
footpath. As Jib raised his eyes in response to the greeting called out by the genial Ashur, his smile faded suddenly and his eyes grew stern, and yet he caught no spectacle
more antagonistic than a pretty, rather pale face, looking
back from the front seat with eyes which tried to be cool
and defiant, and which succeeded instead in being admira-
bly pleading and decidedly pathetic. Jib pushed his hands
farther into his pockets and walked doggedly on, and pathos and defiance alike vanished, and nothing remained
where they had been, save the back of a little red hat which
sped along the whiteness of the way. This change in the
relations which had existed between Jib and Elizabeth was
not that of a moment. It had begun in the early autumn,
when Elizabeth's natural coquetry had made itself evident
among her numerous admirers. The young fellow of whom
Florence had written to Medcott had been one of several
who hastened to declare themselves her victims, and it cannot be asserted that she showed any becoming regret at the
devastations which followed her footsteps. It was some
time before Jib was roused to resentment. His was not a
nature to be speedily kindled into petty jealousy, and, as
has been said, at first the all-absorbing nature of his love
for her left no room for speculations and requirements regarding her feeling for him. Naturally this state of things
had not lasted forever, but certain admissions on Elizabeth's

part having satisfied his unsuspecting trust in her, his security was not easily shaken by the various irrelevancies of his sweetheart. Elizabeth herself, led into these irrelevancies by vanity, a most natural love of experiment, and a genuine liking for amusement and those who provided her with it, watched the effect upon him with a security as great, if not as wise, as his own. Somewhat piqued by his apparent indifference, she had thrown further provocation in his way, and when he was finally roused to remonstrance, she retorted with feminine daring, held out no promise of amendment, and, when he grew angry, waited confidently for his anger to subside and for renewed terms of amity. A wiser woman would have paused before reaching this point, for it was here that surprise lay in wait for her. It has been frequently observed that an unsuspecting nature, once awakened, is more difficult to lull again to slumber than one more easily startled. The outbreak had come just before Elizabeth had left the valley, and frightened and regretful she had gone away without an opportunity to set things right. The fact that she had not dared tell him that the irresponsible Schumacher accompanied her half the way, when he learned it, added confirmation to Jib's distrust, and the summer's idyl was apparently at an end. This had all taken place during the last half of September. What of struggle or regret followed for Jib it was difficult to estimate. Even Rhodope could not do more than guess that it had made a great difference in his life. He returned to his favorite books, and Denver Trent watched him with quiet interest, after half a day of which observation he remarked to Rhodope, as Jib strolled out of the room, that "there warn't no sort of commentaries on any kind of a book, whether it was Scriptures, or whether it wasn't, like a little enlightenin' experience."

The conversation went no further, but Rhodope sighed

unconsciously as she recognized the truth of the assertion
—possibly her mental application of it was not confined to
Jib alone.

The long autumn passed with its gorgeous foliage, its
biting frosts, and its cold winds, as did the first months of
winter, and still, if Jib now and then laid down his book and
gazed idly at the glory of the hills, and then returned impatiently to the page, no one but himself knew that it was
to gaze at a vision in which the heroine of the novel, were
she noble lady, gypsy queen, barbarian enchantress, or village maiden, appeared dressed in bespangled garments,
standing in an open chariot, guiding four prancing ponies
down a dusty street.

In January came a letter from Marcella to her old friend,
Roxana Dust. Elizabeth had never been as well since she
left the valley; Nicholas was going to hunt up a kangaroo
and a few other miscellaneous attractions, and she thought
she would go with him. Would Roxana take Elizabeth to
board for a couple of months, so that she might be at ease
about her and know that she was among friends? So Elizabeth came back to the valley, her brilliant beauty a little
paled; and when Jib first met her at the post-office there was
a new pleading look in the eyes that met his, which affected
the beating of his heart after a manner hitherto associated
only with precipices, battles, and concealments under the
very feet of the enemy; but in spite of it he had lifted his
cap and gone away with the mail, while Elizabeth had stood
looking after him a moment and then climbed into the Dust
sleigh, her lip trembling like that of a well-scolded child.
That was two weeks ago. For one reason or another, or
perhaps with the unreasonableness of one who lets an important decision rest on the turn of a card, she had looked
to this particular Sunday as a day which should clear away
the clouds which lay between them. For one thing it was

Sunday, and Elizabeth still held that simple faith in the Sabbath as an agent for good which is rapidly becoming eliminated from a less hide-bound generation under the enlightenment of Sunday newspapers and sacred concerts. Then she knew that she should see him at church, and that would be a step—she had not been able to go the previous week on account of a storm. Moreover, she knew she should look pretty in that particular bonnet—moreover, she didn't care what was the reason, he would come and speak to her and listen to her, because—because he must. And now she was driving home, and he had not spoken to her, and the snow was hopelessly glaring, and the hills hopelessly high, and life was hopelessly long!

"Those Trents," said Miss Matilda Spore, behind her, "they're the perversest family I ever did see. They'd rather walk than ride any day, just to show they ken do it. I guess when Jib there's got the rheumatism he'll wish he hadn't kicked the snow 'round so much. There ain't no call for a man to have the rheumatism unless he wants to get it standin' round in puddles."

"I dono as Jib's hardly responsible for the snow's bein' on the way to church," said tolerant Mrs. Dust.

"Perhaps he ain't," retorted Miss Spore sharply, "but I suppose he could have rode home with Denver. Look at Denver's left leg." This was evidently mere rhetoric, as Denver's left leg was probably inside his cottage. "That's the way he got it. Fishin' all day, gettin' wet through and trackin' home mud on to the clean floor. I know old Mis' Trent couldn't keep him settin' still noways. Jib'll limp worse than he does." Elizabeth's very ears were scarlet with indignation. Jib never would limp, she was entirely sure of that. He might treat her with positive cruelty, he might be selfish and stupid, and she hated him—but he would never limp like Uncle Denver. She wished that the sleigh would tip over and spill Miss Spore into a good hard place; and as for herself—why, it might kill her for all she cared—but she'd just like Miss Spore *jounced!* In this tempest of emotion it is not strange that she did not trust herself to speak. The sleigh turned off the main road and made its way along a less broken lane. In a few moments they drew up at the rambling farm-house, and Elizabeth sprang down, ran up to her own little room, and broke into a passion of tears.

"There's a party goin' snow-shoein' to-morrow night over to the half-way tavern," said Ashur Dust after the four-o'clock dinner, during which Elizabeth had been unusually quiet. "Ever been, Elizabeth?"

"No, never," she answered; "I wish I could go."

"Well, I guess you can. Some of 'em are goin' around in the ox-cart, and they can pick you up if you get tired. Just get me my pipe, Elizabeth; I guess I'm gettin' kinder rheumatic, or else it's the chair—kinder like to stay settin' after Sunday dinner."

"That's just the way you get rheumatism," said Miss Spore. "If you'd git up and stir around—"

"You just said that was what gave it to people—stirring round!" flashed Elizabeth, wheeling about on Miss Spore. The flame of resentment still burned brightly. There was a moment's silence. Ashur Dust winked with care at his genial wife.

"You did for a fact, Matilda," he said.

Miss Spore had never learned that consistency was the hobgoblin of weak minds, but it held no terrors for her.

"Wal," she remarked to Elizabeth, "I guess you 'ain't got it in your tongue, anyhow."

Notwithstanding the temperate correction of this reply, she secretly entertained from this hour a higher opinion of Elizabeth French.

CHAPTER XIV

" Dearest,
When the mesmerizer Snow
With his hand's first sweep
Put the earth to sleep
'Twas a time when the heart could show
All."

" I'll wipe away all trivial fond records."

BEFORE the hour fixed for the snow-shoeing party, the swift flame which had burst out in Elizabeth's indirect defence of Jib from the aspersions of Miss Spore, and which seemed to scorch her own heart when she was silent, had sunk more than once into the smouldering embers of resentment, and been fanned again into a fire of passionate regret. Now her eyes brightened with the satisfaction of conscious power as she dwelt on the thought that the devotion of at least two of the party was sure to be hers, and she would show Jib Trent—here her train of thought lost coherency and paused in vague triumph, only to be rendered cruelly definite by the reflection that, alas! Jib had been "shown" various things of similar import, and had borne the spectacle unscathed. Then the anticipation would terminate in a sweet but fleeting vision of herself and Jib, standing on the Dust threshold exchanging farewells after it was all over, which was banished by a sudden tide which swept across her consciousness, the simple longing for his presence, for the grasp of his hand, for the care, the ever-watchful tenderness of which she had been conscious, whether expressed or not, for a little of that vanished security in which she had rested and with which she had trifled. Elizabeth was a remarkably concrete person; she had no fancy for abstractions, no taste for self-analysis; almost no thoughtfulness, but she felt the less unmistakably. Through all these emotional variations ran the anticipation of the coming expedition. She clung to that in moods of retaliation and reconciliation alike—that should not pass as had the other opportunities, when she had been less enlightened concerning her own sentiments.

The crust was hard and gleaming. The moon, a little past the full, shed a light, faint and suggestive, rather than brilliant and revealing. The muffled figures stood in a small group at the foot of the lane. Except for a laugh now and then, noticeably that of Elizabeth, it was quieter than seemed befitting a party of pleasure. There was none of that rippling flow of talk, that restless to and fro of graceful movement and verbal interchange which commonly attends such a delay among people to whom social reunions are less detrimental. By and by the natural merriment of youth might lift the curtain of gloom and discover a scene of hilarity, but at present there were few beside Elizabeth who were able to meet the demands of this first ten minutes with apparent light-heartedness.

"Come," said Rhodope, "we are all here at last," and swiftly, silently, her tall, straight figure sped before them over the frozen brilliancy of the shining fields. Jib gave one quick glance over the group, saw Elizabeth in struggling laughter, with an officious instructor on each side of her, and, pushing his thick cap back from his handsome forehead, he followed his sister, and in straggling groups and halting couples the whole company spread itself over the snowy fields.

For a while Jib and Rhodope kept side by side leading

the way. They did not speak. Each of them, in different ways, lay under the spell of the time and scene. Night and snow clothe even the best-known ways with strangeness. Moreover, in their mode of progress itself there was an element of unreality. They followed no beaten track of travel, they went about for no windings of brook or fence or marsh; they kept their way, as the crow flies, over hollows and stone walls, hidden by deep drifts, across fields whose sudden treacheries made them in summer-time pick a careful way. On the smooth, hard crust upon which a light snow had fallen, their snow-shoes slipped along, transformed, from the long, awkward hindrances they appeared, into light, floating supports, which kept them above the lower earth, with its difficulties and pitfalls. Their course lay across the valley and gradually downwards. Before them the white plain stretched itself until it was indefinitely lost in the mistiness of the pale moonlight. It seemed possible that it stretched on into a land of eternal ice and snow. There was a dim, cold uncertainty waiting for them beyond there, where the gleaming hill cut off part of what in spring was a green meadow, and was now only a vague white level. Suggestions of the ice-palaces and the frozen courts of the snow-queen floated through Rhodope's mind. Apparently far on the horizon, but in reality near at hand, twinkled an occasional light, but they seemed no indication of human companionship and neighborhood. When now and then the voices behind them ceased altogether as if muffled suddenly under the veil of mystery, it was very, very still. One strained one's ears unconsciously to catch, if might be, the distant tinkle of reindeer's bells, speeding, speeding northward to the fortresses of continual winter.

Certainly Medcott had told the truth when he assured Davenant that he had uttered no word to disturb Rhodope's peace of mind. No thought of falseness or injury mingled with her remembrance of him. Her nature was too sweet and large to be always bringing looks and words and actions to the bar of personal application. Her unconscious dignity forbade the thought to cross her mind, that he had selfishly sought an idle pleasure for himself and let the cost of it fall upon her heart. In her memory he stood always courteous, strong, and true. But there were days which it seemed to her were all remembrance. There were days whose light seemed only that of earlier mornings and afternoons when the whole world had been warm and sunlit; days when even this pale reflection seemed dying away into colorlessness. She did not fight against it or ignore it. Neither did she grow peevish and fretful under the strain of the sudden weariness that now and then overcame her, but simply turned, as it were, and faced this shadow which had darkened her world. Regarding it with calm and clear, if a little saddened, eyes, she found that within it life was quite livable, and that though the glory of noon had departed, there was still light enough to give their true colors and dimensions to the many dear things that had always been hers. There was something touching in one of her beautiful youth, in this quiet acceptance of what had been laid upon her shoulders. It was the burden of which youth is generally most impatient and which it strives most wilfully to shake off—this of resignation to the loss of the glow and color of life. Possibly it came in part from the absence of the analytical tendency. She never said, If this had been otherwise— Why did I do this? Why did he say this?—or any why? or when? or where? The experiences of her life came to her naturally and inevitably as winter succeeded summer. But more than this, it arose from the sweetness and nobility of her spirit. Nevertheless, there were times when an unusual depression seemed to make more clear what had slipped away. To-night the realization of the change was strong. As they skirted the outlying trees of a clump of bare aspens, she remembered that it was within that dreary, dark wood, with its gaunt tree-trunks, snowy earth, and frozen streams, and which had then dozed in midsummer greenness and plashing waters, that she had first seen Medcott, lying on the ferns. Over beyond there had been the landslide—they could not have gone so near it if there had been no snow. It was as if all the dear by-ways and familiar scenes of her summer wanderings lay with their memories, their warmth and their fragrances, covered up and silent under this cold, crushing, mysterious mantle of white, and henceforth her way lay over them, above them, across them—but never again within them. With a quick little sigh she turned and put out her hand.

"Jib!" she said. Then she paused, almost frightened. Had he failed her, too? He was no longer by her side, apparently she was alone in this waste of snow. In another moment she smiled at her own fear—they were all just behind her, hidden for the instant by a wall of rock; now they appeared, black figures, moving on in all varieties of grace and awkwardness. It was but two or three minutes earlier that Jib had turned back. It had been in obedience to a sudden impulse which, had he paused to consider, he would have disregarded. He had heard Elizabeth's voice raised in distress. It had not been raised very loudly, nor was the distress very poignant, but it came to his ears with entire distinctness. It did not mingle with the other voices in the least. It was as if the two were alone, and she had spoken—so he turned back. They were all laughing when he met them.

"Elizabeth's down," called one girl to another, as she looked over her shoulder. Jib paused and they passed him. A few feet farther were two dark figures clearly defined like everything else this pallid night. One was that of a good-looking boy of the neighborhood, whose reputation had fallen of late somewhat below the easy standard of a country village.

He stood turned away from Jib, stooping over Elizabeth, and attempting to raise her to her feet. He held both her hands, and they were both laughing—Elizabeth uncontrollably. The treacherous snow-shoes, which had been such valuable allies, had been transformed into the most malignant of foes. Elizabeth, unused to their vagaries, felt that each was the size of the traditional barn-door and as impossible of dexterous management. Jib stood watching the little episode, while the jealous anger, which had seemed no part of his quietness these last few months, almost choked him.

What right had that fellow to hold her hands? How could she laugh like that? Had she no heart, no sense— nothing but a spirit of coquetry and a talent for frivolity? Inarticulately these questions surged through his brain. Poor little Elizabeth looked hopelessly pretty as she crouched on the snow, the demoralized snow-shoes turned, twisted, and defiant. Her companion dropped her hands, and, leaning over, his head close to hers, lifted her to her feet. There was a quick exclamation from Elizabeth, a laugh from the young man, and they stood an instant silent, she clinging to his arm, and looking up smiling into his face. That he had kissed her and that he stood unrebuked, Jib was as sure as that there was but one thing for him to do, to turn and go silently and swiftly back to the others, his hot anger changing into a sudden cold, deceptive contempt. But he did not go.

"Oh, Jib," called out the young man, whose education had been fragmentary in certain directions, though somewhat too consecutive in others, "come and fix this here snow-shoe. I don't know what's happened to the blamed thing!"

This was an appeal not to be resisted by the authority on all such difficult points. Jib went skimming back to the spot where Elizabeth stood, the laughter all gone from the red lips, which trembled a little as she looked at Jib's eyes, that did not meet hers, and then down at his handsome head and shoulders as he knelt at her feet. The shoe was so loosened and twisted that it must be unstrapped and put on again.

"Don't wait for me, please," said Elizabeth, with her prettiest smile, to the young man who waited rather uselessly about. "I can stand very well by myself now, and we will come on after you as soon as it is fixed."

Not for want of a little boldness should this opportunity be lost, though her heart failed her as Jib added no word of assent as he carefully unwound the leather strap. But right down there on the road beyond the next field waited General Jim Downing with the ox-team, and she would be driven the rest of the way, and be as thoroughly separated from Jib as though the mountains divided them. With a laughing "all right," the young fellow accepted the suggestion—perhaps he knew something of how matters had formerly stood between these two—and they were alone. Still Jib knelt in silence, taking off the shoe, untwisting the leather strap. At last her foot was free.

"Oh!" she said with a sigh of relief, "I thought I should always have to walk backwards."

He did not answer, and Elizabeth, taking her courage in both hands, placed her disengaged foot—which looked ridiculously small by the side of the other—firmly on the ground.

"Jib," she began. He raised his head, and looked at her for the first time. Her foot went down a little into the crust, but she jerked it out and went on. "I will have you speak to me!" she asserted bravely.

"What should I say?" he asked indifferently. There was a pause.

"Put your foot here," he said, holding out the shoe. The foot, in its moccason, had gone down a little into the snow again, and she was obliged to put her hand on his shoulder to steady herself while she obeyed him. He was more conscious of that slight pressure than if it had been fifty pounds, but he gave no sign. Elizabeth felt bolder while his eyes were down.

"You used to have things to say," she said, as he tightened the strap again.

"Yes," he answered. "Does that hurt you?" He waited for her to answer before fastening it; her hand was still on his shoulder.

"You wouldn't care if it did!" she burst out passionately. Jib started a little. Not care whether he hurt her or not? The idea of her suffering any physical pain was like a blow. But he was cruel enough to be silent, except to say after a moment,

"You have not said if it does."

"No." Her eyes had filled suddenly in the most exasperating fashion just as she needed all her coolness. Jib rose.

"It's all right, I guess—we can go on," he said, without looking at her.

Side by side they went on, the others, by this time, some distance in advance. All the bitter reproaches and the special pleas which had been on Elizabeth's lips ready for just such an occasion—what had become of them? It seemed to her that she could think of nothing except how not to cry. She was tired, poor child, the unaccustomed exercise was using her up. It was all so new and unfamiliar. She was tired of hearing how easily they went over fences. She didn't believe there were any fences there. They kept telling her that she was just over a pond ; she was afraid to go across ponds that way without knowing it. There wasn't much moonlight, and things might happen—everything was so queer, anything might happen. She didn't know where she was in this unfamiliar world. Yes, she did—oh ! yes, she did ! Just before them was the last field before the road and the ox-cart, and this was the last chance she should have—it might be the last time she should ever, ever walk with Jib Trent. Her heart grew very heavy. How desperately quickly they went ! Now they were in the field. The General was already exchanging humorous greetings with the advance guard. Those long, strange white stretches were really very short.

"You used to love me, Jib." The words fell from her lips in a breathless, sudden little way which touched on pathos, it was so destitute of her usual coquetry. Jib turned towards her for the first time since they had started. All the curbed anger, all the jealousy of the last months, of the last hour, all the suffering which had been unuttered and more bitter, thrilled through his slow words.

"Yes, Elizabeth, I used to love you," he said. "Do you remember my telling you once that I should never be ashamed of loving a woman as Uncle Denver loved your mother ? Well, I never thought the time would come, but, after what I've seen to-night, I'd be ashamed of loving you."

He did not know how cruel the words were. He saw in Elizabeth's pleading dejection only another phase of the same thoughtless trifling with his deep feeling which, to do him justice, had not been infrequent. He thought only of the kiss that he fancied she had just given before his very eyes to another man. But to her it seemed that she had had hard measure; that for her small iniquities the punishment dealt to her was of the cruelest. His casual reference to her mother deepened the pain with a thrust of homesickness—her mother, who loved her and was not ashamed of her.

But never had she loved Jib as she did then. She would have thrown herself at his feet if that would have done any good. But a single glance at that set mouth, whose firm lines were generally hidden by the sweetness of his smile, at the stern, unfriendly eyes which met hers, was enough—it would have been worse than folly.

"Wal, here ye are," said the General. "Chuck her in, Jib! I declare, I guess she's clean tuckered out." And the slow oxen started up under many instructions and much encouragement, and the one cowbell jangled, and slowly and irregularly Elizabeth's little red head-covering—this time it was a hood—disappeared again over the hill.

CHAPTER XV

> "If you saw yourself with your eyes, or knew yourself with your judgment, the fear of your adventure would counsel you to a more equal enterprise."

> "Beloved, in the noisy city here,
> The thought of thee can make all turmoil cease."

THE occasional glimpses of blue water had vanished. The uninteresting stretches of flat, sandy country, varied by sudden transits through manufacturing towns, where grimy faces were pressed against the windows as the train flashed past in what seemed dangerous proximity, had been left behind. The delusive rusticity of well-kept lawns and graded roads had given place to the rough and tumble of squalid dwellings, heaps of refuse, and occasional tall brick buildings, the pioneers of the steady upward march of what the nineteenth century has decided to call civilization. The early lights began to appear in straight, if somewhat broken, rows, instead of sporadic twinkles. Rhodope was drawing near to a great city. It was all so new to her, so absorbedly interesting, the country through which she had passed; those towns where it seemed to her people could not have room to breathe, the atmosphere was so heavy with something a little less tangible than smoke; and afterwards prettier, open, freer places, where the green of trees and grass softened the aspect of brick and granite. The people on the train were not the mere travelling public to Rhodope. They were individuals with most special lives and histories, to whom a railway journey was as a matter of course, more or less important. There was a girl of about her own age who read persistently, only now and then glancing up indifferently when they stopped at a station or some one passed down the aisle. How hard it must be for her, thought Rhodope, to fix her mind on her book amid all this excitement —she must be obliged to prepare a review of it or something, within a given time. Across the aisle, some women, with little shopping-bags, talked incessantly, and showed each other samples of dress-goods and discussed shades of trimming; apparently to them the great city was only a well-furnished emporium. Two men, one of whom had read newspapers while the other made figures in a memorandum-book, rose and took down their Gladstones from the rack, and the newspaper reader put up his silk travelling-cap, and put on a stiff hat, all with an air of routine that was impressive. In a moment they would leave the train for the city street. So men face danger, any stirring possibility whatever, when it is but a matter of routine! Peril becomes merely a factor in the general whole for which they prepare themselves. A handsome gray-haired woman who had occupied the seat with Rhodope from the last station now looked at her, hesitated a moment, and turned away. In a moment she looked again, and half smiled, and Rhodope responded with the charming, frank smile that was an inheritance from Denver Trent.

"You have some one to meet you, I suppose," said the gray-haired woman.

"Yes, thank you," said Rhodope, in her sweet voice; then she added, "You are kind."

"Not at all," disclaimed the other. "I thought I would ask, it would do no harm," and she said no more.

Rhodope looked out of the window at the vistas of the long streets which were now flitting by, thrilled by the unwontedness, the mystery of the spectacle. The strange roar of the city grew in her ears; they were slipping into the station. A sense of loneliness, of insecurity, overwhelmed her suddenly. Where was she going? What should she do? Whom should she meet? There were so many people, and she was but one! A glance at her companion reassured her. Amid this hurry and rush there were human sympathy and interest—else why had this woman cared to ask about her comfort?

It was not strange that the conventional self-absorption had yielded to something unusual in Rhodope's appearance. There was that besides beauty that drew the eyes of several people to the quiet, dignified, yet evidently untravelled girl who sat watching and listening and interested as the train swept on.

Florence Needham's letter of invitation had come, and, strangely enough, Uncle Denver had taken the matter into his own hands, and said that Rhodope should go. If it had been left to her, perhaps the decision would have been otherwise.

"Wants you to go to see her, does she?" he had said. "Thinks it may be of pleasure and perhaps of benefit! Wal, I'm not cert'in that that's what she thinks, but neither am I cert'in that it ain't so."

"I think I will stay at home," Rhodope had said; "I know what things are so, here."

"I d'know as you do," said Denver. "Things look different in different places, but one may be as true as t'other. Guess you'd better go along."

"You don't want me to come home and tell you what you ought to think about the mountains, do you, Uncle Denver?" she asked with a smile.

"I guess I can stand it—it don't never trouble me. And you ought to see something outside the valley; 'tain't all of God's earth there is—I've been out of it more'n once.

And when you get tired flaxin' round down there, you can come home."

Rhodope hesitated. If a new life and new scenes held new pleasures, they might, as she had learned, hold also a new pain. And though she was not wise enough to distrust Mrs. Needham, as she should have been distrusted, she was not happy with her.

"But Mrs. Needham—does she really want me?"

"Yes, she does," declared Denver, shrewdly. "I ain't sayin' what she wants you for, but she really wants you. There ain't no call to ask you if she don't. And what she wants you for, she'll get it, don't you worry about that. And her husband's a good feller. He's about as easy in his mind as a katydid, but I like him in the main. I'd ruther you'd go, Rhode."

Just why he was so decided he might have found it difficult to explain. But with the indifference to modifying circumstances and possible complications, which is distinctly a masculine characteristic, he wished her to accept the opportunity that lay before her. Perhaps the Arcadian simplicity which was united with his native shrewdness saw in the singular beauty of his niece the assurance of her urban triumph.

"But she may get tired of me—we don't get tired of people, you and I, Uncle Denver," and she leaned over his shoulder, the letter in her hand, "but in the city there are so many more people, it is natural they should get tired of each other and—of me."

"Wal, if she does, she'll leave the railroad tracks down, I guess, and you can come back as quick as you went."

His persistence weakened her own misgivings, and suddenly a flame of longing leaped into her heart. It was his world that he had talked about that evening at the stile. Why should she not see it with her eyes? Perhaps she

was unwise in her shrinking from Mrs. Needham. It was
not hard for her to re-establish a shaken belief in people's
disinterestedness. The natural, youthful, warm eagerness
for both the certainties and the uncertainties of such an experience swept aside her hesitations. She would go, and—
as Uncle Denver said—she could come back.

Encouragement and discouragement had attended her
going forth. General Jim Downing had shaken his head
mournfully, and stated with gloomy reiteration that New
York was an awful place. "It's an awful place. I went
there once," he said.

"What's the matter with it, General?" inquired Abijah
Stetson.

"There's such an awful lot of folks," he replied.

"And they didn't give you a comp'ny nor anythin'?"
Mr. Stetson spoke with humorous extravagance, and the
General did not answer directly.

"I didn't know where I was," he went on. "You don't
know where you be, Rhode. I didn't hardly know what had
happened. It's an awful place."

On the whole, his prognostications sounded very much—
barring the hint of personal experience—like the somewhat
vague speculations of orthodox theology concerning a future state. But Tim's comments were all of an opposite
nature.

"Never you mind, Rhode," he admonished, "what anybody does, or about crossing the streets. The p'lice 'll get
you across."

"The police!" exclaimed Rhodope in alarm.

"And the horse-cars, they'll take you anywheres you
want to go—you just tell the conductor where you're bound
for."

This gave Rhodope an undefined impression that a
horse-car was something to be obligingly tossed about by

every wind of personal convenience at a suggestion to the conductor. "And then there's the tunnel—but they light the lamps, and you'll get through all right." It must be confessed that Tim's experiences were limited to one outlook five minutes long from the Forty-second Street station, and his reassurances were somewhat tinctured by the peculiar features of that locality. Nevertheless, his assistance was practical, for he took charge of Rhodope to the junction where she made her final change of cars, which was as far as his assorted duties took him. The first strangeness wore off within the shelter of his presence; and when he came and sat with her for a few moments, in the glory of his gilded uniform, it lent her more than a transient distinction in the eyes of her companions, most of them of the simpler country sort.

"New York isn't any great shakes," declared Miss Matilda Spore. "No, haven't ever been there, but I know all about it. Seen New-Yorkers enough up here, and precious glad they be too, to get away from their own city. There ain't nothin' particular about 'em either, except the way they walk and their thinkin' the whole American continent's built on Manhattan Island."

But protection, apprehension, and sarcasm alike, Rhodope has left far behind. She stands committed to the new thing, as she comes along into the mysterious, thrilling, magical precincts which have hitherto seemed to her more distant than to the modern traveller the wilds of Abyssinia —the heart of a great city. Riding backwards, and therefore facing Rhodope, upon one of the seats just beyond her on the other side of the aisle, had been established for an hour a small, small child. She held on gravely to the arm of the seat with one diminutive hand, the other lay in her lap, which was bounded with almost disconcerting suddenness and finality by a small pair of buttoned shoes, forced by the width of the seat into a strictly horizontal position. She looked straight before her, seeming to feel no need of amusement.   Her mother sat opposite her, with a man who had just come into the car, and, taking his seat beside her, greeted her like an old friend.   They were evidently people from one of the ordinary little towns on the way.   The man finally became somewhat ill at ease under the aged steadiness of the child's small gaze, and proffered a few awkward, if well-meant, attempts at entertainment.   He chucked her under the chin with sudden impulsiveness, and it seemed almost disrespectful.   She smiled absently, but did not respond.   The older ones laughed and talked with a good deal of rural and innocent intimacy, and the child observed them incidentally, while she thought of other things. There was something irresistibly droll in the baby's calmness as contrasted with the triviality of her elders' lightheartedness.   She never looked out of the window; she was neither irritated nor amused.   At last the man, driven to desperation by this Lilliputian majesty, presented her with a mundane cooky from a paper bag, while the mother looked on smiling.   The child received it willingly, but without enthusiasm, and ate it slowly, still grasping the chair-arm with one hand and being very careful not to scatter crumbs. When she had eaten it she returned to her former Buddhistic calm, and sat perfectly erect, her small toes straight out in front of her and her hand in her lap.   After this, the man desisted from further attempts to disturb her dignified repose, and only looked at her now and then askance, in the pauses of the conversation, as at a mysterious divinity, not awful, but impressive.   Rhodope had watched her with fascinated eyes.   What sort of a generation was this of which the infants of three gazed forth upon the incidents of a railway journey as unemotionally as the very old look upon life !

When Florence Needham had decided to act upon Davenant's suggestion to have Rhodope visit her, it had been with the intention of carrying it into immediate effect; but as is usual with intentions whose date of fulfilment rests entirely with ourselves, month after month slipped by before the letter of invitation was written. She had not announced the expected arrival of Rhodope to those who were the most interested in it, although before its time was fixed she had let Davenant perceive, on more than one occasion, that she had not forgotten the delightful if vague results to be expected from her presence, at which he had so skilfully hinted. Davenant had amused himself with observation of Florence Needham this winter, more than was perfectly consistent with his convictions. He found it often convenient to go to her of an afternoon for a cup of tea, or to listen to her reflections on her neighbors at an evening reception. How much this weakness was due to the half-conscious hope of seeing Rhodope, how much to an ease and familiarity which was unavoidable after their early relations, and how much to the vanity of his analytical inclination, flattered by the readiness with which she responded to his touch upon her mental tendencies, it would be difficult to say. Certainly he did not lose his keen-sightedness where she was concerned. It amused him infinitely to catch the motive of her most careless reflections. With reprehensible enjoyment he introduced now and then a flavor of the bitterness of doubt into some cup of social nectar. It was not quite an ill-natured pleasure, because there was no draught, however skilfully prepared, that Florence could accept without a glance at that of her neighbor to see if hers had other superior ingredients; but it was certainly not done in a spirit of missionary enterprise. To Davenant the literary faculty brought its usual danger, that of the loss of all wish to change or uplift, in the amusement derived from the observation of human faults and foibles as well as human virtues. Moreover, as he asked himself once or twice, who was he that he should resist the always effusive welcome of a pretty woman?—the less dangerous, he might have added, in that with unsparing rigor he assigned its effusiveness entirely to what she thought he possessed, not in the least to what he was.

In the frequency with which he drifted to her side, Florence naturally continued to see a return to his old devotion. She had never really lost him then! A faint melancholy now and again touched her words to him as she thought of his successful grappling with the world's problems. She conveyed a half-regretful, half-tender emotion in her glance as he came to her after an interview in which he had basked in the smiles of a recognized social leader. But even Davenant did not know just when Rhodope was coming, for he had been out of town for a fortnight. Perhaps this very absence spurred Mrs. Needham's indolence with its suggestion that some time he might stop coming entirely. It was then that she wrote to Rhodope, and it was then that Rhodope came into this atmosphere, all unconscious of the currents and counter-currents that surrounded her; looking forward into this strange, new life with some bewilderment, and shrinking before so many, many people, but with no fear that the time would come when the confusion should grow to be that of strange tongues.

She was grateful to Needham for the evident sincerity of his welcome. Where everything was so unknown, the man whom she had seen half a dozen times, and who had known her in her own home, having talked and smoked with Uncle Denver, and fished with Jib, was like an old friend; and from the moment of that first meeting in the station there

existed between the two an odd sort of friendliness undisturbed by Rhodope's seriousness or Needham's volatility.

Florence had been surprised by the interest her husband
had shown in Rhodope's arrival. He had extolled the suggestion from the very first. He was usually indifferent concerning her guests with the exception of two or three marked
aversions, but evidently the idea of Rhodope's presence
was an unusually pleasant one. Of late he had even been
urgent that the visit should take place, and had abandoned
an important engagement to meet her. He had been
rather irritable at home for the last month. His accusations of insincerity and humbug were flung more violently
and frequently against those whose opinions were not his
own. Occasionally he would insist upon her acceptance of
an invitation to which Florence herself was indifferent,
would accompany her to the entertainment and return,
railing against its every detail. Another time he would be
filled with a fine scorn of all social functions whatever, and
find fault with his wife's taste for them. Altogether, he had
been difficult, and Florence would have found in this fact
a greater significance if she had not had more important
things to think of.

Austin Medcott stood at the ticket-office on his way by
train to keep an evening engagement. As he waited impatiently his turn in the eager crowd, he looked across the
confusion of the railway station and caught a sudden glimpse
of a woman's face. He stood motionless in amazement.
Here, in this turmoil, jostled by the pushing, hurrying men
and women, her beautiful eyes wide open in wondering observation, a little frightened by the unwonted press and
struggle, here in the New York station, was Rhodope Trent!
He made a quick step forward, then, turning to go back, he
was hemmed in by the railing and the line of ticket-buyers

Where was she going? What was she doing here? Could he never get to her?

"Now, sir," said a voice, impatiently. Somebody's elbow was precipitating matters from behind. Mechanically he bought his ticket and pushed on. But it was the most crowded hour of the day. He fell over bundles and across umbrellas. When he reached the door he was just in time to see her put into a carriage by Charlie Needham and driven away. But this reassured him—he could find out, then, where she was. He regretted that he was leaving the city for even a few hours. Now that it held Rhodope, it was strangely attractive. He must see her soon—how had he lived without seeing her so long! Her beautiful face rose before him again, and instead of a cool, dark background, with slender, tall, white birches gleaming here and there through its dimness, he saw it against the dusty, grimy, sordid atmosphere of a railway station. It was a revolution.

CHAPTER XVI

"The appurtenance of welcome is fashion and ceremony."

"Thou art not for the fashion of these times."

FLORENCE had long ago laid aside the subject of the profundity of her husband's attachment to herself as one upon which speculation was unnecessary, else she might have been piqued by his evident admiration of Rhodope. That the day would ever come when the fancy which she without effort had taken possession of, and which she had taken no step to develop into something deeper, might wander away and refuse to be recalled, she never dreamed.

Meanwhile, in Rhodope's presence, Needham was more like his old self than he had been for many days; restless to be sure, sometimes petulant, but not uncompanionable, and evidently willing to please. He showed her little attentions to which she was unused, brought her flowers and candy, and saw that, when it was possible, she was with the people whom she liked. This friendliness stood her in good stead in this new sphere where her presence was to lend glory to Florence Needham's position, for he manifested more tact and sympathy than entered into the arrangements from his wife's point of view. Mrs. Needham was not guilty of overt rudeness, but she never forgot that Rhodope had been brought there for a purpose, and in the tenacity with which she clung to this it was most natural that she should disregard the claims of the girl herself.

The first days of her visit passed, days of observation for both Rhodope and Florence, though after a different manner. To Rhodope everything was new, and the adjustment of internal to external relations was a perplexing thing. It seemed to her that none of the old cables held good, and that if she could be content to drift, things might be easier; but she could not drift, she must learn and know, and with a conscientiousness, sometimes ludicrously disproportionate, she questioned every current and every breeze. Florence could not see that any immediate and startling result followed the discriminating informality with which she presented Miss Trent to a limited circle. But neither was she convinced of the futility of the arrangement. There was, in the uncertainty concerning the direct object, a certain attainment of indirect ones distinctly gratifying, although there were even now many loopholes of doubt through which subsequent disappointments and chagrin were to make their way. Rhodope had produced no social sensation, but her beauty was indisputable, and a few people found out that she was charming, when the shyness, which was not self-consciousness, vanished, and she talked or listened, gravely, with a puzzled little air of half-comprehension, arising from her mental comparison of the ideas gleaned from books and her own thoughts with those she found in the new environment. Those who made this discovery spoke of her to Florence with that inflection of flattery that implies that only delicate perceptions would have brought such qualities to light, which was satisfactory. As for Medcott's artistic and Davenant's critical appreciation, they had been unmistakable from the first moment. Neither suffered diminution now that Rhodope was in another place. In the frequent meetings that took place on various pretences, Florence found the assurance that, in part, at least, her tactics were successful. Medcott disdained to disguise the interest that he found in Rhodope under any veil of general attention, but real feeling rendered Florence less clear-sighted than usual, and she saw in the ordinary civility he showed her evidences that this feeling was shared, and found in his companionship the satisfaction she had formerly sought in vain. It was Rhodope that brought him, she told herself, but it was she that made him stay.

It was at an evening reception that Davenant first began to doubt a little the success, possibly the wisdom, of what his conscience made bold to tell him was his experiment. Over the heads of the people he caught a sudden glimpse of Rhodope seated on a sofa, not far from Mrs. Needham, who had temporarily abandoned her. Just before her sat a young and pretty woman, the waist of whose gown suggested no extraordinary outlay, and by her side a young and beautiful man whose ideas were disproportionate in moral grandeur to that of his shirt-front. Davenant had a sensation of artistic pleasure in the incongruity, touched with sympathetic regret. Rhodope regarded the youth with a smile of compassionate interest as he expressed himself at intervals concerning the latest verities of New York life. She had seen shy boys before, and she knew they needed sympathy. Moreover, she fixed her eyes on him in part to spare the embarrassment of the woman whose shoulders were so near. The young man, who was of course not shy, but only weary of life as Mariana, continued his Delphic utterances with the consciousness that for once in her life this good-looking country-girl was learning what society of the best kind was. Davenant nearly laughed aloud.

"Mrs. Needham is looking very fit this evening," he overheard the oracle say, as he drew near. Rhodope looked slightly alarmed as she glanced across at Florence, wondering vaguely if the adjective applied to her yellow brocade or to possible apoplectic danger. While she wondered she perceived that Davenant stood by the sofa, and she smiled in unconscious relief. They had already met. He had called with Medcott a day or two after her arrival, found her at home with Mrs. Needham, and the four lingered about the tea-table in more or less satisfied frames of mind. Rhodope had said little, but Medcott had watched her with deep satisfaction in her naturalness and beauty, while Tom and Florence had done most of the talking. Davenant had watched Rhodope too, and inclined to the opinion that it had been a good thing to get her here. But to-night he began to have misgivings.

"I am invited to come and see you again to-morrow afternoon," he said, while the young man took the elevation of his intellectual standpoint, with that of his collar, elsewhere. "We are going to have a party, and my advice is to be considered in the matter of certain invitations."

"Will it be like this?" asked Rhodope.

"It will be something like this, only worse, because you will have to stand up and be presented."

Rhodope considered this fact with becoming gravity.

"Are you coming?" she asked. "And is Mr. Medcott coming?"

"We wouldn't either of us miss it for worlds," he replied confidentially, "but we shall come late and look awfully bored when we do come, and as if we'd rather be anywhere else. I tell you this so that you won't be misled by what are just our city manners."

"I am learning all the time, Mr. Davenant," she answered, with a commendable pride in her progress. "I have been listening to the talk of that young lady who plays the piano so beautifully, and I have found out that when you do anything very well, that that isn't the thing you must talk about doing well, or "—she hesitated, for it was difficult for her to express contradictions.

"It's always safer to talk as if you did everything well, only you didn't have to do anything," he suggested vaguely.

" No, that isn't it—but you must talk as if something else was what you really did well—something that nobody knows you do at all." She looked at him triumphantly.

"You have mastered one of the great secrets of social life," he assured her. "What does the piano-playing lady pride herself innocently upon?"

"A way she has of shuffling cards and dealing. She says that you ought to see her do it."

"And you—you are a number of things, patently and evidently," he said, " but what are you going to pride yourself on?"

" Pop-corn balls," she nodded, "I can make them."

A large, be-diamonded woman in velvet passed through the room, and all eyes followed her.

"That," said Davenant, in a tone of hushed respect, "is Mrs. Andrew F. Rimmon."

"I never heard of her," said Rhodope simply. Davenant looked about him apprehensively.

"Oh, my dear Miss Trent, how fortunate that you said that to me and to no one else! If there's any one you must acknowledge not having heard of let it be—er—Adam, or some one of that class; never, never—Mrs. Andrew F. Rimmon!"

"What has she done?" asked Rhodope, looking after the somewhat heavy vision of gorgeousness.

" Nothing—never anything at all—that's her claim to consideration—though of course there are always ill-natured people to assert the contrary. She doesn't even spend her husband's millions—gets some one else to do it for her. And here comes the literary woman of the evening. The fashion of her gown is chastened, you observe—when you see chastened fashion, it means a vocation of some sort— usually literary."

"Does she write books?" asked Rhodope with some awe.

"Oh, no, she doesn't write—but she knows people that do, you know, and she—in short, she is extremely literary. That is a poet with her now; he writes Fragments principally; you could easily pick up twelve basketfuls—at the book-stores."

"I don't know what Davenant is saying," said a voice just behind them, "but I know from the fatuous amiability of his expression that he is abusing his neighbors."

Rhodope looked up quickly at Medcott; Davenant watched her so closely that if she had not been unconscious of it she would have found his scrutiny merciless.

"The magnanimity of my designs is beyond your limited comprehension, Medcott," he said slowly. "I am seeking to guide Miss Trent's wayward footsteps away from the pitfalls that surround her. That my reward will come later I have faith to hope."

"Everything there but charity," and Mrs. Needham's frequent, rather loud laugh rippled close beside him. "You never have any of that to spare."

"No, but I always know where to go to find some," he said with grateful appreciation. Before she had entirely made up her mind what her object had been in approaching the group, she was pacing the conservatory with Davenant, leaving Rhodope and Medcott alone.

Davenant was still doubtful, and the more observant, the next day, as they sat in the Needhams' library and discussed Florence's forthcoming entertainment. This room was called the library because it held a low bookcase at one end, decorated with a row of china bowls and containing a set of Thackeray, an encyclopædia, several recently published novels, and Moore's poems; also a centre-table upon which stood a silver inkstand, two or three pen-handles, a Japanese paper-knife, and an immaculate blotter. A fire burning in the low grate enhanced the literary atmosphere.

"So you are going to have the Eagers, are you?" inquired Davenant from where he sat in front of the fire. Rhodope was across the room in a straight-backed wooden chair very much like one in Denver Trent's living-room. Medcott lounged in the deep window-seat, while Florence played with the paper-knife. She laid it down as Davenant asked his question.

"Yes," she said, "I thought I'd have to; they go everywhere. Perhaps they won't all come."

"Yes, they will," responded Davenant, "and they do litter up a room dreadfully—there are so many of 'em."

"I don't see how I could have helped it"—Florence was vaguely troubled by his partial disapproval. Perhaps everybody didn't have the Eagers, after all.

"I guess you couldn't," Tom reassured her.

"What shall you wear, Miss Rhodope?" asked Medcott.

Rhodope started and blushed a little. She was beginning to realize that the question had not hitherto held its proper place in her life.

"I haven't anything but a white dress," she said—"the same one."

"That's right," commented Medcott, with the freedom of a man whose business it is to study the picturesque.

Florence looked up sharply. Why hadn't he asked her what she was going to wear? She did not like the way his eyes dwelt on Rhodope.

"Did you suppose I should allow the *ingénue* to wear anything but white?" she laughed.

"One is never disappointed in you, Mrs. Needham," he answered.

"I saw Eric down-town," remarked Davenant. "He

spoke of coming. I am glad you asked him. I think that, like the Merchant of Novgorod, when he isn't asked to anything, he goes and sits on a blue stone and plays the harp."

"The Merchant of Novgorod?" repeated Rhodope, with greater interest than she had shown in the Eagers. "Who was he, Mr. Davenant?"

"Blessed if I know," answered Davenant frankly, "but he has figured in story, and that's what he did, anyhow, when he didn't get his invitation—and a very sensible thing, too."

"Clara Eric brings that man she is engaged to."

"Is that girl engaged? Where's the man from, that's going to marry a girl with such a voice?"

"Oh, the West, or Rhode Island—or somewhere," replied Florence, passing under a succession of impressions.

"She sings, too," went on Davenant, "as well as talks. I'd rather marry a calliope."

"Aren't any of your friends coming?" asked Rhodope seriously. She spoke not with suggestion of reproof, but in some mental perplexity.

"Why, of course—" began Florence, and then stopped. Medcott threw his head back on the pile of cushions and laughed.

"I'm beginning to be afraid you won't do," said Tom sadly. The door opened and Needham entered. "What you laughing at, Medcott?" he asked, in his quick, nervous way; and, not waiting for an answer, he went on, "Thought you'd have some tea, Florence; I'm tired—don't often want tea, but I've a headache. You're always saying it's good for a headache. What are you all talking about? They're not chaffing you, Miss Rhodope, are they?" and he sat down by her.

"She's chaffing us," said Davenant. Needham looked at him as he spoke, and then glanced immediately away.

"She thinks our friendship is fraudulent," Tom added.

" Fraudulent?" repeated Needham quickly. "Why is that? Why do you say that, Miss Rhodope? You believe in mine, don't you?" There was a note of earnestness in his voice that no one but Davenant noticed. A servant was bringing in tea, and Medcott had risen to offer some assistance to Mrs. Needham.

" Yes, I believe in it, certainly," said Rhodope, smiling. " And I have not been saying anything against their friendship. That is one of your fashions here," she went on, half to him, half to herself, "to accuse people of things you know they have not done."

" That is true," exclaimed Needham with sudden violence; "they are always making accusations. I must go and dress," he said, starting up. " Don't let me disturb you, but I have an early dinner at the club to-night."

" Here's the cup of tea that you wanted. I wish you'd wait and take it," said Florence with a touch of not unnatural exasperation. The servant was going about lighting the lamps. The cold afternoon light was fading swiftly, and the fire-light twinkled distantly on the gilding of Moore's poems with their own delusive warmth. Needham hesitated a moment, and then, taking the cup from his wife's hand, sat down again near Rhodope. Davenant watched him curiously. He was more restless than usual. When he joined in the conversation, it was generally a remark too late, which made Florence look at him with annoyance mingled with surprise, and produced a slight break in the interest. Perceiving this, he reiterated his statements with nervous emphasis, that they might appear more to the point. Rhodope had not accustomed herself to look upon a cup of tea at this hour as a normal thing. She did not drink tea anyway, but she had learned that it was easier to make a pretence of it, so she took a cup and saucer when the rest did, and sat straight in her high-backed chair, holding it in a stiff little way as if she were afraid it would spill. Medcott drew up a chair, and under cover of the general conversation spoke to her in a low tone. Florence saw it and was irritated. She thought it was Rhodope's way of holding her cup that irritated her. Why couldn't she at least play with her teaspoon like anybody else?

"We said something about friendship once," Medcott had said; "do you remember?"

Rhodope looked into his eyes. How long ago it seemed—that morning, by Shadow Pond! She felt as if she had been so much younger then.

"Yes, I remember."

"And you thought then that our friendship was not worth much."

"No," she said slowly, "I guess I didn't think that. I only did not understand. There are a good many things in the city I don't understand. For instance"—and she spoke more lightly—"I do not understand when I am amusing—like that time a little while ago when you laughed. I do not mind it, for you are not ill-natured, but I do not know when it is that I say funny things. I have found out that it is very important to say funny things," she added sagely, "so I am glad that I do."

"It is only because we have all agreed, we superficial people, that when a thing is so true that it might be disturbing, we shall laugh at it—that is all."

"And I—am I so true that I might be disturbing?" she asked in all seriousness.

"You are," he answered emphatically.

She paused a minute, considering this.

Florence dropped her sugar-tongs with a little clatter. Davenant stooped and picked them up for her.

"I think," Rhodope said, "that you do not use words here in the same way we do."

"Perhaps not—and perhaps it is only where there are so many more people we have to spread our feelings thinner—such as friendliness, you know."

While he said it, he was conscious that knowing a number of people had done nothing to diminish his feeling for her—it was strong and indivisible—but he was watching his words and looks lest they should say too much.

"I think that is it," said Rhodope. Suddenly it had come to her that what he said half in jest was true. Everything here, of course, must go a great way, and that was why it was all on the surface. She liked her way best.

"And it is better at home with Mount Marvel and Mount Innocence and Mount Charity, is it not?" he said. She wished he did not so readily answer her thoughts, that he did not remember so well. It made it more difficult to recognize the superficial nature of the friendliness.

"Yes, I think it is," she answered quietly. Medcott sighed as he rose. God knew she was right—better for her, if not for him!

"I'm afraid you don't like your tea, Rhodope," said Mrs. Needham from across the room. Rhodope started a little and then put her cup down smiling. "For two reasons," went on Florence with a glance at Medcott, "first, you are not drinking it; secondly, you look unhappy."

Rhodope wondered what she had done. Ever since she came she had had this undefinable consciousness of being obliged to parry something that meant attack.

"It is not unhappiness," said Davenant, regarding her critically, "it is perplexity. She can't see why we don't go, Medcott. I've learned to recognize that look, and my sensitive nature cannot disregard it like yours. Good-by, Mrs. Needham."

"Are you fellows going?" said Needham, starting up. "I guess I'll go with you."

"I thought you had to dress," said his wife.

"To be sure—that dinner—no, I can't go. I must dress —well, another time." He spoke hurriedly, almost incoherently. "Wish I didn't have to go. I'd enough rather dine with you and Florence, Miss Rhodope." Davenant looked back at him as he followed Medcott out of the room.

Needham stood looking down at Rhodope, frowning and nervously playing with a cushion on her chair. Then he started, met Davenant's glance, dropped the cushion, and went with his guests to the door.

CHAPTER XVII

" Society seems to have agreed to treat fictions as realities and real-
ities as fictions."

" There's no clock in the forest."

" To meet a few friends," soliloquized Davenant as he
stood in the corner of Florence's crowded drawing-room,
and watched the new arrivals salute their hostess with that
mingling of indifference and courtesy which in its varying
proportions marks the social case of the passing guest.
There were those to whom a grasp of their hostess's hand
was but the necessary prelude to excitements and delights
beyond, indefinite and entrancing; these were for the most
part very young. There were those who clung to her with
persistence, and conversed with juvenile animation, conscious that, after they had left her side, the chances were
against meeting anybody else who would feel obliged to be-
stow upon them equal attention. There were those who
went through it as a necessary form, the mere initiative of
various necessary forms, all to be gone through creditably
and without reluctance, and with as little wear and tear as
possible. " A few friends," thought Davenant—"that's what
she told me—and, by Jove! she was right. She's asked
all the people whom a self-respecting person ought to ask,
and there are not four people in the room whose friendship
for her amounts to the value of a brass farthing. She has
sown her crop of social seeds, and now she is reaping and
gathering into barns. How do you do, Miss Helena!" he
added aloud, with a respectful bow to the *nuque* of a very

young woman who had just placed herself in front of him, and whose apple-green ball-gown was admirable with the white skin and coil of golden hair which were presented to his view. The girl faced about and offered for further inspection a face whose irregular prettiness was very attractive. "For a girl who had picked up her features here and there, just as it happened," Davenant had said on a former occasion, "Helena Screed was a most successful-looking girl."

"Oh, thanks be where they are due!" she exclaimed; "it's you, Mr. Davenant," and without fruitless timidity she wedged herself backward and stood by his side. "I tell you I'm glad to see you," she went on in lively tones that still were not loud; "I just cast my eyes helplessly about; the way one does, you know, when you've said good-evening, and not a soul did I see that I'd waste a minute of this new gown on, and not even anybody that I'd just hang on to a moment till I found something better—kind of life-preserver, you know—except Henry Waterford, and Edwina's got him; and I'm sure I'm glad of it and welcome, for if Edwina *does* get anybody and *keep* him—why, it's nothing but a special dispensation—they have to drop down out of nowhere—'out of the everywhere into the here,' you know—and be *left* right in front of her, or she doesn't know enough to take notice—and I was just thinking it was going to be an awful party, when you spoke, and thank goodness you did. How did you come to be right there, anyway?"

"I was waiting for you to come and take care of me."

"I fancy you didn't know whether it was I that would come and take care of you or not," laughed Miss Screed with the utmost gayety. "You'd better be pretty thankful it is nobody worse."

"What I want to know now is whether or not I'm a life-preserver or a permanent anchor."

Helena glanced around the room with apparent indifference and a good deal of actual sharpness.

" Well, I don't know," she admitted with some frankness, " that depends on you."

" It does and it doesn't," returned Davenant, with the evenness of his temperament. " You might as well tell me now who it is you want most to have talk to you. Of course I know you'd rather have me than anybody else, but who comes next ?"

At this point Miss Helena slipped her hand through his arm and imparted a most energetic though dissimulated impetus to his frame, which brought them both nearer the corner and gave them the effect of making their way through the crowd. She looked up into his face with an expression of blinding innocence, but her low tone was impassioned to a positive degree.

" Whatever you do," she murmured—" whatever you do, henceforth and forever, don't you leave me now !"

A tall, thin, studious-looking young man, whose manner was not that of light-hearted youth, and whose dress-coat appeared to have been assumed for purposes of disguise, wearing eye-glasses, his head slightly bent forward, and his mild gaze wandering over the tops of most of the people, had suddenly discovered in Helena an objective point of evident importance. With fixed attention and flickering smile he had begun to make his way towards them, when her sudden tactics caused him to halt, and then move somewhat aimlessly in another direction, convinced that it was in vain to pursue them.

" Has it gone ?" inquired Helena feverishly, as she moved her fan with the coolness of restraint.

" I think it has," said Davenant, glancing about ; " there isn't anything coming."

" I thought it was all over," she sighed in relief. " He's

the kind you have for the evening, you know," she explained; "they don't let them for a shorter time. There!"
she commented, in a tone of distinct scorn, "he's run up
against Edwina. She might have known he would, and
she's let Henry Waterford just *drift* off with that Schemer-
horn girl. I never witnessed anything so pitiful. Well, she
may just as well sit down and do her sewing now, for he'll
stay till she goes home."

"You don't care much for your sister's methods, do you?"
asked Davenant. He seldom failed to find Miss Screed
amusing.

"Methods!" she repeated with contempt. "She hasn't
any! It's just hit or miss with her. She isn't sure enough
when she's having the best kind of a time, anyway, to keep
hold of it. I'm the only one that knows what either of us
is at."

"Well, you haven't told me yet, you know, what I'm to
do."

"Haven't I? I don't want you— Gracious!" she broke
off as she caught a glimpse of herself in the mirror that her
change of position had brought her in front of. "Did you
ever see such freckles! Such awful ones and so many!
Just all over my nose! Can you see *anything* else?"

Davenant surveyed, at his leisure, the bridge of her small,
unclassified nose, while she awaited anxiously the result.

"Yes," he said deliberately, "remains of features still
survive and even assert—"

"I never expected to find you two people in a corner!"—
Florence's light tones were close at hand. "Helena, is it
possible you didn't know that there are several recesses
across the hall, where discreet seclusion reigns?—that I
find you here in the garish light of gas-jets?"

Florence was very beautiful to-night. She wore glistening, gleaming white, with diamond ornaments, and her

blonde hair, blue eyes, and charming complexion glistened and gleamed with a sheen of their own.

Helena's frank eyes dwelt upon her with admiration unsoftened by affection.

"Are there, really, Mrs. Needham? But I should know that you would provide for all your guests! But you and I —and Mr. Davenant—we like bright places best, because we look so nice. And Mr. Davenant has promised to look after me till—well, till I want to be secluded and discreet." Florence's eyes grew a little harder; she did not like Helena, and she always had an odd sort of jealousy of Davenant's companions, though less poignant than her feeling where Medcott was concerned.

"I don't know," went on Helena with charming candor, "how he'd be *after* that, do you?" Her gray eyes rivalled Florence's blue ones in their quiet innocence as her voice fell into the question—one would never dream that she had heard any reference to the early or later relations between this man and woman.

Florence glanced involuntarily from her to Davenant and bit her lip.

"I should never dare to offer any suggestion to so well-informed a *débutante* as Helena Screed," she said as she was obliged to turn away to greet some late-comers.

"After the conclusion of which amenities," said Helena, as if she were finishing a story, "they both returned to their respective duties. What do you suppose she wants you for? She needn't try to take you away as unblushingly as that again."

"I don't think she wanted me at all."

"Yes, she did"—time was wasted, always, in arguing with Helena. "I think it was to go after that tall Miss Trent, who has just left the room with Austin Medcott. She didn't like her going—I saw that the time I looked in the glass."

Davenant shrugged his shoulders a little, and then he laughed.

"You're something of an observer," he said.

"I don't let much go by me," she assented complacently. "Edwina raves over that Miss Trent, you know. She thinks she's a perfect beauty, and so grand and stately, and so truthful and so—oh! you know Edwina."

"Yes, and her superiority to you. And I know Miss Trent, too."

"And so you rave over her?"

"Yes," he assented again. "They talk of putting me under personal restraint, but—"

"So far you've escaped?—yes—well, I think she's beautiful too, but I don't care very much for her, because she doesn't know it herself. If there is anything that vexes me it is for a woman like that not to know the value of her own looks, and to go about just as if she were—why—*plain*. What's the good of being a beauty if you don't know it?" She paused for rhetorical effect. "It may be all very well in the woods where Edwina says she came from, but I say it's worse than useless here."

Davenant smiled at the truth of her observation. This wise young woman had hit upon the very thing that had struck Medcott and himself—that Rhodope's advantages were turned, in this environment, to her disadvantage.

"Then she has such a way of trying to get at your point of view, don't you know. Edwina gave a luncheon for her the other day, and I talked with her a long time. If she only thought her point of view was better, like a Boston girl, you know, then you could resent it and everything be pleasant. But she doesn't think hers is better; it is only that you know in your soul it is, and she tries to get to yours, and it's awful."

"I've found that same difficulty myself," said Davenant.

"Well, if *you* have, think of the rest of us! It's your business, as it were, to get at people's points of view, but Florence and I, now! By the way, however, does she get on with Florence Needham? *I* can get even with Florence, you know, without any trouble, but Miss Trent! why, *she'd* have to come down three flights of stairs to get even with her. Oh, I'm so glad she wore green!" The transit of a dark, colorless young woman in a green gown aided Davenant to follow his companion's sudden change of theme.

"I should know you would be," he remarked as he noted the costume's distinct unbecomingness. "I don't know the circumstances, but I should know you would on general principles."

"You see," said Helena confidentially, "she thinks she can wear anything that is the fashion, and Walter Mevans"—and her fan fluttered almost imperceptibly in the direction of a fine-looking young fellow who had entered the room five minutes earlier—"has been inclined, of late, to think her handsome—dangerously inclined. He's looking at her now—and by and by when he looks at me"—an unmistakably confident glance at the mirror completed her sentence.

"So it is he that is the anchor and the port and all the rest of it, in preparation for which I have simply been keeping your head above water?" asked Davenant, as one beyond sense of injury.

"Well, if he should happen to stray over here I wouldn't have you bore yourself with us," she admitted with her usual frankness. "He's young, you see, and crude—oh! very crude—and, of course, I know how much you care about talking to *me*," and she laughed at him over her gauze fan.

"So the gown won't be wasted on him," he remarked, looking her over.

"No, I think it won't — speaking after the manner of men," she acquiesced. "I don't mean it shall."

"It hasn't been wasted on me, by the way. It strikes me as an extremely good one."

"I think it is," she agreed with pleased alacrity. "It's just out of the custom-house, and I've seldom fancied myself more in anything."

"Good-evening, Miss Helena," said a strong, youthful voice, whose intonation somehow betrayed that the speaker fancied her in it, too. Helena started violently and looked back over her white shoulder with an adorable turn of her eyelashes. He was very tall, and he continued to look down at her smiling.

"It is not the Fourth of July," she objected; "boys are forbidden to scare the timid public on other days. Why do you come disguised as a torpedo?"

"I never frightened you yet," answered the young man with some penetration.

"But you have me," interposed Davenant. "Good-by," he added to Helena, "and think where you might have been, if it hadn't been for me."

As he passed Florence, she called him back.

"Tom," she said, with an insistent inflection that was not unflattering; "please find Charlie for me. I want him to talk to at least three women — three perfectly impossible women. He never helps me out of anything."

There was a plaintiveness in her impatience which implied that there were times when sympathy was itself an assistance.

"Am I not fitted to cope with one or two of them single-handed?" he asked. "Where do they lurk?"

"No," she said, "I'm not going to squander you on them. Find Charlie and send him over to that woman on the sofa. She came with Miss Unwin. No matter about her name. I didn't hear it, anyway."

"The one with the beads about the foot of her neck? I must have an itemized description."

"Yes, yes," said Florence, laughing; "make haste—do! She has been alone for hours, and I have a dreadful suspicion she is somebody important—and, then, please come back."

It was some time before he found Needham. He looked into the supper-room, but did not see him, and went on to the others. He was in none of them; but as he passed a second time the door of the supper-room, he caught sight of him with a glass of champagne in his hand. As Davenant entered and came towards him, he flushed and put the wine down untasted.

"So you were looking for me?" he said, with not entirely suppressed impatience.

"How did you know that?" asked Davenant, surprised. "Did you see me here before?"

"Oh, I was looking after the wine. I stepped out for a moment," answered Needham confusedly, "and I saw you go by a moment ago."

Evidently he had said more than he meant to. He was nervously uneasy, and his hand trembled as he pushed a glass towards Davenant.

"Not now, thank you," said Tom; "I was looking for you, as it happens. Your wife sent me to find you. She wants you to talk to some people." He wondered why Needham had attempted to evade him, and he did not understand his manner, but it was no time to seek an explanation; there were several people in the room; besides, it didn't matter much, Charlie Needham was always restless and more or less unaccountable.

"I don't want to talk to people," said Needham, fortunately in a low voice, but savagely. "Isn't it enough for her to have the house full of a lot of them that wouldn't remember her day after to-morrow, if it wasn't worth their while, without dragging me into it!" He put down his glass, empty this second time. Davenant watched him, wondering how many glasses he had already emptied; not many, he concluded—it was not the result of that sort of excitement.

"Shall I go and tell her you are not in just the humor for a rout?" he inquired dryly. "Or that you are slightly indisposed?"

"No, hang it! I'll go with you," he exclaimed. "May as well see it through. You know I don't mean you, Tom," he added as they sauntered out of the room, "or anybody else that's a friend—but now and then I get sick of the whole cursed business." The frown on his forehead was reduced to its usual indentation as they went on towards Florence. Evidently Davenant was the only one of his guests whom he intended to allow to perceive his ill-humor. There was no hesitation in Florence's manner as she laid her hand on Davenant's arm. She knew precisely the direction in which she wished to go, and she took it, although she paused here and there to speak to her guests, and maintained a certain apparent inattention to any object she might have in view which did not deceive her companion. As she preceded him in the doorway through which Rhodope and Medcott had disappeared half an hour ago, she turned and looked back at him as if for approval of what she had not even hinted she was about to do. Her hands fell before her, lightly clasped about some flowers she was carrying, her blue eyes, voluntarily softened, and her small mouth gave her beauty a look of extreme youth, which the somewhat too full outlines of her figure failed to efface. Her hand was on the Oriental portière, which in its mingling of colors made an effective background for the whiteness of her gown, her arms, her throat, and her dia-

monds. There was no one very near them—as nearness
goes in a crowded parlor. The room was full of the din of
many voices, which swept to their ears and ebbed from
them like the meaningless sound of inarticulate utterances.
As far as eyes and voices went they were alone. Davenant
looked down at her with an expression that she did not understand. He was a little troubled by Needham's manner;
knowing what he knew, he saw trouble ahead for this woman whom he had once loved, and to whom, in her brilliant,
somewhat hard beauty, trouble would come like a stinging
blow rather than a stern discipline. Nor was this all. His
knowledge of these underlying possibilities, with the inconsistencies and the ordinary social insincerities, which
usually sat lightly enough upon his shoulders, seemed to
make unstable at the best, perhaps impossible, the happiness of another woman, whose happiness he would gladly
have assured. All this lent his expression, as he looked at
Florence, something which was not usually to be found
there. His glance was less cynical, a slightly troubled look
softened the keenness of his eyes, and Florence's consciousness thrilled with sudden satisfaction. She was con-
sumed with jealous impatience to find Medcott and take
him away from Rhodope, but the emotion she felt for him
could not blind her to the brilliancy of this illumination.

"You are coming with me?" she said, her hand still on
the portière. It was not a question; it was only that she
wished to speak.

"Oh, yes, I am going with you," he answered, and she
went on. "I'm going with you until it seems to me time
to stop," he added. She turned quickly and met his
glance. The amusement with which he usually surveyed
her had come back, and the softness had vanished under
it, but she laughed back at him—she was so sure she had
not been mistaken; it had been there a moment before.

When Medcott went up to Rhodope where she was standing at Florence's side, with that tendency towards tropical expression characteristic of lovers, he had thought that she seemed a tall, white, fragrant lily, such as grow in old summer gardens, placed in the midst of an artistic but artificial arrangement of beautiful, brilliant exotics. The fact that the suggestion lacked something in novelty did not in the least annoy him; he was convinced that it could never have been, on former occasions, so entirely appropriate. He had greeted her formally and then gone away, to wait until he could claim her for something more than a moment's interview. As he stood aside he watched her carefully, and briefly put together the conclusions he had drawn during the two or three weeks of her stay. She had changed, he thought. In reality she had changed more than he guessed, more than could be accounted for by the new influences she had been placed under of late. She was paler, and the uncomprehending look that shadowed her eyes when she was faced by problems that she could not solve had grown to be their most usual expression. It had saddened her a little, he thought, this want of harmony between her own ideas and those of the people around her; it could not but be unhappiness for her, he sighed, as one who faces conclusions he is not altogether prepared to abide by. Rhodope saw him enter the room, watched him make his way through the crowd, smiled, and gave him her hand when he reached her, and then was conscious that he moved away as she spoke to the next person whom Mrs. Needham presented. That was all that there had been of their meeting, and it was a disappointment far removed from that which it would once have been. She was no longer the girl whose vivid color leaped into her face, and whose shy eyes fell in the presence of this man, whose power over her was nevertheless not dispelled. Lonely months of calm thought and brave recognition accomplish with certain characters what social training does with others. Though she had not escaped the shadow of regret that marked the passage of what might have been so much and was so little, she had learned that such regret was no unusual and unbearable thing. After even this short experience of new conditions she instinctively submitted to the unwritten laws that possibilities were ignored in this atmosphere, and that the superficial and the patent alone were recognized. It had all been a disappointment—there seemed to be very little else. So she greeted Austin Medcott with calm evenness, and knew that he went away from her, and thought without rebellion, only with that same regret, that she should not see him again that evening. She looked down at the sweet-peas she held in her hand; she had not even had the opportunity to thank him for them. It had touched her inexpressibly that he should have sent them to her. Would he think she had forgotten? As she had opened the box and seen them lying in it in their pink and purple daintiness, how that sunny morning came back to her, when she had given him that bunch of them at the open window! She almost caught the scent of the meadow-grass as it had mingled with the fragrance of the blossoms. She closed her eyes and caught the clear, grand, peaceful outlines of Mystery. Would he think for a moment that she had forgotten! Now, she looked about the room, answered something Mrs. Needham said to her, saw Charlie Needham, laughing, break off a rose from a mass of them near him, and give it to a pretty girl who pinned it in her dress, and then noted, without understanding, the fretful impatience of his face as soon as the smile left his lips. So this was the world—the real world. And the cold solitudes of mountain and valley, where were Jib and Elizabeth and General Downing and Abijah Stetson and the store, were but wastes, almost unpeopled, where the sounds of real existence scarcely penetrated. She smiled, half amused, half sympathetically, as she remembered the General's apprehensive warnings. There were a lot of folks—and it was all brilliant and beautiful enough certainly—this real world. The fitful stir of perfumed fans, the sparkle of gold and silver, the superb contours of arms and shoulders, the harmonious coloring and graceful drapery of silk and velvet, the misty daintiness of gauzes and laces, the light voices and gay laughter, the studied deference of some men, the cool observation, the pronounced admiration of others—this was the world, and she was not of it—it was not hers.

"Miss Rhodope, will you come with me? The social waters have ceased to break and recede at the base of your and Mrs. Needham's immobility. Really, you need not stay here any longer."

She looked up quickly into his face—she had not seen him approaching. Suddenly this world took on a new aspect; after all, it meant existence too—even for her.

"Yes," she answered, "I will come."

Medcott led her through the rooms into the potential library, and beyond to a smaller room, whose retirement had been more than once gratefully invaded by the wisdom of men which is sometimes foolishness, but was for the moment undisturbed. It was sweet with a great bowl of flowers, it was far enough removed from the music to have that seem an accompaniment to conversation rather than an audacious defiance. It was lighted by shaded candles in many-branched sconces. Altogether, it was a satisfactory product of civilization. He seated her in a large armchair, and then, in the midst of this delicate, almost poetic suggestiveness,

"I am going to bring you some supper," he baldly announced. Rhodope laughed her rare, sweet laugh.

"Is it to be sandwiches?" she asked, thinking of their morning at Shadow Pond. Suddenly all that time had drawn nearer. It did not seem only a remembered dream; instead it was a part of the present. She was again in the freedom of an atmosphere where looks and words and tones were not a shield and a disguise.

"Sandwiches!" he exclaimed; "I would not dare to offer them to you. Sandwiches like those of Shadow Pond do not flourish hereabouts—they are a different thing altogether. But we must have a makeshift."

They were together a long time.

"I am going to the valley next summer," said Medcott, as if it were a thing of course. "I am thinking of going up earlier to get spring effects in the woods." He almost smiled at his own matter-of-fact way of stating it. Of course he would go, as soon as she would let him. From the moment that she had turned with him from the reception-room that evening, he had had no manner of doubt that he should tell her he loved her. All doubts, questionings, fears for her happiness, had vanished and were as if they had never been. What in her absence seemed dark disadvantages looming in the foreground, in her presence sank into their natural place of unimportant accessories. As he looked at her in her low chair under the pink light of the candles, a touch of weariness in her attitude, utterly foreign to the buoyant strength of the woman that had gone with him to Shadow Pond, he wondered that he could ever have hesitated. What had led him to dream that he could restrain at will this headlong sweep of feeling that made it the purpose of his life to be near her, to hear her speak, to watch her eyes, to tell her he loved her? It had been the thought of her possible unhappiness, to be sure, that had held him back, but if she cared for him she should not be unhappy—they would go somewhere where her happi-

ness should not be tampered with. If she cared for him!
He observed her with a certain diffidence. Notwithstanding her quietness, she was more like the Rhodope of the
hills than she had been before, since he had seen her this
second time. She was as quick to respond to an idea that
pleased her, as direct, as fearless in her speech, and now
and then the odd little turn of language came back, but
less frequently, for the more conventional influences had
already affected her in this respect But the subtle change
was there, that a less observant man might have missed. If
she cared for him!

"You ask me once in a while if I remember this or that,"
he said. "Do you suppose I have forgotten anything?"

Rhodope weighed the meaning of the inflection.

"It was different with you," she said, "it was not so new."

"Yes, it was," he answered boldly, "it was utterly different from anything I had ever known." He did not mean
to tell her here in this blaze of light, in Florence Needham's presence, as it were, and in the midst of surroundings so foreign to their truest lives; but he could not keep
his voice from tenderness, and his words from straying on
the borders of confession.

"Do you remember the lion, too?" she asked.

"Certainly I remember the lion," he answered readily;
"one does not easily forget royalty." But what he remembered was her figure as she stood in front of the cage, and
how he had felt himself chained by circumstances, with an
impatience equal to that of the brute. What had become
of those hampering restrictions? Had they ever been?

"I would like to have had that lion care for me," said
Rhodope thoughtfully—"really have a regard for me."

"You women all have a passion for bringing into sub-
jection. What would you have done with him? Would
you like to lead him about like a spaniel?"

"No!" she said quickly, "never! Why do you say 'you women'? Do you think all women are alike?" she questioned gravely.

"Heaven forefend! But you all like to hold in leash something stronger than you are." Rhodope thought this over with that serious simplicity that perceived no possible personal application, and which Medcott found so charming.

"I do not know whether that is true or not."

Medcott laughed. "Your disposition to accept my simple statements is flattering."

She laughed a little too, but said, still seriously,

"I would like to accept everything like that, if I could. But I cannot. It is not safe. One is mistaken."

Nothing was further from her thoughts than any hint of reproach, but Medcott felt something in her words that was not there.

"I know now what one should do," she went on with the assured air of discovery that she had had often of late. "One should appear to believe, and laugh at it afterwards, if one does not."

"Would that Davenant might hear you!" ejaculated Medcott.

"But I have not learned it yet," she concluded. "It is not easy."

The confession was very near his lips that truth, and truth only, was possible with her, and that truth meant love. He bent over her, her hand was near his, it was perilously easy to take it when he spoke. Rhodope turned her eyes and looked at him. She colored a little to find him so near, his eyes on her face, something deeper in them than the attention with which he always listened to her. In his simple presence there was an emotion stronger than any other that had stirred her life, but she had learned to look upon it as one which should not extend itself. She had met him over and over and had been confirmed in her acquiescence. But what did this mean?—this sudden disturbance of their calm relations, which yet were just what they had been. She, too, felt that some barrier had been swept away in that moment, and that they were together with nothing to keep them away from each other, as it had been that last evening in the valley when they had watched the sun set and the moon rise.

> "We're sunk enough here, God knows!
> But not quite so sunk, that moments
> Sure, though seldom, are denied us,
> When the spirit's true endowments
> Stand out plainly from its false ones—"

He paused a moment, the words still unsaid; not that he doubted if he should say them, but not here and now. In the moment Rhodope rose.

"What are you going to do?" he asked, dismayed that his hour of happiness was to be cut short.

"I must go back," she said uncertainly. It was not that she dreaded unfriendly criticism if she stayed with him longer; it was with no thought of any conventionality whatever. Perhaps it was that conscientiousness which suggests that entire happiness cannot be dissociated from moral dereliction. Perhaps it was born of a fatalistic desire to go away before this happiness be disturbed as it must be.

People had been coming into and going from the library while they talked—sometimes there were a dozen people in it and sometimes more. Just now that, as well as this smaller room, was empty, save for themselves. She stood before him gravely regarding him, her gray eyes with their moving shadows suggesting the sunlight rather than the shade.

"Rhodope," he said, coming nearer. Her eyes fell before his. There was a sudden exclamation, a flash of light, and he had caught her in his arms, and her head fell on his shoulder, why and how she did not quite know. It was just at this moment that Florence and Davenant appeared at the distant library door. The two figures started into prominence like those of a picture at the end of a skilfully managed vista—Rhodope in Medcott's arms.

"Well!" exclaimed Florence in a curious hushed tone unlike her usual light voice, "I think it is as well that I am looking after my guests." Between unreasoning fury with Medcott and utter disgust with himself for allowing Florence to make him a participator in this scene and with her for bringing him, for an instant Davenant was silent. In that instant he saw Medcott put Rhodope aside and tread upon the vivid flame of a burning shade. Rhodope stood white and silent watching him, and as Medcott turned back to her, evidently with some inquiry, the look in her eyes, which Davenant felt rather than saw, was one he would have given all he possessed not to have Florence see, and which, to tell the truth, he would willingly have dispensed with seeing himself. Medcott stooped to look at Rhodope's dress, and in so doing saw Mrs. Needham and Davenant. The latter was already coming towards the little room—he had seen it was too late to go back.

"Oh, I think I will not go in," said Florence in a loud, gay tone meant to reach the ears of the others, and she turned back with an affectation of dismay.

"You must," said Davenant with an intonation that, quiet as it was, silenced her, and she went on with him.

"Arson," declared Tom firmly, as they reached the door of the smaller room, "and in the first degree. The defendant was discovered secreting burning paper in the hangings, while his accomplice undoubtedly supplied the matches. "

In a swift glance Medcott perceived what impression

had been made, but before he had time to speak Florence walked up to him, her head thrown back, her voice defiant.

She ignored Rhodope entirely; it was as if no one but Medcott were in the room.

"My candle - shades are not sufficiently guarded for such emotional outbreaks, Mr. Medcott," and she laughed. "They should be protected by wire netting—but I really hadn't thought them within arm's length before." Her temper was rapidly getting the command of the situation—she hardly knew what she was saying. Medcott, however, did not lose his; he was as sure as Davenant that it was very important to keep it.

"Gratitude!" he demanded, laughing. "I refuse to have your improvidence usurp the place of my prowess. That burning candle-shade fell upon Miss Trent's gown, which, if I mistake not, is of the material usually recognized as diaphanous, and consequently inflammable. Had it not been for my promptness—I forbear to say my personal bravery —what might not have happened!"

"We saw what happened," said Florence, still defiantly but less confidently. Medcott's carelessness, the apparent absence of any emotion on his part—above all, Medcott himself, the man for whom her feeling was so complex and so strong—had subdued her into some self-control.

"And we see—it is bad enough as it is!" said Davenant solemnly. He had been making investigations. "One candle-shade, undoubtedly expensive, done for entirely; one spot burned on the carpet, but which can be judiciously covered by yonder small table, now acting merely as a pitfall; one hole in Miss Trent's gown, small and easily concealed by a—a gather."

"Oh, is that all?" said Florence, with exasperating incredulity.

"And I hope not Miss Trent's arm permanently dislocated," said Medcott, speaking for the first time to her. "I did not stop to think that I might hurt you."

"He did not stop to think," said Florence under her breath.

"I am not hurt," said Rhodope in a low voice. "I might have been but for you—this second time."

"You would have been a crisp," said Davenant with terrible lightness. He felt something must be done to get Rhodope away. He wondered when the first time had been, but with noble self-abnegation he did not wish his curiosity gratified at the expense of gratifying Mrs. Needham's too. "Having thanked your deliverer, you will now come with me where the uneventful gas-lights are predominant, and candle-shades are not."

The whole episode had been barely five minutes long.

Rhodope and Davenant found the rooms still full; people were not thinking of going home.

"How high-minded of him to take her away!" said Florence, her voice vibrating harshly, as she stood where Rhodope had stood just before, facing Medcott.

CHAPTER XVIII

" Wormwood !   Wormwood !"

" Though you fret me you cannot play upon me."

THERE was the noise of voices raised in sudden, sharp contention, of quick words of entreaty, wild, untrained, pleading, in a woman's tones; the rough, brutal reply of a man; the dull, yet startling, sound of what might be a blow; detached, violent syllables, some of which were curses; "For God's sake, Bill!" in passionate outcry; the unlicensed, uncontrolled savagery of speech, and perhaps action, which comes with such terribly strange, palpitating force to ears unused to its evidences; all this came up from the street below, through Rhodope's open window, waking her from a broken sleep into horrified attention. A distant church-clock struck three—the slow, heavy step of a policeman turned down a neighboring street; the voices ceased, and it was still, save for the approaching signal of municipal watchfulness. Rhodope sprang up and went swiftly in the darkness to the window, and, drawing aside the curtain, looked out. The street was empty to her eyes, though what the black shadows might conceal she knew not. The block of houses opposite rose tall and dark, save that, here and there, a light, probably that of a sick-room, gleamed behind the hangings. The more distant towers and steeples were massed against the sky and its already paling stars. All was stately, orderly, civilized. She felt as if a brief whirlwind had swept through the street and left no disastrous trace, as she went back, shivering a little, with apprehension as much as with cold, to sleep until daylight. But sleep did not come immediately. The commonplace incident had served to emphasize the mood into which she had fallen. What did it mean? Was there a fellow-creature out there in distress or terror which that slow, heavily-treading guardian would know nothing of? These things, as well as others, happen in the world and in a world quite as real as that of brilliant reception-rooms and well-bred, soft-speaking guests. This truth, which appalls the stoutest hearts, oppressed Rhodope in those early morning hours when the night itself has grown weary waiting for the day.

It was due in part to the reaction of the evening before. She knew, with the clear-sightedness with which her entire trustfulness endowed her, that the moments before that one in which Medcott had snatched her out of the way of the flame had been moments of as nearly utter sincerity as souls are vouchsafed in one another's presence. She felt it now as clearly as she had then, that underneath the sometimes light, sometimes serious words that they had said to one another, there had been a current of strong feeling in which they had understood each other, independently of speech. When she had rested an instant in his arms she had been as sure of his love as she had been of her own. It was a moment which she could never put away from her again—and how lightly he had put it away! To Rhodope, with her intensity and directness of feeling, the scene which followed had been jarring in the extreme. She had been stirred to the soul, and so she was sure had he, yet he had met jest with jest, had faced an angry woman with an assurance equal to, though calmer, than her own, and had apologized to her—to her!—for grasping her roughly—that was all. To her exacting perceptions it had been so miserably inadequate. Did it need only the presence of Florence Needham to destroy the simplicity of her relations with Medcott? Rhodope was not jealous of Florence; she would have felt it degrading and disloyal; but she had learned the larger value of much that had once seemed to her of slight importance. She saw her deficiencies by the side of Florence's completeness; the perfection of her dress, the luxury of her environment gave Mrs. Needham, she perceived, something that she lacked. The picture of her first view of Florence flashed before her eyes with a certain insistence—her charming blonde head beside Medcott's in the farm-house window. Did her approach bring suddenly to bear upon him all the tradition, the association, the necessities of his life, outside of which seemed to be Rhodope's place? Had she a power in what she represented, to close his lips and harden his heart?

Florence, Rhodope, and Needham were together at the late breakfast—a not entirely normal occurrence.

Breakfast is perhaps as great a strain as civilized people are subjected to with any frequency. There is that subdued air of being under the sway of duty, not inclination, about it all. The probabilities are that we did not wish to get up in the first place, and the necessary grip on the natural man has not had time to relax. It is only the most satisfactorily constituted organizations that welcome the idea of food for its own sake, and a decent amount of conversation is an unnatural drain upon the intellectual forces which refuse to be marshalled until later in the day. Any determined cheerfulness on the part of an individual is regarded as arrant Pharisaism, and put down to his or her account accordingly. Now and then a phenomenon like Thoreau turns up to preach early morning, but most of us look upon it, as the worldly look upon heaven, as undoubtedly all that it is represented to be, and endlessly refreshing, but something that we prefer to leave unseen until we have to depart from all that we hold most dear—and take an early train. To the actual incapacities of the breakfast-hour were added this morning some special disadvantages. Needham was more out of temper than usual, owing to the gayety of the evening before. Florence's nerves were on edge—the result of a variety of causes, and Rhodope's oppressive visions had not been altogether banished by the sunlight. Moreover, the efforts of the servants had not yet entirely reinstated the house in its usual atmosphere of order and well-being.

"Len Wright has shot himself," said Needham suddenly, laying down his paper. Florence looked up from the note of invitation she was reading.

"Those Wrights are always committing suicide," she observed. "Was it his brother or his cousin last? And then there was his uncle."

Rhodope looked from one to the other with shocked eyes.

"Is it some one you know?" she asked in a low tone.

"Dined with him night before last at the club," replied Needham briefly, as he rose and walked to the window, where he stood looking out, his hands in his pockets.

"Why, you saw him, Rhodope," said Florence. "He was at that musicale Wednesday—a tall, good-looking fellow who was talking most of the time with Helena Screed." She was quite interested in helping Rhodope to identify him.

"Yes—I remember. Is—is he dead?"

"Oh, yes, killed instantly," said Charlie from the window.

It seemed to Rhodope a horrible thing, too horrible a thing to dwell on.

"What was the matter?" asked Florence. "What did he do it for?"

"Financial embarrassment."

Florence picked up the paper.

"Oh, yes—couldn't pay his debts—books found wrong;" she glanced over the notice. "Well, I suppose it was the best thing he could do. The Wrights' position won't be so much injured as if he'd gone to prison or anything," and she tossed the paper carelessly aside. Needham did not answer. Florence tore open another note.

"How nice!" she exclaimed an instant later. Her cheeks were flushed with pleasure. The constraint which had marked her manner each time she had spoken to Rhodope that morning had momentarily vanished.

"Mrs. Rimmon has invited us to dinner," she announced in a tone which almost crossed the line that separates satisfaction from triumph—"to dinner, Charlie, to meet those English people. She has never asked us to dinner before," she added, that he might not miss the full significance of the fact.

"Well, I dare say the cook could get us something at home if she hadn't asked us this time," said Charlie disagreeably, without turning around.

"You can be as rude as you like now," returned Florence, with a contempt which did not, however, shadow the illumination of her spirit, " as long as you are civil then."

She turned to Rhodope with a return of her former coolness. "Mrs. Rimmon says nothing about you," she said. "She does not know you are here, perhaps."

"Oh, never mind, never mind," said Rhodope eagerly, " I couldn't bear to go—it would give me much greater pleasure to be at home." She rose and pushed back her chair. Life, death—they were nothing to these people. What was it to them that the man who had been next to them had shot himself in despair—so long as there were dinners to go to. Naturally enough, she underestimated the force of familiarity.

"It is some days off," said Florence coldly. "We can make other plans for you."

Rhodope had seated herself by the fire. She cared more to be by a fire here than she had in the cooler climate of her home. It remained warm and friendly, and so appealed to her.

"I am afraid something terrible happened here last night," she said slowly.

"What? For Heaven's sake!" demanded Florence, turning a little pale, "was anything the matter in the supper-room?—I didn't go into it once." Even Charlie turned his head to listen.

"No, oh no, not in the house, "said Rhodope, "but outside. I heard a man's voice and a woman's. I was almost afraid."

"*When* do you mean?" Florence had a dreadful vision of the Adells not being able to get their carriage, and their consequent reflections on her bad management.

"Early this morning—very soon after I fell asleep," said Rhodope.

"Oh!" breathed Mrs. Needham, relieved. "A street row," and she poured more cream into her coffee. "We are always hearing them here—it's a perfect disgrace, too! Why can't they confine their disturbances to their own neighborhood?"

"Yes," sighed Rhodope, "a street row, I suppose." She began to perceive its trifling position in the drama of life.

"Don't you like to dine out, Miss Rhodope?" asked Needham, facing around for the first time.

"I have not done it often," replied Rhodope thoughtfully. "I have attended but one very formal dinner, I think."

"The Mevans, you know," interpolated Florence; "only the best people were there."

16

"I did not enjoy that," went on Rhodope frankly; "they talked altogether about themselves. If I had known them I might have been interested too," she added, with her usual justice.

"I'll lay you five to one you wouldn't," Needham laughed scornfully.

"It is very singular you did not enjoy it," said Florence with measured disapproval. "It was given in part for you, and Mrs. Mevans was very kind to ask us."

"She was very kind," admitted Rhodope simply; "I think perhaps it was only that she did not know how to make people enjoy each other."

"Not know how—Mrs. Rodman Mevans." Mrs. Needham's tone was indescribable.

"No." Rhodope felt the unfriendliness of her hostess, but she was answering Charlie, and she regarded him seriously while she explained. "You see, she did not tell me who anybody was, and I knew but one person, and when I addressed myself to her, saying that I had seen her at Miss Screed's luncheon, she said, 'Indeed, you have a good memory,' and that was all."

"It was a beastly shame," broke out Charlie indignantly. "She ought to have her ears boxed."

"Charlie!" said Florence, "it was Miss Arne!"

"Then she ought to have known better!" was the retort. "She considers herself well-bred, I believe. Where was I at this dinner that I couldn't help you out?"

"It was a woman's dinner—you weren't asked," answered Florence.

"A woman's dinner!" repeated Charlie, as though he had said "Fire and water."

Rhodope had not meant to be critical, only to explain, but Needham's encouragement drew her out. She laughed a little now.

"But one lady spoke to me at the table," she said, "and she asked me, 'Who is your favorite photographer?' and I could not answer."

Charlie burst out laughing. "Why didn't you ask her what was her favorite trout-fly," he asked, "and she could not have answered you."

Florence rose and left Charlie and Rhodope to their flash of ill-regulated gayety. Such criticism was to her on the level of the profane jokes in the lower order of comic papers. Perhaps it was to her disapproving presence that the flash was due, for, after she left, the gloom of the winter morning fell again upon the other two. Needham went back to his absent-minded gaze out of the window; then, conscious of his want of civility, fidgeted about the room, beginning a sentence or two which lost themselves in the vagueness lying in wait for absent-minded people, and finally said good-by, and went out of the house. Rhodope sat silently before the fire while the servant removed the breakfast things and withdrew. A light snow was beginning to fall—the houses opposite looked oppressively high—the rumble of a crowded thoroughfare was distantly in her ears—the shrill whistle of the postman sounded a few doors off. Now and then she caught glimpses through the window of passing figures, but she did not watch them— she had never seen one of them before in her life—she should never see one of them again. For the first time she realized that she was wretchedly homesick.

In another room of the house sat Florence Needham. She had heard her husband go, and she knew that Rhodope was alone, but she had no thought of joining her; she had been there long enough to know the ways of the house; she could not be running after her all the time. If there were reasons why she might think any neglect this morning intentional—she did not care—she was not un-

willing to have her think so. Florence was in her worst
mood. A variety of causes which would have made quite
a respectable showing by themselves were all merged in
that one great cause, the incident of the previous evening
and its result. To be sure, these lesser causes had each
their detrimental and positive effect, and she dwelt on them
that she might not lose herself in the anger that throbbed
in her veins when her thoughts reverted to the other. In
the first place, Rhodope had not been a remarkable success;
the fact that she was not included in this invitation of Mrs.
Rimmon was an evidence of it. Florence owed the satisfaction of the day to her own diplomatic charms and not
in the least to Rhodope, who had not created the ripple that
she had thought possible; she had been noticed by some
people, of course, and she was thought beautiful, but Florence Needham was just where she would have been without
her. She needed to cast no such bait for discriminating
favor anyway—had not Mrs. Rimmon asked her to dinner?
To be sure, there was Austin Medcott. Instead of ignoring
her almost entirely, he had dropped into the position of an
habitué of her house. Yes, there was Austin Medcott!
Florence sat at the library table, upon which there still
stood a bowl of magnificent roses. She snatched a handful
of them and pulled them rapidly to pieces, scattering the
bruised petals over her dress and about her feet; then
with a violent gesture she sprang to her feet, shook herself
free from them, and paced rapidly up and down the room.
She would have liked to break china, to have smashed
ornaments. The shallow, violent nature of the woman
longed for an outbreak—it was only her conventionality
that held her in any sort of check. Finally she paused
at the door of the smaller room—just where she had stood
and faced Medcott last night.

"You fancied yourself still at the farm-house of one

Israel Clock, perhaps," she had said, the angry light in her eyes; "or up at Uncle Denver's—or by the cascade—or at the stile?" Her voice grew more contemptuous with each suggestion. "You forget that something besides the etiquette of the valley is in force here. You forget—" She stopped because she did not dare go on. There was an expression of answering contempt in his eyes which warned her—the liking of this man was so much to her! Medcott watched Rhodope disappear with Davenant.

"I do not forget that I am in Mrs. Needham's house," he said, with entire civility, paused a moment, and went on smiling—"and consequently subject to her interpretation of etiquette. Apparently I have transgressed. If I have kept Miss Trent too long from your other guests—at least Davenant has remedied my mistake for me."

"I fancy she has not been generally missed," said Florence with an angry shrug.

"Then my present guilt is the greater—for I am detaining you."

The determined lightness of his tone, the unmeaning flattery which he offered her, as he would a child sweetmeats, exasperated her.

"You have been making love to that girl," she said suddenly and sharply. His expression changed and his eyes grew sterner as they looked straight into her unreliable blue ones.

"You are mistaken, Mrs. Needham," he said briefly. "I have not yet had the opportunity."

His frankness was a stab to her vanity and through that to her heart.

"It looked very much like an—an opportunity," she said with a disagreeable laugh.

Medcott had not Davenant's coolness, and he was very angry, but not only his strength of will, but the scene itself helped him to be apparently unmoved. The sound of the music which was just beginning again, the hum of the voices, the brilliancy and sparkle, instead of disturbing or bewildering him as it had disturbed and bewildered Rhodope, held him in his place and contributed to the maintenance of the proper key of conversation.

"Then I am slow at recognizing effects," he answered carelessly; "I brought Miss Trent her supper and protected her incidentally from a burning bit of paper, but neither occasion seemed to me a favorable one." He waited a moment—while Florence looked up at him with her hard, incredulous smile—not in doubt, but to make his next words more unmistakable.

"But allow me to say, Mrs. Needham, as Miss Trent is at present in your charge, that I shall seek an opportunity to tell her that I am in love with her as soon as may be."

Florence turned swiftly away in a rush of mingled impulses that forbade present speech. If Rhodope had been there she could have found words for her; to Medcott she could say nothing. The kindled insistence of his usually somewhat indifferent manner, the suggestion of haughtiness which indicated his resentment of her impertinence while he yielded to it, the strength and distinction, physical and mental, of the man, made his attraction for her the more absolute.

As Florence recalled this instant of the interview, she flung aside the portière near which she stood with a violence which rattled sharply all its many rings, the sudden sound of which was like an angry exclamation. She had gone a few steps away from him under the stress of her dismay. With a second ill-considered caprice she had come back to his side. She stood close to him, her eyes raised with a look of softness, deeper than even Davenant was allowed to perceive in them, her round cheek almost touching his

arm, the exquisitely dainty tints of her complexion flushed
by the momentary excitement, the diamonds gleaming about
her white throat.

"Why don't you make love to me?" she said, in tones so
low that her voice was almost sweet.

Her beauty had never had for Medcott even the fascination that Davenant cynically allowed himself to perceive in
it. In those early days at the Clock farm-house, before he
found a stronger interest, it had not swayed him in the
least. He looked down at her smiling.

"I am not of that stern stuff," he said; "I cannot declare war upon so many. There is no room for another
aspirant. Would you have me prove it in bitterness of
soul?"

The banality of the reply accomplished what it was meant
to do. She drew away from him. and, resuming her ordinary
gayety, she said a few words of laughing retort and preceded him out of the room.

Medcott knew that he might have done more wisely according to the children of unrighteousness. If he had detained, instead of following her, had stayed with her there
in the half seclusion that an hour before had been so grateful, and had said some of the things she wanted to hear
him say—it would not have been a great matter after all,
and he might have found his path the smoother for it.
It would have been a rational and becoming proceeding,
viewed from the standpoint he was accustomed to occupy.
But a standpoint is not Gibraltar—even for the individual,
and his had suffered modifications. Unconsciously a singular and stern simplicity had been begotten in the cool,
silent shadow of Mount Marvel, Mount Innocence, and
Mount Charity.

Mrs. Needham's gayety, however, had not deceived Davenant when he went with Medcott to bid her good-night.

"Embers," he remarked, with that sententiousness he liked to treat himself to, as he caught her expression as she spoke to Medcott. "Large embers. The blaze is over, but there must have been a pretty one." .

He even went so far as to make an entry in his note-book after he reached home. "Disturbed vanity," he wrote. "Pre-empted lover. General conflagration begun by lamp-shade. Embers not so extinct as to be incapable of bearing a hand at reconstruction. Mixed metaphor, but will do something with it when I have time."

"I wonder what kind of a mess Medcott made of it,". he mused as he replaced his pencil. "He's safe to have experimented. But I don't know as he could have helped it," he admitted pensively. "It was a pretty severe situation for—as old Denver Trent used to say—just the ordinary one-headed man."

Davenant was quite right. The flame had barely been kept under. This morning all Florence's cruel resentment was directed towards Rhodope. Freed from the elevating restrictions of self-control, she descended to the essentially low level of her ordinary aims, impulses, and inclinations. It indicates with critical clearness the state of her mind to say that she would have liked to have turned Rhodope out of the house and then to have slammed the door. It was while she yielded to this access of irritation that she remembered that a day or two earlier, in unacknowledged consequence of some remarks of Davenant and Edwina Screed, she had urged Rhodope to remain through the month. She felt choked by complications. The knob of the library door turned and she faced Rhodope.

"Well?" she said, with an unfriendly intonation she had not hitherto permitted herself. Rhodope was too free from self-consciousness, too physically at ease to appear timid; but tall, straight, and beautiful as she was, as she caught the chill of Mrs. Needham's manner she felt helpless and alone. It recalled the day of the picnic, when she had felt that an unmeasured distance separated her from her kindred. Her voice trembled a little under the weight of strangeness.

"I think I will go out to walk," she said. "The snow has stopped, and I should like to be outside."

"Oh, very well," said Mrs. Needham, indifferently.

"You would not care to go?"

"I? No, I never walk if I can help it."

Rhodope turned to leave the room. Florence came to a sudden resolution.

"Rhodope." The perceptible hostility of the tone brought the tears almost to Rhodope's eyes, but they did not fall.

"Yes," she said, coming back into the room. As she did so she saw the scattered rose-leaves. They suggested the sudden extinction of what had seemed beautiful and vital the night before.

"Last night you were here a long time with Medcott—Austin Medcott."

"Was it a long time?" questioned Rhodope with entire simplicity.

"Yes; I think I had better tell you that he is a man who is dangerous, from the very artistic appreciation that makes him so—so delightful."

"He is delightful," she said gravely again. Her calm acquiescence was rather disconcerting to Florence's artificial temperament.

"I thought, perhaps, from your having seen so much of him last summer and all that, you might think it was something—something special. He admires you—as an artist"—the implied flattery did not fall from honeyed lips—"but he is a man who—who goes no further." Florence was finding it difficult to say what it was he did not do, with the memory of his last night's deficiency so keenly present. "That is, he talks to every woman as he talks to every other." She was losing the justice of her analysis in her wish to heal her own vanity.

"I think he does not talk to me as he talks to every other woman," said Rhodope, with the same somewhat sad gravity. Her confidence amazed while it exasperated her companion.

"I did not think matters had gone so far," she exclaimed angrily. "I see my warning has come too late! If you already think that he says to no one else what he says to you—why, the harm is already done."

"I think you are not just to him."

"Don't flatter yourself that you are!" Florence interrupted angrily.

"And," concluded the other, with a proud little inflection, "I do not think you are just to me."

Mrs. Needham could not realize that her sense of the situation was the finer and truer one, but she felt the imperturbable sincerity of the recognition of it, and her irritation increased.

"Justice is not what either of you want," she retorted. "You had better go for your walk now," she added, with the air of concluding the interview, and Rhodope went slowly out of the room.

CHAPTER XIX

"She says she hears there's tricks in the world."

"This love just puts his hand out in a dream
And straight outreaches all things."

IT was about noon, and, the snow-storm being over, the air had softened into one of those freakish days of late winter, when the sun shines with a freedom that sets the bondage of cold at defiance, and makes us feel that spring is an actual presence that has for the moment drawn nearer, and the flutter of whose garments is almost perceptible as she passes.

As Rhodope walked through Madison Square her eyes fell upon a group of four—two men and two women. They had paused at one of the benches, and were showing one another tintypes. They had so evidently come from the country into the full enjoyment of metropolitan pleasures, that it was impossible not to look upon them with friendly eyes, and some curiosity to see the tintypes. There was something in the manner of all of them that suggested that the acquaintance was not of long standing. Instead of the calm serenity of those who have sat up with each other for successive evenings, there was a conscious, blushing, timid audacity in their giggles, exclamations, and unevasive flattery that indicated something innocently irregular in the proceedings. A careful observer would have surmised that the two men had been having their pictures taken, when the girls came in, and that there had been mirth in conse-

quence, which had resulted in this wayside meeting for
mutual confidences.   It was altogether an innocent, pleasing spectacle, not unedifying to the jaded observer.   Rhodope felt for them a throb of sympathy as she drew near
them on her way across the square.   It was with such
simple folk as this that she was happiest.   One of the men
might have been Tom Furwin himself.   She remembered
that he had had a tintype taken, and the subsequent satisfaction on higher than artistic grounds of his immediate
circle.   She had come out this morning to fling off this
load of homesickness that had oppressed her, and here it
faced her again on the city square.   Under its influence she
put aside the suggestions of a deeper, more exacting, more
intoxicating happiness; yes, it was with people like these,
in their own homes, that she belonged, not here in this
brilliant, noisy, confusing, heartless city, where people had
no time to wonder whether or not women were cruelly in-
treated, or what had led their friends to suicide, and where
one's deepest feelings were tossed aside with a smile that
befitted one's most trivial.   It was characteristic of Rhodope that nothing that Florence had said, nor her own dissatisfaction with Medcott, had led her to doubt the genuineness of the feeling he had had for her during those moments when they had understood one another.   The tintypes were replaced, and the four people strolled up one of
the wide park walks with the shrinking bravado of couples
promenading country lanes, heedless of mocking, cynical,
indifferent, busy New York.

With a certain irresolution, Rhodope turned again up-
town.   Suddenly she felt the hopelessness of going farther
after light-heartedness.   It was better to be in the house,
even with Florence Needham, away from other observation,
than here where there was subtle mockery in the very sun
and air, and where a little, harmless idyl, like that she had

just witnessed, was as distinctly out of place as though it had been a bit of real Arcadia. She recalled the instant that her head had rested on Medcott's shoulder, with sudden half-frightened but unashamed consciousness, and caught again the revelation that that moment held—for them both, she had thought—nay, she was sure—for them both. It was only that for him it was quickly hidden again by the close-pressing illusions of outside things; for her, it would remain forever unobscured.

"Good-morning, Miss Trent," said a man behind her. "This is better luck than I dared to hope for." For an instant his voice carried her back to the brief confidence of that moment, and then she met his glance with a gravity which startled him. His thoughts had been dwelling on that last interview, but without her perplexity and misgivings. They walked on through the square and turned up Fifth Avenue. The day had become fairly brilliant. The city had already assumed that gala air which it lays aside only under protest, now and then, and which it is always ready to take up again at a moment's notice.

"I am coming to see you as soon as I may," said Medcott. "When shall it be?"

"I do not know," answered Rhodope, her eyes straight before her as she walked swiftly, yet without hurrying, up the street. "I do not know, for I do not judge of things right. It is not for me to say when you shall come."

There was a sense of distance conveyed by her tone.

"It is for you to say what I shall do always," broke out Medcott, "always, if you will."

The color surged into Rhodope's cheeks, and she did not meet his eyes.

"You all have a way of speaking here," she answered gently.

"But you do not believe that it is only a way of speaking," he exclaimed. "Oh, Rhodope, you know what I am coming to tell you! You know what was so near my lips last night—"

"Last night?" she took the sentence up. She made no pretence of not understanding, but the joy, the deep, throbbing emotion she had felt the night before had gone. She seemed conscious only of a sort of impatient sadness. "Yes, I know—perhaps. But it was not said, and it was better that it was not." Now she turned and met his protesting eyes.

"It shall be said," he interrupted briefly, "even if it is in a city street."

"It is so easy for you to say another thing," she went on. "It is not such a great matter."

Medcott's intuition seized the impression that was in her mind.

"Do you say that because I found it possible to say something else last night?" he demanded. "Because I thought the feeling I had for you was too sacred a thing to be then revealed or lightly acknowledged?"

"It is always easy," she repeated, "to say something that conceals. Why is it not easy to say what *is*—always—any time? Would it not be better?"

He knew her utter unreasonableness, and yet its seriousness disconcerted him, as it had done before. This sudden failure of a common ground in the very midst of what seemed extraordinary mutual understanding had been to him a part of Rhodope's exquisite and unusual charm. Before he made answer she went on:

"There is some reason for it all, but I have not found it," she said with a somewhat pathetic earnestness. "Mr. Davenant said once, in the higher civilization it is not half the matter what one does as what one says." Medcott almost laughed in the midst of his perplexity to hear her quote one of Tom's cynical maxims as if it were a simple copy-book rule of good conduct, suitable for the instruction of the young of both sexes.

"But is it"—she paused a moment—"is it of so much importance what one says? Does one even *say* what one feels?" There was something a little affecting in her evident wish to adapt her comprehension to new codes, that she might judge fairly, even while she could never wish to make them her own. Medcott could not know that her confusion was the result of increasing bewilderment, her disappointment in him, and her wish to defend him even to herself. He felt constrained to answer her according to her own fashion.

"It is of every importance," he said gently, but with a strong feeling perceptible through his words that Rhodope could not but be conscious of, "what one says to some people at all times. I told you once no one would ever tell you anything but truth. No word, no look, no slightest action of mine towards you has been meant to convey anything but truth. But I have not told you half of it, that is all. Half-truths we know are dangerous. What I feel for you has a length, a breadth, a depth that you must learn to know, for I cannot tell it to you." He paused. Rhodope was swayed and thrilled, but the conflicting currents of the night's and morning's experience had tried her courage. Unconsciously she had been subjected of late to a nervous strain of which she did not know the meaning or the effect. She dared not let herself trust to what she would once have accepted as utterly trustworthy.

"It is not that I do not believe you," she said, with a sincerity that she did not mean to be somewhat cruel. "It is that I do not think you understand. I think that what I have grown up to believe great, deep, sad, and terrible is not that to you who live where there are so many people.

I have said before, I do not understand your language sometimes. That is what makes it hard for you and me."

Medcott felt with sudden heaviness that she was saying in her own way what he had said to Davenant, and often to himself. The evident wavering of her faith in him hurt him deeply; he saw that what had been his natural wish to spare her the evening before had seemed to her simplicity almost a denial. And he knew that she was unjust to him; he knew that his subsequent interview with Florence had been a test and a witness of his truth to her which she could never understand. But the overbearing, stormy flood of passionate love refuses to be long held within barriers of abstractions and misgivings, or veiled in the mists of misunderstanding.

"Rhodope," he said suddenly, "I love you. I love your eyes, your heart, your doubts, your distrusts, and the sound of your voice! I love the way you move and speak! I love you for those things in which you are like others and in which you differ from them! You may judge me and condemn me, and weigh me and find me wanting, but you shall believe me. I love you!"

It was a strange place for such a confession. To have walked with this woman in the sweet silences of forest, field, and country roads, to have watched with her the moon rise and listened with her to the song of the wood-thrush, and then to tell her that he loved her in the dimmed brightness of a winter noon on a city street, where they met and passed strangers, and now and then acquaintances, equally observing and indifferent, was an incongruity Medcott was one of the first of men to be conscious of. But he had not willed it so and it had come, and even his artistic temperament was in abeyance. To be sure, they were now in a quieter part of the avenue, but the rush of carriages and the evidences of crowded, hurrying, swift, and audacious life made it hard for the individual to realize that it was all, after all, but made up of individuals and individual hopes and fears.

Rhodope did not answer. She found herself in the midst of something that dismayed and inspired her. It was as if she had stepped from a dusky night into the brilliant light of many lamps, and was half blinded by the illumination. They were almost at the corner of the street where the Needhams lived. She longed to be safely there, but she felt that, after all, here was protection; but, as the moments of "uncertain glory" passed, she was again perplexed, buffeted, and alone. She turned to Medcott, and her eyes were full of tears. For the first time in her life she was thoroughly unnerved.

"I cannot forget it," she said. "No, I can never forget it. But it is not like anything I have ever known. I want to be alone and to think. Oh!" she exclaimed, with a quick sigh of longing, "I want to be at home, where it is quiet, and where the nights are dark, and the stars shine, and then I shall know what to say."

She was outwardly calm, strong, serene, save for the unshed tears, but her sweet peace was disturbed. It had felt the shock of something stronger than death.

"You shall answer me when, how, and where you will," said Medcott quietly, with the generosity of strength. "But I wanted you to know that I can speak the truth."

The evenness of his tone brought back her usual repose. She felt no longer the wish to hurry away. His presence ceased to be disturbing—it held again its old assurance of delight. They walked on up the holiday street, the air always full of the sound and life of wayfaring humanity. Drivers of heavy drays blundered out of the way. The stages followed their serpentine course with an odd sort of regularity. Picturesque children, from the long-trousered

17

but diminutive sailor-boy to the faltering confidence of broad-hatted and voluminous-skirted two-year-old girls, enlivened the sidewalk. Carriages, with every variety of occupant, and footmen of British haughtiness, rolled swiftly up and down. All were but the common sights and sounds of a city thoroughfare, but to Rhodope that portion of the avenue, measured by a few blocks, was ever filled with a certain radiance that lifted it above the commonplace. There was a freedom in the wind which blew in little eddying whirls at the corners of the cross streets, tossing the feathers and ribbons of the women, that she had missed before.

He had said she need not answer him; for the present she would not even think nor reason. A man crossed the street towards them, threading his way with careless alertness through the stream of carriages. It was Needham. It was an unusual hour for him to be up-town, but he offered no explanation as he greeted them. He had come up as if he had something special to communicate, but as he turned and walked at Rhodope's side he seemed rather to be waiting for them to speak. His manner was at once absent and nervously alive to certain impressions, as it had been often of late. It was not easy for any one of them to maintain the conversation. Rhodope was too strongly moved to talk quietly of ordinary things. Medcott was resolved that she should not a second time accuse him of denying the situation, by putting its meaning lightly aside. Needham himself was blind to anything unusual in their attitude, and frowned abstractedly at men and things, save when he roused himself to reply to some half-diffident speech of Rhodope's. But in spite of his abstraction, his influence was potent. He brought Rhodope back to the contradictions and doubts of her disturbed existence, to what she had been fain to believe were not, after all, the eternal verities, and had restored to them their apparent immutability.

"Good-by—for a few hours," said Medcott in a low tone, as he held her hand in a strong grasp at the Needhams' door, which Charlie was opening with a latch-key.

"Good-by," answered Rhodope a little tremulously and with troubled eyes.

"She does not understand—she has no far-away conception of what it means," Medcott said to himself, as he looked back at her as she followed Needham in, "but she knows—we have one secret—she knows!" It was almost enough for the moment, this sense of understanding, and he was almost untroubled by the half-apprehensive recollection that "by and by is easily said."

CHAPTER XX

"A sad tale best for winter."

"Those compensations that, like angels of justice, pay every debt."

ROXANA DUST had led a monotonously cheerful life hitherto. Possibly the good temper that had become identified with her personality was more nearly the result of circumstances than of actual disposition—peradventure not nature's work, but fortune's. At least, it had been fostered rather than tested by the various experiences through which she had passed. Child of good-humored parents, she had grown up in the midst of good-humored brothers and sisters, and had married the most good-humored of men. It would seem that having arrived at an age when the trials of life are apt to be looked back upon rather than anticipated, she might feel that she had escaped the danger of deterioration. But the laws of compensation were not inoperative, and with becoming humility she began to distrust her own ability to support their action.

"Land sakes alive!" she remarked one February noon to Mrs. Clock, an old and valued friend, who had come over to know if she would lend her some saleratus. "They useter say I was easy as 'n old shoe, but as I says to father, take and put pebbles and prickles inter even 'n *old* shoe, and it ain't a-goin' to be a sight easier 'n a new one. Goodness knows I ain't begrudgin' Matilda anythin', and I wouldn't say as much to anybody else as I'm sayin' to you, but I do say that now and then I'm most put about."

"Isr'el says," remarked Mrs. Clock, who was by nature a conservative and seldom gave utterance to decided sentiments on her own undivided responsibility, "that Matilda's one of them women as is bound to ketch holt of a kittle spout first and then git mad because she can't pour out o' the handle."

"Well," answered Roxana, "I dono but what there's conside'ble truth in that."

Miss Matilda Spore having come for a week's visit, had been detained by lumbago under the Dust roof for the better part of a month. She had shut up her own house, Tim was away nearly all the time now, and there was really nothing to interfere, practically, with an arrangement so productive of social advantages.

Notwithstanding Roxana's depression resulting from this particular manifestation of hospitality, it was not precisely even now what the journalistic spirit of our great country has agreed to call a "walk over" for Miss Spore. Elizabeth French was also a member of the Dust household, and from their first encounter Elizabeth had arrayed her forces, regular and irregular, against the encroachments of Matilda Spore. And although Elizabeth French had lost much of the gay, glowing audacity that had distinguished her when she first visited the valley, she was by no means a foe over whom one could afford to triumph without fear of reprisals.

"You hadn't ought to take it so much to heart," admonished Tim on his last visit, when he had been invited to take dinner at the Dust's. "You'd ought to take a kind o' interest in what Aunt Matilda'll *find* to say."

Elizabeth was mixing a Sally Lunn after one of Mrs. Dust's generous recipes, for the early supper. She gave the spoon a little vicious twist.

"It isn't interesting any longer," she exclaimed. "She's

picked flaws ever since she came. I don't take it to heart,
but Aunt Roxana"—Elizabeth had turned the near friendship into a relationship—"will keep trying to please her.
You might as well try to please a—"

"A hornet," supplemented Tim, as Elizabeth hesitated,
"just eggzactly. You'd hardly believe it," he went on
modestly, "but she ain't pleased with me." Elizabeth
laughed.

"After all, you get along with her better than anybody
else," she said.

"That's because she don't ever faze me," he went on
with the conscious power of a Talleyrand. "She gets up
early the mornings I'm home, so's to have more time to
find fault. Before night comes she's clean tuckered out
and I'm fresh as a daisy. I don't let her wear on
me."

"I suppose that's the best way," admitted Elizabeth.
"But I wonder what'll be the matter with this Sally Lunn.
I s'pose it'll be too brown or not brown enough."

"I'll bet you a fourth piece"—Tim was a born speculator
—"that there'll be something the matter with it that you
never thought of."

"Well, if it's too many eggs, I've thought of that."

"All right, check it off."

"And if there aren't enough eggs, I've thought of
that."

"Go ahead."

"And if we'd had it yesterday it would 'a' been better."

"Three of 'em."

"And if it tastes of baking-powder."

"Yare."

"And if you can't raise it without baking-powder."

"I tell you, you know Aunt Matilda," chuckled Tim.
"Is that all?"

" And she likes Sally Lunn better for breakfast than tea."

" That's six.   Do you take me up ?"

" Well, you wait till it comes out of the oven," said Elizabeth with the wisdom born of experience, " and I'll tell you."

When the Sally Lunn did come out of the oven it was such a beautiful brown and so irreproachably light that Elizabeth, moved by a not unnatural pride in her own handiwork, was filled with the confidence of a still buoyant nature, and whispered to Tim as supper was ready,

" I'll bet you my fourth piece."

Tim waited with an air that would not have disgraced the knowledge of a Mephistopheles concerning the short-comings of humanity. Miss Spore, in a chair cushioned to suit her infirmities, was pushed to the table.

" You was sayin' the other day," said good-natured Roxana, " that you liked Sally Lunn, and so I had Elizabeth make one. Give Elizabeth my receipts and she can do every bit as well as I can." This was high praise, and Elizabeth looked gratified.

" Some uses receipts," said Miss Spore in discriminating criticism, " some cooks just as well without 'em."

" Wal, I d'ruther have one of mother's receipts," said Ashur, who was fond of Elizabeth, " than King Solomon's guessin' at it."

The Sally Lunn was cut, and Tim had gotten well into his second piece, but with still unshaken confidence, and the blow had not yet fallen. Elizabeth was beginning to feel triumphant.

" Well, now this is real good, Elizabeth," said Roxana.

" This was baked in a shaller pan, warn't it ?" asked Miss Spore.

" Yes," replied Elizabeth, avoiding Tim's eye with deliberate intention.

"I'd used the deep ones for somethin' else," and Roxana grew somewhat depressed, "and I said to Elizabeth I guessed these was just as good."

"And I don't see but what they be," said Ashur.

"I thought 'twas baked in a *shaller* pan," went on Miss Matilda ruthlessly. "It always has a different taste to me baked in a shaller pan. It ain't as good. I've known a good many folks as made Sally Lunns," she went on thoughtfully, "and I never knew any of the partickler ones to bake in shaller pans."

"I guess, Elizabeth," said Tim, with studied restraint, "you may as well give me that piece. You've had three."

It was some weeks since the incident, but Elizabeth was thinking of Tim and his bet this evening, as she brushed up the kitchen after another supper. It had been a more trying meal than usual. The continued presence of Miss Spore was beginning to reconcile Elizabeth to the prospect of her own early departure. What if, in leaving the valley, she left behind her all that could have made her life a happy one—still she would be taken away from this constant heart-wearying querulousness and fault-finding, which she resented more on account of her host and hostess than on her own. Her father and mother were coming after her some time during this week, and she would go away with them and—yes, she was glad of it! Only those who under the pressure of a real sorrow or a deep regret have been obliged also to submit to the petty injustice of little daily unreasoning plaints and innuendos can appreciate Elizabeth's state of mind. Since the night of the snow-shoeing party she had exchanged little more than a word with Jib Trent; her own dignity, after his final repulse, as well as his attitude, had insured that. But she still loved him. His contemptuous indifference had accomplished what his continued devotion would have failed to do—it had fettered her waywardness with the chains of unsatisfied longing. Now that the final sting of his cruel words had passed away she was even ready to pardon them and to assume and bear the chief burden of the blame. If only she might hear him say that he loved her! With the splendid recklessness of her youth she thought that were that granted she would demand of life nothing more!

And it had been an unusually trying evening meal. Elizabeth had made another Sally Lunn, which had recalled Tim and his ribaldry. Mindful of its former shortcomings, she had baked it in a deep cake-pan, and had been rewarded by the suggestion that if it had been baked in a shaller pan it would have been crustier, and most folks liked 'em crustier. Evidently Miss Matilda wished it understood that she belonged to this class.

There had been one passage-at-arms which would have gratified Tim with a single-minded gratification impossible to overestimate, and which had brought even to Elizabeth's wounded spirit a slight uplifting. It was anent a certain jam that had graced the board.

"No, I won't take any more, thank you," Miss Spore had said, with a tinge of reproof. "It's currant, ain't it?—clear currant."

"Yes," said Mrs. Dust; "ain't it good? It ain't tetched anyway, is it?"

"Well," replied Miss Spore, with an effort to be indulgent, "it ain't as good as what has rosberries in. I always eat twice of that. Currant jam without rosberries ain't ever just the thing to my taste."

Elizabeth held her peace religiously until the fiat had gone forth.

"Aunt Roxana," she said, with an innocence worthy of better things, "I meant to tell you, when you sent me for a glass of currant, I went in the dark and brought a glass of currant and raspberry instead.   I didn't see it until it was opened.   This, Miss Matilda," she added kindly, "is currant and raspberry."

Ashur laid down his knife and winked at Elizabeth.   It was his usual way of expressing his appreciation of a crisis. There was an instant's silence while Miss Spore fell back upon her reserves.

"Medder rosberries, ain't they, Roxana?" she inquired, ignoring Elizabeth and her ill-advised supporter Ashur. "Grew in the west medder, didn't they?   In that big patch of bushes?"

"Well, I dono but what they did," admitted Mrs. Dust.

"I thought they grew there.   Them medder rosberries never had the real rosberry flavor—I could 'a' told you that."

"Wal, Miss Matilda," observed Ashur, without affectation, "I guess 'bout the only kind of rosberries that'll suit you is those as grows in kingdom come."

Miss Matilda had triumphed, to be sure.   Elizabeth had found Mr. Dust's reflection appropriate but inadequate, and she was too depressed to retaliate further, though after all she had a certain glow of success in driving her from her first position.   But even this had faded as she seated herself at the little kitchen window, and, resting her chin in her hand, looked out with a sudden, passionate longing that the peace of the scene might enter into her soul and make it still.   The pangs of unrequited love which are so rapidly losing their early simplicity, and threatening to become archaic, were making of ungoverned, capricious Elizabeth a rebellious, heavy-hearted woman.   The days were growing longer, and it was not yet quite dark.   The sun had set, and left a clear, pale gold above the hills.   Against this the trees stood straight, motionless, and dark.   They were still far from the full leafage of summer and from even the delicate tracery of the budding leaves of early spring, but neverthe-less there was an undefinable suggestion of something that was not all of winter in their clear outline. A small moon burned palely in the east. Spring was not here; she was still afar off, but the trees on the luminous mountain-tops could catch a glimpse of her approach.

But to Elizabeth the spring brought no promise of re-newed hopes and blossoming happiness. It meant to her but that absence should be added to despair—to what she called despair, for she did not yet know how hard hope is to kill, and that, so long as she was near Jib Trent, she would have an unrecognized hope of reconciliation. Let them come and take her away! Let the new birth of spring come and be but the beginning of a greater weariness!

There was the sound of steps upon the snow outside. Elizabeth turned her gaze from the hill-tops to the path that led to the kitchen door, and saw Jib coming towards her. Instinctively she sprang to her feet to hasten to open the door—it was as if the golden light behind the moun-tains suddenly pulsed with a wave of deeper radiance. Then she paused in sudden dread. Whether it was that something in his face, as he looked up and saw her at the window, warned her; whether it was that a realization of the strangeness of his coming thus alone, at dusk, when he had not trodden that path in long, long weeks, startled her into a presentiment of evil—whether it was one of these things, or something more subtle than either, she was over-whelmed for an instant. Recovering herself, she went on and opened the door, standing silently, framed in the low doorway, while he drew nearer, silent too, his eyes on hers. In them was no hesitation, no contempt, no reproof. Neither was there questioning, petition, or forgiveness—nothing but an unutterable tenderness. As Elizabeth looked into them, the peace, for which she had looked towards the sunset in

vain, flooded her soul. All at once she was quiet and at
rest; there was to be no misunderstanding any more, one
look at Jib's face had told her that. But there was something to come after? Had this sudden joy come to her
without explanation, without reckoning — a visitation of
God? A visitation of God—the quaint phrase stayed in
her consciousness. She had heard it on Sunday evening.
Did it not mean pestilence, earthquake, and sudden death?
Were not these things for the most part called visitations of
God? Her happier, natural creed reasserted itself against
the associations of a gloomy one. No — whatever might
come after, whatever chastening was before her, this deep,
unalterable, enfolding love was the true visitation of God!

Jib took both the hands which she had instinctively extended to him, and led her inside the door. Then he drew
her into his arms.

"My darling," he said gently. His voice had a strange
huskiness, unlike its usual sweet, somewhat hesitating utterance. Moreover, the term of endearment was foreign to
his New England undemonstrativeness. "I am yours, and
I am all you have in the world." She raised her head from
his shoulder and looked up at him frightened. He forgot
even how hard it was to tell her. He thought only of her.

"There has been an accident," he said, his voice steady,
but infinitely gentle. "A bad railroad accident. The news
has just come to the valley. Your father and mother, Elizabeth, are among the killed."

Her head fell again on his breast, as a great darkness enveloped her. There was absolute silence for a moment,
and then she stood upright and drew away from him. He
let her go instantly, and she steadied herself a moment, her
hand on his arm, and then walked back to the window, which
looked out to the yellow light, now grown pale, but forth
from which stars were shining. Here she sank into a chair.

Jib watched her head fall on her hands, and then went towards the door leading into the sitting-room. Before reaching it he paused a moment.

"Elizabeth," said he, "I want you to remember that it was very sudden—there was no suffering." She did not answer, and he went on into the next room. The lamp was burning, but Mrs. Dust stood between it and Jib, throwing the doorway into shadow. She was engaged in lighting a candle for Miss Matilda, and Ashur had laid down the weekly journal to watch her success with the paper lamp-lighter she held over the lamp-chimney. No one of the three perceived Jib's entrance.

"Well," Miss Matilda was remarking impartially, "don't seem 's if you'd ever git it lighted."

"Wal, I calc'late even mother can't make paper burn afore it gits hot enough," said Ashur conciliatingly.

"That candlestick is the awk'ardest thing to hold I ever came across," went on Miss Matilda.

"It's your own candlestick," commented Roxana, with what threatened to become tartness under further provocation.

"Yes, it is," admitted Miss Spore, who had momentarily overlooked the fact, "and it's all dish."

"You was sayin' the other day you couldn't abide one of them narrer candlesticks that let the grease drop all over," said Mrs. Dust. She had lighted the paper twist, and was now struggling with the candle-wick. Jib still stood in the shadow. He dreaded to interrupt them—perhaps a more fitting moment might come.

"No more I can," said Miss Matilda, undisturbed. "Tim brought me that one last time he come home, and says I, 'Wal, it's big enough to set in the tabernacle.' 'Wal, now, Aunt Matilda,' says Tim, 'I thought you'd like this, 'cause it can't drip, and you said the old candlestick was always drippin'. That candlestick,' says he, 'couldn't drip, not if it *rained* spermacity.' 'Perhaps not,' says I "—Miss Matilda fell easily into narration, and to do her justice it was seldom devoid of a certain interest—"'perhaps not, but I never said that I wanted to carry round a candlestick like John the Baptist's head on a charger.' Them was the last words I said to Tim just as he was goin' off—"

Jib brushed his hand over his forehead and stepped forward.

"Miss Matilda," he said.

Roxana nearly dropped the candlestick.

"For the land's sake!" she exclaimed, turning around with the deliberation her size demanded, "I didn't hear you comin' in."

"Nobody heard him comin' in!" asserted Miss Matilda with the spitefulness naturally engendered by being startled. "It's my belief he didn't want us to."

"I guess Jib Trent ain't a burglar," said Ashur, with humorous intention. Then he paused. All of them were suddenly struck with the unnaturalness of his being in that house after so long an interval. With the unconscious directness of her simplicity, Roxana spoke.

"Where's Elizabeth?"

No one answered her. Jib had come forward into the light, and they saw his face. He was pale and his features were contracted. The exaltation of his care for Elizabeth had passed away, and he was confronted by the load he had undertaken to bear. He felt himself a messenger of death. Ashur rose with the slowness of hard-worked age from his wooden chair.

"For the Lord's sake, Jib," he said, "what has happened?"

Before he answered Miss Spore spoke.

"What'r' you lookin' at me that way for, Jib Trent?" she

demanded harshly, straightening herself in spite of her rheumatism.

"Elizabeth's father and mother have been killed on the railroad," he said with difficulty. Roxana gave a sudden cry and ran towards the kitchen.

"Poor child, poor child!" she sobbed.

At the door Jib's voice arrested her.

"And Tim," he said with a further effort.

"Wal, Tim—Tim *what?*" Matilda's voice was sharper than ever, though it trembled. "Why don't you say what you've got to say?"

"Tim was on the same train."

"And he's with 'em? With Marcella and that good-for-nothin' Nicholas?"

Miss Spore rose to her feet for the first time in weeks unaided.

"Matilda!" exclaimed Ashur, "don't call him that!—he's dead."

"You keep still, Ashur Dust," said Miss Spore contemptuously. It was as if her great fear brushed aside all the lesser moralities. "He's with 'em, I say—Tim is with 'em—helpin'?"

"Yes, he's with 'em," said Jib heavily, "but not helping—he's with 'em—wherever they are."

The young fellow was almost overborne with his own tidings. He was unused to such a vicarious weight of sorrow. Moreover, she was looking at him as though she held him accountable. At last she understood. She sank back into the chair again. Roxana had slipped out into the kitchen to Elizabeth.

"The last words I says to him," repeated Matilda Spore mechanically, "the last words I says to him—"

Jib, avoiding the room where his love sat hopeless and helpless—beyond even his help for the present—went towards the other outside door, and Ashur Dust, his trembling hand on his shoulder, followed him. They went out, closing the door after them, and spoke in low tones. Miss Spore sat there alone, facing her loneliness. It is given to no one of us to alienate our fellow-creatures, one by one, by our own wilfulness, counting, meanwhile, on some one affection as our right, and therefore inalienable.

The candle burned by her side in Tim's candlestick. It flickered in the draught of the open door, but did not go out. When Roxana came back into the room some time after, the little flame was still there, and Matilda Spore was tearlessly gazing at it. It was as if three strong lives had been snuffed out since it was lighted, and its feebleness still burned on unharmed and unresisting.

The night passed. Roxana spent most of it with Elizabeth. Her passionate, overwhelming grief she could understand and try to soothe, but the placidity of Roxana's nature, itself undisturbed by excess, was ill at ease in the presence of Matilda Spore's undemonstrative bitterness. She declined all suggestions of repose. No, she didn't want to go to bed; she'd set where she was. As Roxana moved about the room in a sorrowful, inconsequent way, preparing for the night, she was uneasily conscious of Miss Spore's scrutiny. She knew that her clumsiness—the clumsiness of preoccupation — was noticed. Grief seemed to have softened none of the asperity of the glance that followed her from the old arm-chair. At last, with a word or two of final remonstrance, coldly received, she took up her candle and went back to Elizabeth, leaving the lamp burning and the stove filled with wood.

"I guess," said Miss Matilda as Roxana reached the door—"I guess if Tim had 'a' held on he would 'a' been saved." Mrs. Dust waited, not knowing what to answer. There was a slight contraction of Miss Spore's throat.

"He was always a dretful heedless boy," she added. It
was the last protest against fate that she uttered. According to the habit of years, somebody must be found fault
with, but it was a feeble flash of the ruling passion, after all,
lacking the searing, irritating quality that she excelled in,
and as such was not without pathos.

It was a melancholy vigil, that of this lonely old woman
sitting alone in the familiar room, giving to its familiarity
an aspect of tragedy, in spite of the friendly lamp and the
nearly articulate stove. It is almost always a mistake when
it is asserted that an individual who is of a rough and indifferent behavior is one of a nature of deep tenderness
and unusual sensitiveness. "As much virtue as there is, so
much appears." Specially unsatisfactory are those people
who flatter themselves that for a rude and injurious daily
conduct they stand ready to atone at certain crises by unusual steadfastness and devotion. Our neighbor is not always lying by the road-side robbed and left for dead, when
he is in the greatest want of strengthening ministrations.
Moreover, "in times of trial," as Meredith says, "great natures alone are not at the mercy of their instincts." Ice
does not form in a warm neighborhood. Cold manners are
apt to be the manifestation of a cold heart. Therefore
Miss Matilda Spore did not in all probability suffer from
actual grief at the loss of the only human being that was
bound to her by nearer ties than those of a common humanity, as deeply as might have a more loving woman.
But there were added pangs of defeat, rebellion, perhaps
remorse; and, after all, her lonely, unappealing, spare figure
represented a suffering of its own, lonelier and more tragic
in that it was unlovable. Tim had been all that belonged
to her, and though his claims had appeared to be chiefly
upon her faculties of rebuke, she had now and then acknowledged others. If an unusual softness of mood came

over her, it was Tim that had the benefit of it in added dainties of the table—that he might have now and then suffered from hunger less easily appeased, she had never cared. If she would not admit that he was worthy, she always denied that any of his companions were less unworthy. And there was a stout, robust, New England fibre in her nature that had stood her brother's child in good stead.

The lamp burned dim, the stove grew silent, she drew her shawl closer around her angular shoulders. She had slept, though she did not know it—she looked out towards the grayness of the dawn and remembered that Tim was dead.

Early in the morning, Jib, in his sleigh, drove up to the door to take Elizabeth over to North Lanes, where her mother and father were lying. There had been no question from the first of Jib's right to take upon himself all of Elizabeth's burden that could be borne by another; the care and direction of most of the details had been left to him. There were no conventionalities to be infringed, no heedless speculation concerning their relations to be dreaded. The whole population of the valley was shocked by the terrible accident, and in its shadow all lesser difficulties were forgotten, and Jib reassumed his place by Elizabeth's side without comment. Miss Spore, with the fortitude of her undemonstrativeness, insisted upon being wrapped up in shawls and buffalo robes and also driven over. That she suffered intense pain weighed not a straw in the balance with her invincible will. Ashur took his seat in the front of the lumbering sleigh and drove the two women down the sharp descent from the farm-house, while Jib and Elizabeth went fleetly on before. Denver Trent had expected to accompany them, but the old man was suffering from increased lameness, easily contracted in his exposed life and less easily thrown off each year of his advancing years, and Jib had peremptorily forbidden it. Jib was so rarely peremptory that Denver Trent had yielded. The cold, crisp air, the unblinking sunlight, seemed but to increase the sadness of the long drive. Elizabeth and Jib scarcely spoke for mile after mile. There was no room in her heart for anything but passionate sorrow. It was not until long after that she knew what his presence and constant care had saved her from. If she had been called upon to sustain this terrible blow in the unrelieved loneliness that she had felt closing about her, as she stood at the window looking towards the darkening hills, if she had not felt unconsciously but keenly the strength of another love close at hand, it seemed to her, later, that she should have died.

As they drew near the little town of North Lanes, Jib said,

"Will you go now, Elizabeth, or wait for the others?"

"I will go now," she said.

As they passed swiftly through the crooked streets a wave of remembrance rushed over them both. They were the same streets through which Elizabeth had driven her ponies in the audacity of beauty and skill, and where Jib had first caught sight of the vision that should be to him forever the glory and the dream. Poor little Elizabeth! From so dazzling a pageant to so sad an errand! One year had held for her what a long life finds enough to compass—triumph, love, and sorrow.

Jib did not follow her into the house whither she was led with the kindness and sympathy which strangers do not withhold when it is needed. He drove away and learned about the accident. It had not been one of those railroad horrors which fill a column of the daily papers with heart-rending descriptions and a terrible list of the killed and wounded. Only five people had been killed and only one or two others badly hurt. The car in which had been Nicholas French and his wife was the only one that had suffered. Officials were going quickly hither and thither. The business of the road must go on, the obstruction of the wreck was being removed as quickly as possible, but a heavy curtain of gloom was over all the little community. The accident had occurred a mile or two from the town. It was as if Death had come visibly among them.

"Where is Tim?" asked Jib, his voice unsteady.

"The newsboy? He is over there," answered a brakeman whom he addressed. "They think he must have been thrown from the platform; he wasn't in the car. He was a plucky little feller," he added, with the roughness of unaccustomed sympathy—"all hands liked him." To this man it was a serious accident and solemnizing, but it was not the awful catastrophe that it was to the less experienced dwellers in North Lanes. This sturdy brakeman, who had seen death before, near at hand, and had been in more terrible scenes than this, perhaps would have been satisfied to expect some such eulogy himself some time—"All hands liked him." At the door Jib met Miss Spore and Roxana, and they entered together. Tim lay in the best room of one of the neighboring houses. Possibly the scene never lost for Miss Matilda an underlying suggestion of satisfaction that the best room of a not unimportant neighbor, and one keenly alive to the sacredness of a best room, had been freely offered on this occasion. There was nothing distressing in the sight. It was so unusual to see Tim absolutely still— that was perhaps the most startling thing at first. The look of precocious knowledge had vanished from his face, leaving a childishness that was sweeter. His cap, that gold-laced cap, the source of so much innocent pride, which had marked such official distinction, lay beside him, battered and soiled, upon the floor. Miss Matilda pointed to it, and Jib picked it up and gave it to her, and she stood there holding it and looking down at its owner. Some one passed under the window; the voice, though not the words, penetrated the silence of the room with a touch of sacrilege. A boy who had always envied Tim's position looked in at the door, and, frightened, went quickly away. Roxana, crying quietly, came out with Jib and closed the door, leaving Miss Spore within. In the outer room the wife of the not unimportant neighbor, with sympathy unclouded by any sense of strangeness in the circumstances, gave them some things that had been taken from his pockets. Among the rest—the usual preparations for impossible emergencies germane to a boy's pocket—was an envelope with a little money in it, addressed to his Aunt Matilda, a book bearing the inscription " For Jib Trent—the best yet," written in a round, school-boy hand, evidently for the pleasure of making an inscription—an amusement which had no opportunity to grow stale in Tim's life—rather than as an actual aid to recollection. There was also a note to a brother official— the news agent whose duty it was to conduct the business on alternate days; it ran as follows:

" DEAR FRIEND,—Miss Rhodope Trent will be coming on the 78 along about next week. If I ain't on the 78 you look after her. You've seen her with me at the Stashun. She's the nicest girl Lady there is, but she ain't much on the travell. You watch out for her, Sid, and don't you forget it. Yours truly, TIMOTHY SPORE.
"(News Agent.)"

Not so many, after all, have gone to their last account with more to the credit side in the way of unselfish thought for others than Timothy Spore, News Agent.

CHAPTER XXI

" But he is not your lover after all—it was not you he looked at !"

" A woman of the world—
—if she loves at last,
Her love's a readjustment of self-love,
No more, a need felt of another's use
To her one advantage."

MEDCOTT rose from his easel with a sigh of impatience.

" It's no use," he said, " I've been trying to think it's the light, but it isn't; it is my hand that is the trouble—or my brain. I haven't been able to paint for a week past. It is ' out of me, out of me,' like poor Andrea, this afternoon."

" Your mind is ill at ease," remarked Davenant sententiously.

" I'm afraid she thinks I'm a dilettante sort of fellow," said Medcott abruptly. " With her admiration for being and doing, that would be fatal."

" If she thinks so—and I don't believe she does—it is because of her ignorance. There are enough people to enlighten her."

" Oh, it isn't that—" and he paused.

" It is only that you think it would seem more like real work to her if you—well, followed the plough. Now, I don't believe she has any idea of its being your duty to follow the plough, or would like you better if you did. Probably she has before this ascertained that even those who are habitually engaged in following the plough are not thereby rendered entirely superior to human frailty."

Davenant was talking on in his lazy fashion, that seemed to have no application other than one of general philosophical interest. Perhaps he was getting a little tired of the subject. Medcott laughed.

"How do you like this thing yourself?" he asked.

He had reseated himself at the easel, notwithstanding his dissatisfaction.

"I like it," answered Davenant. "I don't know anything about technique, but I know a great deal about sentiment—I like it." He did not move from his easy-chair and walk wisely about for different coigns of vantage, but he spoke positively.

"I have hopes of it myself," said Medcott, and he painted in silence for a few moments. It was a small picture, a bit of moonlit landscape—a deeply-shadowed lane with a profusion of flowering shrubs near two figures, a man's and a woman's, leaning on a stone wall, all suggestive of youth, summer, emotion—and off to the left a little graveyard, one or two of the headstones shining palely in the moonlight. He called it "The happier, they." It had been suggested by Browning's "De Gustibus":

> "Hark! those two in the hazel coppice—
> A boy and a girl if the good fates please—
> Making love, say—
> The happier they!
> Draw yourself up from the light of the moon,
> And let them pass, as they will, too soon,
> With the beanflower's boon,
> And the blackbird's tune,
> And May, and June!"

"I wonder if Charlie Needham is going to the devil," speculated Davenant in a tone of unemotional inquiry.

"Not faster than a good many other people, I guess—by freight, perhaps."

"I don't know," went on Tom, watching the smoke of

his cigarette. "I think it's getting almost too late to whistle down brakes—to carry out your unworthy metaphor."

"What makes you think so?" and Medcott paused an instant to face his companion.

"Oh, one thing and another," said Tom carelessly.

"I'm sorry if it's so. Charlie Needham has the makings of a good sort of fellow—what he needs is a balance-wheel."

"What might you consider a balance-wheel?" inquired Davenant. "We all have our little ideas. The student of human nature likes a crack at them all."

"Enthusiasm for the beautiful," answered Medcott promptly, "whether in character, art, nature, morals, or purpose. Something besides a critical attitude towards life."

"Not an altogether original conception," commented Davenant, "but 'twill serve."

"If a man hasn't that," continued the other, "he's in a fair way not to have anything. I came across a remark of Holmes to that effect the other day. He says—wait a minute"—and he rose and picked up a book from the table—"he says, 'You remain an idealist—I sometimes think it is the only absolute line of division between men—that which separates the men who hug the actual from those who stretch their arms to embrace the possible. There is no profit in discussing any living question with men who have no sentiments—we don't talk music to those who have no ear.' There it is for you! I say, Charlie Needham doesn't admire anything he can't do or be himself—that is what is the matter with him—and there is no salvation in—*Kleinigkeiten.*"

"That's true enough," assented Davenant. Medcott went back a second time to his painting. "And I never thought you much of an analyst either. You are too fond of the abstract."

"I suppose there is an occasional point where the abstract touches human nature," scoffed Medcott. "Don't be an ass." •

This gentle admonition drew a smile of toleration from Davenant and the further concession of silence.

"I wonder why she won't let me see her," exclaimed Medcott suddenly.

"Austin," said Davenant gently, "you are getting to be a bore. When you have anything to tell me about Miss Trent, I shall be glad to listen," he went on generously, "but this inanity of speculation, guesswork, and over-statement is rapidly alienating my affections."

"I'm sure it is intentional," asserted Medcott without the slightest regard for his guest's remonstrance. "I've been trying to see her for ten days."

"Is that all?" sighed Davenant.

"I can't get a word with her. I saw Mrs. Needham once, and she told me Miss Trent was out."

"I wonder if she was."

"Then I wrote to her, and I haven't heard a word. There is something going on behind the scenes—there must be."

"It is my firm knowledge and belief," declared Davenant, "that man wants but little here below, but wants that little long before he gets it. Don't consider yourself exempt from the common lot."

"I don't!" replied Medcott, starting up. "But I mean that I shall learn whether I am to get it at all from the lips of one person only, and that a league of evil spirits, however clothed upon in the flesh, is not going to turn me off! I know why you are smiling—you are thinking of my doubts and hesitations. Well, they are over! I've never prided myself on being consistent."

"I have always felt that the reason that consistency is termed a jewel," considered Davenant, "is that it is sometimes useful for ornamental purposes, and costs a good deal more than much more valuable things."

"I wish you wouldn't be always getting your confounded note-book off on me," objected Medcott.

"I've pretty nearly given up my note-book," answered Davenant with a touch of seriousness. "Life has grown too interesting—I need all my aphorisms for daily use."

Medcott looked at him in some surprise as he laid aside his palette and brushes. He was not sure that he understood him.

"Come out for a walk," he said. "It's too dark to work any longer. It really is the light this time."

"What you want," said Davenant, as they turned into the street, now darkening, very like the stage, as a preliminary to a future blaze of electric light—"what you want just now is a female relative. It's a great pity that your mother is on the other side; she would know just what to do. Where's Mrs. Harrow?"

"Mrs. Harrow would not understand," said Medcott briefly. "The best of women will not sometimes."

Davenant nodded. Mrs. Harrow was a devoted friend of Medcott, but he suspected her of having views of her own for his future.

"A man is more or less wax in the hands of a woman like Florence Needham," he said. "A clever woman is a particularly inflexible kind of granite."

"I shall not be wax in the hands of Mrs. Needham," said Medcott.

Davenant's smile contained a suggestion of applause.

"But I wish, too, that my mother were here," went on Medcott. "I'd like her to see Miss Trent. Even Bertha might be of use."

Davenant shared the misgiving indicated by the form of her brother's reference to Bertha, but, notwithstanding, he thought, too, that Bertha might be of use. He knew Medcott's family as he knew his own—of whom only his father was left for him to know now.

"Bertha is very apt to come around to doing the right thing," remarked Medcott, smiling. "My mother does the right thing at first, because it's polite, but Bertha has to work up to it by following the path of duty which, ten to one, starts in the opposite direction, but, to her surprise, fetches up at the same place with the conventionally courteous."

"Bertha would like Miss Trent."

"Yes, but Miss Trent would seem to her singular. People often seem singular to Bertha. What a comment it is on our civilization that she should seem singular to a good woman like my sister!" he exclaimed. "We are so overlaid with affectations that we suspect truth of being in masquerade. Because Rhodope is absolutely direct, single-minded, unaffected, and unspoiled, she strikes everybody as unusual."

"Yes, yes," said Davenant, a little hurriedly. "But most things are comments on our civilization, you know. One runs across them everywhere."

Medcott laughed. "All right, Tom," he said, "I won't tell you anything more about Miss Trent till I have something to say."

When Davenant left Medcott he had not told him that he was going to dine with Florence Needham that evening, but he resolved that he would then make some effort to discover the cause of the silence that Rhodope seemed determined to maintain between herself and her lover. Ten days is a short interval in the complex lives of those who dwell in cities, but it is a long time to elapse between such words as Medcott had spoken and a reply. Knowing Florence as he did, Davenant felt that this interval might

not be entirely due to a natural sequence of events. It
was a fact that he had neglected his note-book; that is,
that he had ceased to be the philosophic observer, always
on the watch for material, and had become involved in the
underlying emotions of these three or four lives to an
extent he had not anticipated. Scientific research is in
danger of losing its quality of dispassionateness when it
is devoted to the development of human thought and
feeling.

As Davenant took a car going up-town, he thought of
Medcott's apprehensions. He understood perfectly why he
feared that, to Rhodope, art would not appear a serious aim
in life.

"He thinks that to her practical and yet ideal concep-
tions," he said to himself, "he will seem to belong to the
category of the decorators of paper-knives, a calling that
appeals neither to the practical, nor satisfactorily to the
ideal."

Yet Medcott was an unusually hard worker. He had all
the fine contempt of an earnest laborer for those who seek
a trifling success in what is but an amusing one's self with
art. He believed that nothing but the taking of infinite
pains brought assured results, and that a serene and high
purpose were inseparable from a worthy devotion to the
production of the best. Altogether, he was very far from a
dilettante. He would not have been anything but dissatisfied with the reputation of a person of excellent taste, and
he had won much more already. Success was within his
grasp, and only those who have worked thus realize how
rarely such success is the result of accident. Davenant
was so interested in reflecting on this that, although the
car was crowded, and while he stood, the conductor, on his
wedging way through the car—whose brute force really
should have had its usual accompaniments of half-backs

and rushers—planted his elbow firmly in the small of his back, thus steadying himself while he made change, and although, after he had acquired the seventh part of a seat, the large man next him persistently sought for small coins in a rear pocket, thus effectually pinning his face flat against the pane—though these things happened, he bestowed upon them an attention even more cursory than they usually receive.

He had been told that there were to be no other guests, but he was surprised that he did not see Rhodope. When dinner was announced, and they went to the table without her, Florence somewhat negligently explained that she had been invited to spend a few days with Edwina Screed, and would remain with her until the day after the next—as she was not going to the Rimmon dinner, she would stay until it was over.

"Great fuss people are making over that Englishman," said Charlie.

"Oh, well, he is rather a good specimen, after all. For Heaven's sake, if people make a fuss over a reputable Englishman, Needham, give 'em your blessing. This man really has enlightened instincts, and has shown it in Parliament."

"Yes, that's just it, in Parliament—the House of Lords. It isn't on account of his enlightened instincts they ask him to dinner."

"I'm sure Mrs. Rimmon would never give a dinner for anybody that is not worth knowing," observed Mrs. Needham decidedly. We have seen that there were some subjects that Florence would never admit were not placed outside the realm of legitimate criticism. There was a pause as the fish was removed.

"Are you going to Mrs. Rimmon's dinner?" asked Florence suddenly.

"Yes," answered Davenant carelessly. "I met some of Lord Ayforth's people abroad, and they let me know he was here, so I've seen something of him."

Florence crumbled her bread during a moment of absence of mind. This was the sort of thing that Tom Davenant was falling into all the time. She was exceedingly agreeable during the rest of the dinner. Needham had an engagement almost immediately after it, as usual, and Davenant perceived that the *tête-à-tête* that followed had not been unexpected.

Florence sat in one of the low-cushioned drawing-room chairs, beneath a tall lamp, whose shade spiritualized her beauty with its soft coloring. Davenant, not far from her, leaned against the corner of a heavy screen, his thin, almost delicate face, with its frequent rather melancholy smile, turned towards the open fire. With his air of perfect breeding, and apparent indifference to any effect he might produce, his attractive cynicism and his real cleverness, he represented a great deal to Florence Needham. She was quick enough herself to admire his talent, but she never dared to dwell on that too much, lest it should not be that, but a certain undefinable something else, that made him so admirable to the authorities.

"Have you seen Medcott lately?" he asked, turning his eyes from the fire to hers. Her face hardened instantly.

"No," she said; "he has been here, I believe—but we were out. Speaking of Medcott, did you see that little sketch of the Clock piazza? He gave it to me a month ago. There it is."

Davenant glanced in the direction indicated by her eyes.

"No," she said laughing, "you can't see it unless you stand up. It is on the other end of the shelf."

"Why should I rise to look at the Clock piazza?" objected Davenant. "I saw it for the better part of September most of the time. By what right am I turned out on the Clock piazza?" Nevertheless he rose, and crossed in front of the fire. By the side of the sketch was a letter. It was placed against an ornament of the chimney-piece in such a way that Davenant read the address on the envelope instantly and inevitably—" Miss Trent "—in Medcott's singular and unmistakable handwriting. Before he could take up the sketch Florence sprang to her feet and snatched the letter out of the way. The whole performance occupied scarcely a minute, but it was a minute that she would gladly have recalled. The next instant she stood with the letter in her hand, her invariable laugh on her lips, but conscious of her mistake, and Davenant, after one glance at her, was quietly examining the sketch.

" It is very good," he said. " I can almost see the griddle-cakes through the kitchen door. Dost remember those griddle-cakes ?"

Florence tossed the letter down on the table.

" Why don't you say I've behaved like an idiot, Tom ?" she said.

Davenant put the sketch back in its place.

" I never allow myself to get beyond implication of that sort," he said indifferently. " How do I know but that you might consider idiot actionable ?"

Florence laughed again. Laughter was her resource always in social difficulties.

" I don't know why I should have minded your seeing the letter," she said, rather inadequately.

" That is not the difficulty," he replied composedly. " It is that, if you had minded, you should have put the letter away before. I read the address unavoidably in the critical moment."

Florence seated herself with an effort to regain her former manner.

"But there really is no objection to your knowing that Medcott has written a note to Rhodope."

"And that you have been keeping it a week undelivered," he added quietly. He had made up his mind to interfere if the opportunity came in his way. He gauged pretty accurately his influence over Florence, and the fancy for testing it, not unusual in the philosophic temperament, was an additional reason for using it for the general good. She instantly recognized that evasion would be useless.

"Well," she said, defiantly.

"Well, what objection is there to my knowing that too? And why should you have fancied that there could be one?"

She came to a sudden decision, led to it by a variety of causes. In the first place, her flame of resentment towards Medcott sought an outlet; and her jealous dislike of Rhodope had become unbearable in silence; and the vexation of the whole situation was extreme. There is a certain relief in giving utterance to such a complication of feelings to a person thoroughly cognizant of all the circumstances and personalities concerned, even though this very knowledge makes the listener a disapproving one. Moreover, there were other more gratifying influences at work. She felt the intoxication of confidence to-night. She had reached an advantageous eminence in the social range. She was going to-morrow to dine with Mrs. Rimmon. Below her were the smiling but unimportant valleys of undefined but cheerful location; below her the slopes of precarious but rewarding effort; above her, a little nearer than ever before, gleamed the lofty, if somewhat icy and unresponsive, peaks of English society. This consciousness gave her an almost uncalculating recklessness. And in Davenant's presence there was always the stimulus of a sentimental past and an emotional present. She felt sure that she could sway Tom Davenant as it had been given to no other woman to sway him.

All her cleverness could not save her from this danger of personal vanity—that of overestimating the power which her beauty placed in her hands.

"And suppose all that you suspect is true?" she demanded, rising again and coming nearer him, her eyes on his. "Suppose that I have been keeping this letter from Rhodope, hoping that it may lead to misunderstanding? Suppose that I did succeed in preventing him from seeing her when he called? Suppose I would like to break off all communication between them? What of that?" Her voice rang with audacious defiance. She let the storm announce itself.

Davenant looked at her critically a few moments before he answered, contemplating his own attitude with an impulse of curiosity greater than that with which he regarded hers. Passionate, brilliant, confident as she was, suddenly she stood before him divested of the slight charm which, with cynical tolerance, he had yielded to her during these last months. And yet he was conscious, too, of a quick appreciation of the added interest that this flash of overmastering feeling lent her. It was the touch needed to lift her beauty above the trivial.

"If that is true, it will convince me that in moments of some excitement I have not overrated your capacities for evil," he answered at last, with the increased slowness of utterance he was apt to use on occasions which seemed to call for rapid speech.

"It is true. I would give a great deal," and she clenched her hands with an impulse that was half natural, half theatrical, "to keep them apart—to make mischief."

"You have very respectable gifts in that line," said Davenant appreciatively.

"I hate her," said Florence with a little stamp. "I tell you I hate her!"

"Oh, no, you don't, Florence. Hate is one of the strong emotions. You are not the sort of woman that hates."

His tone was rendered contemptuous by his feeling for the woman of whom she spoke, but what he said was true. There was lacking in all she said the dignity of a passionate hatred. Even an unusual stress of feeling scarcely lifted her above the commonplace of a pretty, capricious, jealous woman who resents the praise of a rival.

"Why shouldn't I hate her? She has come between me and so much. Last summer you were all so foolish about her, do you remember? And this winter—what has she done? She has made no friends. She has attracted no attention. She has been difficult—oh, difficult does not express it!"

Florence did not realize, in the suddenness of this outbreak, how she was exploiting her own motives. Davenant smiled as he listened.

"You may laugh, but she has been a burden—a positive burden, I tell you! Even Charlie thinks her superior to me—as if I cared for that!" and she laughed—"but that is what the people think who have liked her—that she is superior! Do you suppose I asked her here to be my superior? They have thought her that—but she has made no sensation. Unless you consider that Austin Medcott is securely entrapped—that—"

"That will do, Florence," said Davenant suddenly, and she paused. "You have a certain vivacity of expression," he went on, "an ease in asserting and in contradicting yourself, with a general ardor of frankness that is pleasing—"

"Oh, how I hate you when you talk that way!" and Florence flung herself again into her low chair.

Just how much she was acting, how far she was natural, he hardly knew. Her anger was real, her expression of it, though not studied, was conscious.

"But there is a limit to what is pleasing even in that line, and I think you have reached it. Medcott has certainly fallen in love with Miss Trent"—she would have interrupted him, she was so unwilling to hear him say it, but he would not be interrupted—"but you know as well as I do that it has been singularly without provocation beyond that perennial and legitimate provocation of beauty, nobility, sweetness, and truth."

She was silenced in spite of herself, but she was the more angry. She had hoped to carry him with her in the sweep of her indignation, and she had but driven him to array himself on the side of her rival.

"If he succeeds in winning her he will be fortunate beyond even his deserts."

"I'd like to have his mother and sister hear you say so!" she exclaimed.

"It is a pleasure that the future very likely has in store for you. In the meantime I insist that you cease your disinterested efforts to preserve his peace of mind intact." He came close and leaned over her chair. "I insist, Florence," he repeated.

She looked up at him defiantly, but her heart misgave her. She realized with a shock that whatever might be her power over him, his was stronger than ever over her. Unconsciously what he had grown to represent to her had added its increasing weight to the old domination, and even the strength of her attachment to Medcott dwindled beside her feeling towards this slight, pale, indifferent, half-contemptuous man.

"And suppose you do insist?" she said, angrily still. "Suppose that I prefer to win, if not the future gratitude of Austin Medcott himself, at least the present gratitude of his mother, sister, and other friends less blinded by prejudice than you are?" He did not answer her, but he regarded her more seriously than usual, while the lines of his mouth grew more determined.

"Think of it, Tom, for a moment!" she went on, sitting erect in her chair. "Just think one moment of the folly of it—the utter folly of it! That country-girl and a man like Austin Medcott—critical, artistic, oh—*finished*, everything that she is not!"

"We won't discuss it on general principles, but I want you to give up your present policy of obstruction."

"And if I do not?"

"If you do not, you will not do the least real harm— which ought to be a consideration to you—but you may cause some unhappiness."

Davenant felt truly that while Rhodope was here she would feel herself absolutely dependent upon Florence Needham's treatment of her, and that therefore Florence held a certain command of the situation which he and Medcott could neither of them disturb by any direct appeal to Rhodope. She looked him steadily in the face a moment, and then her eyes fell. If Davenant had wanted revenge for the pain she had made him suffer years ago, he might have found it then; but he had not cared for revenge. Neither was he a vain man, but he was not blind, and he perceived the working of his experiment.

"She shall have her letter to-morrow," she said with an attempt at sullenness. "I can't send it to her to-night."

"And she shall see Medcott if he comes?"

"I shall take no steps to prevent it."

Then there was silence. He saw that she was still angry, but she had yielded. With all the keenness of his perceptions, however, he could not tell just how much this yielding promised for the future. He went back and seated himself where he had been before he rose to look at the picture. He would take leave in a few moments, but he did not like to have the air of vanishing on the wave of triumph. Florence turned her head towards him, where it rested on the rich coloring of the chair. Her whole manner was changed, her voice was softer; she had laid aside her vexation.

"I should not think you would so misunderstand me," she said—"you, who once loved me."

Davenant was distinctly conscious of a wish that she had not said it, but he smiled with an entire absence of apparent disturbance.

"I don't think I ever thoroughly misunderstood you, Florence—I who once loved you."

Had she been a wiser woman that would have been enough.

"Yes, you have," she persisted.

"I wish I misunderstood her now," he thought. "Why will women never believe in a past?"—"What do you want me to say?" he asked aloud.

It was a question he was always asking her, and the transparency of its deference usually disconcerted her and made her petulant. To-night, in the new exaltation of her spirit, it stimulated her to a reply.

"I want you to say that you have forgiven everything, but not—forgotten everything." The relationship between a tear and her half-smile could easily be traced.

"I have forgiven everything long ago," he answered, "and I have forgotten—nothing."

He had obeyed her literally, but she was not satisfied.

"What have you remembered best?" she demanded with a pretty childishness.

"How pretty you were," he answered promptly. "But then I disclaim any credit for that, because I have been constantly reminded of it since."

As usual she could not withstand a compliment to her

beauty. Her smile this time was further from the line that divides pleasure from grief.

"What did you do after you went abroad?"

"You tempt me to be autobiographical, and I hate it."

He spoke honestly, but it is a question whether at another time he would have admitted that anybody ever hates to be autobiographical.

"That is what I want," she said.

"She will have it and she deserves it, but it seems particularly brutal just now," he said to himself, as he rose and stood by the table on which she leaned her half-bare arms, her chin in her hands, waiting for him to speak. She hardly knew what she expected. She had not recovered from her surprise at the revelation of his new power.

"I fell in love," he said briefly.

She let her hands fall one on the other and opened her eyes wide.

"With some one else!" she exclaimed.

"Would you have had me go on falling in love with you —you who preferred Charlie Needham?"

For the time all Florence's pique and disappointment were swallowed up in simple curiosity.

"And she—did she not care for you?" she asked.

Davenant's expression changed.

"Yes. She cared for me—and she died," he answered. There was a moment's silence. A lump of coal fell noisily apart in the heart of the fire.

"It is a long time ago," he went on quietly. "It has become a memory rather than a sorrow, perhaps. Rhodope Trent reminds me of her."

He was apparently perfectly unmoved. He would tell Florence Needham the fact since she asked for it, but he was not bound to show her anything beyond. With her natural selfishness she saw only its relation to herself.

Perhaps no more stinging blow could have been devised. Not only had he not been faithful to his first love, his second had resembled not her—but Rhodope Trent. With feminine intuition, she caught the realization of just what her subsequent power over Davenant had been, and how trifling it was. Later it would be obscured by jealousy, vanity, self - love—just now she saw it in a flash of revealing illumination. All the disappointment, the consciousness of what she had irrevocably lost so long ago, linked itself with one of his last utterances.

"And I—I preferred Charlie Needham," she repeated almost mechanically. This gave Davenant the opportunity he wished for.

"Yes," he said, "and you were wise enough. And as we have come round to Needham, let me say another thing —look out for him. He doesn't seem to be like himself lately."

"He is cross," she admitted absently.

" Perhaps he has some reason to be cross—he may be ill."

It was natural that she should follow his lead back again to the level of friendship. She was always quick to adapt her mood to his and find the reason afterwards. Moreover, it was a part of their singular relation. Florence was beginning to realize that, however he might wound her vanity, she could never be angry with Tom Davenant. She did not think of it, but she was made aware that so far as concerned these two, this power to wound and not be hated had passed forever from her hands into his.

" He talks about extravagance—fancy !—extravagance— to me ! As if I could live without extravagance !" and she laughed.

" There are people who do, I have understood." Her lightness irritated him into being didactic, for he knew something of Needham's state of mind.

"But they have not done what I have done," she said with a little toss of her head. "Charlie ought to be grateful to me."

He knew she was caught up into a vision of the Rimmon dinner.

"And he is, no doubt. So am I," and he held out his hand—"Good-by."

"Why are you grateful to me?" she asked, giving him hers.

"For what you have done," he said enigmatically. "And I expect you to do more," he added, smiling. "I expect you to save me from the approach of Mrs. Eunam to-morrow night. She will be there, and she continually spreads a net for my feet, and, having caught me, forces me to listen to recitations. They are from a book she is getting out, which she calls 'Extracts from Some of our Neglected Authors.' I have ascertained that it is made up exclusively from her own works. So is her sorrow turned into joy. Good-night."

Florence sat where he left her for some time. The evening's conversation, while it had perhaps gained for Rhodope some practical advantages—for it had shown Florence that Davenant was on the watch for unfriendliness, and would resent it, and she dreaded his resentment—had but increased the load of her offendings. The whole fabric that she had reared of his long devotion to her and his newly-awakened susceptibilities had fallen, leaving in its place a new image that was in the similitude of Rhodope Trent.

Davenant reached home late that night, having kept one or two other engagements after leaving Florence. Going to his desk, he picked up his neglected note-book, and wrote half a page:

"Melancholy Adventures of a Young Man who would

fain play Providence.   His Assumption of the Rôle.   His various Incapabilities.   His dreary Failure."

Such was the general statement, and he developed it somewhat further: "Who suggests to one woman to bring another woman and a mutual friend into more intimate relations.   Mistake No. 1, though maybe all for the best.   By judicious management of the circumstances makes one woman the deadly enemy of the only one he cares about.   Mistake No. 2.   Who eggs on the mutual friend into dangerous committals, and produces a great deal of misunderstanding.   Mistake No. 3, but not serious, because it would have happened anyway.   Who clinches the situation by diplomatizing, bullying, and instructing the woman he once loved through an assumption of rôles varying from that of Mephistopheles to that of the excellent Jane Taylor.   Mistake No. 4.   Gloomy reflections of the Young Man who would fain play Providence."

CHAPTER XXII

"No man has learned anything rightly until he knows that every day
is Doomsday."

> "'Faithless and faint of heart,' the voice returned,
> 'Thou seest no beauty save thou make it first;
> Man, Woman, Nature, each is but a glass
> Where the soul sees the image of herself,
> Visible echoes, offsprings of herself.'"

"Hardly know which way to turn. Guess you'd better
come along home.—UNCLE DENVER."

Such was the despatch that Rhodope read as she stood
by the window in the Screed house, with Edwina and
Helena both waiting with the undisguised curiosity per-
missible regarding other people's telegrams.

"Uncle Denver wants me at home," she said; "I hope
nothing has happened."

None of the sad news of the valley had been communi-
cated to Rhodope. Denver Trent, with his usual common-
sense, had insisted that if there was no call for her to come
home, and as she couldn't bring the dead to life, she
shouldn't be told and kep' awake nights, wonderin' if there
was anythin' she could do. "If there was anythin' tryin'
to human natur' it was wonderin' if you couldn't do somethin' when you was far away," thus had he enlarged upon
the subject, and he guessed "'twas more 'n likely Rhode 'd
find there was enough things in New York to worry about,
without worryin' 'bout the valley too."

Needham had read a notice of the accident in the daily

paper; but though he saw it was somewhere in that neighborhood, had not connected it with valley interests at the
moment, and the next moment it was forgotten. As for
Rhodope, she had not learned to regard the presence of
papers whose numerical strength so far exceeded that of
the valley supply, and Florence shared the prevalent feminine conviction that while newspapers were the natural
pabulum of man, a fact no more to be questioned than
other mysterious dispensations of Providence, and undoubtedly suited to his special needs, they were not worthy the
abiding attention of woman, wisely bestowed on more important interests.

"Oh, I don't believe so," said Edwina quickly. "You'll
have a letter perhaps to-morrow. That telegram doesn't
sound—well—immediate."

"That telegram," said Helena impressively—"that telegram settles it! I shall marry Uncle Denver."

Rhodope smiled. It had been Helena's custom for some
days to express admiration of Uncle Denver. Her professions before Walter Mevans and others in a similar situation were nothing less than wanton in their indifference to
possible misconstruction.

"No, you needn't look at me like that, Edwina, and I
don't care if Rhodope does from this moment devote herself to a serpentine policy of defeating my plans—I tell
you I shall marry Uncle Denver. Any man that will write
such a telegram as that, conveying to the remotest shade
of feeling what he means to say without a thought of expense—that man would be an ideal husband!"

"Is it very expensive?" asked Rhodope, somewhat surprised.

"Expensive!" exclaimed Helena. "I don't believe the
cattle-kings ever send a telegram of more than ten words."

"Oh, yes, they do," said Edwina, with the fine literalness

with which she opposed her sister's exaggerations. "There is the Associated Press—"

"The Associated Press is a corporation! We are taught in our nurseries that 'Thou shalt not' does not apply to corporations, only to individuals. No one," she repeated, "but a cattle-king and Uncle Denver would have sent that. I like a man when he is going to make an outlay to *make* an outlay. Do you suppose a man that sent that telegram would ever ask you what you did with the change of a thousand-dollar bill? Rhodope," she went on, having satisfied herself that her extraordinary inconsequence had left room only for a consideration of ways and means, "when will you wish to start?"

"Oh, to-morrow—to-morrow early."

"Then you shall be driven round to Mrs. Needham's this afternoon instead of to-morrow. It is too bad about your lonely evening, but it will give you time to pack and be ready to leave in the morning."

It was growing dark when Rhodope ran up the steps of the Needham house and rang the bell.

"Good-by," called Helena from the carriage-door. "Don't forget to tell Uncle Denver that I am coming up to marry him. I'm afraid it may slip your mind. Good-by."

The servant who admitted her said that Mrs. Needham was still out. He was not sure if Mr. Needham was at home, but he thought not. Miss Trent had not been expected that afternoon, as no one had known of a telegram except the servant who had received it at the door and sent it around to Miss Screed's on his own responsibility. He hoped he had done right. Quite right—and Rhodope went upstairs to her own room. There she began to make her arrangements for leaving, quickly, though not hurriedly, for she had the whole long evening before her. She occupied herself with a certain eagerness that she might not have too

much time to think. Notwithstanding Helena's nonsense
and Edwina's sensible representations, she could not help
being somewhat anxious concerning the motives of the telegram.

At last, all the preparations made that could be attended
to just then, she seated herself in the dusk before the fire
to wait until she should hear that Florence had come in.
She was tired, and the open fire made her think of that in
the living-room at home. Uncle Denver was probably sitting by it, thinking of how she would come on the morrow.
What was the cloud that perhaps hung over his spirit?
Surely Jib was there and a book with a frontispiece of horrors that but whetted the appetite for further disclosures,
and with which he was absorbed at the littered table—both
elbows amid the rest of the things that covered it in a confusion fostered by her absence. Now and then the lamp
smoked unnoticed, until Uncle Denver, becoming suddenly
conscious that something was wrong, roared at Jib, who in-
attentively, as though it were a thing little worth doing,
turned it down. The homeliness of the scene, its familiarity, its closeness to those who were her very own, whom she
loved and who loved her, the dear accustomedness of it,
came over her with that strength of longing that threatens
to be heartbreak, and she burst into tears. They were over
in a few moments, and she sank back in her chair again,
quieted by the happy knowledge that she should see it all
to-morrow. Her lips still drooped a little; the heavy masses
of her hair had fallen lower in her neck; she had been
paler of late, and her fatigue added to her pallor to-night.
She was far from the free, brave, strong, unsaddened dwell-
er in the forest she had seemed to Medcott that day so
long ago—that spirit of the woods. Instead, she was but a
woman whose beauty and strength could not save her from
doubt, perplexity, and sadness. As she waited she remem-

bered a book she wished to take away with her, and that
was in the library. As she rose to go and look for it, a
maid entered with lights.

Did Miss Trent know there was a letter for her in the
library?

"A letter!" exclaimed Rhodope, with a sudden surge of
color, invisible in the uncertain light, that showed how near
the surface was a supreme delight, in spite of her misgivings. Yes, it was in the library, she would fetch it. No,
Miss Trent was going there for a book; she would find
it for herself. The last gleams of day made the library
window a square of dim and clouded light visible in the
semi-darkness. The corners were in deep shadows, and
the tables and chairs were vague dangers in otherwise open
spaces. As Rhodope opened the door—its being closed was
a little unusual—and stood in the doorway a moment, she
was surprised at the darkness and wondered why there were
no lamps. Even the fire was out, and the room had a look
of desolation in consequence. She could dimly discern a
half-burned log in the grate, which was just opposite the
unsheltered window. She hesitated in doubt whether she
could find her book and her letter or not. Not till she decided that she could did she turn towards the clouded light
of the library window. She then saw against its coldly il-
luminated panes the outline of a man's figure. Vaguely
startled, in an instant she recognized it as Charlie Needham's, and perceived that he had not heard her enter. He
stood with his back towards her, apparently looking out, as
he had stood that morning when they had breakfasted together; she had hardly seen him since, and she had an odd
sensation that he had been standing so all that time. His
hands were not in his pockets now, however; one rested on
the window-sill, in the other he held something that she
did not see. She stood still, with a curious, strained sort

of attention. She had no impulse to speak; as far as she was conscious of thinking anything, she wondered what he could be looking at. The window did not open on the street, but on a little-used alleyway, beyond which was a high fence and a new building going up. It was an unfinished-looking place, and there was nothing to see there, now that the workmen had gone home. Suddenly Needham raised his right hand and paused again. Something gleamed in the dying light of the day—the silver mounting of a pistol. Rhodope no longer hesitated. With a swift, silent movement that seemed to place her at Charlie Needham's side with a single impulse of motion, she laid her hand on his arm, and with a strength for which he was, of course, entirely unprepared, brought his arm down, and while with a quick curse he turned towards her, before he could recover himself from the startling interruption she took the pistol from his loosened grasp.

"Rhodope!" he exclaimed in amazement. "I would not have said that to you," he added quickly, ashamed of his outbreak.

"No," she said, gravely regarding him, "I know that."

It was as if the trivial, conventional aspect of the incident were the more important; as if its lamentableness lay not so much in the fact that he was going to shoot himself, as in that he had been guilty of swearing in her presence. But this very triviality marked an important transition. He had returned instantaneously to normal conditions. Had he been still confronting death, not even the shock of this interruption would have led him into such impatience. There was barely light enough for them to see one another's faces, as each gazed with an intentness that sought to read the thought and purpose in the other's expression. He was pale as death, his eyes showing the nervous strain that had brought him to the wretchedness of this

resolve. Rhodope's were like stars in the excitement that
kept her quiet instead of agitating her. She looked the
very incarnation of purpose, calmness, and strength.

"Why didn't you let me do it?" he asked at last.

"Because God sent me to prevent you," she said quietly.

Five minutes earlier Needham had been resolved to take
the step which should precipitate him into a future which,
however far he had slipped from his childhood's teachings,
he could not think of as empty of a Power that was God.
He had been hurrying to confront this Power, and yet, with
the inconsistencies of such natures and such resolves, this
calm reference to a God who was present, acting, and omniscient touched him with a fear of which he had been
destitute before.

"I thought that you were away," he said, seeking in the
commonplace an evasion of his own feeling. "I did not
think that you were coming back. I thought I was alone."

"I came back for this," she answered.

He had stepped back into the room, and she, the pistol
still in her hand, went close to the light, and let the hammer
down softly and steadily with a skill the result of frequent
practice with Jib and Uncle Denver. The gravity, the
quietness with which she met the situation, had an effect
which nothing else could have had upon Needham. Had
it been a man who had taken his weapon away from him
and made it less dangerous, as if he were a child that might
be permitted to look on but not to interfere, it would have
irritated him beyond endurance. Had Rhodope become
hysterical and sought to alarm the house as Florence might
have done, it would in the present state of his brain and
nerves have confirmed him in his intentions; but when it
was Rhodope Trent who faced him with this temperate
firmness, he yielded with an acquiescence which, though
petulant, was entire.

"Now," she said gently, as she put the pistol down, "will you tell me why you wanted to do it?"

Needham threw himself into a chair that stood near, and put his hand over his eyes.

"Because I am ashamed not to."

"Is there nothing else that you could find to be ashamed of, that you should think it so poor a thing to go on living?"

He looked at her in silence.

"You are fortunate," she added softly.

"Fortunate!" he burst out with a short laugh. "How little you know! Fortunate! It is a long time since that word could be applied to me!"

"And is it a wise thing, when fortune slips away from a man, to throw deliberately his life and his courage after it?"

Whether it was a question or not, he did not answer it.

"And a man is ashamed not to do it—because—because it is such a fine thing to do?"

Needham was amazed as well as stung. He had never fancied her capable of mercilessness.

"Rhodope," he said, "you do not understand—"

"No," she said, shaking her head, "I do not understand. It seems such a pitiful thing to me—always—always to take the easy way."

"Whatever you believe," said Needham sullenly, "I beg you to believe that my way has not been an easy one. It has been a cursed hard one," he concluded stormily.

"It is well, perhaps, that you found that out. If it had been an easy one you would have gone on—and on—no matter what way, if it was only easy. Is that it?"

Beneath her calmly questioning eyes, whose glance he felt rather than saw, the glow of intensity and fierce reck-lessness faded from the picture of his folly. He grasped at the old excuse, "It was the best thing I could have done—

you remember young Wright, and what everybody said—
what Florence said. It was the best thing I could do," he
repeated bitterly. "Ask my wife."

Rhodope lifted the small weapon from the table, looked
at it, and laid it down again, and shook her head.

"Oh, no," she said with a little smile, "the best thing you
could do—you, a grown man—that? Oh, no."

Suddenly it appeared to him trivial too.

"It is the only way out of it," he said.

"How do you know it is a way out of it?" objected
Rhodope.

Charlie stared a moment.

"You mean they would talk. But I should not hear
them."

"How do you know you would not hear them?"

Needham paused. Had his carefully considered prem-
ises been insufficient?

"Then it would not be death," he said.

"How do you know what death is?" she questioned se-
renely.

Needham shuddered—he had been so near to finding out.

"Besides," said Rhodope, with a sweet pitifulness that
softened the rebuke, "people who are brave do not just
want to get away and not hear."

"That is what people always say," he said sullenly.
"Then I do not claim to be brave."

"But you admire those that are, do you not?"

"No!" he exclaimed savagely. "I don't. If people
seem brave it is all the result of accident. There is no
such thing as bearing hard things voluntarily. Men do
things that are called brave, because they are forced to do
them, or because they want to have people praise them—
that is what your great men amount to—a crazy wish to be
talked about—the rest is all luck."

Rhodope looked at him as she might have looked at a child who denied the alternation of day and night.

"And that is worse than being afraid of being talked about?" she questioned, going back to his own position.

He did not give her an answer, although he sought for one.

"Will you tell me about the trouble?" she said again.

"Yes," he replied, with sudden apathy, "I will tell you." He paused a moment. "I am sick of life," he said with the triteness of every-day fact. "I have lost my money. What is there to do when you have lost your money? It is all people care about really—how much money you've got. I've lost my money, and, what is worse, I've lost other people's. I can't pay my debts. I can't borrow. Davenant pulled me out once. I'd look well asking him to do it again! I haven't any friends—I know men who will drink with me. What is the use of living? It means disgrace. How is Florence going to bear disgrace? If I'm out of the way people will be sorry for her and make much of her, and she'll like that. They may forget now and then that she hasn't any money. Anyway, I would not hear her reproach me—I'm sure of that, no matter what you say."

He did not realize how pitiless was his analysis of Florence's position, but Rhodope did, and shivered a little, for she recognized its truth, and a harsh truth to be faced is a more terrible thing to some temperaments than any number of startling falsities.

"But it wouldn't be good for her any more than for you," she said with her accustomed acceptance of facts with which most people would be inclined to temporize.

"I've gotten past what is good for her or for me," he answered bitterly.

It was quite dark now, and he rose to light the gas. Rhodope watched him as he struck the match and, with the quick illumination, brought the room back from the shadows that had come so near deepening into those of the valley of death. Now it was bright, unveiled, commonplace.

"I put out the lights after the maid had gone," he said in restless explanation, "and told her I didn't want any fire. I thought it would give the servants something to remember, you know, after the—the catastrophe. ' The last thing he says, says he, "I won't have no lights." ' And I should have gone under with the imputation of bad grammar after all— ' " I won't have no lights," says he ' !"

The change to the commonplace had had its effect upon him. He became uneasily conscious of the tinge of the ludicrous that is apt to attach itself to the defeated suicide, and his usual egotism was enhanced by the common American anxiety to be at all hazards the first to perceive a point made against one's self. But Rhodope was not so to be diverted from the solemnities.

"You do not seem to think what is best for anybody," she said seriously. "Perhaps you don't believe there is a best."

" Well, and if I don't?" he said, not roughly, but with an irresistible yielding to the genuineness of her interest.

"Don't you honor a great man?"

" I have told you that I don't believe men are great," he answered moodily. "Why should I honor another man whom nothing but circumstances have made appear greater than I?"

He had said it. He had struck the key-note of his weak, variable character ; one of those characters to which failure is predestined from the beginning, since they will not see that half the load they stagger under is belief in the impossibility of true success.

" Have you no enthusiasm for people who do brave things, wise things, true things ?" she asked.

"Enthusiasm!" he exclaimed scornfully. "There is no room for it."

It flashed across Rhodope's mind with what a difference Medcott had talked of these same things that night on the hill when he had spoken with such freedom and such conviction. This man was complaining of the complications and the want of simplicity, and yet her creed was too simple to meet his difficulties—hers and Austin Medcott's. Involuntarily she glanced towards the mantel and saw her letter. Then she turned again to Needham, but she was faced by the very impossibility Medcott had stated to Davenant. There was no way of making this deaf man understand. There are vibrations too high in the scale of sound to reach the human ear, and in the souls of certain men lofty emotions wake no response. And these men say that there are no such emotions. Verily they have ears and hear not.

"It is a pity," said Rhodope sadly.

Something in the real sorrow of her tone touched him more nearly than anything she had said.

"Rhodope," he said, "you do not know what my life for a year has been. You do not know what it is to have cheated others and to go right on cheating them. You do not know what it is to have spent money that does not belong to you—but that belongs to men that are poorer than you ever dreamed of being—men like—" he pulled himself up short, and then burst out, "I will tell you! Men like Denver Trent! I say I have ruined your Uncle Denver! I have ruined you!"

Rhodope, who had risen to go away before he began to speak, paused startled. Ruin is a terrible word. It was something she had never thought would come near her or hers with its implied destruction. Uncle Denver ruined! A picture of an old, broken, helpless, hopeless man, who should be Uncle Denver stopped her breath for an instant. Was this the shadow that had fallen upon his spirit? Should she find him thus? Then came the revulsion. Denver Trent could never be like that—never!

"After all, it is only a matter of money," she said.

Perhaps none but a person ignorant of many of the important facts of life could have said it with the sincerity of her indifference; one who had never realized that much of the misery, the hopelessness, the cheer, and the peacefulness of life is only a matter of money. But illogical as it was, it was, perhaps, the one thing that she could have said that would give Needham a new courage. In imagination he had been facing those whom he had injured for weeks; he had fancied their reproaches, their accusations, and their despair, and had resolved to turn his back on them. Now he had flung the truth at the feet of one of them, and she had answered him thus. He did not stop to remember that she was unusually ignorant; she seemed to him unusually wise, and she had assured him that he had not bereft her of everything. Perhaps it was not so irreparable as he fancied. Perhaps he had not lost his grip, after all. He looked at her in a wonder that was nearer the admiration of which he professed to be destitute than he knew, as, without further speech, she crossed the room and picked up her letter. At that instant the door opened, and Florence stood on the threshold. She wore a long carriage wrap trimmed with silver fox, her cheeks were reddened by the outside air, her eyes had the hard brightness that belonged to them.

"They told me you had come, Rhodope," she said. "A telegram? Is any one ill?" She came into the room as she spoke, and put her small foot on the fender. "Why is there no fire?" she exclaimed, without waiting for an answer. She had barely looked at her husband, who, after a single glance at her, let his head fall on his hands again in sullen indifference.

"I do not think any one is ill," said Rhodope slowly.
" But I must go home to-morrow."

Something not quite natural in her voice made Florence
pause with her hand on the bell she had moved aside to
ring, and she scanned her keenly and then turned towards
her husband. His attitude and silence deepened the impression.

"What is the matter with you two?" she demanded.
"What has happened?" Needham did not answer.

"It did not happen," said Rhodope hastily. "Nothing
has happened."

"It came deuced near it, though," said Charlie, whose
worse nature was apt to come forward at his wife's touch.

"What came near happening?" and Florence left the
bell and came to the centre of the room. "Will you be
good enough to explain yourself with a little more ac-
curacy?"

Rhodope, seeing that an explanation was coming,
through Florence's awakened curiosity and Needham's
recklessness, went quickly towards the door.

"Wait, Rhodope!" said Florence imperiously.

"Miss Trent found me amusing myself with that play-
thing," and Needham pointed to the table.

Florence looked down and recoiled with the common in-
stinct of women.

"What!" she screamed. She did not need further explanation. Davenant's warning recurred to her.

"Yes," he went on rapidly, as if anxious now to get it
over, "I had conceived the somewhat played-out project
of blowing my brains out."

With a hysterical cry Florence threw herself down on a
sofa.

"Oh, Charlie, how could you!" she wailed. "How could
you! Oh!" and she caught her breath in long sobs.

" And to-night of all nights! When we are going to the Rimmon dinner-party."

Charlie sprang to his feet.

" The Rimmon dinner-party be—" he began savagely. Then he paused, half shamed by the nearness of the crisis through which he had passed, half silenced by the sight of Florence, in her rich dress, her flushed beauty, and her abject distress—and Rhodope slipped from the room as he waited. Miserably inadequate as was Florence's grief, it was actual grief, and such as she was in her beauty, her folly, and her shortcomings—indeed, for these very things— he had loved her; she was the woman he had promised to make happy.

" Oh, Lord !" he exclaimed, wearily and not altogether profanely. "Let it be the success it ought to be, and we'll go to it and be happy ever after. Come, Florence, stop crying.   I won't shoot myself again before dinner-time, anyhow."

Florence pulled herself together, and looked at him, still fiercely gripping the sofa pillow in which she had buried her face, and fetching short, gasping breaths.

" How did you happen not to do it this time ?" she asked nervously.

" Rhodope Trent stopped me."

" Rhodope Trent!"   Her accent was little less than furious.

" You seem grateful," remarked Needham dryly.

" I owe Rhodope Trent more than I can ever repay," said Florence, with a violence that told its own story.

" So do I, unfortunately," he rejoined with a short laugh.

He was more angry at his wife's feeling towards Rhodope than he had been at her want of it towards himself.

" A good deal more. Though I mean to pay some of it if I live," he added between his teeth.

"What do you owe her?" demanded Florence, feeling there was something still unsaid.

"Money," he answered laconically.

"Money!"

"Yes, or I owe it to Denver Trent—it's the same thing. He gave me money to invest and I've spent it—that's all."

It seemed as if Charlie was bound to overwhelm her with a sense of his iniquities, if he could not with that of his unhappiness.

"I'm going to dress now," he concluded, walking towards the door, "for the Rimmon dinner."

Florence's cup was running over. The Fates had united to besiege her ears with the name of Rhodope Trent. Was it not enough to have robbed her of Medcott's devotion? To have fascinated the man who had once been all hers? To have made her the unwilling victim of a lurking sense of inferiority? Must she snatch back her husband from the gate of death, and did she owe it to her presence that she should sit that night among the few who were chosen for the Rimmon dinner? The money question sank into insignificance save as a weapon.

Rhodope was sitting in her room with Medcott's letter before her. After the scene through which she had just passed, and which had been more agitating than she had realized, it overpowered her. It was infused with that sense of personality that strong emotion sometimes lends to even written words. It was as if he leaned over her while she read, and took her hand and made her listen to him. She felt, with a thrill of pride, the contrast between his nature and aims—and that discontented, pettish, aimless individuality with which she had just been brought in contact, and which even tragedy failed to dignify. Now as ever there was no doubt of her love for him. It had become the strong force of her life, but it had been checked and thwarted in what might have been its even flow, by mis-understanding and apprehension, until she distrusted its power to carry her on with it to a sea of happiness. While for him—what if his letter did read as if there was but one thing that was best for him? Could she make him happy, not at the cost of suffering—she would not have minded that—but at the cost of the sacrifice of what was the very warp and woof of her nature, not because he would demand it, but because his life would demand it? It was a strange, questioning mood for a girl to be in while reading her first love-letter, but it was the not unnatural result of the many forces which had been at work, the vague anxiety concerning Uncle Denver's telegram and the afternoon's discovery of the mockery of what had been outwardly so fair. And yet—blind-ed by the possibilities of what might be—Rhodope threw her head back and closed her eyes. There was a knock at the door, and without waiting for a response Florence came in and walked quickly across the room to where she sat. There was a suggestion, in the swift gracefulness of her approach, of preparation for a hostile spring, which was increased as she paused suddenly, still wearing her long velvet, fur-trim-med wrap, before the girl who had raised her head and waited. Florence's face bore the traces of her recent burst of hysterical grief. The elegance of her dress was at variance with the stormy flush of her cheeks and the tear-stains about her eyes. But her voice was unsoftened.

"You have been treated to melodrama this afternoon, I hear." Rhodope knew that she was hard, but this cynicism shocked her. "But the melodrama seems to have turned out almost, if not quite, a farce." Rhodope remembered Charlie's face as he sat with his head on his hands. Had this woman really no heart at all?

"Don't say that!" she exclaimed, "a farce is something we laugh at!"

"A farce is something that turns on other people's absurd mistakes," declared Florence. "Charlie has made several. Possibly even you have not been exempt"—she paused to make what she meant to say more effective.

"I have made a great many," said Rhodope. "Perhaps I made one in coming here," she added unconsciously, in a half-whisper.

"Possibly that was one," Florence admitted calmly. "Another may have concerned Austin Medcott. This afternoon has at least revealed the secret of his alleged fondness for you!"

Rhodope shrank from the cruelty of her choice of words.

"Tom Davenant knows, and of course Mr. Medcott knows, that Charlie spent Denver Trent's money. That means that you may be at any time without support. It puts a different face on a flirtation, for an honorable man."

The inspiration which seldom fails to come when we are resolved to do our worst was standing Florence in good stead.

"It is astounding what pity will do with the artistic temperament," she paused to laugh, not quite naturally. "It disposes it to undreamed-of chivalry in the case of a good-looking woman. Has Austin Medcott been asking you to marry him, my dear?"

Perhaps only the insolence of the last words would have roused Rhodope to reply. She was so hurt that she had no wish to retaliate, only a longing that her enemy might feel that she had dealt blows enough. Moreover, it is the prerogative of such violence as Mrs. Needham's to silence a gentler nature. But as Florence waited for an answer with what she meant for a smile, but which was a half-hysterical distortion of her lips, Rhodope spoke. The fire-light was dancing across their faces with an air of light-heartedness that contradicted their expression. Rhodope's pure profile threw flickering shadows on the opposite wall, where Florence's figure lost its daintiness and became grotesque.

"I cannot answer you," her voice was low and unbroken, "for you do not understand Mr. Medcott or me. We speak the truth."

"You will wish some time that I had not spoken the truth," Florence said shortly.

"No," said Rhodope gently, "I shall never wish that." She moved nearer Florence, her hands clasped in front of her. "Would it not have been better," she asked, "to have had more truth from the first? Would it not have been better to have let me have my letter when it came?"

Florence shrugged her shoulders without speaking.

"He spoke to me that day we met in the street—the day after your reception," went on Rhodope.

"What did he say?" asked Florence contemptuously. "The sort of thing that a man says to a pretty woman when he is sorry for her?"

"I shall not tell you what he said," returned Rhodope gravely, "but they were not the things that he says to you." She did not know it was a thrust, but Florence paled under its truth. "Perhaps you are right, perhaps he was sorry for me. But at least he wrote. And I have not known that he had written. I wondered why," she said simply. "But I soon thought that he was leaving me to think it over."

"He was thinking it over himself," sneered Florence. "Even an artist may know when he is quixotic."

"I am telling you about it," said Rhodope calmly, her eyes on Florence, who let hers fall unwillingly before them, "in order that we may have truth now, at least. I have thought it over," she went on, "and I had grown to think that his life was really very far apart from mine, that what seemed to me a great thing—his love for me"—Florence

looked at her, astonished by the fearlessness of her words—
"was not a great thing to him—that like so many other
things, I had not understood. But now I have his letter.
He had written, and while I was wondering, he was wondering too. I think it would have been better to let me
have it."

Nothing could have silenced Florence like this utter
frankness, it was so foreign to her own nature. But she
saw her way now to emphasize her suggestion.

"And do you not see," she exclaimed, ignoring Rhodope's question, "that he, too, knows that you are far apart?
that you look at things differently? that you never could
make him happy? You are not a stupid woman, Rhodope,
with all your refinements about truth and Heaven knows
what all!"—and she laughed with the scorn she felt—"and
you must know that but one thing could bring Austin Medcott to such a foolish step—the knowledge that you loved
him and that you have become dependent."

Rhodope's hands clasped each other more tightly under
the lash of the words. She walked over to the fire—the
fire that made her think of home—and looked down into it.
Florence stood watching her, playing with an end of her fur
trimming, her lips set in harsh lines.

"Uncle Denver said, Mrs. Needham," Rhodope raised
her eyes and met hers as she spoke, "that whatever you
wanted from my being here you would certainly gain it."
It did not soothe Florence to know that Denver Trent had
a not incorrect idea of her character. "I would like to
know that you have it. I would like to go away thinking
that it has not all been a mistake. Have you gained it,
whatever it may be?"

In Florence's angry consciousness Rhodope was driving
her to a confession of failure. She entirely lost the pathos
of the half-indignant, wholly sad, question.

"What could you do for me!" she exclaimed. "I wanted nothing of you. I have not failed in anything. But," and she turned towards the door, "do not be too sure that you have succeeded."

It was with a certain sense of defeat that she closed the door; but she might, nevertheless, have revelled in the consciousness of one who has fought a good fight. Her blows had told. Without shedding a tear, Rhodope sank into her chair and closed her eyes again, utterly weary. As a beautiful dream suddenly changes into a strange something that frightens and oppresses us, so other doubts, other thoughts, intruded unaccountably, and were imposed upon what had been a dream of love. She opened her eyes after a while and looked about her. Her trunks stood ready for departure, the room looked strange and inhospitable. What had she done to this world, into which she had gladly come, that it treated her so as she was going away from it alone? What had she done?

CHAPTER XXIII

" 'Tis a kind of good deed to say well."

" Oh, sing them back, as fresh as ever:
  The sunshine and the merriment,
  The unsought, evergreen content,
    Of that never cold time ;
  The joy that like a clear breeze went
    Through and through the old time."

" These two shall have their joy."

THE Rimmon dinner was distinguished, as usual, for that union of the elegant, the stately, the depressing, and the superfluous that makes a Rimmon dinner the Mecca of social pilgrims.

By the wise ordering of an all-comprehending Providence, the sense of elation that filled the rightly constituted heart at the realization of its owner's privileges in thus sitting at meat with a ruler, made up for the lack of less subjective enjoyment, and established an equilibrium as gratifying to most of the guests as to the imperturbable soul of Mrs. Rimmon herself. But into even this empyrean circle unregenerate impulses made their way, and among its members was at least one exception to the rule of perfect satisfaction. It was that of Medcott's mother, who, while he was expressing a wish for her presence, had unexpectedly cut short her visit at the German baths and was on her way home, and made on this occasion her first reappearance in New York society.

" I am growing Bohemian," she sighed inwardly, as she

turned her intellectual face to the man on her right, who was giving her a spirited account of something—just what, she had not heard—after a lapse into actual, if unmarked, inattention.

"These short and frequent trips to the other side, with their irresponsibility, are the unmaking of me. By all the traditions of my bringing up I ought to be permeated with happiness, and I'm not. Yes," she said aloud, with that attentiveness which made her so charming to even younger men, "no wonder you were interested. As you have said, it is in exhibitions of that kind that the future tastes, and really the safety, of the present generation lie."

She watched him with feminine readiness to take back or to alter any of her words in case they proved to be sadly inappropriate, for her idea was of the vaguest concerning what seemed to be something in the line of Art, complicated by technical terms. The stout and sanguine gentleman, who had been telling of a recent athletic exhibition, was confirmed in his impression of her extreme intelligence.

"So I say, so I say," he responded. Mrs. Medcott was a fine-looking woman, of that distinguished appearance which white hair, a youthful face, and dark eyes go far to establish. She had to perfection that art of being mistress of the situation, without undue insistence on it, which some women never learn even after long experience. She knew her world thoroughly, but that was not all she knew. She had looked over into other people's ; and though, in the long run, she preferred her own, she was not ignorant that there were certain others, inhabited by rational beings. Of decided views, she had the fine tolerance which, in its perfection, is the result only of wide experience and a keen intelligence.

"I shouldn't be so outrageously absent-minded if it were not for this business of Austin's," she went on in an undercurrent of thought that did not seriously interfere with the duties of the hour. " But to come home to find that one's only son has fallen in love with a milkmaid is enough to call out one's worst traits. If Bertha doesn't get me away early I shall acknowledge to myself that I am bored. After that I might as well give up, of course. To admit that one is bored at a dinner like this is social burial. Of course she isn't a milkmaid, by the way. I never saw a milkmaid in my life, and I don't believe Austin ever did. I know nothing about them except that they get up very early with three-legged stools. But I have an idea Violet Harrow didn't write me the worst, after all. She is something terrible, of course. And I was so sure of Austin's taste. I've always said that Bertha would be saved by her sense of duty and Austin by his taste. It shows the uncertainties of even religious convictions. Bertha will make up her mind to this because it is her duty, and because earthly advantages are really nothing. And I shall never make up my mind to it because Austin gets his taste from me, and I know earthly advantages are a great deal. Oh, indeed it is," she observed to her neighbor on the other side, who had sprung suddenly into prominence in the scientific line, and whose views had not yet been tempered by the chastening atmosphere in which he found himself. He had been asked because the Englishman had expressed a wish to meet him, thereby causing Mrs. Rimmon a bad quarter of an hour's speculation concerning his possibilities. " Indeed it is. It develops one mentally, this living in a country where eminence is the direct result of real force. What could America do with artificial standards ?"

As the scientist, charmed by the insight of one who had at first appeared to him merely the unexceptionable woman of fashion, was led to enlarge upon the benefit of democratic institutions, Mrs. Medcott went on with her reflections.

" How easy it is to make nonsense sound like sense,"

she thought, as she observed the avidity with which her remark had been seized upon. "Austin would say that wasn't
nonsense, after all. I don't see how he keeps that faith in
the promises of life when he goes to places like this. I
have a fancy he doesn't go any oftener than he can help.
I'd like to have him see that pretty piece of completeness
talking to the titled Englishman. Her conception of republican ideals is that of being sufficiently elevated to look up
to a lord. By the way, it just occurs to me that that is a
Mrs. Needham, and that Austin mentioned a Mrs. Needham
as the person responsible for the social introduction of the
milkmaid. I've an idea I've heard who she is, or was, or
something. Bertha will know. It might be well to burn a
sort of noncommittal incense to the guardian angel. I'll
make Bertha find out for me after dinner. Tom Davenant
would know, but I can't get hold of him in time."

Mrs. Rimmon—who even in her own house produced
something of the solemn effect of Buddha, and who was
accustomed to have her proceedings waited upon with the
same earnest watchfulness, as possible manifestations of
divinity—had gathered her guests in the drawing-room. It
was just after their entrance that Mrs. Medcott had found
an opportunity to say to her daughter,

"Bertha, find out if that woman is a Mrs. Needham, and
if Mrs. Needham isn't the woman—"

"She is, mamma." Bertha spoke with her enlightening
manner; she was accustomed to interrupt her mother when
necessary, and at present their interview must be short.
She was a girl of a good deal of immobile beauty, which
announced its own inability to charm at the same time that
it asserted its claim to respect. "She is a Mrs. Needham,
and she has a Miss Trent staying with her. She was a Miss
Evans, and Tom Davenant was at one time engaged to her.
I mean to speak to her about Miss Trent."

"Your memory for names and your principles are as admirable as ever, my dear," said Mrs. Medcott, "and I have fallen into a way of depending upon both instead of my own; but I think this time you had better let me speak to her rather than do it yourself."

"Very well, mamma," replied Bertha, who had long ago recognized in her mother a certain felicity which she herself lacked. Bertha's memory for names was undoubtedly excellent, but possibly if it had been a less reliable one she would not have found it difficult to recall the name of the woman to whom Tom Davenant had once been engaged.

It could not perhaps be asserted that Florence had thoroughly enjoyed the dinner, but then the sense of repose inseparable from absolute enjoyment is impossible upon a dizzy pinnacle. But she felt that she ought to be enjoying it, which, though less gratifying to the natural man, is of a loftier and more securely founded order of experience. As Mrs. Medcott had divined, her republican simplicity looked no further into the claims of her English neighbor to distinguished consideration than that of his title. And though to the ordinary observer this one talent seemed, from its barrenness, in danger of being buried in a napkin, she felt that he was in the position of the man to whom had been committed fifty, and who might be expected at any time to bring in fourfold. She did not allow herself to be distracted from the matter in hand even by the sight of Davenant, who, in direct contradiction to the statement that in vain is the net spread in sight of any bird, was listening resignedly to a favorite bit of one of Mrs. Eunam's " Neglected Authors." Only now and then, as she had glanced down the table at Charlie, with his pale face, nervous frame, and irreproachable evening-dress, a slight sense of giddiness oppressed her as she began to realize that the solid earth might "fail beneath her feet." And once or twice her nerves thrilled with a sudden rush of hatred of Rhodope. It was not without a sensation of satisfaction that she was presented, after dinner, to Mrs. Medcott. She had made all her life that grievous mistake of not recognizing a difference in the point of view; in this instance it had led her into considering Mrs. Medcott's interest as another tribute to the secure exaltation of her present social position.

"It is with you, I think, that Miss Trent is staying," said Mrs. Medcott quite naturally, after the exchange of a few preliminaries. "My son wished me to call upon her. I think he was fortunate enough to be under the same roof with you both last summer—when I was stupid enough to be ill and break off his holiday—was he not?"

Florence was fanning herself slowly with a superb fan; the thick plumes quivered a little in her hands as she answered.

"Under the same roof with me?" she laughed. "Under no roof at all, most of the time, with Miss Trent. They were both famous for out-of-door expeditions."

Mrs. Medcott's ear was too keen to miss the harsh note.

"Austin has contrived to put her on the other side," she thought.

"I am an old woman," she said with a smile that threatened to belie the words, "and Austin ought to think of it. When he talked to me of Mrs. Needham, I did not remember that she was once the Miss Evans whom people were not expected to forget." The manner, the smile, seemed to make it in this case a flattering thing to have been forgotten.

"I am surprised that Mr. Medcott should have mentioned me at all," Florence said with an affectation of indifference. However gratified by his mother's graciousness, she could not help showing her pique at the son's shortcomings.

"Austin knows my taste for personalities," smiled Mrs.

Medcott. "He knows that nothing entertains me like hearing of his friends. Is Miss Trent still with you?"

"Yes, she is still with me." Florence recognized that an opportunity to revenge herself might be at hand. "But she goes to-morrow."

"To-morrow? I am sorry."

At this moment the titled Englishman drew near to be presented to Mrs. Medcott, who knew "some of his people at home." It is impossible to exaggerate the importance attached to this latter fact both by the Englishman and Mrs. Needham.

"I am at home on Thursday," said Mrs. Medcott before she turned away. "Perhaps you will let me make your acquaintance even if I am cut off from Miss Trent's."

"If I am not mistaken, there is an infusion of the mammon of unrighteousness in that young woman which it will be well to make a friend of," she remarked to Bertha as they drove home that night. Her mother's forms of expression often struck Bertha as exaggerated.

"She wore a pretty gown," she observed with literalness.

"It was an irreproachable gown. Another testimony to her being a dangerous woman."

"Tom Davenant was said to be very much in love with her," said Bertha thoughtfully. She found no difficulty in discussing the subject. Davenant was the only man except her brother and two cousins that Bertha called by his Christian name.

"Tom Davenant is too clever to have been in love with her," said Mrs. Medcott promptly. "He may have been in love with his idea of her."

"How did you make a friend of her?" asked Bertha.

"A friend of her!" exclaimed Mrs. Medcott. "My dear child, I wish you would be more careful of your expressions."

"You said it would be well"—began poor Bertha.

"Oh, well—Bertha, you have a terrible way of telling people what they said," interrupted her mother impatiently. "I may make myself a friend of the mammon of unrighteousness, but I am not yet hardened enough to call it friendship."

"Are you going to call on her?"

"No, the rare bird flies to-morrow. But she is coming to see us on Thursday. Then I shall find out all she can tell me—more than she means to."

"I was thinking—" began Bertha, thoughtfully still— "then she won't wait for us to call on her?" To Bertha questions of this sort formed a large and legitimate interest in life.

"No, my dear," replied Mrs. Medcott with conviction. "She won't think it worth while."

"May I ask," said Mrs. Needham to her husband that night, "when the world is to know the result of these financial operations of yours?" She spoke with a chilling intonation that was the immediate result of her contemplation of her position in Davenant's eyes, on her way home in the carriage. Needham had admitted, during their stormy interview of the afternoon, that Davenant had helped him. To be a pensioner of Tom Davenant! It was too much.

"The world, as you call it, will probably know it in about a week."

Charlie threw himself down in an easy-chair, lit a cigarette, and scrutinized with contemptuous irony the luxurious fittings of the room, and finally the exquisite costume of Florence herself as she stood before him. She saw what he meant to convey by this silent examination.

"And they will say your wife ruined you," she said.

"I don't know—perhaps." He was tired out mentally and physically. The dinner had bored him intensely.

"They will forget what I have done for you," she said angrily.

"They may."

"Does it mean that we shall have no more money?"

"Not enough to get you gowns like that."

Florence moved and stood more directly in front of him. It seemed to her that the whole universe was threatened. She heard the solar system, as it were, clattering about her ears.

"People fail," she said, "or are bankrupt, or whatever you call it, and have money left. They go on. Can't you do that? Isn't there some money—somewhere—that you can get—can take?"

Needham looked at her with a sort of admiration.

"I've taken it," he said half to himself, "I've done the very thing. But somehow I never had the coolness to say it to myself like that."

She did not heed his comment.

"Isn't there?" she persisted.

"No," he answered shortly.

Florence threw her arms wide with a gesture that was nearly tragic.

"Oh," she exclaimed passionately, "I will not be poor! It means—it means death and burial—nothing less. Who will come to see me? Who will talk about me? Particularly if you have cheated somebody."

Needham winced, but to Florence the deed itself was so trifling beside its consequences that she did not notice it.

"Everybody will drop me. What good has it all done? —my efforts and my success!"

Elements of real tragedy were here, but she had seized upon the ignoble qualities, and threatened to make it a farce.

" I wonder you haven't thought of that before.   What *is* the good of it ?"

But this was an appeal to a sanity beyond which Florence had passed.   The fact that she could have asked such a question was but to announce the blackest despair.

" Do you think it is I that am to blame ?" she asked, not remorsefully, but with a determination to understand.

" No, I guess not," he answered wearily.   " I've chucked it away as fast as you have."

" And you haven't as much to show for it."

" No, I suppose not."

Florence gathered up her fan and gloves and swept to the door.   There she paused.

" Is there no way out of disgrace ?   No chance of escaping it ?"

" No—yes, one chance.   No certainty."

" What is it ?"   She was at his side again.

" Nothing but another speculation—foolish enough, the Lord knows — but they say it may turn out something. What's the use of telling you ?   It won't.   It's those chances that I've waited for and staked on, and that have always come up blanks.   It is because I didn't want to wait for one more that I tried to cut the whole business."

" If it succeeds, what will it do ?"

" Give me enough to tide over a nasty place.   Perhaps give me a fresh start."

" The idea of a man's giving up when he has one chance !"

Florence spoke in her hard, deliberate little way.   " You would have put yourself hopelessly in the wrong ; you would have brought dreadful disgrace upon everybody belonging to you, and all when there may be a way out of it."

" And I would have kept you home from the Rimmon dinner."

"It was a cowardly thing to do." She was unmoved by his sarcasm.

"Well, Florence, I guess I am a coward," he said, tired of the whole subject. It was as if the nervous petulance of the discontented man had deepened into real sorrow and disappointment. Florence crossed the room again to the door. It would have been better if she had been a little more gentle in her regret. Possibly not even in the days of courtship would Needham have valued a caressing word or gesture more than he would have now. But she gave neither. She had listened so long to the suggestions of one side of her nature that other impulses had become numbed and powerless. For the seventy and seventh time, perhaps, she had stood at a parting of the ways, but she did not even see it—such was the pitifulness of her punishment.

That night left a deep void in their relations that was never bridged over, and which later Florence learned, with a certain discontent, to realize was impassable by her most concentrated effort.

"I do not think we shall be poor," was all she said as she went away and left him. As it happened she was right. Poetical justice demanded that they should be, that a spoiled child like Florence should be corrected by the rod of privation. But there seems to be a justice beyond even the poetical, and perhaps it was a keener, more scathing sentence that allowed her to go on in the way she had chosen, without let or hindrance — the lesson she might have profited by unlearned.

When the next morning's paper announced the success of the mining scheme of which Needham had spoken so discouragingly, and later operations relieved him from the most pressing of his engagements, in Florence's eyes the world rolled on as before. There were questions asked, suspicions were aroused among men who knew and had watched Needham's career; but there was no overt failure to meet liabilities, no noisy creditors, nothing that came to the ears of the city at large. On the whole, Needham's conduct, whatever it was, was by common consent of the wise lifted from the sphere governed by the laws of ethics to that higher and less easily attainable one of "smartness." He had been pretty smart, they said; they didn't know he could do it. But not many weeks later he wrote Denver Trent a letter, accompanying it by certain transferences of property which occasioned some astonishment.

"Darn it!" said Denver to himself at last, "it was a close call. But what's the use of getting as old as I be if I'm going to be s'prised at things?" With which the matter ended.

Meanwhile Rhodope was gone, and Florence could give her whole mind to the interview that she was to have with Mrs. Medcott. It was with a delightful sense of abandonment that she gave herself up to rough mental drafts of the interview, and to the subsequent touching up and toning down of light and shade. She resolved to go early, that she might have some consecutive conversation, for naturally she was clever enough to perceive that Mrs. Medcott's object in asking her was to find out about Rhodope. She hastily reviewed Uncle Denver's limp, and a pair of unregenerate overalls in which he was wont to appear upon week-days; the little wooden house, with its living-room adorned with the various stores connected with eating, fishing, hunting, and other domestic economies; then Jib, with his lazy drawl and high-minded indifference to the conventionalities.

"Good-looking, of course "—she knew just how she would say this—"with an uncultivated sort of beauty, like his sister's." The social amenities of the valley and its peculiarities of speech she could hit off very well. As for Elizabeth, the future sister-in-law, her affinities with the circus would be sure to please the fastidious taste of the Medcotts. She thought it would be a fair construction of the truth to imply that these affinities had not been confined to private life. Austin Medcott's sister-in-law jumping through a hoop was a spectacle his mother could not fail to dwell on with satisfaction. She was doubting whether to hint darkly at tights—pink silk tights—as she put on her bonnet to go to a concert which she was to attend on her way to Mrs. Medcott's. To be sure, she could not assert positively that she had ever seen Elizabeth in pink silk tights, but there was a delicious concreteness in the suggestion as an argument in Rhodope's disfavor that she was loath to abandon. She rolled it as a sweet morsel under her tongue as she entered the concert-room. Florence had never been susceptible to music. Perhaps it was that it never appealed to her primarily as music. She went to hear some one sing, because people just then talked about that person's voice. She attended certain orchestral performances because the best people showed there. She conscientiously sat through evening after evening of the fashionable opera, possibly upheld by that relic of superstitious belief which so many of us unconsciously cling to—the suggestion that it will be made up to her under future discipline in another world; perhaps only as one of the numerous company whose feelings, while there, coincide with those of the celebrated Bishop of Rum-Ti-Foo in his arduous struggles to learn the dance of which his instructor assures him,

> " ' The attitude's considered quaint.'—
> The weary bishop, feeling faint,
> Replied, ' I do not say it ain't,
> But " Time !" my Christian friend!' "

This afternoon, however, Florence underwent a new experience. It was the lightest kind of music to which she listened in company with the fashionable audience that had made this leader the fashionable conductor of the day. The programme consisted of nothing but dance-music, gay, regretful, swinging, passionate, reminiscent waltzes. It was as if the shallow nature, that was unstirred by the depth and grandeur of the harmony of the great masters, was cast into a strange ferment at the touch of an inspiration that it could understand. As she listened she found herself growing curiously softened. The melodies were full of the spirit of youth, its short-sighted, unheeding gayety, and its bitter, brief regrets. It was the same music to which she had danced night after night, a few years ago, with Charlie Needham, Tom Davenant, and hosts of others. She had danced often enough since, but it had been a different thing. In the balls of to-day she found none of that sweet intoxication that once made the ball-room a world of its own, beyond which there was nothing that need be taken thought of. Unconsciously she found herself thinking of Needham as he had been then, not as the harassed, petulant man with whom she had hardly exchanged a word at breakfast. She recalled a particular box of roses he had sent her for a certain ball. A pretty but rather faded woman leaned over and spoke to her.

"I never hear 'One heart, one soul,' Florence," she said, "without thinking of poor George Ralston. Do you remember when we all went together to that dance?"

Florence nodded. "Yes," she said.

Her limited soul was filled with a passionate regret for those days of youth and ignorance. George Ralston had gone away to the West and had died there. It had not occurred to her then that anybody of her own age could die. Well, she was glad she had had it all. In this new, strange mood it seemed a more actual benefit to have had those

pleasures of youth and beauty than the more diplomatic
and valuable ones of later years.

The leader rose on the tips of his toes, describing a complete titillating circle, pointing his baton now at one and
now at another of the players with a gesture imploring,
beseeching, commanding by turns; now and then he took a
violin himself, and as he drew his bow across the strings it
was as if he said, "Go as you please now, I am playing."
Then he laid it down. "Now I am not! Look what you
are about there—*you—you!* Now you wait till it is your
turn," the baton indicated with fury. Was he really silent?
Had these little beseechings, these impatiences, not been
spoken aloud? Were they but the expression of his elastic
poses?

Florence watched and listened, fascinated. Yes, she had
had it! She had lived and revelled in that ball-room
world of delight and intoxication and emulation. Suddenly
she thought of Medcott and Rhodope, and with a new softness. Perhaps the newly awakened domination of Davenant's nature over hers had weakened Medcott's hold on
her fancy. She wondered now if it were worth while to interfere with their happiness? Had she not done enough?
Could not they, too, have their holiday? That despairing
minor wail that breaks now and then through the gayest
music came to her ears like an overwhelming reproach.
George Ralston had gone away and died. After people died,
so little mattered. The leader rose on his toes and pointed
high in the air, as to the rising star of progress or the first
faint flush of dawn. You were spiritually elevated in spite
of yourself. Then down again into the orchestra. "Can't
you get more 'go' into it? *Can't* you? So! So! So!"

It was not music to stir the soul, but it stirred the fancy
and those upper strata of emotion which take the place of
depths in women like Florence Needham. Tom Davenant

had loved her then. He had been near her always; he didn't care for dancing as much as she did, but he always danced with her. Poor Tom! She had treated him badly. Why should she want him to care for her any longer? Why not be willing that he should have a relief from what had been the fever of that intense, longing, gay, reckless time of youth?

The leader was in the attitude of Hamlet adjuring his father's ghost; but you knew that this distinguished gentleman had never seen any ghosts—save perhaps delicate, dreamy, feminine ones of a deserted ball-room, ghosts with broken fans and bits of torn tarlatan and a pretty, sad, suggestive, pathetic grace of fleeting smiles, mocking flattery, and passing youth—and would not have followed them if he had.

Florence went straight from the concert-room to Mrs. Medcott's. On the way she was surprised to find the day cold and gray, she had been so long amid the light, the perfume, and the figures of the ball-room. There was almost no one there. Bertha was talking with one or two people at the tea-table. Mrs. Medcott was saying good-by to an old lady who was evidently of importance. She greeted Mrs. Needham with just enough cordiality, and in a moment she was seated by her on a small sofa, the tea-table talk barely reaching their ears.

"You will want to know about Rhodope Trent," said Florence. Mrs. Medcott was rather shocked at the bareness of the proposition.

"I have heard about her already," she smiled. "Helena Screed has just been here."

"But I knew her at home," said Florence hastily. Her cheeks were flushed, and her eyes had that evanescent softness that sometimes made them dangerous. Mrs. Medcott came to the conclusion that she might be a more attractive woman than she had been inclined to believe.

"She is what Mr. Davenant would call tremendously fine."

It showed Davenant's influence over her, that she chose his expression rather than her own when she was moved.

"She is not like other people—not in the least like me, for instance."

"I was afraid so." Mrs. Medcott still smiled, but she was more curious.

"No—no, I don't mean like that. But she sees things differently. She dresses queerly sometimes, but after all it—it suits her." This attained to positive heroism. "She is very handsome and very good. You will like her."

"I have no doubt of it." Mrs. Medcott was very curious.

"At home—at her home—it is not like this, you know, but it is not bad."

Bertha rose and came forward. Her guests were taking leave and others were coming.

"You will not forget," said Florence in a low tone, "you will like her."

"No, I shall not forget; thank you for telling me."

For almost the first time Mrs. Medcott nearly doubted her own impressions. The conversation was diverted and the spell was wearing off as Florence said good-by, but it had done its work. For an hour she had thought and acted without taking thought of the morrow.

Just before dinner Austin came in. There was a letter for him on the table. He held it a minute in his hand before opening it. He had not seen his mother for several days. She watched him as he walked over to the fire to read it. His face flushed and his hand tightened over it as he finished, otherwise he was quiet.

"Your Miss Trent cannot be a mere wild-flower, Austin," said his mother, going up to him. She had a wonderful fascination of manner. "She must be a rare and delicate orchid, which, as we all know, is not only a beautiful thing, but a fashionable—"

Medcott sighed impatiently, but she went on, her hand on his arm: "for she has won the discriminating praise of Mrs. Florence Needham."

"After she has let her go," broke out Austin impatiently.

"But did you not know she was going?" asked his mother, surprised. "We heard so a day or two ago."

"No, I did not know."

He felt disproportionately overwhelmed. There had been such a succession of things between them, and just as he thought they were brushed away, just as even the spiteful woman who had done such repeated harm had yielded—she was gone! He could not reach her, and the sad little note he held in his hand, while it thought itself an obstacle, but filled him with renewed longing to speak to her face to face.

"She must be a remarkable woman," repeated Mrs. Medcott later to Bertha. "I have hopes of her," but she sighed.

"I suppose it would have been our duty any way not to oppose it if she is really interested in Austin," reflected Bertha.

"It would not have been mine," said her mother sharply. "It would have been my duty to break it off, and if I hadn't succeeded, never to become resigned to the ways of Providence. And it will be now, if she is an ordinary person. Of course she is interested in Austin! Women always have been since he was five! That is no sign that they were made for each other!"

Medcott read Rhodope's note over and over again, seeking to read all that there was between the lines. It was a short note and she had sought to make it absolutely truthful.   Its force was all in what it left unsaid.   Altogether it touched Medcott inexpressibly, though he did not know all the circumstances.

"I do not think it will be best," she had written. "I am going away. Do not think I do not understand. I shall not be miserable. Please do not write to me again. It was good of you to think of it.
"Yours truly,
"RHODOPE TRENT."

22

CHAPTER XXIV

"Why else was the harmony prolonged but that singing might issue
   thence?
Why rushed the discords in but that harmony should be prized?"

> "Oh, world as God has made it, all is beauty,
> And knowing this is love, and love is duty.
> What further may be sought for or declared?"

"AIN'T it most time for that teaspoonful of medicine?"
asked a feeble, querulous voice from the bed.

"No, Miss Matilda." The answer came in Rhodope's
quiet tones. "It isn't time for half an hour yet."

"I dono as it does any good anyhow," observed the
querulous voice, its flavor of acidity diluted, but not destroyed, by physical weakness. Rhodope made no reply,
and the former silence fell upon the sick-room. It had
been a silence of an hour's duration. A small lamp burned
dimly on the table with its usual sick-room litter of bottles,
glasses, and spoons, causing curious shadows to fall here
and there in unexpected places, illustrating, after the fashion of shadows, undreamed-of possibilities in the forms of
well-known and altogether normal objects. But the table
and the shadows were the only notes of disorder in the
room. The patchwork counterpane was a marvel of well-
regulated lights and shades. The virginal simplicity of
Miss Spore's chamber was uncorrupted by any hint of luxury save that of a braided mat at the side of the bed, and
a framed canvas representing in colored lithograph certain
Masonic emblems of an order to which the father of Matil-

da had once belonged. The detached but impressive eye, the square and compass, the altar, the visible lightning, all of these symbols had exerted their influence upon Miss Matilda's development, and perhaps contributed to the severity of her moral nature. A child whose early recollections of parental hours of relaxation are attended by the vision of the altar, the lightning, and the square, could not well grow up to take a light-minded view of social recreations. It seems hardly necessary to say that this masterpiece belonged in the parlor, but since her illness Miss Matilda had craved its presence before her eyes. Since infancy she had gazed upon it with varying emotions of awe, curiosity, mystification, and admiration. Of late years these had yielded a large place to the calmer satisfaction of family pride. In the restless helplessness of illness, amid the limited resources of the unimpressive wall-paper and the green window-shades, she found in contemplation of its glories much of the same distinct, if evasive, comfort contained in the pronunciation of Mesopotamia.

The rest of the room, as has been hinted, appealed less to the æstheticism of the observer. That it was spotlessly neat and somehow suggestive of the tightly drawn back hair and unornamental collar of its occupant, need not be stated to such as have cared to observe Miss Spore's tendencies. Rhodope glanced at the small but remorseless clock on the top of the chest of drawers, and then rose a little wearily, and, walking to the low window, knelt on the floor, and, drawing away the calico curtain, leaned her head against the pane. It had been stormy, but the wind and the cold rain had ceased. Before her the mountains loomed dark and silent. Above her the stars looked down with clear-sighted solemnity upon the earth beneath. Below her the street in the outskirts of the little town lay hushed and empty, as though it were a street of that other village where

> " All the villagers lie asleep;
> Never a grain to sow or reap;
> Never in dreams to moan or sigh;
> Silent and idle and low they lie."

She was alone with the silences that she loved. Her thoughts could lie at peace or raise themselves reverently to high things under the guardianship of the night. She was far from the mocking, thwarting disturbances that had troubled and hampered her. And yet? Her eyes grew sad as she pressed her forehead more closely against the cold pane. Had she come back to them in vain? Had they for the first time no help for her—those everlasting hills? Her forehead slipped down into her hands as she knelt facing a great unrest, that seemed to widen out before her into a pitiful loneliness without bounds, and over which she could not pass, save wearily and in many years.

The clock hasted not, nor halted, but ticked on steadily; for was not this night as other nights, and why hasten or retard its hours, that led but to a day that should be as other days?

Miss Matilda had been very ill. The nervous strain, the long, chill watching, the overtaxed strength, had resulted in a sudden sharp attack of fever. She had insisted upon going back alone to her empty house, where she had broken down, and been discovered helpless and unresigned by the child of a neighbor who brought in the morning's pitcher of milk. It is safe to assert that that child, though in no wise shielded from the vicissitudes of mature life, will never forget, in the light of subsequent experiences, the details of that morning. Miss Matilda gave her directions as to what she wanted done, and the child tried to follow them to the best of her not-skilled, and perhaps somewhat slow-witted, ability. Miss Matilda told her to make a fire, and then found fault with the disposition of each stick and bit of

paper in a sharp, weak voice, that came with singular vivid-
ness, from the stiff lounge whither she had dragged herself,
to the ears of the frightened child.

"There ain't any draught," moaned Miss Matilda.
"'Ain't your ma ever told you you can't make a fire without a draught? Put them sticks crossways 'stid of len'th-
ways—not *them* sticks, the little ones! Open that little slide
at the bottom. Land o' grief! that ain't the slide—it's the
door! Do you want to put out all there is?"

With panicky fingers the child pushed the wrong way,
and the slide refused to open.

"Did you know there was a nose on your face?" inquired Miss Spore with irritated inelegance. "Push it the
other way! There! You do beat all for awk'ardness. Now
blow a little. Mercy on us!" And her voice rose in a feeble shriek. "Don't roll your eyes so, and don't blow the hull
stove out o' doors! You'll give me the apperplexy. Now
fetch the kittle. For goodness' sake! That ain't the kittle—that's the saucepan—don't *any* of your ma's children
know a saucepan from a kittle?" So the directions had pro-
ceeded till the poor little ignoramus, whose errors had been
rather those of alarm than of natural thick-headedness, escaped to send in her mother, who speedily sent, in her turn,
for the doctor.

"I want to see Denver Trent," said Miss Matilda to
the doctor, "and you sha'n't stir me a step till I do see
him."

The doctor, like most of her acquaintances, had no wish
to push matters with Miss Matilda merely for the pleasure
of theoretical demonstration, and he sent for Denver Trent
as soon as might be. Jib drove Denver over and waited
for him while he limped up the steps of Miss Matilda's little house, which grew right up from the street, with only
room for a fence between, probably because, when it was

built, front-door yards might have been had for the asking. Matilda still lay on the sofa, her cheeks burning with fever, the counterpane looking fairly scandalized at thus being brought into public notice, and a blanket shawl wrapped about her spare form.

"Wal, Denver," she said hastily, "I guess you're wonderin' what on airth I sent for you for."

"Well, I was—consider'ble," answered Denver frankly. "I'm sorry you're sick, anyhow, Matilda."

"I dono as I'm sick," she said shortly.

"I thought you sent for me because you was sick," said Denver, without the slightest heat.

"Wal, I did," she assented.   "You know about Tim?"

"Yes," he answered soberly.

"Wal, I 'ain't got anybody to look after me now."   It would have been a triumph for poor Tim if he could have heard his aunt acknowledge by implication that he had looked after her.   "And I don't seem to think of anybody but you that's ever been much of any friends with me. Not that you was ever any great shakes of a friend."   Miss Spore's eyes had a gleam of something that was not fever. "You allers liked Marcella Brown best."

Denver Trent's eyes glistened.

"Seems 's if you was goin' back a good ways, ain't you, Matilda?" he asked gently.

"Mebbe I am.   You did, didn't you?"

"Well, yes, I guess I allers did," he answered simply.   "I liked her better 'n anybody else."

There was silence for a moment.

"I knew it," said the forlorn old woman, whose voice was growing weaker from fatigue.   "But you've allers been pretty frien'ly to Tim and me, and I want you to git somebody over in the valley to come over and take care o' me. I don't want anybody here.   'N' I want you to kind o' keep your eye on things if I'm very sick. I'll feel better if you do. That's all, Denver."

And Denver Trent came away, having promised, and soon thereafter despatched his reckless telegram.

It would be hard to say why she had sent for him. Whether it was the old sentiment which suddenly asserted its survival, or the old jealousy seeking an opportunity to observe what wound had been made by the death of her rival, or a sudden realization of her unloved, unliked helplessness and Denver Trent's steadfastness of character—whether all or any of these, or but the vagary of feverishness, even she herself could not have told, but it was this that she did.

"Blowin' like Statia, ain't it?" Denver had said as he helped Rhodope, half frozen, out of the sleigh. "I guess it came hard for you to come away. But land! Rhode, I'm glad to see you back. What with my leg givin' out just when it did, and one thing and another, I felt kinder like a woman with a jack-knife—more I try to do things right, more it looks as if I'd never done 'em before, and wasn't ever goin' to do 'em again—and yet wantin' to do somethin'." And Rhodope stood in the middle of the little living-room, and looked slowly and lovingly about her at the big open fireplace; at Jib kicking the snow from his boots into the hissing flame; at a paper-covered novel on the red table-cover; at the crocheted mat, and the framed wreath of immortelles that had lain on her mother's grave; at all the other dear, familiar things; and lastly at Uncle Denver himself, smiling as he balanced himself against a chair to save his lame leg, and then she went up to him and put her arms around his neck and said,

"Oh, Uncle Denver, it is never a hard thing to come home !"

"I guess it's more 'n half an hour, now," said the restless

voice from the bed. Miss Matilda had not been asleep, but had been lying staring at the counterpane and the Masonic picture, which, though invisible in the shadow, revealed to the eye of familiarity its salient features. Rhodope rose and went to the bedside.

" In two or three minutes it will be," she said gently. " I had not forgotten." She seated herself and looked down at Miss Matilda. A great pity for her filled her heart. Here was a life as empty, as self-despoiled, as any that were lived amid the manifold hindrances of the city. Was there so much to choose between the stony places, incapable of fostering the good, and those where thorns sprang up and choked it ? She was so unloved that she needed pity. To Rhodope it seemed a terrible thing to be unloved. She wondered if she should ever get to the point where she would not care.

" You can tell that Elizabeth French," said Miss Spore with sudden sharpness, " that that warn't a bad Sally Lunn she made."

" Very well," said Rhodope, " I will tell her." She did not understand, but she recognized a wish to make amends. She felt that Miss Matilda must feel that she was going to die. She really was drawing near to convalescence. Rhodope rose, and taking from the table a bottle and spoon, poured out a few drops.

" Is that the right bottle ?" asked Miss Spore with fretful anxiety.

" Yes, this is the one."

" Lemme see it. Lemme take it."

Rhodope placed it in the thin hand, which was almost too weak to hold it. This was an almost invariable proceeding, Miss Spore never hesitating to show distrust of her nurse's ability.

" That's it," she allowed.

Rhodope gave her the medicine ; as she lay back she looked sharply at the spoon.

" Is that the spoon you've been using right along ?" she asked.

Rhodope admitted that it was.

" 'Tain't really a full spoon.   It's under-sized.   If you've been givin' it to me in that, you 'ain't give me enough."

" The doctor used this spoon," explained Rhodope.   " He showed me how much."

She was tired and the night had been long, but she spoke with the utmost patience.

" There never was a man that knew anythin' about tea-spoons," murmured Miss Spore as she grew drowsy under the anodyne.

Rhodope went back to the window and knelt down again. She was not in the least afraid of growing sleepy.   She reviewed every episode of her friendship with Medcott.   He seemed so far away from her now, and yet so near, so intimately present, that every word spoken, every sight seen, seemed to come to her touched by his personality.   And she herself had turned the page and refused to read to the end of the beautiful story.   She saw clearly every word of the note she had written him, which had been meant to close the chapter.   And those words had already acquired the obstinacy, almost the incontrovertibility, that the very act of writing down seems to impart to a hitherto perhaps shadowy sentiment or intention.

What if it had been a mistake ?   She had yielded to the cruelty of Florence's suggestion, in the strange contradiction of things, just because her soul had rebelled against it. But now she was away from the contradictions, and she could think.   In the presence of the grand quietness of the mountains and the stars, still one emotion rose stable, strong, and immutable—her love for Medcott.   The pettiness of jealousy, the confusions of life, the falseness of appearances, fell away from her spirit; but love stood clear and enduring, a mighty fact of existence, no mirage of dazzling foreign skies. Artificial laws of existence could not destroy it, though they might now and then deface its image, and the grandeur of nature could not shut it out. It was in the world, and was the healing of nations. As the faint, pale luminousness of the coming day stole over the hills, Rhodope knew that she must always see it and recognize it, though she had chosen to go forth alone to meet it, not in the companionship that might have been hers.

There was the sound of the click of the outer latch, a soft footstep crossed the hall, and Rhodope raised her head to see, in the early gray of the morning, coming into the room the woman who shared her watch.

"You go to bed, Rhodope Trent," she whispered, "and get an hour's sleep before they come to fetch you."

At the door Rhodope paused and looked back at the bed. The loneliness of the figure there touched her inexpressibly, as it had done before. She was unwilling to go away and leave her, so destitute she seemed. Unconscious that with terrible certainty, by the ruthlessness of her selfishness, she had stripped not only the present but the future of what might have made it happy, Matilda Spore was, nevertheless, facing that desolate future, and with returning health it was growing always nearer. The tears came slowly into Rhodope's eyes, so deep was her pity. Her need was but the need of the whole world, though she would never recognize it. What did it matter where one was or what one did? Everywhere is the need, and those that have let them give. It is the world's want—love! love! love! So she slipped out of the room, with its regularly ticking clock and the somewhat fitful breathing of Miss Spore demonstrating the indisputable advantage of pure mechanism unhampered by the restric-

tions of suffering humanity. She tried to follow the advice
she had received, but she could not sleep, and after an hour's
rest she rose, and wrapping herself up, went quietly out of
the door, determined to walk up the road to the valley and
meet Jib and the sleigh. On the doorstep she stood still in
wondering delight. The day before, that had gone out in
wailing and darkness, had been that of an ice storm; and
now, as the sun broke forth, it was into one of those mornings of enchantment that only Nature can provide for this
somewhat *blasé* earth, catching it up into a sort of ecstasy
of artificial beauty, that convinces us that there is no hand
like hers, and that all our boasted human art is but trifling
and infinitesimal when she herself chooses to become spec-
tacular. The trees were gray, nodding ostrich-plumes
tipped with diamonds. The commonplace street, leading
farther into the sordid little town, was over-swept and over-
arched by pendent jewelled sprays and carpeted with brill-
iants. The road which Rhodope turned into, that led her
over towards the valley, was a long vista of drooping laces
sparkling with crystals flung in reckless profusion. The
hills lay laughing under the jewelled ermine that had been
cast upon them. The trees defied the danger that awaited
their straining branches, clad in a shining mail that was
touched by the wand of enchantment, so that it gleamed
and glowed with flames of prismatic glory. As she walked
slowly on over the hard ground strewed with the glittering
points of broken ice, it was as if she were setting forth to
fairy-land on a strange highway that led she knew not
whither, save that it was into fantastic beauty without end.

It was not cold; the world was but waiting for the warmer
touch of the risen sun to pass out of this fairy-land. The
spell of the present enchantment must yield to the dearer
and more potent one. It was still so early that she met no
one until she was past the last outlying houses of the little

town and fairly committed to the loneliness of the hills. She looked up and on, and moving towards her swiftly along the road she saw a man's figure. She paused an instant as if the staff of the wizard had been suddenly laid upon her and made her a part of the motionless frozen beauty. She had not doubted that it was Medcott from the first flash of perception. He quickened his steps as he caught sight of her, and she more slowly moved towards him.

Behind each of them, in the distance, the drooping branches swept so low that they shut off the turns of the road in masses of gray, shining beauty, and the two came towards each other as if they met in a beautiful crystal world that had neither entrance nor exit.

"Rhodope," he said, taking her hands, "you did not mean what you said in your letter. I know that. I do not know that you love me, but I shall not let you go on any such foolish pretext as that contained."

She looked at him in delicious surprise. All misgivings, all doubts of the motives of his confession, all thoughts of anything but what she saw in his eyes melted away. And did he treat that letter so lightly? They had seemed so terribly irrevocable—those written words! It had cost so much to write them!

"No," she said gravely; "I have learned better now."

His heart leaped at her words, but he did not take her in his arms. She should tell him first what the lesson had been.

"What is it you have learned, Rhodope?" he asked. She glanced up at the brilliant blue of the sky, at the rainbow color of the trees, at the shining glory of the hills. It was in such beautiful silences as this that she would have chosen to make her confession.

"I have learned," she said slowly, "that it is not a thing to be interfered with, or perhaps listened to — that love is

not. It is a thing that belongs to everybody everywhere—
there and here. And I love you. I have always loved
you—"

She paused a moment, and Medcott, who had at last
heard the words he had been waiting for, stayed not for
the end. She had said that she loved him. The swift
color stained her cheeks under his kisses. This conclusion
had not seemed to her the inevitable one, as it had to him.
She could not lift her eyes as her head lay upon his shoulder. He kissed her eyelids, which increased their tendency
to stay down.

"There were other things I had to say," she murmured,
half frightened, half smiling.

"And you have all the rest of your life to say them in,
and I to listen, love," he said gently.

The little fur cap she wore was pushed back from her
soft hair, her cheeks were brilliant with color, her grave
lips had taken tender, happy curves, her eyelashes swept
her cheeks. It was the third time that her head had rested
there: once for an instant of danger, when he had first
known her, again for that intense moment in the Needhams' library, and now, beside which time the others were
pale with uncertainty. It seemed to him that their whole
acquaintance had been a steady progression to the flower
of this happiness. He looked from her to the beautiful,
cold, sparkling world about them; it was as if he held
the warmth, the glow, the heart of all the beauty in his
arms. She raised her head and he let her go.

"It came to me last night," she said, meeting his eyes
now that she stood a little away from him, "that there were
some things that are the same everywhere."

"Always."

"And when one wants those things, one need not be
afraid that they will fail."

"Am I one of those things?" he demanded, half laughing, half serious.

"Love is," she answered—" I have told you so. But after all," she went on, "I shall always like it best here. One can be one's self here."

The reverence that Medcott had always felt for her grew within him. He saw in a flash of illumination how both Davenant, the far-sighted, and he himself, who so loved her, had wronged her. How was this nature to be spoiled or thwarted by any environment? It was strong as well as sweet. They both seemed to have lost sight of this in their caution.

"And yet, would you have learned this?" he asked. "Would you have learned so well of the verities if you had not seen some of the mutabilities?" He spoke rather to himself than to her. It was a reminiscence of a conversation with Davenant. She looked at him a little puzzled.

"Perhaps not," she answered, "but both are everywhere. I learned that last night." He did not know what she was thinking of, he hardly knew what she said—he only read in her eyes the promise and the fulfilment of her happiness and his own. They had stood alone in this fairy-land of glistening enchantment, and now faintly came to them, from the distance, the sound of bells. It was a fitting prelude to the breaking of the spell. A crashing branch, over-weighted with ice, fell not far from them.

"Oh, my darling," said Medcott passionately, "is this beauty that has come into my life real? Do you love me? —for to-day, and every day? Or will all the delight melt away as the beauty about us must melt and vanish? I do not like the omen."

"There are no omens in love," said Rhodope simply. "Such things are all outside. Love is for always."

And Jib's sleigh-bells rang nearer across the morning air.

CHAPTER XXV

"Sunshine and love,
Sky blue and spring."

"Four times Cupid's debtor I—
Bankrupt in quadruplicate.
Yet, despite this evil case,
An a maiden showed me grace,
Four-and-forty times would I
Sing the Lovers' Litany:
'*Love like ours can never die!*'"

THE sweetness from trays of violets, lilies-of-the-valley, and jonquils drifted across the corner of the street in gusts of perfume. It was one of those bright, sunny days of earliest spring, when it seems that the flowers might have been plucked by their Arcadian vendors from the door-yards about, and which, with their vagrant sweetness, beguile us into a deceptive pleasure in existence, only that we may be the more cast down by the aggressive hurly-burly of another March day. Davenant had just joined Mrs. Medcott and Bertha, and was walking with them along Twenty-third Street.

"I am glad she is all you say she is, Tom," with a smile that her maternal wisdom modified by a sigh. "I had other ideas for Austin, as well as Violet Harrow, but I have not lived to my present age to fondly believe that one's children grow up for the purpose of carrying out one's ideas."

"I have always meant to invent one of those whoppers— what you might call a secular whopper."

"My dear Tom," expostulated Mrs. Medcott, "I must ask you to speak English."

"Remember I am a newspaper reporter," said Tom modestly, "and, moreover, I know of no synonym. I mean one of those things that you hang on the wall and whop every morning as a sort of calendar and guide for the day. Mine should have on it for one day, 'Nothing lasts'; for the next, 'Nothing is as bad as it seems'; for the third, 'Nothing is as good as it seems'; for the fourth, 'It all comes to the same thing in the end,' and then back to the beginning again—just those four. I think the moral effect would be infinitely supporting."

"You are more cynical than usual this morning," observed Mrs. Medcott.

"It is the atmosphere of spring and youth and beauty. If it wasn't for me you might be cheered up by it all. One has one's responsibilities."

"I don't think the moral effect would be good at all," objected Bertha seriously. "It would influence us to neglect our duties."

"Would it?" asked Davenant, looking down at her with an air of respectful attention. It always interested him to hear Bertha Medcott on the subject of duty. She had gained a pretty color in the warm air, too. "Then I won't patent it immediately."

"I wish you would, and give Bertha one. It is just what she needs."

"Mamma doesn't mean that," said Bertha anxiously. "She would not really like me to neglect my duties any more than anybody else."

"My dear child," said Mrs. Medcott with her usual little shrug of tolerant impatience, "Tom Davenant doesn't need the glossary that you usually provide for my conversation— he heard me talk almost before you did."

As Davenant held open the door of a shop for them, he noticed what a pretty figure Bertha's was, and as she looked back at him, he caught a transient troubling of the serenity of her glance which made him think deeply for a few moments. Mrs. Medcott wouldn't let him come in with them: she said she was only going in to buy hairpins, but she did not know what she might not feel called on to buy before she came out, and she didn't want to be hampered. Just after he left them he met Helena Screed and joined her.

"I know you've been looking for somebody just like me," she exclaimed, "to talk over Mr. Medcott's engagement! It's people like you and me, without partiality and without prejudice, that can be comforts to each other."

"I'm not without partiality," asserted Davenant. "I'm blinded by an eccentric devotion to Miss Trent."

"No, you're not," said Helena shrewdly; "you've never been blinded by anything—that's the trouble with you."

"I object to your adopting the rôle of observer, Helena. Just go on being the simple flower of a high order of civilization that you are. Don't begin to take notice."

"*Begin* to take notice!" she repeated scornfully. "Did you ever know me when I didn't take notice? But I'm not here to discuss my character, but the engagement. I like it for many reasons. In the first place, because Florence Needham doesn't. Oh, she doesn't like it at all!"

"How do you know?"

"How do I know? Do we any of us like to see our fondest hopes decay, and to know that the talk of our lips has tended only to penury? Didn't she do her best to break it off? And now, that she didn't break it off, isn't she trying in vain to get the credit of making the match?"

"You are a contentious woman," remarked Davenant.

"In the second place, I really think they are fitted for each other." Helena was quite undisturbed by his criticism. "They are both on a—oh, a sort of a *plane*, you know. I always said she was an uncommon sort of person, and as for Austin Medcott, he is very uncommon too—he never cared for me in the least."

"He was withheld by a feeling of delicacy," Davenant hastened to say, "because I cared for you so much."

"Do you think so? I'm glad it was nothing worse. Did you know," she went on, "that Mr. Needham is going around telling everybody that Miss Trent saved him from shooting himself?"

"Yes, so I've heard."

"Do you believe it?" Helena's bright eyes scanned Davenant's non-committal face sharply.

"Oh, I think she'd have stopped him if she'd seen him about it."

"But do you suppose he wanted to?"

"The pistol was loaded, I believe. I don't believe he meant to do himself any real harm."

"You are putting me off with a newspaper joke! Never mind. I'll pay you back. I'm going about to say that I have it on your authority, as an *intimate* friend of all parties, that she turned the pistol aside so that the ball but slightly grazed the left temple. Good-by," and she signalled a car and entered it without further discussion.

Even if Florence Needham could have listened to Helena's diagnosis of the situation, it is doubtful if it could have added much to the discomfiture that she was undergoing at this very moment. While Davenant was making his somewhat intermittent way across the city, she had been standing a little at one side of the entrance to the elevator in one of the fashionable apartment houses, waiting for it to come up from a lower story. As it drew near and stopped, and in the moment's pause while the door was being opened, she caught certain words uttered in the clear, not unpleasant, but rather loud voices of many of those women who are compelled to be always talking down the noise of a city.

"Oh, I grant you she has style, beauty—brains of a certain sort if you like, but she lacks—"

"Oh, of course she *lacks*," interrupted the other, "oh! everything, especially distinction; but, for that sort of woman, she has a certain air."

"How you can tolerate her for just that!"

"Oh, *tolerate!* We have to tolerate everybody nowadays that has *anything!*"

The door rolled back, Florence stepped forward, and the two speakers swept out. There was a hurried exchange of greetings, startled on the one side. Quickly as the elegant, socially distinguished women recovered their self-possession, it came a second too late. In the slight change of color, the quick glance interchanged, Florence had read immediately that these undeniable members of the class of dictators had been talking of her. As her carriage-door closed in front of her own house, she was still facing the fact, and she was still angry. If the glow of the feeling that had led her to praise Rhodope had not long since passed away, this experience would have restored her to herself. Her eyes sparkled as she threw aside her wrap. She would live to defeat those women on their own ground. That they should talk of distinction! She reviewed their manners and their connections alike with bitter satisfaction. They should yet sigh for an invitation to her house. So she took up again the struggle to enter that Eden, guarded by an angel who lays aside his flaming sword at the prospect of a sufficient bribe, but the trees of which garden are heavy with the apples of Sodom.

Deserted by Helena, Davenant went on to the editorial office, where he had an appointment. As he waited a few moments in an anteroom he remembered what a serene, admirable woman Bertha Medcott was, and how she had looked when she turned back at the shop door. He thought her mother was a little hard on her. Mrs. Medcott had always cared more for Austin. Then he took out his note-book and scribbled a few sentences.

"Cynical man. Specialty of unrequited attachment. Poses always as an *homme de trop*. Dead failure. Always finding some one to take the last one's place. Finally requited?" After making a large, black interrogation-point after the last word, he put the book back in his pocket, lit a cigarette, and walked absently about the room.

A week later he went to meet Medcott at the station.

"Yes," he said, with a sort of unhurried haste, as the men shook hands, "I know it all, my dear Medcott! You know I've taken the story in instalments. Don't make me read the bound volume too."

They turned into the street and walked towards Mrs. Medcott's house.

"Besides," he went on, "I have my own sentimental confession to make." Medcott looked at him in surprise. "Yes, I've persuaded your sister to look upon me as a duty. In time, I have hopes of making her regard me as a pleasure also."

THE END

BY W. D. HOWELLS.

THE QUALITY OF MERCY. A Novel. 12mo, Cloth, $1 50; Paper, 75 cents.

AN IMPERATIVE DUTY. A Novel. 12mo, Cloth, $1 00.

A HAZARD OF NEW FORTUNES. A Novel. 2 Volumes. 12mo, Cloth, $2 00; Illustrated. 12mo, Paper, $1 00.

THE SHADOW OF A DREAM. A Story. 12mo, Cloth, $1 00; Paper, 50 cents.

ANNIE KILBURN. A Novel. 12mo, Cloth, $1 50; Paper, 75 cents.

APRIL HOPES. A Novel. 12mo, Cloth, $1 50; Paper, 75 cents.

CHRISTMAS EVERY DAY, and Other Stories. Illustrated. Post 8vo, Cloth, $1 25.

A BOY'S TOWN. Illustrated. Post 8vo, Cloth, $1 25.

CRITICISM AND FICTION. With Portrait. 16mo, Cloth, $1 00.

MODERN ITALIAN POETS. With Portraits. 12mo, Half Cloth, $2 00.

THE MOUSE-TRAP, and Other Farces. Illustrated. 12mo, Cloth, $1 00.

A LETTER OF INTRODUCTION. A Farce. Illustrated. 32mo, Cloth, 50 cents.

A LITTLE SWISS SOJOURN. Illustrated. 32mo, Cloth, 50 cents.

THE ALBANY DEPOT. A Farce. Illustrated. 32mo, Cloth, 50 cents.

THE GARROTERS. A Farce. Illustrated. 32mo, Cloth, 50 cents.

BY CONSTANCE F. WOOLSON.

JUPITER LIGHTS. A Novel. 16mo, Cloth, $1 25.

EAST ANGELS. A Novel. 16mo, Cloth, $1 25.

ANNE. A Novel. Illustrated. 16mo, Cloth, $1 25.

FOR THE MAJOR. A Novelette. 16mo, Cloth, $1 00

CASTLE NOWHERE. Lake-Country Sketches. 16mo, Cloth, $1 00.

RODMAN THE KEEPER. Southern Sketches. 16mo, Cloth, $1 00.

Delightful touches justify those who see many points of analogy between Miss Woolson and George Eliot.—*N. Y. Times.*

For tenderness and purity of thought, for exquisitely delicate sketching of characters, Miss Woolson is unexcelled among writers of fiction.—*New Orleans Picayune.*

Characterization is Miss Woolson's forte. Her men and women are not mere puppets, but original, breathing, and finely contrasted creations.—*Chicago Tribune.*

Miss Woolson is one of the few novelists of the day who know how to make conversation, how to individualize the speakers, how to exclude rabid realism without falling into literary formality.—*N. Y. Tribune.*

Constance Fenimore Woolson may easily become the novelist laureate.—*Boston Globe.*

Miss Woolson has a graceful fancy, a ready wit, a polished style, and conspicuous dramatic power; while her skill in the development of a story is very remarkable.—*London Life.*

Miss Woolson never once follows the beaten track of the orthodox novelist, but strikes a new and richly loaded vein which, so far, is all her own ; and thus we feel, on reading one of her works, a fresh sensation, and we put down the book with a sigh to think our pleasant task of reading it is finished. The author's lines must have fallen to her in very pleasant places ; or she has, perhaps, within herself the wealth of womanly love and tenderness she pours so freely into all she writes. Such books as hers do much to elevate the moral tone of the day—a quality sadly wanting in novels of the time.—*Whitehall Review*, London.

BY ELIZABETH B. CUSTER.

FOLLOWING THE GUIDON. Illustrated. pp. xx., 369. Post 8vo, Cloth, Ornamental, $1 50.

The story is a thrillingly interesting one, charmingly told. . . . Mrs. Custer gives sketches photographic in their fidelity to fact, and touches them with the brush of the true artist just enough to give them coloring. It is a charming volume, and the reader who begins it will hardly lay it down until it is finished.—*Boston Traveller.*

An admirable book. Mrs. Custer was almost as good a soldier as her gallant husband, and her book breathes the true martial spirit.—*St. Louis Republic.*

Mrs. Custer has the faculty of making her reader see and feel with her. . . . The whole country is indebted to Mrs. Custer for so faithfully depicting phases of a kind of army life now almost passed away.—*Boston Advertiser.*

The book is crowded with the amusing and exciting details of a life strange indeed to those who have spent their time sitting tranquilly at home. Her observation is so quick, her descriptive powers so picturesque, that the camp and the skirmish seem to live before the reader.—*Springfield Republican.*

BOOTS AND SADDLES ; Or, Life in Dakota with General Custer. With Portrait of General Custer. pp. 312. 12mo, Cloth, Ornamental, $1 50.

A book of adventure is interesting reading, especially when it is all true, as is the case with "Boots and Saddles." . . . Mrs. Custer does not obtrude the fact that sunshine and solace went with her to tent and fort, but it inheres in her narrative none the less, and as a consequence "these simple annals of our daily life," as she calls them, are never dull nor uninteresting.—*Evangelist*, N. Y.

We have no hesitation in saying that no better or more satisfactory life of General Custer could have been written. Indeed, we may as well speak the thought that is in us, and say plainly that we know of no biographical work anywhere which we count better than this. . . . It is enriched in every chapter with illustrative anecdotes and incidents, and here and there a little life story of pathetic interest is told as an episode.—*N. Y. Commercial Advertiser.*

Every member of a Western garrison will want to read this book ; every person in the East who is interested in Western life will want to read it, too ; and every girl or boy who has a healthy appetite for adventure will be sure to get it. It is bound to have an army of readers that few authors can expect.—*Philadelphia Press*

BEN-HUR: A TALE OF THE CHRIST.

By LEW. WALLACE. 16mo, Cloth, $1 50. *Garfield Edition.* Two Volumes. Twenty Full-page Photogravures. Over 1000 Illustrations as Marginal Drawings by WILLIAM MARTIN JOHNSON. Crown 8vo, Printed on Fine Super-calendered Plate-paper, Uncut Edges and Gilt Tops, Bound in Silk and Gold, $7 00. (*In a Gladstone Box.*)

Anything so startling, new, and distinctive as the leading feature of this romance does not often appear in works of fiction. . . . Some of Mr. Wallace's writing is remarkable for its pathetic eloquence. The scenes described in the New Testament are rewritten with the power and skill of an accomplished master of style.—*N. Y. Times.*

Its real basis is a description of the life of the Jews and Romans at the beginning of the Christian era, and this is both forcible and brilliant. . . . We are carried through a surprising variety of scenes; we witness a sea-fight, a chariot-race, the internal economy of a Roman galley, domestic interiors at Antioch, at Jerusalem, and among the tribes of the desert; palaces, prisons, the haunts of dissipated Roman youth, the houses of pious families of Israel. There is plenty of exciting incident; everything is animated, vivid and glowing.—*N. Y. Tribune.*

From the opening of the volume to the very close the reader's interest will be kept at the highest pitch, and the novel will be pronounced by all one of the greatest novels of the day.—*Boston Post.*

"Ben-Hur" is interesting, and its characterization is fine and strong. Meanwhile it evinces careful study of the period in which the scene is laid, and will help those who read it with reasonable attention to realize the nature and conditions of Hebrew life in Jerusalem and Roman life at Antioch at the time of our Saviour's advent.—*Examiner, N. Y.*

The book is one of unquestionable power, and will be read with unwonted interest by many readers who are weary of the conventional novel and romance.—*Boston Journal.*

One of the most remarkable and delightful books. It is as real and warm as life itself, and as attractive as the grandest and most heroic chapters of history.—*Indianapolis Journal.*